Virginia Andrews is a worldwide bestselling author. Her much-loved novels include RAIN, LIGHTNING STRIKES, EYE OF THE STORM and THE END OF THE RAINBOW. Virginia Andrews' novels have sold more than eighty million copies and have been translated into twenty-two foreign languages.

The Dollanger Family Series
Flowers in the Attic
Petals on the Wind
If There Be Thorns
Seeds of Yesterday
Garden of Shadows

The Casteel Family Series
Heaven
Dark Angel
Fallen Hearts
Gates of Paradise
Web of Dreams

The Cutler Family Series
Dawn
Secrets of the Morning
Twilight's Child
Midnight Whispers
Darkest Hour

The Landry Family Series
Ruby
Pearl in the Mist
All That Glitters
Hidden Jewel
Tarnished Gold

The Logan Family Series
Melody
Heart Song
Unfinished Symphony
Music in the Night
Olivia

The Orphans Miniseries
Butterfly
Crystal
Brooke
Raven
Runaways (full-length novel)

The Wildflowers Miniseries
Misty
Star
Jade
Cat
Into the Garden (full-length novel)

The Hudson Family Series
Rain
Lightning Strikes
Eye of the Storm
The End of the Rainbow

My Sweet Audrina (does not belong to a series)

VIRGINIA ANDREWS®

HIDDEN JEWEL

POCKET
BOOKS

LONDON • SYDNEY • NEW YORK • TORONTO

First published in Great Britain by Simon & Schuster UK Ltd, 1996
This edition published by Pocket Books, 2003
An imprint of Simon & Schuster UK Ltd
A CBS COMPANY

3 5 7 9 10 8 6 4

Simon & Schuster UK Ltd
Africa House
64–78 Kingsway
London WC2B 6AH

www.simonsays.co.uk

Simon & Schuster Australia
Sydney

A CIP catalogue record for this book is available from the British Library

ISBN 0-7434-6828-7

Printed and bound in Great Britain by
Cox & Wyman Ltd, Reading, Berkshire

HIDDEN
JEWEL

Prologue

It always begins the same way. First I hear him singing the lullabye. He is carrying me in his arms, and we are walking over marshland where the grass is so tall that neither he nor I can see his feet, only the tops of his high boots. He is wearing a palmetto hat so the brim puts a mask of shadow over his eyes and nose. I wear my pink and white bonnet.

Behind us, the metal monsters do their monotonous drumming. They resemble giant bees drawing the black nectar from the earth When I look back at them, they raise their heads and nod at me and then raise their heads again. It frightens me and I know he realizes it does, because he holds me tighter and sings louder.

Then we come upon a flock of rice birds. They rise out of the grass with grace and beauty, but they are so abrupt and they come so close that I can feel the breeze stirred up by their wings. He laughs. It's a soft, smooth laugh that glides over me like cool water.

Before us, the great house looms against the sky.

1

The house is so big it looks as if it swallowed up the sky and can block the sun. I see Mommy coming down the stairs from her art studio. She sees us and waves, and he laughs again. Mommy starts toward us, walking quickly at first and then running. With every passing moment she grows younger and younger until . . she's me!

I'm standing before a mirror and looking at myself. I am so amazed at the blue in my eyes, the flaxen color of my hair, and the pearlescent luster of my complexion that I smile and reach out to touch my image in the glass, but as soon as I do, I fall backward. I fall and fall until I hear the sound of splashing water and open my eyes to look at a school of fleeing fish. Their absence reveals the twisted roots of an upturned cypress tree. They look like the gnarled fingers of a sleeping giant. They frighten me, and I turn away, only to come face to face with him.

His eyes are wide, his mouth open with just as much surprise that he is down here. I try to scream, but when I do, the water comes rushing in and I gag.

And that's when I wake up.

When I was younger, my gagging would bring either Mommy or Daddy or both of them. But for years I have been able to catch my breath and regain the courage to lower my head to the pillow in the darkness in search of sleep again.

Tonight Mommy must have anticipated the dream, because she was in my doorway moments after I cried out.

"Are you all right, Pearl?" she asked.

"Yes, Mommy."

"The dream?"

"Yes, but I'm fine, Mommy," I assure her.

"Are you sure, honey?" she asks coming closer.

Why does it worry her so? I wonder. Is it because I still have the dream?

2

"When will it stop, Mommy? Will I have the dream forever?"

"I don't know, honey. I hope not." She looks at the doorway. "I can try another candle," she whispers.

"No, thank you, Mommy."

Once, she was so desperate about my dream that she tried one of the old voodoo remedies she had learned from Nina Jackson, my grandfather Dumas's cook, and Daddy got angry.

"I'll be fine, really," I say.

She wipes some strands of hair from my forehead and kisses me.

"What's going on in here?" Daddy demands from the doorway in his pretend gruff voice.

"Just woman talk, Beau."

"At three in the morning?" he asks amazed.

"It's a woman's prerogative."

"To drive a man crazy, you mean. That's a woman's prerogative," he mutters and goes back to bed.

We laugh. In some ways we are more like two sisters than mother and daughter. Mommy looks so young, hardly thirty-six, even though everyone says caring for twin twelve-year-old boys has to be an age maker.

"Dream of good things, honey. Dream about to-morrow. Your wonderful party. Dream about going to college and doing all the things you've wanted to do."

"I will, Mommy. Mommy," I say and quickly grab her hand as she stands.

"What is it, Pearl dear?"

"Will you tell me more? Maybe if I know more, the nightmare will stop."

She nods reluctantly.

"I know you think it's painful for me to hear and you don't want to do anything to hurt me, but I have to know everything, don't I, Mommy?"

"Yes," she admits. "You do." She sighs so deeply, I'm afraid her heart will crack.

3

"I'm old enough to understand, Mommy. Really I am," I reassure her.

"I know you are, honey. We'll talk. I promise." She pats my hand.

I watch her go off, her shoulders slumping a little now. I hate to make her sad, even for a moment, but I am drawn to the dark past almost as strongly as a moth is drawn to a candle flame.

I hope—no, I pray—that, unlike the moth, I will not be consumed and destroyed as a result.

1

The Future Beckons

I woke to the sound of shouting just outside my
window. The extra workers Daddy had hired to
spruce up our house and gardens for my graduation
party had arrived and were being assigned their jobs.
It had rained the night before and the damp, sweet
scent of green bamboo, gardenias, and blooming
camellias floated all around me. After I ground the
sleep from my eyes, I sat up and saw that the sun was
nudging aside whatever clouds remained and dropping golden rays over the pool and the tennis courts. It
was as if someone had lifted a blanket off precious
jewels. Our gardens were dazzling, our blue and
mauve Spanish tiles glittering. Could there be a more
beautiful beginning to one of the most important days
of my life? In seconds all the webs of confusion,
shadows of darkness, and childhood fears were
washed away.

I was seventeen and about to graduate from high
school. And I was the class valedictorian, too! I sighed
deeply and then let my eyes move over my room. Long
ago Mommy had returned it to the way it had been

when she had first arrived in New Orleans. I slept in her actual dark pine queen-sized canopy bed, the canopy made of fine ivory-colored silk with a fringe border. My pillows were so enormous and fluffy I felt as if I sank a foot whenever I lowered my head to them. The bedspread, pillowcases, and top sheet were made from the softest and whitest muslin. Above my headboard was a painting of a beautiful young woman in a garden feeding a parrot. There was a cute black-and-white puppy tugging at the hem of her full skirt.

On either side of my bed was a nightstand with a bell-shaped lamp, and in addition to a matching dresser and armoire, my room had a vanity table with an enormous oval mirror in an ivory frame decorated with hand-painted red and yellow roses. Mommy and I had often sat side by side and gazed at ourselves in the mirror while we did our hair and makeup and had our girl-to-girl talks, as she liked to call them. Now, she said, they would be woman to woman; but soon they would be few and far between, for I was about to go to college. I had been so anxious to grow up and so excited about reaching this day, but now that it was finally here, I couldn't help feeling somewhat melancholy too

Good-bye to my Huckleberry Finn days, I thought. Good-bye to sleeping late on weekend mornings; good-bye to not worrying about tomorrow. Good-bye to wasting time and cramming for tests at the last moment Good-bye to sitting outside in the garden for hours, dreaming away the afternoons. With a sweep of its hand, the clock would thrust me and my fellow graduates forward into the real world, the world of work and serious study in college where the only one looking over your shoulder was your own conscience.

As my eyes retreated from the mirror, I looked at my door and discovered it was partly open. A further

6

investigation revealed my brother Jean on his hands and knees peering in at me and my brother Pierre on Jean's back peering in as well. The two duplicate faces with their cerulean blue eyes under their golden bangs gaped with curiosity and anticipation. What they expected I would do the moment I woke up on my graduation day I did not know, but I knew they were waiting for me to say or do something that they could tease me about later.

"Jean! Pierre! What are you doing?" I cried. The two stumbled sideways. Laughing and squealing, they scurried back to their room, the room that had once been our great-uncle Jean's room, my mother's father's brother. I heard them slam their door shut and all was quiet for a moment.

Most of the time the twins were like two puppies sniffing and poking where they didn't belong. Usually it got them into some sort of trouble, and Daddy, despite his apparent reluctance to do so, had to discipline them. He was very fond of his twin sons, very proud of them, and full of expectations for them, too.

Between the two of them, they did seem to mirror Daddy. Jean had his athletic ability, his love of sports and hunting and fishing. Pierre had his inquisitiveness, his sensitivity and love of the arts, but neither looked down on the other. Rather, my twin brothers were like halves of one brother, a hybrid called Pierre-Jean. What one couldn't do, the other did for him, and what one didn't think, the other thought for him. They were already the Two Musketeers and didn't need a third.

What was amazing to everyone, even the most skeptical, was the way they both came down with the same childhood diseases at just about the same time. If one got a cold, the other was sure to have it minutes later, and I swear, whenever Jean bumped his head or

7

his knee, Pierre grimaced with just as much pain, and vice versa.

They liked to eat the same things and almost always ate the same amount, although Jean, who was growing faster, was beginning to eat more.

"What's going on out here?" I heard Mommy say. She listened for a moment and then came to my door. "Good morning, Pearl honey. Were you able to go back to sleep?"

"Yes, Mommy."

"Were your brothers here waking you up?" she asked with a scowl.

I didn't want to tell on them, but she didn't need me to testify.

"I swear they're like two muskrats getting under everyone's feet these days. I don't know what to do about them. One will swear the other's innocent and do it with the sweetest, most innocent eyes himself." She shook her head. She was complaining, but I knew how happy she was that they were so close. It had been so different between her and her twin. Whenever she talked about her sister Gisselle, she did so with a deep sigh of regret, still blaming herself for not being able to get Gisselle to become the sister she should have been.

"I should be getting up anyway, Mommy. There's so much to do, and I want to help."

"I know," Mommy said, her eyes small and dark. For both of us, but maybe more for Mommy, this was one of those happy-sad days. If she could have kept me a little girl forever, she would have, she said. "It all goes so fast," she had warned me. "Why rush it?"

Mommy always said she didn't want me to lose a day of my childhood. She claimed she had skipped her childhood completely. She blamed the hard life she had for making her grow up so fast.

"I want to be sure you don't struggle and suffer like

me," she told me often. "If that means you'll be a little spoiled, so be it!"

But I knew she couldn't keep me a little girl forever, not if I had anything to say about it. Although I'd loved growing up here, now mostly I couldn't wait to leave and explore the world outside.

"I think I'm more excited today than you are," she said, her eyes beaming. She looked radiant, despite the early hour. Mommy was never one to wear a great deal of makeup or pamper herself the way the mothers of some of my girlfriends did. She hardly ever went to the beauty parlor and was not one to flit from one style to another, although she always looked chic and elegant. But maybe that was because Mommy was one of those special people who set the style. Other women were always interested in what she chose to wear, what colors, what fashions. She was a highly respected artist in New Orleans and her appearance at an art gallery or an exhibition would be noted, photographed, and printed on the society pages.

Mommy rarely cut her rich ruby hair, her namesake. She kept it long and when she wore it down, she had it curled or twisted in a French knot. She told me that simplicity was the keynote to being attractive.

"Women bedecked in expensive jewels and caked with makeup might attract attention, but often they are not attractive, Pearl," she advised. "A pair of earrings, a necklace, should be used to highlight and not overwhelm, and the same is true for makeup. I know that girls your age think it's fashionable and exciting to dab on the eye liner lavishly, but the trick is to emphasize the positive, not smother it."

"I don't know what's positive about me, Mommy," I said, and she laughed.

Then she fixed those emerald-green eyes on me and shook her head. "If God had come to me when I was pregnant and said, 'Paint the face you want your child to have,' I couldn't have done better or thought of someone more beautiful than you, Pearl.

"And you have a wonderful figure, the sort of figure that will make most women green with envy. I don't want your good looks to go to your head. Be modest and grateful, but don't be the insecure little person I once was. That's when people take advantage," she cautioned me, and her eyes grew smaller and darker so I knew she was remembering one of the sadder or uglier events of her life.

Of course, my brothers and I knew that Mommy had been born and brought up in the bayou. Until she was sixteen, her father, after whom my brother Pierre was named, didn't know she existed. He thought her twin sister, Gisselle, was the only child born out of his love affair with Gabriel Landry. He was married at the time, but his wife, Daphne, accepted Gisselle and pretended she was her own when my great-grandfather Dumas purchased her from the Landrys and brought her to New Orleans as soon as she was born. My mother's surprise appearance on their doorstep sixteen years later nearly exposed the grand deception, but the family concocted the story that she had been stolen immediately after she was born and had returned when the Cajun couple who stole her were struck with a fit of conscience.

From time to time, Mommy described how difficult life was living with a twin sister and a stepmother who resented her, but Mommy hated speaking ill of the dead. She had been brought up by her grandmere Catherine, who was a Cajun traiteur, a healer who combined religious, medical, and superstitious methods to treat the sick and injured. She believed in spirits. She told me that her grandmere Catherine and Nina Jackson, the Dumas family's old voodoo-practicing cook, would warn her that if she dragged up the dead with these stories, they could haunt us all.

10

Mommy didn't try to get me to believe in these things; she just wanted me to respect people who did and not take any chances. Daddy sometimes reprimanded her and told her, "Pearl is a woman of science. She wants to be a doctor, doesn't she? Don't fill her with those tales."

But when it came to keeping my twin brothers in line, Daddy wasn't above trying to scare them with Mommy's stories. "If you don't stop running up and down those stairs, you'll wake up the ghost of your evil aunt, and she'll haunt you when you sleep," he warned. Mommy would turn a twinkling eye of reprimand at him, and he would go sputtering off, complaining about a man's home no longer being his castle.

"I wish you and Daddy hadn't decided on such a big party for me, Mommy," I said as I rose to get washed and dressed for the work ahead. Daddy had hired one of the famous New Orleans jazz bands to play on the patio. He had a pastry chef from one of the finer restaurants to make desserts, and he had employed waiters and waitresses. He had even contracted with a film company to record the affair. He was doing so much for my graduation, I couldn't imagine what he would do for my wedding.

But then, I couldn't imagine getting married, either. I couldn't envision having my own home and raising my own children. The responsibilities were so enormous. But what I really couldn't imagine was falling so deeply in love with someone that I would want to spend the rest of my life with him, see him every morning at the breakfast table and in the evening at the dinner table, go everywhere with only him, and be so beautiful and so desirable all the time that he would want to be only with me. I had had boyfriends, of course. Right now I was going steady with Claude Avery, but I couldn't envision spending my life with him, even though he was one of the handsomest boys at school, tall with dark hair and silver blue eyes. Many times Claude had told me he loved me and waited for me to say the same about him, but all I could muster was "I like you very much, too, Claude."

Surely love had to be something different, something more special, I thought. There were many mysteries in the world, many problems to be solved, but none seemed as impossible as the answer to the question What is love? My girlfriends hated it when I challenged their dramatic declarations of affection for one boy or another, and they were always accusing me of being too inquisitive and looking at things with microscopic eyes.

"Why do you have to ask so many questions?" they complained, especially my best friend Catherine Didion. Catherine and I were different in so many ways, it was hard to understand why we were so close, but perhaps it was those very differences that attracted us. In a way it was our curiosity about each other that kept us so interested in each other. Neither of us fully understood why the other was the way she was.

"It's not such a big party," Mommy said. "Besides, we're proud of you, and we want the whole world to know it."

"Can I see my portrait this morning, Mommy?" I asked. Mommy had painted a picture of me in my graduation gown. She was planning to unveil it tonight at our party, but I had yet to see the finished work.

"No. You have to wait. It's bad luck to show a portrait before it's completed I have a little touching up to do today," she said, and I didn't protest. Mommy believed in good and bad gris-gris, and never wanted to tamper with fate. She still wore the good-luck dime that Nina Jackson had given her years ago. It was on a string around her right ankle.

"Now I'd better go speak to those brothers of yours to be sure they don't make a nuisance of themselves around this house today."

"Will you help me decide what to wear and do my hair later, Mommy?"

"Of course, dear," she said just as my phone rang. "Don't spend your morning gossiping with Catherine," Mommy warned before leaving to go to the twins.

"I won't," I promised, but when I said hello, it wasn't Catherine, I greeted, but Claude.

"Did I wake you?"

"No," I said.

"Well, it's here: our day," Claude announced. He too was a senior and he too was graduating, but I knew he wasn't referring only to that. Claude and I had been going steady for nearly a year. We had kissed and petted and once been almost naked beside each other at Ormand Lelock's house when his parents left him alone for two days. We had nearly gone all the way twice, but I had always resisted. I told Claude that for me it had to be something very special, and he had come up with the idea that it would be something we would do on graduation night. I hadn't agreed, but I hadn't disagreed, either, and I knew Claude thought that meant it would happen.

The first time it had almost happened, I stopped him by explaining why it was a prime time for me to get pregnant. He was frustrated and annoyed and fumed as I explained a woman's cycle.

"It starts when an egg is released," I began.

"I go out with you," he moaned, "and find I'm in science class getting a lecture on human reproduction. You think too much; you're always thinking!"

Was he right? I wondered. When his fingers touched me in secret places, I trembled, but I couldn't help analyzing and thinking of why my heart was pounding. I thought about adrenaline and why my skin had become warm. Textbook illustrations flashed before my eyes, and Claude complained that I was too distant and uninvolved.

The next time we were alone he was prepared and proudly showed me his protection. I didn't want to hurt his feelings, but I told him I wasn't ready.

"Ready!" he exclaimed. "How do you know when you're ready? And don't give me some complicated scientific answer."

What was my answer? We had been having a lot of fun together, and all of our friends assumed we were in love. The other students at school considered us a perfect couple. But I knew we weren't perfect. There had to be something else, something more that happens between a man and a woman, I thought.

I watched Mommy and Daddy when they were together at parties or at dinners, and I saw the way they were in tune with each other, reading each other's faces, knowing each other's feelings, even when a roomful of people separated them. There was an electricity in their eyes, a need and a love for each other that made me feel they were secure in their affection. Maybe I was asking for too much from life, but I wanted a love like theirs, and I knew I didn't have it with Claude.

I didn't know how to tell Claude that he wasn't the one, and I almost talked myself into doing it with him just to satisfy him and satisfy my scientific curiosity about sex. But I had resisted right up to this night, the night Claude planned for us to make love.

"It's all set," he said. "Lester Anderson's parents are leaving for Natchez right after graduation. We've got his house for our private party."

14

"I can't leave my own party, Claude."

"Not right away, no; but later, when we're all going out, I'm sure your parents will understand. They were young once, too," he said. He had a way of turning his eyes and looking at a girl from head to foot that made her self-conscious. Most of the girls giggled and felt flattered when Claude did this. During the last few weeks, I'd suspected that Claude was seeing someone else on the side, maybe Diane Ratner, whose gaze followed us so closely down the hallway that I felt the hair on the back of my neck tingle.

"My mother never had a party like this when she was my age," I said softly.

"She'll still understand, I'm sure. You want to go, don't you?" he asked quickly. When I didn't reply immediately, he punched out another "Don't you?" his voice full of desperation.

"Yes," I said.

"Then it's set. I'll see you later. I've got a lot to do before the graduation ceremony, but I'll pick you up."

"Okay," I said.

"I love you," he added and hung up before I could respond. I sat there for a moment, my heart pounding. Would I finally surrender myself tonight? Should I? Maybe I was just finding excuses because I was simply afraid.

Mommy and I had had our intimate conversations, but she never really answered my questions. Instead, she told me no one could.

"Only you can answer those questions for yourself, Pearl. Only you will know when and with whom it's right for you. Make it something special and it will be. Women who treat sex casually usually get treated casually. Do you understand?"

I did and I didn't. I knew the fundamentals, the science, but I didn't know the magic, for that's what love had to be for me, I thought, something magical.

When I went downstairs I found the house at sixes and sevens. People were scurrying to and fro, following Mommy's directions to change this and rearrange that. Flowers were being placed in vases everywhere. The maids were hunting down the smallest specks of dust. Every window was being washed, all the furniture polished. The hum of vacuum cleaners filled the air. Mommy was having our ballroom decorated. A six-foot-long glittering Congratulations sign was being hung from the ceiling, as were multicolored balloons, rainbow streamers, and tinsel. The jazz band had arrived to check out the acoustics and set up their stands and instruments.

"Good morning, Pearl," Daddy called as soon as he came in from the patio. "How's my little intern?" He kissed my forehead and embraced me quickly. Nothing I had done or said had pleased Daddy more than my decision to become a doctor. It was something he had once hoped for himself.

"I went as far as premed," he had told me.

"Why didn't you continue, Daddy?" I had asked. For a few moments it looked as if he wouldn't answer. His lips tightened; his eyes grew small, his face dark.

"Events carried me in a different direction," he replied cryptically. "It wasn't meant to be. But," he added quickly, "perhaps that was because it was meant for you."

What events? I wondered. How can something you desire so much not be meant to be? Daddy was so successful in business, it was difficult to imagine anything he couldn't do when he set his mind on it. When I pursued him for the answers, however, Daddy tightened up and became uncomfortable.

"It was just the way things were," he said and left it at that. Because I saw it was too painful for him to discuss, I didn't nag, but that didn't mean the ques-

16

tions were gone. They hung over all of us, dangled invisibly in the house and attached themselves to the pictures in our family albums, pictures that traced the strange and mysterious turns my parents' lives had taken before and just after I was born. It was as if we had secrets buried in some dusty old trunk in the attic and someday—maybe soon—I would open the trunk and, like Pandora, release the discoveries I would quickly regret.

"I'm afraid you'll have to have breakfast with your brothers only this morning," Daddy said. "I've already eaten, and so has your mother, and we're busier than two bees in a hive."

"I wish you and Mommy hadn't planned quite such a large affair for me, Daddy."

"What? I wouldn't have it any other way. In fact, it's not big enough. Every hour I remember someone else we should have invited."

"The guest list is already a mile long!"

He laughed. "Well, with my business interests and your mother's art crowd, not to mention your teachers and friends, we're lucky it's only a mile."

"And my portrait will be unveiled in front of all those people. I'll be so embarrassed."

"Don't think of it as your portrait, Pearl. Think of it as your mother's art," he advised. I nodded. Daddy was always so sensible. He would surely have made a wonderful doctor.

"I'll eat quickly and help you, Daddy."

"Nonsense. You relax, young lady. You have a big night ahead of you. You won't know how big until it starts And you have your speech to worry over, too."

"Will you listen to me practice later?"

"Of course, princess. We'll all be your first audience. But right now I've got to see about our parking arrangements. I've hired a valet service "

17

"Really?"

"We can't have our guests riding around looking for a place to park, can we? Make sure your brothers eat their breakfast and don't annoy anyone, will you?" he asked and kissed me again before hurrying to the front of the house.

Jean and Pierre were at the table, both looking so polite and innocent that I knew they were up to something. Strands of Jean's blond hair hung down over his forehead and eyes. As usual his shirt was buttoned incorrectly. Pierre's appearance was perfect, but Pierre wore that tiny smirk around his lips and Jean looked at me with his blue eyes twinkling. I checked my seat to be sure they hadn't put honey on it so I would stick to it.

"Good morning, Pearl," Pierre said. "How's it feel to be graduating?"

"I'm very nervous," I said and sat down. They both stared. "Did you two do anything silly?"

They shook their heads simultaneously, but I didn't trust them. I scrutinized the table, checked the floor by my chair, and studied the salt and pepper shakers. Once, they put pepper in the salt shaker and salt in the pepper, and another time, they put sugar in the salt shaker.

They dipped their spoons into their cereal and ate with their eyes still fixed on me. I looked up at the ceiling to be sure there wasn't a fake black widow spider dangling above me.

"What have you two done?" I demanded.

"Nothing," Jean said too quickly.

"I swear if you do anything today, I'll have the two of you locked in the basement."

"I can get out of a locked room," Jean bragged. "I know how to pick a lock. Right, Pierre?"

"It's not hard to do, especially with our old locks," Pierre said pedantically. He had a way of making his eyes small and pressing his lower lip over his upper whenever he offered a serious opinion.

"I can take the hinges off the door, too," Jean claimed.

"All right. Stop talking about it. I'm not serious," I said. Jean looked disappointed.

"Good morning, mademoiselle," our butler, Aubrey, said as he came in from the kitchen with a glass of fresh orange juice for me. Aubrey had been with us for years and years. He was the proper Englishman at all times. He was bald with small patches of gray hair just over his ears. His thick-rimmed glasses were always falling down the bridge of his bony nose, and he would squint at us with his hazel eyes.

"Morning, Aubrey. I'll just have some coffee and a croissant with jam this morning. My stomach is full of butterflies."

"Ugh," Jean said. "They were caterpillars first."

"She just means she's nervous," Pierre explained.

"Because you got to make a speech?" Jean asked.

"Yes, that mostly," I said.

"What's it about?" Pierre asked.

"It's about how we should be grateful for what we have, for what our parents and teachers have done for us, and how that gratitude must be turned into hard work so we don't waste opportunities and talents," I explained.

"Boring," Jean said.

"No, it's not," Pierre corrected him.

"I don't like sitting and listening to speeches. I bet someone throws a spitball at you," Jean threatened.

"It better not be you, Jean Andreas. There's plenty that has to be done around here all day. Don't get underfoot and don't aggravate Mommy and Daddy," I warned.

"We can stay up until everyone leaves tonight," Pierre declared.

19

"And Mommy let us invite some of our friends," Jean added. "We should light firecrackers to celebrate."

"Don't you dare," I said. "Pierre?"

"He doesn't have any."

"Charlie Littlefield does!"

"Jean!"

"I won't let him," Pierre promised. He gave Jean a look of chastisement, and Jean shrugged. His shoulders had rounded and thickened this past year. He was tough and sinewy and had gotten into a half dozen fights at school, but I learned that three of those fights were fought to protect Pierre from other boys who teased him about his poetry. All their friends knew that when someone picked a fight with Pierre, he was picking a fight with Jean, and if someone made fun of Jean, he was making fun of Pierre as well.

Mommy and Daddy had to go to school to meet with the principal because of Jean's fights, but I saw how proud Daddy was that Jean and Pierre protected each other. Mommy bawled him out for not bawling them out enough.

"It's a tough, hard world out there," Daddy said. "They've got to be tough and hard too."

"Alligators are tough and hard, but people make shoes and pocketbooks out of them," Mommy retorted. No matter what the argument or discussion, Mommy had a way of reaching back into her Cajun past to draw up an analogy to make her point.

After breakfast I returned to my room to fine-tune my valedictory address, and Catherine called.

"Have you decided about tonight?" she asked.

"It's going to be so hard leaving my party. My parents are doing so much for me," I moaned.

"After a while they won't even know you're gone," Catherine promised. "You know how adults are when

20

they make parties for their children; they're really making them for themselves and their friends."

"That's not true about my parents," I said.

"You've got to go to Lester's," she whined. "We've been planning this for months, Pearl! Claude expects it. I know how much he's looking forward to it. He told Lester, and Lester told me just so I would tell you."

"I'll go to the party, but I don't know about staying overnight," I said.

"Your parents expect you to stay out all night. It's like Mardi Gras. Don't be a stick-in-the-mud tonight of all nights, Pearl," she warned. "I know what you're worried about," she added. Catherine was the only other person in the world who knew the truth about Claude and me.

"I can't help it," I whispered.

"I don't know what you're so worried about. You know how many times I've done it, and I'm still alive, aren't I?" Catherine said, laughing.

"Catherine . . ."

"It's your night to howl. You deserve it," she said. "We'll have a great time. I promised Lester I would see that you were there."

"We'll see," I said, still noncommittal.

"I swear, Pearl Andreas, you're going to be dragged kicking and screaming into womanhood." She laughed again.

Was this really what made you a woman? I wondered. I knew many of my girlfriends at school felt that way. Some wore their sexual experiences like badges of honor. They had a strut about them, a demeanor of superiority. It was as if they had been to the moon and back and knew so much more about life than the rest of us. Promiscuity had given them a sophistication and filled their eyes with insights about life, and especially about men. Catherine believed this about herself and was often condescending.

"You're book-smart," she always told me, "but not life-smart. Not yet."

Was she right?

Would this be my graduation night in more ways than one?

It was difficult to return to my speech after Catherine and I ended our conversation, but I did. After lunch, Daddy, Mommy, and the twins sat in Daddy's office to listen to me practice my delivery. Jean and Pierre sat on the floor in front of the settee. Jean fidgeted, but Pierre stared up at me and listened intently.

When I was finished, they all clapped. Daddy beamed, and Mommy looked so happy, I nearly burst into tears myself. Graduation was set to begin at four, so I went upstairs to finish doing my hair. Mommy came up and sat with me.

"I'm so nervous, Mommy," I told her. My heart was already thumping.

"You'll do fine, honey."

"It's one thing to deliver my speech to you and Daddy and the twins, but an audience of hundreds! I'm afraid I'll just freeze up."

"Just before you start, look for me," she said. "You won't freeze up. I'll give you Grandmere Catherine's look," she promised.

"I wish I had known Grandmere Catherine," I said with a sigh

"I wish you had too," she said, and when I gazed at her reflection in the mirror, I saw the deep, far-off look in her eyes.

"Mommy, you said you would tell me things today, things about the past."

She nodded and pulled back her shoulders as if she were getting ready to sit down in the dentist's chair.

"What is it you want to know, Pearl?"

"You never really explained why you married your half brother, Paul," I said quickly and lowered my eyes. Very few people knew that Paul Tate was Mommy's half brother.

"Yes, I did. I told you that you and I were alone, living in the bayou, and Paul wanted to protect and take care of us. He built Cypress Woods just for me."

I remembered very little about Cypress Woods. We had never been back since Paul's death and the nasty trial for custody over me that had followed.

"He loved you more than a brother loves a sister?" I asked timidly. Just contemplating them together seemed sinful.

"Yes, and that was the tragedy we couldn't escape."

"But why did you marry him if you were in love with Daddy and I had been born?"

"Everyone thought you were Paul's daughter," she said. She smiled. "In fact, some of Grandmere Catherine's friends were angry that he hadn't married me yet. I suppose I let them believe it just so they wouldn't think I was terrible."

"Because you had gotten pregnant with Daddy and returned to the bayou?"

"Yes."

"Why didn't you just stay in New Orleans?"

"My father had died, and life with Daphne and Gisselle was quite unpleasant. When Beau was sent to Europe, I ran off. Actually," she said, "Daphne wanted me to have an abortion."

"She did?"

"You wouldn't have been born."

I held my breath just thinking about it.

"So I returned to the bayou where Paul took care of us. He even helped me give birth to you. When I heard Daddy was engaged to someone in Europe, I finally gave in and married Paul."

23

"But Daddy wasn't engaged?"

"It was one of those arranged things. He broke up with the young lady and returned to New Orleans. My sister had been seeing him. She had a way of getting whatever she wanted, and your father was just another trophy she wanted," Mommy said, not without a touch of bitterness in her voice.

"Daddy married Gisselle because she looked so much like you, right?" It was something I had squeezed out of Daddy when he had decided to stem the flood of questions I poured at him.

"Yes," Mommy said.

"But neither of you were happy?"

"No, although Paul did so much for us. I devoted all my time to my art and to you. But then, when Gisselle became sick and comatose . . ."

"You took her place." I knew that story. "And then?"

"She died, and there was the terrible trial after Paul's tragic death in the swamp. Gladys Tate wanted vengeance. But you knew most of that, Pearl."

"Yes, but, Mommy . . ."

"What, honey?"

I lifted my eyes to gaze at her loving face. "Why did you get pregnant if you weren't married to Daddy?" I asked. Mommy was so wise now; how could she not have been wise enough to know what would happen back then? I had to ask her even though it was a very personal question. I knew most of my girlfriends, including Catherine, could never have such an intimate conversation with their mothers.

"We were so much in love we didn't think. But that's not an excuse," she added quickly.

"Is that what happens, why some women get pregnant without being married? They're too much in love to care?"

"No. Some just get too caught up with sex and lose

24

control. You can be the smartest girl in school, the best reader, have the highest grades, but when it comes to your hormones . . . well, just be careful," she said.

"It doesn't seem fair," I said.

"What?"

"That men don't face the same risks."

Mommy laughed. "Well, let that be another reason why you don't let a young man talk you into something you don't want to do. Maybe if men knew what it was like to give birth, they wouldn't be so nonchalant about it all."

"They should feel the same labor pains," I said.

"And get sick in the morning and walk around with their stomachs hanging low and their backs aching," Mommy added.

"And get urges to eat pickles and peanut butter sandwiches."

"And then have contractions."

We both roared and then hugged.

Daddy, coming up the stairs, heard us and knocked on the door. "Exactly what are you two females giggling about now?" he asked.

"Pregnant men," Mommy said.

"Huh?"

We laughed again.

"Women are not just another sex; they're a different species altogether," Daddy declared. That only made us laugh harder.

After I had my hair the way I wanted it to look, I picked up the dress I would wear under my graduation gown. Then I opened the box that contained my cap and gown and screamed.

"What is it, Pearl?" Mommy gasped.

"My mortarboard's gone, Mommy."

"What? That can't be." She looked herself and then she lifted her eyes. "Your brothers," she declared and marched out. I followed her in my graduation gown as we descended the stairs, Mommy shouting for Pierre and Jean. They came running down the hallway, Pierre right behind Jean.

"Did you take your sister's graduation cap?" she demanded, her hands on her hips.

Pierre looked guiltily at Jean, who shook his head.

"Jean? Are you telling a fib?"

"What's happening?" Daddy demanded, hurrying up behind us.

"Pearl's graduation cap is missing, and I think these two imps have an idea where we can find it," Mommy said, her eyes still on the twins. Pierre's gaze dropped quickly.

"Boys," Daddy said in a stern voice.

"I saw a hat on the statue of Adonis in the garden," Jean confessed.

"What?" Daddy and Mommy looked at each other, and then we all traipsed out to the garden.

There was my graduation cap on the statue. People had been going past it all day and no one had noticed it or commented on it. Daddy's lips curled into a quick smile and then became taut and thin after he looked at Mommy's face. He got the cap for me and then turned to the twins, who looked terrified.

"How could you pull such a prank on your sister? You both know how nervous she is."

"It was all my idea," Pierre said.

"No it wasn't; it was mine," Jean insisted.

Daddy looked at the statue and then at them. "My guess is that Jean boosted Pierre up so he could put that cap on the statue's head. Am I right, boys?"

Pierre nodded.

"I think tonight you two will go directly to your rooms and miss the party."

"Oh, no!" Jean exclaimed. "We just meant to tease Pearl. We were going to tell her where it was."

26

"Nevertheless . . ."

"It's all right, Daddy," I said. "They'll be little angels from now on, won't you, little brothers?" I said. They both nodded vigorously, grateful for my forgiveness.

"Well, if your sister can forgive you, you're lucky. You should do everything you can to see that this is the happiest night of her life," Daddy warned them.

"We will," Pierre promised.

"Uh-huh. We will," Jean said.

"Get dressed and look very neat," Daddy said. They turned and scurried back into the house.

Mommy and Daddy gazed at each other and then at the statue before the three of us broke into laughter.

It seemed to break the ice that had formed around me. I wasn't as afraid of what was to come.

But maybe I should have been. Maybe it was better to always be a little frightened of the future, so you would be careful. Maybe that was why Mommy believed so strongly in good and bad gris-gris and crossed herself three times if we ever came upon a funeral.

Somehow I knew I would know for sure sooner than I ever dreamed.

2

Just Think
Happy Thoughts

Before I left for school to get ready for the graduation ceremony, Mommy came up to my room and helped me choose the dress I would wear at my party. We styled my hair and she talked a little about her school life in the bayou and her own graduation ceremony. Mommy and Gisselle had attended a private school in Baton Rouge their senior year, but according to Mommy, it was an unpleasant experience, except for her art class and her getting to know Louis Clairborne, a famous musician who occasionally played recitals in New Orleans and always came to our home for dinner when he was in the city. Whenever he came to our house, he always brought the twins and me something special from one of his European tours. I had dolls and music boxes from France and Holland.

"Well, Mommy," I said after Aubrey came to tell me Claude had arrived to take me to the graduation exercises, "Here I go." I followed that with a tiny whimper.

"Stop worrying," she said and hugged me. As I started out, she cried, "Wait."

I turned and saw her sit on the vanity table chair and bend over to untie her good luck dime from her ankle.

"I was going to give this to you before you left for college at the end of the summer, but I want you to have it now, Pearl."

"Oh, no, Mommy. That's your good luck. I can't take that."

"Of course you can. I can pass it on to you."

"But then you won't have it," I warned.

"It's time for you to have it, Pearl. Please take it," she pleaded. "It will mean a great deal to me."

"I know how you feel about this special dime, Mommy," I said shaking my head but moving forward to take it.

"Sit down and I'll fasten it around your ankle," she told me. I did so. "There," she said, patting my knee. "I know you think it's silly, but whatever magic it has had for me it will have for you, too."

"I don't think it's silly, Mommy, but what about you? You won't be wearing it anymore."

"I've had more magic than anyone deserves. Look at the wonderful family I have and the success I've had in my art. Now I live to see you and the boys enjoy your opportunities."

"Thank you, Mommy."

"But don't tell your father just yet," she warned throwing a glance at the doorway. "He thinks I get too carried away with the old beliefs, and he'll only bawl me out for imposing them on you."

Mommy and I never kept serious secrets from Daddy, but there were a few things we didn't tell him.

"We can tell him afterward," she added.

"Okay, Mommy." We hugged again and I was off. Claude was waiting outside by his car, pacing impatiently.

"Hi," I called and hurried down the steps. He

stepped forward to kiss me. Lately he was shoving his tongue into my mouth every time. This time he not only did that but held me so close for so long that I had to pull free.

"Please, Claude. We're right in front of my house!"

He shrugged, brushing off the reprimand as if it were a mosquito on his shoulder.

"Well, the day has arrived. Our release from prison," he declared.

"Is that what you thought school was, Claude?"

"Hey, we won't have adults looking over our shoulders as much from now on. To me, that's a release, and tonight"—he smiled—"is our time to howl, right?" He tried to kiss me again.

"I guess so," I said, stepping toward the car and away from him. Claude's exuberance frightened me a little. He was like a young man ready to march through locked doors.

"Don't look so sad," he said. He opened the car door, and I slipped in quickly. "Only a few others will be at Lester's tonight," he told me after getting in beside me. "No deadbeats. And we might have a little more than booze," he added and winked.

"More than booze? What do you mean?"

"You know." He winked again.

"I know what I don't want to see you do, and you know what I won't do," I added firmly. We had had this discussion before. Claude stopped smiling.

"Ease up. You only graduate from high school once," he said.

I pressed my lips together and swallowed back the words that would surely cause an argument. For now I had more important things on my mind—namely, my speech.

There was so much excitement at the school when we arrived. I joined Catherine and some of our friends in the girls' room for a last minute put-together. Girls were borrowing lipstick, spraying on cologne, dabbing their cheeks with makeup, and many were smoking. Diane offered me a cigarette, and I refused, as usual.

"Right. The little doctor doesn't want to poison her lungs," she quipped, and the other girls laughed.

"That's true, Diane. The fact is, just standing in here and breathing the secondhand smoke is dangerous. That's already been proven."

The girls around me looked glum for a moment.

"That's so stupid. What do you think, you're going to live forever?" Diane retorted. Her friends smiled.

"No, but I know what it's like to get lung cancer. It isn't pleasant," I said sharply.

"Miss Goody Two-shoes. Just listen to her. What a drag. I hope your speech isn't depressing. This is supposed to be a happy occasion." Everyone was looking at me.

"It's not depressing," I said defensively. "Excuse me a moment," I said. "I've got to use the bathroom."

Laughter followed me into the stall. I heard them suddenly quiet down and start filing out. When I emerged, there was no one left. Confused, but happy that I didn't have to argue anymore, I left too. It wasn't until I had slipped my graduation gown on and put on my cap that I realized I must have left my speech in the bathroom. In a panic, I ran back. But it wasn't there!

Maddeningly frantic, I ran up and down the corridor, questioning every girl in the line, but no one knew anything.

"What's up?" Claude asked.

"My speech is missing. Someone took it when I went to the bathroom," I told him.

"No kidding. What are you going to do?"

"I don't know."

I turned to Catherine. She looked as if she wanted to say something but was too afraid. I spun around, desperate. Mr. Stegman, the teacher in charge of the procession, was ordering me to get in place.

"I can't find my speech!" I told him. "I had it with me when I went into the bathroom, but it's not there!"

"Oh, dear," he said and went to fetch Dr. Foster, the principal.

"Did you look real good, Pearl? Go back and check once more," he suggested. "I'll hold the procession back a few more minutes."

I gazed at Catherine.

"It has to be there," she offered. A horrid thought occurred to me. I returned to the bathroom and threw open the stall next to the one I had used. There was my speech, floating in the toilet.

"Oh, no!" I cried and dipped into the water to retrieve it. Many of the words had been washed away. I wiped down the paper as carefully as I could with a towel and then went out to take my place at the head of the procession.

"You found it?" Dr. Foster asked.

I held up the soggy sheets.

"How did that happen?"

"Yes," I said loud enough for everyone in my class to hear. "How did it happen?"

My heart was pounding so hard I thought I was sure to make a fool of myself in front of all the families and guests. I don't know how my legs carried me down the corridor and out the door, but I had no choice.

I really didn't have time to worry about myself. We marched to the stage that had been erected outside for our graduation exercises and took our seats. I tried not to look at the audience. There was so much noise—laughter, chatter, babies crying, small children being warned to sit quietly—that it sounded like bedlam. No one would hear my speech anyway, I thought. Why worry?

We had a warm, bright day for our ceremony with a

light breeze that made the flag flutter and strands of hair dance over our shoulders. The sky was turquoise with patches of fluffy clouds. In the distance I could hear the bellow of the steamboats preparing to carry tourists up the Mississippi.

After the introductions and some short remarks by our principal, I was called to the lectern. My legs wobbled as I stood up. I closed my eyes, took a deep breath, opened my eyes, and walked to the lectern. My classmates were dead silent, all wondering what I would do. I searched the audience until I found Mommy gazing at me confidently, and then the words just came. I didn't need to look at the paper. The words were printed in my head.

To my surprise, everyone had grown quiet. I raised my head, took a deep breath, and began. I thanked the principal and then, addressing the faculty and our parents, families, and friends, began in a voice that grew stronger and stronger as I delivered the speech I had composed over the past few days. Amazingly, once I started, the words flowed. From time to time I gazed at the faces in the audience and saw that people were really listening. Most wore sweet, appreciative smiles. The twins were staring up at me, both with their mouths slightly open, neither fidgeting.

When I concluded, the applause boomed in my ears, and when I looked at Mommy and Daddy, I saw the glow in their faces. Even Pierre and Jean looked impressed. They stopped clapping at the exact same moment, and when I returned to my seat, I gazed at Claude and saw him smiling proudly and elbowing his buddies to make them jealous. Diane Ratner and her friends looked devastated, but Catherine hugged me quickly.

"That was great. I knew you could do it, no matter what I actually listened to the whole thing, even though I didn't understand some of it."

"Thanks," I said dryly. I didn't want her to think I was satisfied with her weak demonstration of friendship. She had disappointed me.

I sat back as the principal and our class adviser went to the lectern to hand each of us our diploma. When I rose to get mine, the audience gave me another thunderous ovation. Daddy was snapping pictures, and the twins were waving and cheering.

"Nice job, young lady," the principal said. "Good luck."

I thanked him and smiled at my parents one more time for Daddy's camera.

After the ceremony I was inundated with compliments on my speech. All of my teachers stopped by, as did some of my classmates and their parents, to offer their best wishes. I was happy to see that my aunt Jeanne—the sister of Mommy's half brother, Paul—and her husband, James, were there and were waiting to congratulate me, too.

Aunt Jeanne was the only member of the Tate family who had anything to do with us. She was about an inch or so taller than Mommy, with dark brown hair and almond-shaped eyes. Mommy said that Aunt Jeanne looked more like her mother, Gladys, than her father, Octavius, because she had her mother's deep, dark complexion, sharp chin, and nearly perfect nose. I liked her because she was always pleasant and sweet to us and especially sweet to me.

"I loved your speech, Pearl honey" Aunt Jeanne said, hugging me.

"It was something," Uncle James added, nodding. He shook Daddy's hand. "You have a lot to be proud of, Beau."

Mommy and Daddy were beaming so brightly, I got chills up and down my spine.

"How is your family, Jeanne?" Mommy asked, a dark shadow crossing her face.

"Mother's got the gout on top of her arthritis. Daddy never changes. He buries himself in his business." Aunt Jeanne smiled. "My sister Toby's youngest turned sixteen, you know. I'll be going to another graduation soon."

Aunt Jeanne and Uncle James had never had any children. I wasn't sure why not. If Mommy knew, she never said.

"You're coming over to the house, aren't you, Jeanne?" Mommy asked her.

"Of course. We wouldn't miss the party for the world," she said. "You knew I would be here, Ruby," she whispered, but loud enough for me to hear. I saw the way the two of them gazed into each other's eyes, and I felt the unspoken words that passed between them, words I knew were all about my mother's half brother, Paul, the man in my strange dream. "Paul would have been so proud of her," Jeanne continued. Tears came to Mommy's eyes as she nodded. They hugged again.

Mommy turned to look for the twins, who were amusing themselves by weaving in and out among the crowd and teasing some of my girlfriends. For once, I was happy about their behavior. Mommy shouted for the boys to come along. It was time to go home and get ready for the party. Mommy threw her arm around me, and we all went to the limousine.

"I'm so proud of you," she said.

I didn't want to tell her about the prank my so-called friends had pulled on me in the bathroom. "I was so nervous. Didn't it show?"

"Not a bit. I told you that once you got started, the words would roll off your tongue. And they did," Mommy declared.

In the limousine, the twins teased me about the way I had shifted my eyes after certain phrases in my speech, but Mommy chastised them, and they smoth-

35

ered their giggles. My stomach wasn't filled with butterflies anymore. Now it felt positively cavernous. I couldn't wait to get something to eat. I had been too nervous to eat much of anything all day.

Some of our guests were already at the house, and the musicians had already begun to play by the time we arrived. The atmosphere was festive. I hurried upstairs to change into my party dress and repair my hair. By the time I descended the stairs, the other guests had begun arriving, all bearing graduation gifts. A corner in one of the sitting rooms had been designated for the presents, and the twins eyed the pile, eager to satisfy their curiosity by tearing through the wrappings. Mommy warned them to stay away, and they shot off to play with their friends.

An army of servants began to serve hot and cold hors d'oeuvres with glasses of champagne. Daddy's business friends gathered in the ballroom, and Mommy greeted some of the important members of the art community, including other artists and gallery owners. The crowd was a Who's Who of the society pages.

My portrait remained covered on an easel, near the four-foot-high layer cake with "Good Luck, Pearl" written on it in red icing. Both the portrait and the cake were under a spotlight. Daddy wanted to make the unveiling a special moment after all of the guests had arrived.

Claude came late with Lester Anderson and some of his other friends, and I knew immediately why they were delayed. I saw from the way they swaggered and laughed that they had already had something alcoholic to drink, and when Claude came over to kiss me, I smelled the whiskey on his breath.

"Is the punch spiked?" he asked me.

"Of course not," I said. He winked at Lester, a tall, lanky boy who always looked as if he had just done something mischievous. Lester idolized Claude and would do most anything he suggested.

"Should I?" Lester asked me and revealed a pint of rum in the inside pocket of his jacket.

"Lester Anderson, don't you dare," I warned. All the boys laughed. Claude put his arm around my waist and tried to kiss me on the neck.

"Claude, stop. Some of my father's friends are looking at us."

"Let's step into the den for a few moments," he whispered. "I haven't congratulated you properly."

"No. Just be patient," I said. He was disappointed, but he retreated and behaved.

A short while later, Daddy asked the musicians to stop playing for a few moments, and he took center stage to announce the unveiling of my portrait.

"We have a special present for Pearl tonight," he began. "Actually, this is all my wife's doing, but one of the reasons I married her was that I knew she was talented and would be able to do these sorts of things."

Everyone laughed. I gazed over at Aunt Jeanne, who appeared to be exchanging secret glances with Mommy. Daddy took hold of the cloth covering the painting, and I felt my heart pounding. It was almost as nerve-racking a moment as I'd had rising to make my graduation speech.

"Pearl," Daddy said. I stepped out and the guests applauded. Mommy stayed beside Daddy when he went over to the portrait and, with a little drum roll from the band, slowly pulled away the cloth to reveal a painting that took my breath away. Mommy hadn't just painted a portrait of me in my graduation outfit Behind me she had painted another portrait, this one with me dressed as a doctor, a stethoscope around my neck.

There was a gasp of appreciation, and then everyone applauded, some rushing over to shake Mommy's hand.

"It looks like twins," Pierre cried.

"Just like us, there are two of you," Jean squealed. Everyone laughed.

"It's beautiful, Mommy," I said when we hugged. "I hope I live up to it."

"You will, honey."

"You better," Daddy said and kissed me, too.

After that, the party went into full swing. The musicians paraded around the house as if it really were a Mardi Gras celebration. The food was brought out and set on the tables. There were platters of turkey and roast beef, baked stuffed shrimp in oyster sauce, shrimp Mornay, and stuffed crabs as well as crawfish étouffée. Everyone was impressed with our elaborate spread, and when the desserts were wheeled out on serving wagons, the guests uttered exclamations of joy and hovered about the tarte aux pêches, banana nut bread, crêpes, pecan pie, orange crème brûllée and chocolate rum soufflé. My graduation cake was cut as well, and wedges of it were served.

The grand menu added to the festive atmosphere. People were dancing everywhere, even in the hall-ways. I circulated as much as I could and spoke to many of Mommy's and Daddy's friends. Suddenly, when I paused in the ballroom to catch my breath, I felt someone come up behind me.

"Good time to slip out of here," Claude whispered, his hands on my hips.

"I can't yet, Claude." I stepped away.

"Why not? You were here for the big event: your unveiling. And we've all gorged enough on the food." He paused, his blue eyes fixed on my face suspiciously. "Didn't you tell your parents you were going to another party?" He waited a moment and then quickly added, "You didn't, did you?"

"I was going to tell them, but they were so excited about my party, I didn't have the heart. Just give me a little while longer," I pleaded.

Claude scowled and reluctantly returned to his friends, who, as they had threatened, had spiked some of the punch for themselves. Now they were sharing it with Catherine, Marie Rose, and Diane Ratner. Diane had always been after Claude. I saw she was taking advantage of my having to visit with Daddy's and Mommy's friends. She had her arm through Claude's and was whispering in his ear constantly. Whatever she said obviously pleased him, but he kept his gaze on me. I saw that he was growing more and more furious with every passing moment. It made his silver-blue eyes glitter like stones in a cold stream.

I was going to speak to him again when Aunt Jeanne tapped me on the shoulder. "So what will you be doing this summer?" she asked me.

"I'm going to work at the hospital as a nurse's aide. Daddy thought it would be good experience for me."

"You're really serious about becoming a doctor, then?" she said with a smile.

"Yes, very serious."

She nodded. "Perhaps that's meant to be," she said, which made me think of my great-grandmother Catherine.

"Did you know my great-grandmother Catherine, Aunt Jeanne?"

"I knew about her. She was a very famous traiteur. I wish she were still around to help my mother. She's been seeing a traiteur, but this woman apparently doesn't have the healing powers your great-grandmother had. You don't mind being around sick people, seeing illness and blood?"

"No," I said. "I feel good whenever I can help someone who is ill."

She smiled. "Then perhaps Catherine's gift has

been passed on to you." She stared at me with wondrous eyes and nodded. "Good luck, sweetheart, and someday come to see us in the bayou."

"I will," I said and swallowed. Mommy and Daddy had never forbidden me to go there, but their reluctance to return to the bayou made it seem like taboo.

"We've got to be going soon, but I wanted you to have this first," Aunt Jeanne said and handed me a small box. It wasn't gift-wrapped.

"Thank you," I said, a little surprised. Why hadn't she wrapped it and put it with the other gifts?

"Go on, open it," she added. I looked across the room and saw how Mommy was staring at us, her face full of fear. Her expression made my fingers tremble, but I finally opened the box to find a silver locket.

"There's a picture inside," Aunt Jeanne explained. I pressed the release and opened the locket. There was a picture of Paul holding me as an infant in his arms, and he was wearing that palmetto hat. For a moment I couldn't speak. It was exactly the way I always envisioned him carrying me at the start of my recurring nightmare.

"I thought you would like to have that," Aunt Jeanne said.

"Yes, thank you."

"Do you remember him at all?" she asked.

"Just a little," I said.

"He was very fond of you, and you were very fond of him," she said wistfully. Then she took a deep breath and covered my hands with hers, shutting the locket at the same time. "But this isn't the time for any sadness. Put it someplace safe and look at it from time to time," she asked. I thanked her again, and she went to say good-bye to Daddy and Mommy.

Mommy came over to me immediately afterward. "I saw her give you something," she said.

I showed her, and she gasped. "I just knew it had something to do with Paul."

"Do the rest of the Tates really hate us, Mommy?" I asked.

"Let's just say we're not on their A-list," Mommy replied. She gazed at the picture again. "He was a very handsome man, wasn't he?"

"Yes."

She gave the locket back to me.

"It was nice of her to give you this, and it's right of her to try to be sure Paul is not forgotten. Keep the locket with your most precious possessions."

"I will, Mommy."

She smiled softly and returned to her guests.

A little while later, while I was talking with Dominique, a gallery owner who was trying to persuade Mommy to display my picture in his front window, Catherine approached.

"Claude's getting very upset. We all want to leave, Pearl. Lester and the others have already gone to his house. Are you coming or not?"

I bit down on my lower lip. A part of me did want to go, but another part argued against it. I looked across the room and saw Daddy laughing. The twins were gorging on strawberry shortcake with their friends. I could slip away without causing too much of a stir now, I thought.

"Let me talk to my mother," I said.

"Good. I'll tell Claude," Catherine said

Mommy rarely missed anything happening around her. While she and her art world friends talked, she had her eyes on me. As I started toward her, she stepped away from the others.

"What is it, darling?" she asked. "You want to go someplace with your friends?"

"I guess," I said.

She looked at Claude, Catherine, and the others and then fastened her gaze on me. "Your heart's not fully in this for some reason, Pearl," she said with the assurance of a psychic. "What is it, honey? Is it going to be a wild party?"

"Maybe," I confessed.

She nodded. "You know what growing up is," she said, nodding like someone who had finally reached a conclusion. "It's knowing when to say no. Nothing more than that, I think," she added. "You decide. It's all right for you to leave if you want to. It's your night, Pearl. Daddy will understand."

We hugged, and I turned back to my friends. Claude raised his eyebrows and smiled. I started to nod and stopped. Once I left this house and went with Claude to Lester's, saying no would be harder than graduating from medical school, I thought.

"Coming now?" Claude asked anxiously.

"Why don't you and I stay here, Claude?" I suggested. "We can have plenty of privacy."

"Here? Are you serious? Everywhere you go, there are servants loitering—unless we slip up to your room," he proposed, his eyes lustful.

"Claude, I don't like being rushed into anything," I said.

"Rushed? We've been going together for nearly a year That's like being married nowadays," he protested.

I started to laugh, but he continued, his anger building. "You don't know what it's like for me, lying to all my friends, pretending you and I are really lovers. All my friends have girlfriends who aren't afraid to make love."

"You mean you make up stories about us?" I asked.

"Of course. You want me to look like a fool?"

"Is that what you would be if we didn't sleep

together, a fool? What about caring for me and my feelings?"

"That's what I want to do," he said stepping closer. "Care for your feelings. Come on, let's go with the others."

"I'd rather stay here, Claude," I said after taking a deep breath.

He shook his head. "You're never going to make love with me, are you?"

"I'm not going to make love just to keep some high school kids from thinking I'm a fool. It has to be something more serious."

He nodded. I saw that his eyes were a little blood-shot. "I think you should give me back my ring," he said. "It's just wasting away around your neck."

My heart was pounding to have such a dark and unhappy thing happen on this night, of all nights.

"Well?" he said. "What is it going to be?"

I undid the chain that held his ring on my bosom and handed it back to him.

He was surprised and clutched it roughly in his fist. "I should have listened to my friends. They all told me you were just a brain with no feelings. You probably went home and wrote a report after every date we had, didn't you?"

"Of course not," I said.

"I feel sorry for you," he continued, shaking his head. "You'll always be dissecting people. What did you do, take your temperature and decide tonight was a prime egg night?" he asked with his lips twisted into a sarcastic smirk. His words were like darts aimed at my heart. Tears burned under my eyelids, but I wouldn't permit myself to cry in front of him.

"Are you coming, Claude?" Diane Ratner asked as she crooked her shoulder suggestively.

"You're damn right I am," he said and smiled at

43

her. Then he put his arm through hers and embraced her tightly around the waist. She squealed with glee and flashed a look of satisfaction at me. I could just hear her bragging: "You might be our class valedictorian and you might have this big house and great party, but I have your boyfriend.

"Satisfied?" Claude asked me.

"Yes. If this is what you've decided is most important, then I am very satisfied. I made the right decision," I said.

His smile faded quickly. "Go read a book," he snapped.

"A dry one," Diane added. Their peals of laughter trailed after them as they joined the others and headed for the front door.

Catherine came running over to me. "What are you doing?"

"The sensible thing," I said. She shook her head and looked toward the others. "Go on. Don't worry about me. I'm all right."

"This was supposed to be our night to howl," she whined.

"We all howl in different ways, I suppose. Why did you let them destroy my speech? I thought we were close friends."

"It was just a joke. I knew you would be all right," she said but she averted her gaze.

"Friends protect and look after each other, but I suppose that takes some maturity," I added dryly.

Her eyes snapped back, full of fire. "I don't know what to think about you anymore, Pearl. Maybe you're too full of yourself for the rest of us. I'm disappointed," she added and turned away to hurry after the others. I watched them all leave the house, and for a moment, all the music, all the chatter and the laughter, faded. I heard only Claude's angry words and Catherine's disappointment

44

I bit down on my lower lip and sucked back the sobs that clamored to escape. Even though I had eaten, I had a hollow feeling in my stomach. *Was* I too much of a goody-goody? *Was* I just a brain?

I looked back at my party. Everyone was having such a good time, and Daddy had never looked younger or happier. Mommy was in a conversation with some of her gallery friends. All of my classmates had gone. Why, on this, the night I was supposed to feel so wonderful, was I standing here feeling devastated? I hurried out the side doors and walked down the patio toward the pool and cabana, leaving the jolly sounds of laughter, music, and chatter behind me.

I folded my arms under my breasts and walked slowly with my head down. Suddenly the twins and two of their friends jumped out of the hedges at me, all of them screaming, "Boo!"

"Get away from me!" I cried harshly.

Pierre's jaw dropped, but Jean kept laughing.

"We were just fooling, Pearl," Pierre said.

"I don't have the patience for the two of you right now. Leave me alone!" I yelled at them.

"We're sorry," Pierre said. He seized Jean's arm. "Come on. Let's go see if we can get some ice cream."

"What's the matter with her?" Jean asked, confused.

"Let's go," Pierre ordered. Although Jean was stronger, he obeyed his brother, and the four of them scurried back to the house, leaving me with my shadows.

Above, the sky that had been mostly clear with stars gleaming was growing increasingly overcast. It was as if the clouds were being drawn from one horizon to the other like some great dark curtain to shut out the heavens and shut away the happiness I had experienced this day. I planted myself on a lounge chair and

45

listened to the sounds of the city that drifted over our walls.

"What's wrong, Pearl?" I heard someone say a short while later. I looked up to see Mommy standing in the shadows.

"Nothing."

She stepped into the pale glow of the patio lights. "I know you too well, honey, and you know I feel your sadness," she said. She did, too. We were so close at times, it made Daddy shake his head in wonder. "I carried you inside me. We're too much a part of each other not to know each other's deepest feelings. What happened?"

I shrugged. "I said no, and everyone left. They think I'm a goody-goody, a brain without feelings."

"Oh, I see." She sat down beside me. In the increasing darkness, her face was hidden in shadow, but her eyes caught the pale light and glimmered with sympathy. "I know it's painful for you to drive your friends away, but you have to do what your heart tells you is right.

"Once, a long time ago," she added, "I said no, and I think I saved my life."

"Really? What happened?"

"My sister and a boyfriend came by in a car and asked me to go along with them. They had been smoking pot, and I saw they were already high, laughing, being reckless. They thought I was a party pooper, too, and I remember wondering if maybe there wasn't something wrong with me, maybe I was too old for my age."

"That was the night of the accident that crippled Gisselle?"

"Yes and killed the boy. I'm not saying something terrible has to happen all the time, but you've got to follow your instincts and believe in yourself."

"It was fun being with Claude sometimes; he's the

46

most popular boy in school. But I didn't have a strong enough feeling for him. The fact is, I haven't had a strong feeling for any boy yet, Mommy. Is that odd? Am I too analytical? Am I just a brain?"

"Of course not," she said, laughing. "Why do you have to become seriously involved with someone while you're still so young?"

"You did," I said quickly and then regretted it.

"It was different for me, Pearl. I came from a different sort of life. I told you that. My childhood was rushed. I wish I had had more time to be young and carefree."

"But you did fall in love with Daddy soon after you met him, didn't you?"

"I suppose." Even in the darkness, I could see the tiny smile on her lips as she remembered. "We had our first kiss out here, in that cabana, a kiss that changed my life. But that doesn't mean it has to be that way for everyone, especially for you," she continued quickly. "You're going to have a career, and you're dedicated to higher things than most of your friends are," she added.

"Is that good?" I wondered aloud. "Will I miss something important?"

"I don't think so, honey. I think you're destined for more important things, and when you fall in love and someone falls in love with you, it will be a greater relationship than you can imagine now."

"I almost feel as if I should go to Marie Laveau's in the French Quarter and get some love powder," I said, and Mommy laughed.

"Who told you about that? Don't say I did," she added quickly

"No, I read about it. You never did anything like that, did you?"

"No, but once in a while I'd burn a candle or Nina Jackson would burn some brimstone to keep away evil spirits she thought might be hovering about me. I suppose you think that's silly," she said. "And maybe it is."

"I don't know. Maybe if I were less scientific, I'd be happier," I said. "I know my friends would like me more."

"Nonsense. Don't be someone you're not just to please someone else," Mommy warned.

"Hey," Daddy called from the patio doors, "are you out here, Ruby?"

"Yes, Beau."

"Some of your friends are leaving and want to say good night."

"I'm coming."

"Something wrong?" Daddy asked when he saw I was with Mommy.

"No."

He stood there, skeptical. "Are you sure?"

"I'm fine, Daddy," I said. "We're coming in." I rose, and Mommy put her arm around me.

"And you are fine, too," she said squeezing me. "I'm proud of you, not just because you were the valedictorian and made a wonderful speech, but because you're sensible and mature. You don't know how wonderful it is to have a daughter you can trust and rely upon."

"Thank you, Mommy." I kissed her on the cheek and smelled her hair and perfume and felt my heart lighten. I was lucky, and I would not let anything darken this wonderful day and this wonderful night, I thought.

After our guests left, the twins whined and begged for me to open some of the graduation presents. Mommy wanted them to go to bed, but Daddy said it was a special night and they could stay up a little later, so we all went into the sitting room, and I unwrapped some of the gifts.

48

There was clothing for college and some expensive reference books. Dr. Portier and his wife had given me the latest edition of *Gray's Anatomy*.

The twins became bored with my presents rather quickly. The two of them sank back in the larger settee, resting against each other, Pierre's arm over Jean's shoulders, Jean's eyes blinking and battling the weight of his eyelids. Finally Daddy nudged them and ordered them to bed. They had no resistance left and stumbled along. He guided them upstairs, and Mommy followed to be sure the two of them were all right.

Daddy returned first. "Happy, princess?" he asked.

"Yes, Daddy."

"It was the happiest day of my life," he said.

"No, it wasn't, Daddy."

"What?"

"The happiest day of your life was the day you met Mommy."

He laughed. "That's different."

"But it was your happiest day, wasn't it?"

"I didn't know it at the time, but yes, it was. I met her right outside this house, and I thought she was her sister in a Mardi Gras costume."

"How does a man know when he's in love, Daddy? Do bells really ring in your head?"

"Bells?" He smiled. "I don't remember bells. I just remember that my first thought every morning when I awoke was of being with your mother." He stared at me. "Trouble with Claude?" I nodded. "The problem is simple, Pearl. You're too mature for him."

"I'm too mature for all the boys my age."

"Maybe."

"Does that mean I'll be happy only with a much older man?"

"No," he said, laughing. "Not necessarily. And don't you bring home anyone who could be your

49

father," he warned. Then we hugged and started upstairs. At my bedroom doorway, he kissed me on the forehead.

"Good night, princess," he said.

"Night, Daddy."

"When you were opening your gifts downstairs," he said, "I thought I saw something around your ankle. Is it what I think?" I nodded. He shook his head. "Well, they say if you believe in something hard enough, it will happen. Who am I to disagree?" He kissed me again, and I went into my room.

Mommy came to say good night, too. I told her Daddy had seen the dime.

"Now he'll tease me to death," she said. "But I don't care. I've seen my grandmere do things that defied reason and logic."

"There's so much you still haven't told me about the past, isn't there?"

"Yes," she said sadly.

"But you will now. You'll tell me everything, won't you? The good and the bad. Promise?"

"Just think happy thoughts tonight, honey. There's plenty of time to open the dark closets." She kissed me and stared down at me a moment with that angelic smile on her lips, and then she left.

I could hear music in the night, trumpets and saxophones, trombones and drums. New Orleans was a city that hated to go to sleep. It was as if it knew that when it did, the spirits and ghosts that hovered outside the wall of laughter, music, and song would have free rein to wander the streets and invade our dreams.

At Lester's house Claude was probably kissing Diane. It was supposed to be my kiss.

My kiss was on hold, waiting in the wings for the lips of my mysterious lover. But maybe that was just a dream, too. Maybe there was no lover and never would be. Maybe one of those curses Mommy feared were left at our doorstep was a curse designed for me.

I reached over to the nightstand and opened the locket Aunt Jeanne had given me, so that I could gaze at myself being held by Paul. Love could be painful, too, I thought.

I had graduated from high school as class valedictorian, but at the moment I felt I didn't know very much. I closed the locket, turned off the lights, and closed my eyes.

Then I fell asleep to the sound of the applause I had received when I ended my speech saying, "Today is commencement, and commencement means a beginning."

Was it the beginning of happiness and success or the beginning of loneliness and error?

"Don't look down," Mommy had once told me. "Be like a tightrope walker and keep your eyes focused on the future. You have to have more trust in yourself, Pearl."

That was what I would try to do.

3

A Brave New World

The first official day of summer vacation declared itself with record heat. Temperatures cleared the one hundred and five mark and the humidity was so high, I imagined I could see droplets forming in the air right before my eyes. I had only a few blocks to walk to catch the Saint Charles streetcar, which would take me to Broadmoor General Hospital, where I was to work, but by the time I stepped into the car, my clothes were sopping wet and my hair felt glued to my forehead and scalp. Everyone looked subdued by the heat and humidity and sat with drawn, tired faces, anxious to get into their air-conditioned workplaces. Even the canopy of spreading oak, usually high and regal, appeared weighted down and exhausted, the leaves drooping sadly. The birds that normally flitted about joyfully, looked stuffed and stuck to these branches, not wasting their energy.

But despite the weather, I was bubbling with excitement. Although I didn't expect to do much more than aid the nurses and run errands, I was still looking forward to being around the medical staff and seeing and hearing the business of caring for the sick. For the first time in my life, really, I would be part of that mysterious, magical world in which doctors and nurses, with wisdom, knowledge, and insight, determined the treatments that would heal people and save lives. It wasn't too much of a stretch for me to understand how and why Mommy's Cajun relatives believed in the power of traiteurs. Even though medicine was a science, doctors and nurses were magicians in the minds of most people. They listened to and viewed our insides to discover where our bodies broke down and what tiny enemies had invaded us to do us harm.

Broadmoor General had been constructed on a grassy knoll. Two pairs of tall, full sycamore trees stood out in front, and patches of Queen Anne's lace ran alongside the driveway. The gardens were filled with azaleas, yellow and red roses, and hibiscus. Trumpet vine ran over the lower gallery, and purple wisteria peeked through the scrolled iron fence. Off to the right was a small pond, the water the color of dark tea.

The original building had been a mansion seized by the Confederate army during the Civil War and converted into an emergency hospital. The facility had been expanded and modernized over the years, but it wasn't one of the city's biggest. However, Daddy thought I would get more out of working in a small hospital because it would be more personal.

The streetcar stopped about a block away, and I walked quickly to the front entrance. The lobby was tiny compared to those of the more modern hospitals in the city. The old chandeliers had been replaced with bright, antiseptic-looking fluorescent lights, and the beige walls had been freshly painted. The tile floor had just been scrubbed; a small sign warned about it being slippery. I paused at the information desk to get directions to the personnel office. An elderly lady in a pink uniform directed me to the short corridor on the right and told me it was the first door on the left.

I found a tall, dark-haired woman slamming file cabinet drawers closed while she kept her eyes on a duplicating machine that was spitting out forms. When she turned to see who had entered the office, I noticed a thin blue ink stain on her chin. She was at least six feet tall with very hard, bony features. Her collarbones were prominent under her dark blue blouse. She had long arms and hands with slender fingers.

Her smile was a quick rubber-band tightening of her lips, a pale red line slashed across her face. She tweaked her slim nose and widened her dull brown eyes, the lids of which had been drooping to the point of shutting completely. She gasped before speaking as if she had to suck in enough air to make speech sounds first.

"Yes?" she asked, not disguising her annoyance at being interrupted.

"I'm looking for Mrs. Morgan," I said.

"I'm Mrs. Morgan."

"Bonjour! I'm Pearl Andreas. I'm reporting to work today," I said. "Mr. Marbella, the hospital administrator, said I should come here as soon as I arrived."

"You have to fill out these papers," she said, gesturing toward a small, narrow table on my right. There were stacks of forms on it.

"All of them?" I asked.

"Start at the left and fill out one form from each of the first three stacks. Be sure to put down your Social Security number. I can't issue a release to the financial office so they can issue your first paycheck unless that's included. And be sure it's correct."

"Yes, ma'am."

"As soon as you have all that completed, go see Mrs. Winthrop on the second floor. She's the head nurse on this shift. You can take the stairway at the end of the hall and make a right. She'll issue you a uniform and explain your duties."

"Yes, ma'am."

"Your uniform doesn't belong to you," she lectured. "It belongs to the hospital. You can take it home, if you like, and you are responsible for keeping it clean and in good shape. A ten-dollar deposit will be held against your first week's salary."

She leaned over the desk and looked down at my feet. "You can wear those sneakers today, but tomorrow you should wear soft-soled white shoes. You can buy them at Medical Supplies on Canal Street. You have to pay for them yourself."

"I understand," I said.

She sighed again; this time it looked like her body would simply collapse inside her blouse and skirt, the hem of which was so low it brushed the floor when she walked. "Is this your first job?"

"Well, actually . . ."

"I'll explain all about FICA, withholding, medical, food allowances . . . after you complete the forms," she said and shook her head. "My assistant is out sick again. She usually handles new enrollments. She works in a hospital and she's constantly out sick," she added. "I haven't missed a day's work in twelve years, but people don't have the same attitude about their work anymore. Younger people are very lackadaisical when it comes to responsibilities."

"I'm not," I said. "Actually, I'm very excited about working here this summer. I'm going to become a doctor," I told her.

"Really?" She bit the inside of her cheek and tilted her head. "I myself have never gone to a woman

55

doctor, and probably never will." She snapped her head straight and nodded toward the desk as if someone had poked her to remind her she was at work. She jabbed her long right forefinger toward the stack of forms. "The quicker you fill those out, the quicker you can earn your pay. You have to punch in and punch out every day right over there," she said nodding toward the opposite wall. "I'll have your temporary card for you before the day's over. For today I'll write in when you actually begin. Don't expect to get credit for the time it takes to fill out the forms."

"Yes, ma'am," I said and went to the forms. After I completed them all and handed them to her, she rattled off the information about my pay voucher slip, explaining everything so fast that I barely had time to hear, much less comprehend.

Then she leaned toward me, pursed her lips for a moment, and said, "Do your work and don't put your nose into anyone else's affairs and you'll do fine."

"Thank you, ma'am," I said. She stood back and nodded toward the doorway. I hurried out and up the stairs to the second floor. The nurses' station was located near the center of the corridor. A nurse who looked about fifty with curly gray hair and friendly blue eyes turned my way as I approached. A short, slim black girl with large round eyes stood beside her.

"I'm looking for Mrs. Winthrop," I said. "I'm Pearl Andreas."

"Oh, yes, dear. I'm Mrs. Winthrop. We've been expecting you. Sophie will take you to the linen closet and find you a uniform," she said, nodding at the slim black girl, who looked no more than sixteen. Her hair was cut very short, and she had a tiny but prominent scar on the left side of her jaw. She came around the desk quickly.

"This way," she said. She stared at me hard, dropping her eyes to my feet and raising her gaze to my face. When we were far enough away from the nurses' station, she spun around. "What do you want to be a nurse's aide for?" she demanded. "You look rich."

"I want to work in a hospital during my summer vacation because I hope to study medicine," I told her. "I want to get as much experience on my own as I can."

"You want to be a doctor? How long do you have to go to school to get your degree?" she asked, looking friendlier than before.

"You go to college and medical school for about seven years, and then you do your internship in a hospital. I'll be in my late twenties before I can practice on my own."

"We've got one of those," Sophie said.

"One what?"

"An intern. Dr. Weller. He's not a full doctor, though. He's got years to go yet."

"Well, it does take years and years of hard work. I hope I can stick it out," I said.

She narrowed her eyes again. "You sure you want to be a doctor?"

"I'm sure."

"I've never seen a woman doctor here."

"Well, maybe I'll be the first," I said and smiled.

She looked at me thoughtfully for a moment, then narrowed her eyes skeptically. "You ever give someone a bedpan?"

"No."

"You ever cleaned up vomit?"

"Once, when one of my brothers got sick," I replied.

She leaned toward me. "You ever seen blood, lots of blood?" she demanded.

"I've seen blood," I assured her.

"And guts?"

"I've dissected animals and I know what's inside a human being," I said.

Sophie stepped back, shocked. "Where did you do that?"

"In school in the lab. Didn't you?"

"I only went to school through the fifth grade," she told me, "and we didn't have a lab, but I clean the lab here, so I've seen blood and guts and smelled it, too. You got to have a stomach made of iron. I do. Nothing makes me throw up anymore," she added proudly.

"I'm glad," I said. "It would be hard for you to come to work every day if you got sick to your stomach all the time."

She nodded. "The other girl, the one who come here last Friday, she got white as chalk the first day and puked in the bathroom for half an hour before Mrs. Winthrop sent her home. I'm glad you're here because I've been doing twice the work ever since that girl left."

"I won't throw up. I promise," I said.

She looked satisfied and led me to the linen room. There weren't many uniforms. The ones that were there were either way too big or too small. The best fit was so snug I had to leave the top two buttons of the bodice undone. "I guess this will have to do for now," I said.

"What's that around your ankle? Is it a dime?" Sophie asked.

"Yes. It's a good-luck charm."

She eyed me suspiciously for a moment. "Who gave it to you?"

"My mother. Someone special gave it to her a long time ago."

"My mama says people who wear a dime around their ankle be practicing voodoo."

"The dime is good gris-gris, if that's what you mean, but I don't practice voodoo."

"Does your mama?"

"No, not really," I said, but she continued to eye me warily.

"How old are you?" Sophie asked.

"Seventeen. I'll be eighteen in two months. How old are you?"

"The truth or what I tell people here?"

"The truth."

"I'll be fourteen next August, but they all think I'm going to be seventeen. Don't you tell," she warned.

"I won't."

"Let's go see Mrs. Winthrop."

"Is that the best fit you can find for her, Sophie?" the head nurse asked immediately.

"The others are much smaller or much, much bigger, Mrs. Winthrop," Sophie said. "We tried them all."

"I'm afraid this is the best," I said.

"Well, I'll ask Mr. Marbella to order more uniforms. Now that you're here, Pearl, we'll divide the floor between you and Sophie. You take rooms 200 to 205; Sophie will see to the rest." She checked her watch. "It's time to bring the patients their juice and refill their water pitchers. Sophie will show you where things are."

Sophie took me to the kitchen where we found another, much younger nurse talking with the intern. He was sitting with his back to us, and she was leaning against the counter. They were laughing when we entered.

"'Scuse me," Sophie said and did a small curtsy. "We got to start on the juice."

The nurse smirked and moved away from the refrigerator. I saw from her name tag that she was

Mrs. Crandle. She had light brown hair trimmed at the nape of her neck, hazel eyes and a firm mouth that dipped with annoyance at the corners. She wasn't unattractive, but her nose was a little too sharp and too long. The intern spun around in his chair and smiled widely when he saw me.

"Well now, who have we here?" he asked.

"She's the new nurse's aide," Sophie explained. "Her name's Pearl."

"Well, hello," he said. "I'm Dr. Weller. My mother always thought I should be a doctor because of our name. Get it? I make people weller." He laughed, but Mrs. Crandle grimaced as if it pained her to hear his joke again.

"Hi," I said. He rose to his full five feet eleven inches and extended his hand. He widened his smile to show me his very white and perfect teeth. His dark eyes sparkled wickedly when I put my hand into his. He folded his fingers over it quickly. His skin was as fair as mine, though in contrast to his dark hair, it made him look a little too pale. His strong chin sported a devil's cleft and another dimple in his right cheek flashed in and out apparently at will.

"About time we dressed up this place," he said, still grinning from ear to ear. He shot a look at Mrs. Crandle, who raised her eyes toward the ceiling.

"Just what we needed," she remarked, "another thing to distract you from your work."

"Don't mind her. I'm never distracted from anything I put my mind on," he said, keeping his gaze fixed on me. He dropped his eyes slowly and raised them with a look of appreciation. "That's the sexiest nurse's aide uniform I've seen," he added.

"There aren't any that fit me better, but . . ." I began, feeling my face grow warm as my cheeks turned crimson.

"Hey, I didn't say this doesn't fit you." He laughed. He was still holding my hand.

"We've got to start bringing the juice to the patients," I said.

"Sure." He flashed another amused smile and released my hand.

"She gonna be a doctor too," Sophie bragged.

"Is that right?"

"Yes," I said.

"Not a nurse, a doctor?"

I looked at Mrs. Crandle who had turned back to me sharply when he asked the question.

"I think nurses are just as important," I said, "but I'm interested in practicing medicine outside the hospital too."

"Oh? Very ambitious." He frowned, putting ripples in his forehead. In a deeper voice he asked, "How are your grades in school?"

"I was class valedictorian," I said.

He raised his eyebrows. "Impressive. We better watch our p's and q's, Mrs. Crandle," he joked.

"I would say you should watch the whole alphabet and not just the p's and q's," she remarked. "I have an I.V. to hook up. Don't you have anything to do, Doctor?"

"Whoa," he said. "Yes, I do. Well, good luck, Pearl. Please don't hesitate to ask me any questions," he said and reluctantly followed Mrs. Crandle.

"He's always making jokes," Sophie said. "Mrs. Crandle says some of his patients will laugh themselves to death. Can people do that, laugh themselves to death?"

"I don't think so," I said. She looked unconvinced, but nodded and then showed me where everything was located. I loaded my cart and began my rounds.

There were two elderly women in my first room, one

of whom was on a heart monitor; a man with a broken leg in the second, and a woman in her thirties undergoing tests for a stomach problem in the third. Her name was Sheila, and she was obviously very nervous and concerned. "I have to fast for a day," she told me. "Tomorrow morning I'm having another test."

"What's wrong with your stomach?" I asked.

"I get terrible pains right here whenever I eat," she said, pointing.

"They're looking at your gallbladder?"

"Yes. How did you know? Did the same thing happen to you once?" she asked hopefully.

"No. I just know that's where it is and that's where you would feel pain if it was acting up. But that doesn't have to be the reason," I added quickly.

"I know," she said sadly. "It could be something else. It could be something far more serious."

"Don't get yourself upset. Wait for all the reports. Most of the time, our imaginations make more of it than it is," I told her. I had overheard our doctor say that to Mommy once when Pierre and Jean both came down with a bad case of whooping cough. Sheila smiled, and I fixed her bed and made her more comfortable.

When I turned to go on to my next room, I saw Dr. Weller standing in the doorway, a slow grin forming around his lips. He stepped back into the corridor as I emerged with the juice cart.

"I overheard what you said." He leaned toward me. "If Mrs. Winthrop heard you giving patients medical advice, she would send you right home."

"I didn't give—"

"You let her believe it might be her gallbladder. Uh-uh-uh," he said, wagging his forefinger. Then he laughed. "It's all right. Chances are very good that you're right. Actually," he said, leaning back against the wall and folding his arms, "you did a smart thing deciding to work in the hospital during your summer vacation. You'll pick up a lot just hanging around and listening."

"That's what I thought, too," I said.

"You know, I'm studying and learning every day myself. I'm interning here under Dr. Bardot. He's constantly testing me." He smiled. "I bet you can help me," he said, nodding with a thoughtful look.

"Me? How?"

"You can be my study partner. You know, ask questions, test me on stuff. Do you have a heavy social schedule?" he asked.

"Social schedule?"

"Do you punch a clock with a boyfriend, too?"

"Oh. No, not anymore," I said.

"Good. Maybe you'll give me some time, then. I promise you'll learn a lot too," he added. "And I don't mean just medical information. I can fill you in on what to expect, how to prepare your applications, interviews. It's getting harder and harder to get into a good medical school in this country, you know. There are a lot of valedictorians out there competing for the same spaces," he warned.

I thought a moment. Learning about all this was why I had wanted to work here.

"Okay," I said. "Do you study during breaks?"

"Oh, no. We'll do it after work. I don't live far from here. It's a small apartment I took near Tulane University. That's where I attended premed and med school. You expect to go there?"

"I might, yes," I said.

"Fine. I'll fill you in on all the nitty-gritty. What's your shift tomorrow? Same as today?"

"Yes."

"I'm free about the same time. We can start right away—if that's all right with you, that is," he said.

63

I hesitated. I liked the idea of working with an intern, but why had he chosen me and so quickly? "Wouldn't you rather work with someone who is already a medical student?" I asked.

"They want to study only what they need." He smiled again. "Hey, I won't bite you, and even if I did, I'd treat the wound," he added and laughed. "But if you think you'll be uncomfortable or—"

"No, it's all right."

"Great. And don't worry about getting home afterward. I'll see to that. I'll even make you dinner, if you like. Nothing fancy, of course. I'm not living on a doctor's salary yet. Fact is, and you better know it now, interns are medical slaves. But we all gotta pay our dues. See you later." He winked and walked down the corridor.

I wondered if I had agreed too fast to help him. He was already an intern. I probably wouldn't understand half the questions. Surely I would just be wasting his time and my own, I thought, but then I thought, He should know that, and yet he still wants me to help him.

"This isn't exactly a place to daydream," I heard someone say. Mrs. Crandle was standing in the doorway of my next room.

"Oh, I'm sorry," I said and hurried on.

Sophie wasn't exaggerating about the problems we could encounter as aides. An elderly man in room 205 messed his bed, and I had to clean it up. I must have swallowed a hundred times and held my breath for an hour before I was finished. Mrs. Crandle made me wash down the bed frame and scrub the floor around the bed as well.

Sophie and I had to run down to the laundry and carry up fresh linens. I emptied a half dozen bedpans and cleaned bathrooms. I thought my first day at the hospital would be relatively uneventful and just the sort of work I had expected, but shortly before my shift ended, Mrs. Conti, the elderly woman in room 200, had a heart attack. Mrs. Crandle called for a Code E Blue, and Dr. Weller came running from the other end of the corridor. I watched them wheel in a defibrillator. Another doctor came from the third-floor cardiac care unit. They worked and worked, but Mrs. Conti's heart had stopped dead and didn't start again.

Her roommate, Mrs. Brennen, cried hysterically and had to be sedated. There was a flag of mourning on everyone's face. Mrs. Conti had been dozing when I had delivered her juice and had barely opened her eyes when I returned to freshen her water pitcher and see if she needed anything. I had seen and heard her heart monitor, and Mrs. Brennen had told me that Mrs. Conti had been upstairs in the cardiac care unit for ten days before being brought down to the second floor.

"Why wasn't she still upstairs?" I whispered to Dr. Weller when he emerged after the failed effort to revive her had ended.

"They sent her down two days ago because she had made enough progress and they needed room for another patient." He shrugged. "Can't always predict it," he said and then flashed a challenging smile. "Still want to be a doctor?"

I looked back at the room in which the dead woman still lay. Her family didn't know yet, but I was sure she would soon be mourned and missed. When I envisioned the saddened children and grandchildren, I felt anger boil in the base of my stomach. If I had been her doctor, she wouldn't have been moved out of the cardiac care unit.

"More than ever," I replied.

65

He tilted his head back and laughed. "Maybe you're the real thing. Something tells me I've found the right study helper." He looked back at the room and sighed. "Gotta go do the paperwork," he said. "That's a part of being a doctor you'll soon learn to hate too."

Maybe I was naive, but I thought there was no part of being a doctor I would hate.

I hadn't done all that much, but when my shift ended, I felt exhausted. Most of it was from the tension of starting the work and the emotional strain that resulted from seeing someone die. I changed back into my street clothing and left the corridor with Sophie. She and I stepped into Mrs. Morgan's office to punch out.

"How did you do?" she asked and looked at Sophie.

"She did fine, just fine," Sophie said quickly. "She didn't throw up once."

Mrs. Morgan smiled. "Well, that's an accomplishment. Here is your regular card. Punch in when you begin your shift and punch out when you end, and remember to buy some white shoes," she reminded me.

"Yes, ma'am."

Sophie and I left the hospital. The humidity hadn't diminished a degree, but the sun had gone down enough to lower the temperature.

"My mother says I'm lucky because I work in an air-conditioned hospital," Sophie said as we started down the driveway.

"What does she do?"

"Laundry."

"What about your father?"

"He works in the Quarter. He's a cook. I got two younger sisters still in school and a brother who's in the army. What about you?"

"I have twin brothers, twelve years old. Where do you live, Sophie?"

"On the other side of the Quarter. I take the car to Canal Street."

We waited for the streetcar together.

"How long have you worked in the hospital?" I asked her.

"Little more than a year."

"Don't you want to return to school? There's a lot more for you to learn," I said.

She dropped her eyes quickly. "Can't," she said. "Gotta work."

"Why? Doesn't your father make good money as a cook?" I knew good cooks in the Quarter were valuable.

Sophie shrugged. "Maybe," she said. "We don't know for sure."

"What? Why not?"

"He doesn't live with us," she told me just as the streetcar came around to our station. She hurriedly boarded, I sat beside her, and we both looked out the window as the car rattled down the track. "He doesn't even come to the house anymore," she continued. "He just sends some money around from time to time. If I want to see him, I have to go down to the restaurant, but he never has time to talk much."

"I'm sorry," I said. When the car approached my station and I stood up, Sophie looked very impressed.

"You live in the Garden District?"

"Uh-huh."

"I never even walked down here," she said.

"Maybe one day you can stop off and have dinner with me," I suggested.

"Really?" Her smile faded. "I usually gotta get right home to help Mama."

"Maybe you can work it out," I suggested. "See you tomorrow. Thanks for helping me get started. Bye."

"Bye," she called.

When I got home everyone wanted to hear about

my first day at work. The twins made faces and groaned when I described some of the cleanup work I had to do, but when I told them about the death of Mrs. Conti, the twins' eyes lit up with interest.

"You saw a dead woman?" Pierre asked.

"Yes."

"Did you touch her?" Jean said.

"No."

"Did she smell?"

"I think we can change the topic until after dinner," Daddy said. "Don't you, Pearl?"

"Yes, Daddy."

I went on to tell them about Sophie, but the twins weren't interested in anything except Mrs. Conti. When I told Daddy about Dr. Weller, he sat back and looked at Mommy.

"He just met you and he wants to make you dinner?" she asked.

"I guess because we aren't going to study until after work. Why?"

Daddy looked troubled.

"I'm sure he's just impressed with Pearl, and since she's shown an interest in medicine . . ." Mommy said.

Daddy thought for a moment and relaxed. "I suppose you're right, Ruby. You usually are when it comes to people. Your mother's going to have a new exhibition in two weeks," he added proudly. "And your picture is going to be part of it."

"That's wonderful, Mommy."

We talked about Mommy's artwork, and after a dessert of crème brûlée, Daddy took me to buy some soft-soled shoes, and Mommy went to work in her studio.

"Well," Daddy said in the car, "after being on the front lines, what do you think?"

"I think I want to become a doctor even more, Daddy." He nodded. "What really stopped you, Daddy?" I asked again. I knew his family had the money to put him through medical school and that he had been a very good student.

"My family was upset with me, especially after your mother became pregnant. I was very upset with myself for leaving Ruby, and for a while I was self-destructive. I drank heavily while I was in Europe, and I wasted my time and talent. And then . . ."

He paused and I saw how his eyes focused on a memory. "And then I heard that Ruby had married Paul. I soaked myself in self-pity, cut classes, and wasted time. Suddenly one morning there was a knock on my apartment door. When I opened it, I found your aunt Gisselle standing there. For a moment I thought she was Ruby. They had such identical faces. I let myself imagine, and your aunt Gisselle encouraged my illusions. The rest you know. Gisselle and I were married, and I returned to work in the Dumas enterprises.

"That's why I am so happy you are pursuing the career I cast aside," he said, turning to me with tears burning behind his eyelids. "I know you will be a wonderful doctor, Pearl."

"I'll try, Daddy," I said, my heart aching, my throat closing as I swallowed my tears. "I'll try."

After we returned home, the twins pleaded with me to tell them more about Mrs. Conti and what it was like to see a corpse. I finally pulled out some of my books on anatomy and let them look at the pictures. They were fascinated with what was inside their bodies, but Jean was upset about it as well.

"I'm glad we have skin covering everything," he remarked. "So I don't have to look at it."

Pierre laughed, but I closed the books and lectured

69

both of them about how wonderful the human body was. "The human body is one of the most perfect creations in the universe," I explained.

"If it's so perfect, why do we get sick?" Jean demanded.

"It's perfect but not invulnerable," I said.

He grimaced with confusion.

"She means you can't stop the germs from flying up your nose or into your mouth," Pierre said. "Unless you walk around with your nose plugged up and your mouth taped shut. But then they could get in your ears, right, Pearl?"

"So we'll plug up our ears," Jean said.

"Then you can't hear."

"So we always get sick," Jean concluded sadly.

"But that's why we need doctors, right, Pearl?" Pierre asked.

I smiled. "Yes, Pierre."

"Couldn't the doctors stop Mrs. Conti from dying?" Jean asked.

"She was old. Her body was tired."

"She was worn out, like our tricycles," Pierre explained.

Jean nodded, and then he suddenly burst into a flashbulb smile. "We'll have a doctor living with us and keeping us from getting too sick all the time. We'll have Pearl!"

I laughed. "It will be a while yet, Jean."

"And she won't be living with us. She'll be grown up and married with her own children," Pierre explained.

Jean's smile faded.

"But I promise. I'll always look after you two," I said, which restored the brightness to Jean's face. "Now go up and get ready for bed. Everyone, especially a young person growing a foot a day, needs rest."

"Aw . . ."

"Or else those organs in your body will shrivel up," Pierre threatened. Jean's eyes widened and he turned to me.

"No, they won't," I assured him. "But go on."

They jumped to their feet.

"Good night, Pearl," Pierre said.

"Good night, Pearl." Jean smiled impishly. "I hope you don't have a nightmare about Mrs. Conti."

Pierre pulled him out, and they scurried up the stairs, laughing.

It wasn't too much longer before I followed them to bed myself. I had just crawled under my covers when the phone rang. It was Catherine. We hadn't spoken since graduation night. I sensed a formality in her voice. There wasn't any of the warmth and excitement of our former relationship.

"Did you start working in the hospital?" she asked.

"Today."

"How did it go?" she asked with little real interest.

"I think I'll learn a lot," I said. "An intern asked me to help him study."

"Oh? What's he look like?"

"It's nothing like that. He just wanted someone to help him keep sharp. An intern's really still a student. It's a great opportunity for me, too."

"Good for you." After a moment she said, "Everyone's still mad at you for not going to Lester's. They think you're a snob."

"I'm not running for political office," I said dryly.

"You shouldn't forget who your real friends are," she said. "Even if you are the smartest girl in the school."

"I never forgot them, but as I told you, real friends protect and look after each other."

"Everyone is the butt of a joke sometimes, Pearl. Don't you think you overreacted?"

"No."

She was silent a moment and then decided to fire with both guns. "Claude had a good time with Diane. They went into one of the guest rooms and didn't come out until morning. They're seeing each other regularly now."

"Then maybe that was meant to be," I said.

Catherine sighed with frustration. "I swear you are the hardest person to be friends with," she concluded.

I was speechless for a moment. Was she right? Things that interested most girls my age didn't seem to be as important to me. Was that a curse or a blessing?

"Anyway, we're going away for our summer holiday. I won't see you for three weeks. I suppose you don't care."

"I said I was disappointed about what happened and what you did, Catherine, but I hope you will see my point and we'll still be friends."

"And I hope the lifeguard I met last year is working at the beach again. He thought I was too young for him, but maybe he'll change his mind this year."

"How old was he?"

"Twenty-three. I know. You think he's too old for me," she said quickly.

"No. That's not too old for you."

"Really? I don't think so either." She lowered her voice. "But my parents wouldn't be happy. How would your parents feel about it?"

"I don't know," I said. "I suppose if we really cared for each other, they wouldn't complain."

"Your mother's so understanding. Well, maybe I'll drop you a postcard."

"Do that, Catherine."

"Don't give anyone the wrong pills," she warned.

"I'm not permitted to dispense medication. I'm just an aide."

"Well don't give anyone the wrong aid," she said

72

and laughed. "Look. I'm sorry. Maybe you're right. Maybe the girls went too far and I should have told you right away, but I didn't want everyone to hate me, too."

"Too?"

"You know what I mean. Anyway, I said I was sorry."

"Okay. Thanks. Have fun."

"I will," she promised and we hung up. I sat there for a moment thinking. Somewhere in the back of my mind I heard the voice of a little girl trying to hold on, trying to keep me from being so serious. But it was a voice that was dwindling and barely audible anymore.

Whether I liked it or not, I was rushing headfirst into adulthood now. And there was nothing to do about it but sit back and enjoy the ride.

I fell asleep quickly after Catherine and I spoke, but I did have a nightmare about Mrs. Conti. I saw her eyes pop open when I returned to her room, and they were glassy and milky white. Then I thought about Dr. Weller and his impish smile. "Still want to be a doctor?" he had challenged.

"More than ever."

I mumbled it in my sleep.

"More than ever."

4

Life Lessons

"If you and I are going to be study partners," Dr. Weller said as we left the hospital the next day, "you should call me Jack. Dr. Weller is too formal after we walk out of there," he said, nodding back toward the hospital.

"Jack?"

"That's my name. Oh, my real name is Jackson Marcus Weller, which is what I will hang on my shingle. I was named after my great-grandfather on my mother's side. I'd rather be just Jack, though, especially to people I admire and people I hope will admire me," he said. Then he put his hand on my waist to turn me to the right. "My apartment is just a few blocks this way," he said. "You don't mind walking, do you?"

"No." His hand lingered on my hip, his fingers pressing with authority.

"I have a car, but I seldom use it. Driving is such a hassle in the city. I'd much rather walk or use public transportation." He drew his hand away when we started to walk again.

"Did you grow up in New Orleans?" I asked.

"Grow up?" He smiled and then laughed. "Most of my relatives and friends think I haven't. They think because I'm going to be a doctor, I should look, act, and feel like an old man. Who trusts a young doctor these days? In almost every other profession, youth is an advantage, but in medicine . . ." He paused and turned to me. "My ex-roommate actually dyes his hair gray. Do you believe that?"

I shook my head.

He stared at me a moment and relaxed his lips, a look of pity in his eyes. "Actually, I feel sorry for you. It's twice as hard for a woman to become a doctor. You've got to be twice as good. But," he said, winking, "I think you might just have the grit to make it. Now," he said holding up his hand, palm toward me, "don't tell me anything else about yourself. Let me guess."

We continued, strolling at a slower pace. It wasn't quite as humid as it had been the day before. The sun was low enough to leave the eastern sky a darker blue so that the billowing clouds looked as white as milk. Toward the south a single-engine plane was dragging a banner that advertised a jazz and dinner special in the French Quarter. We could hear the streetcar rattling along past the palm trees behind us. The birds were twittering noisily. I imagined they were filled with news that they had stored up like acorns during the impressive heat and humidity. Now that they were cooler and able to gossip, they did so nonstop.

The street lanterns were just flickering, it not being dark enough to turn themselves on full. Less humidity seemed to free the scent of camellias and of the banana and magnolia trees that grew along and behind the pike fences of the houses we passed as we ambled along the sidewalk, which in New Orleans was known as a banquette. Most banquettes were built two to three feet high, mainly to keep water out of houses. Across the way I saw three Tulane summer school coeds giggling and walking while two boys in a convertible followed slowly and tried to get their attention.

"You're not an only child, and you're not spoiled. That's for sure," Jack Weller began.

"I have twin brothers, twelve years old."

"Uh-huh."

"But I am spoiled," I admitted.

"Sure. All spoiled young women agree to work as nurse's aides for peanuts and are willing to clean up after sick people," he remarked. He gazed at me again. "You're not spoiled."

"I'm spoiled, but I'm determined," I replied.

He laughed. "I like that. You're from a well-to-do family, right?"

"Yes. But did you really guess that or did you cross-examine Sophie?" I fired back quickly.

He laughed again. "You are a bright girl. All right. I'll confess I asked Sophie some questions. Just down here," he said seizing my hand and turning us into a side street toward an apartment building with a canopy that sagged in the middle. The gray stucco walls were badly chipped and cracked and the front door was in dire need of paint or wood stain. "I want to prepare you," he said as we approached the entrance. "I have only a studio apartment. Someone from the Garden District won't think much of it, I suspect."

"I'm spoiled, but I'm not a snob," I said.

His smile widened again and he opened the door. We stepped through a short entryway into a small lobby, the walls of which were faded and smudged. Here and there the dark brown tile floor was chipped. The only furnishing was a rickety table with an oval mirror in a dull white frame above it. The aroma of shrimp gumbo filled the air.

"The stairs are faster than the elevator," he said, nodding toward them. I followed him up three flights, the old, worn steps moaning complaints at our every step. "At least I have a little view," he said putting his key into the lock.

I was prepared for a small place with inexpensive furnishings, but I wasn't prepared for the mess. The door opened immediately to the living room—bedroom. The settee to the right was covered with books and papers, and there were books and papers on the floor as well. There was also a coffee cup, still with some coffee in it; the dish beside it was crusted with leftover pasta. The windowsill was caked with dust, and the rug was frayed clear through in spots.

"I got up late this morning and didn't get a chance to clean up from last night," he explained. "Otherwise, it's comfortable."

Comfortable? I thought. It would be easy to become claustrophobic here. We had closets bigger than Jack's apartment. There was only one narrow window in the living room—bedroom, and the room itself was barely big enough to contain the settee, the bed, a table, and two chairs. Through an open doorway I saw a tiny kitchen with dishes piled in the sink and a small trash can stuffed so full that a take-out pizza box popped up and over the side.

Jack scurried about, clearing off the settee, chairs, and coffee table.

"Just give me a minute," he asked. He carried the dishes into the kitchen and then hurried back to straighten up the bed. "Bachelors," he said with an emphatic shrug. "This is the way we live, but you don't know any real bachelors yet, I imagine," he said. When I didn't reply, he stopped and looked at me. "Do you?"

"What? Oh, no." I couldn't get over how messy his

apartment was. A doctor should be concerned about cleanliness, I thought.

"I wasn't raised to be a slob, if that's what you're thinking," he said, reading my mind. "Just wait until you start your internship. You'll see how little time you have for yourself. Unlike you, I come from modest means. My father worked on the oil rigs in Beaumont and was laid off so often that I used to think he was rich and had to work only a few months a year. Medical school is pretty expensive, you know," he added.

"How did you manage?" I asked, feeling guilty for condemning him so quickly.

"My grandmother left a trust for me. When she first left it, it was worth something, but inflation ate up a lot of it and the cost of medical school climbed, so I had to borrow money. I'm in debt up to here," he said holding his hand an inch or so above his head. "It's a great advantage to attend medical school and not have to worry about financing," he said. "But you've got to have more than money to become a doctor. Only thing is . . ." He stopped cleaning up and stared at me, shaking his head slowly.

"What?" I asked, concerned.

"You're really too attractive."

"What?"

"Seems like a waste," he added. "You should be a doctor's wife, bedecked with jewels and furs, running social and charity affairs," he said and then laughed. "Just kidding. Although the only female doctors I've known could scare the germs away." He patted down his bed, which was covered with a plain light blue quilt and two pillows. "Would you like something cold to drink? I've got orange juice, tonic water, and Dixie beer."

I gazed at the kitchen. It looked contaminated.

His face broke into a laughing smile. "I'll wash the glass first. I promise," he said.

"Orange juice will be fine."

"Great. Sit anywhere you like. Sit on the bed if you want," he said and went to get my juice. I sat on the settee and started to peruse the medical books.

"I know it's too soon, but have you considered what you want to specialize in?" he asked from the kitchen.

"I was thinking about pediatrics."

"Good one," he said returning. He had juice for me and a glass of beer for himself. "Especially for a woman. Mothers find it easier to deal with a woman."

"I wasn't thinking of it because of that," I said with some testiness in my voice. "Women are capable of becoming good surgeons, good cardiologists, good—"

"Okay, okay. I'm sorry. I'm not a male chauvinist. I'm just practical," he said, handing me my glass of juice. He sat beside me on the settee. "Hungry yet?"

I had been, but the sight of the room had churned my stomach and driven away my appetite.

"Not yet," I said. I was thinking now that I would study with him for a while and then make my excuses and go home, where I could enjoy some of Milly's leftovers.

"I happen to be a pretty good cook. All that chemistry," he said smiling. He gazed at me and then let his eyes drop softly, moving like invisible fingers over my face, down my neck, and across my breasts. "I bet a beautiful girl like you has had lots of boy-friends, right?"

"No."

"No? I thought girls were more promiscuous these days, collecting male trophies the way boys used to when I was in high school," he said.

"I have always had more important things on my mind, although I did go steady for a while this year."

"What happened? I don't mean to be personal. I'm just curious about young people today," he said.

"Let's just say I wasn't as committed to our relationship as he thought I was."

"Uh-oh. I think I know what that means. Was he your first steady boyfriend?" he asked with a licentious smile.

"Yes, but as I said, it didn't last that long."

"I see." He nodded, his right forefinger and thumb squeezing his chin. He was making me feel as if he were a doctor of romance and I had come to him for a love checkup.

"What do you have to study tonight?" I asked, feeling a little uncomfortable under such intense scrutiny.

"Hmm." He thought a moment and then reached under the settee and brought out a textbook. "I know just the topic. During office hours, we had a female patient today who suffered from dyspareunia. I don't suppose you know what that is," he said thumbing through the book.

I shook my head.

"Another term used is vaginismus, affectionately known as the honeymoon injury," he said, his smile widening. "Enough hints?"

I felt myself blanche.

"Now, now. Someone who wants to be a doctor must be comfortable with every aspect of the human anatomy. Our patient," he said sitting back, "was a nineteen-year-old girl who had been recently married. You understand what dyspareunia is now, don't you?"

"I think so," I said. My heart was beating rapidly, but I felt as if my lungs had stopped working.

"Painful or difficult coitus," he recited. "You shouldn't be uncomfortable discussing any aspect of the human body," he repeated. "Or any of our normal functions."

"I'm not," I insisted. I felt my spine harden into cold steel and sat up sharply.

"Good. Dyspareunia may be the subject of back alley and barroom jokes, but to us doctors it's just another medical problem to solve, another form of suffering for us to end," he declared with the dedication and authority of someone who had been part of the medical profession for decades. "You understand that, don't you?"

"Of course." In my secret heart I wished he had chosen a different subject, but I wasn't going to let him see that this topic disturbed me. That was just what he would expect, and he would tell me how my attitude illustrated why it was so difficult for a woman to become a doctor.

"Let's continue, then." He leaned forward. "The patient confided in me after Dr. Bardot had left the examination room. She felt more comfortable talking to someone younger. She said she had been raped when she was twelve years old."

"Raped! How horrible."

"Yes, and that left her with some deep psychological damage." He handed the textbook to me and stood up. He started to pace like a college medical instructor giving a lecture. "This was important for me to know, because dyspareunia can be caused by psychogenic spasms. Please turn to page 819, top right corner." I did so quickly and then looked up at him.

He paused and closed his eyes, grimacing hard as he searched his memory. "When dyspareunia is not due to local causes, or when local symptoms are overshadowed by nervous symptoms, it indicates a psychologic defense mechanism developed by the patient." He opened his eyes and looked down at me expectantly.

I read the first lines. "That's right," I said.

"Good. Let's continue. The defense may be directed against sex and intercourse in general. The possibilities are listed: excessive egotism, ignorance of the anatomy and physiology of the reproductive organs, fear of pregnancy, aversion to the partner, possibly due to a previous love affair or something discovered after marriage. I think it says that even halitosis might form the basis of such an aversion, right?"

"What?"

"Bad breath," he said. "You know. You're in bed with someone, and he turns to you and—"

"Oh." I read and looked up at him. "Yes."

"So if you read between the lines there, before someone marries someone, she should be very familiar with him. They should conduct some test runs, don't you think?"

"I don't know that that's necessarily the inevitable conclusion," I said quickly.

He laughed. "Well, let's use you as a case in point," he said and sat on the settee. "Reading between the lines concerning what you told me about your boyfriend and you, I assume that you and he never made love. Correct?"

"I don't want to discuss my personal life," I said.

"You have to become purely objective, even about yourself, if you want to be a good physician. That's why I say that some people are just not psychologically prepared to become doctors. They might be smart —valedictorians, even—but if they can't bridge the psychological gaps—"

"I can handle the psychological gaps," I snapped.

"Fine. Then you shouldn't have any trouble discussing yourself. You're human, right? Every reaction you have, other people have, too, people you're going to examine and treat. When a man touches you, your body does the same things another woman's body does when a man touches her," he said and shrugged. "Don't you see that?"

"Yes, but . . ."

"So. Let's continue. It's much better to work these problems out with real subjects than just to recite lines from textbooks. You might be suffering from frigidity," he said nodding firmly.

"What?"

"It's a medical term for the incapacity of the female to derive normal pleasure from sexual intercourse. It's right there in the textbook, bottom of the page on the right side." He indicated the passage with his right forefinger.

My eyes fell to the page, and I read it just as he had recited it. Then I looked up and shook my head. "That's not my problem. I don't even have a problem. I just didn't feel—"

"Let's not jump to any diagnosis just yet," he said holding up his hand. "All right? We might have to refer you to a psychiatrist."

"What?" I started to laugh, but he shook his head.

"One of the most important things you'll learn as a medical student is when to recognize that your patient's problem is beyond your ability and requires the attention of a specialist. Doctors get themselves and their patients into trouble when they don't recognize that," he added. "Are you following me? I don't mean to go too fast."

"I follow you. I just don't see how I'm helping you study by talking about myself and why I broke up with my boyfriend."

"Oh, but you are, because it's a situation with which I must be familiar. As I said, we had this case just today, and I'm sure Dr. Bardot is going to test me on this first thing tomorrow. So," he continued sitting back, his arms folded across his chest, "you never slept with this boyfriend. Correct?"

"Yes."

"Have you ever slept with anyone?" I blushed an

even deeper red and hated myself for it. "I'm asking purely as a physician, not as a gossip columnist," he added.

"No."

"Aha!" he said, a sickly arrogant smile forming across his lips. "I'm sure you had ample opportunity, so what prevented you?"

"I don't sleep around, and I'm not interested in sex for the sake of sex. For me it has to be part of something bigger, something . . ."

"What?" he pursued.

"Magical. Love. And don't laugh," I told him sternly.

"I'm not going to laugh, but you might just be rationalizing, making up excuses for your deep fears, your frigidity."

"I am not frigid," I insisted, practically bouncing on the settee for emphasis.

"You don't tighten up when a man touches you?" he asked. I simply stared at him. "You do, don't you?"

"No. *No!*" I emphasized.

"The lady doth protest too much, methinks," he said with a snide smile.

"You can be very infuriating," I said.

"I don't mean to be. Look, I'm a doctor and you want to become one. There's nothing about your physiology I don't know, and from what I already know about you, I feel safe in saying you are pretty well informed. A little knowledge can be a dangerous thing, however."

"What's that supposed to mean?"

"Maybe because you are so intelligent, you are too aware of what's going on, and therefore you lose the magic you claim to want so much. Maybe you are doomed never to find it. Maybe when you think of a human heart, you think only of ventricles and arteries."

I felt my throat tighten and tears burn under my eyelids.

"Am I striking a sensitive note? Because if I am, I'm doing a good job of analyzing your problem," he said.

"I don't have a problem," I replied, but not as firmly as before.

He reached out to take my hand. I started to pull it back.

"Relax," he said. "I'm not going to hurt you."

He made me feel like a little girl going to see the doctor. I let him keep my hand in his. His fingers began to stroke the backs of mine.

"Let's walk through this together," he suggested, moving closer to me on the settee. "I bet you vividly remember the first time you kissed a boy, don't you?"

I did. Freddy Mainiero and I had gone to the movies, and he had kissed me good night. I was only twelve. It was only a quick touch on my lips, but it sent a shiver of excitement down my spine, and I went running up to my room to look at myself in the mirror. My face was crimson, and my heart was pounding so hard that I thought it might split my chest open. I had always thought my first kiss would be long and romantic like the ones I'd seen in the movies, but after this, I couldn't imagine surviving one of those luscious extended kisses.

"Tell me about it," Jack Weller asked. He was only inches from me, his own lips softening, his eyes bright with interest.

"It wasn't anything. Just a little kiss."

"So, you felt safe in that sort of environment, having that simple and innocuous an experience, but alone with a young man, someplace where the lights are low and music is playing softly . . . when his hand touches your shoulder." He let his hand touch my shoulder, and I cringed. "Relax. Easy. I know just what I'm doing."

85

His fingers continued until he was touching my neck, and then they moved down to trace my collarbone. "You know about erogenous zones, I suppose," he whispered.

"I haven't made sexual activity a concentrated area of study," I replied.

He smiled and nodded. "You can't be afraid of your own body and how it reacts. Those feelings are only natural."

"For the last time, I'm not afraid."

"Actually, you're lucky that you and I met. I can help you overcome this problem so you can be assured you will have a normal, active sex life. It's very important when you get married," he continued. As he spoke, his fingers found the buttons of my blouse and undid them. "Relax. Close your eyes and just sit back a moment. You have wonderfully healthy skin."

My heart was pounding. His fingers slipped inside my blouse and traced the top of my bra into my cleavage as he leaned forward and kissed my neck.

"Your pulse quickens bringing the blood to the surface. It's like a knock on the door. You can't be afraid of answering it, Pearl. Go on."

"Wait," I said, but his hands moved under my arms and around behind me, where, with a surgeon's swift skill, he undid my bra and quickly swept his fingers under the elastic, lifting it way from my breasts.

"Yes," he said lowering his lips to my exposed nipple. "Pearl . . . Pearl," he murmured, sending tiny electric chills down my spine while his hand sought to stroke my thigh. "Everything is going along right; it's all as it should be. Try to relax."

My head was spinning. He had moved so quickly and so gracefully. I couldn't believe I was half undressed in moments. My heart was pounding. Actually, it felt funny, as if I were betraying someone. I started to resist, to push him back. He stopped kissing me and looked into my eyes. We were only inches apart.

"From what we just studied, you can see how important the first time is. I'm glad you're still a virgin. If the first time is clumsy and rough, it can scar you, give you dyspareunia, cause psychological damage that will affect your life forever.

"But with me it will be gentle, perfect. I just want to help you. I just want to make sure," he continued and again, as he spoke, his fingers moved over my clothing, unzipping my skirt and gently lifting my body to slide it down my legs. "Your body is preparing itself. You're ready."

I felt a wave of weakness ripple through me, my resistance diminishing as his lips continued to glide over my neck, my cheeks. The tips of his fingers were slipping under the elastic band of my panties.

Finally that part of me that had been overwhelmed with his aggressive, smooth approach, regained a foothold. I heard myself question what was happening. Reality like a flash of lighting shot across the clouds of confusion, and I lifted my legs to press my knees into his abdomen to push him away, crying out at the same time. "No! Stop it!"

He lost his balance and tumbled off the settee.

I quickly pulled up my skirt and closed the zipper and buttoned up my blouse. Then I swung my legs over him and stood up. Still on the floor staring up at me, he looked foolish and my resolve strengthened.

"You didn't ask me here to help you study," I snapped.

"Of course I did." He sat up. "I just thought while we were at it—"

"You would seduce me," I finished.

"Oh, come on. Don't get melodramatic. I merely saw that you have a problem."

"I don't have any problem." I backed farther away from him.

He pulled himself onto the settee and sat there smiling at me. "I think you do."

"How many other girls have you tempted up here using the same phony excuse?" I accused. "You're the one with the problem."

"Are you sure? Really sure? You wanted it for a few moments there, and then your frigidity took control. If you'll only give me a chance," he continued, reaching toward me.

I stepped back again. "Don't touch me!" I cried and grappled for the doorknob.

He pulled his hand back and smiled. "Okay, okay. You don't have to leave. I won't try to help you, if you don't want my help. A patient has to want the doctor's help."

"I'm not a patient and you're . . . you're no doctor!" I screamed and pulled open the door.

"If you change your mind, I'll be here," he cried after me.

I slammed the door behind me and flew down the steps, tears streaming down my cheeks as I charged across the lobby and burst out of the building, nearly knocking an elderly woman over in the process. I apologized and hurried away, nearly running now to catch the next streetcar. Right behind me, Jack Weller's smile and laughter lingered. It wasn't until I was almost home that I felt my heartbeat slow to a normal pace. I wiped away the streaks on my cheeks, took a deep breath, and stepped off the streetcar.

When I entered the house, I paused and leaned back against the front door, hoping to regain all of my composure; but something inside me, something that felt as dainty as china, was shattered and all the king's horses and all the king's men couldn't mend it. A doctor, as young as he was, had tried to deceive me. A member of the profession I idolized had filled me with disappointment and disgust. How could anyone study and work to be a doctor and then do what Jack Weller had done? How could he care about other people, their feelings, their pain, their suffering?

Mommy stepped out of the sitting room and stopped, surprised to see me standing there so quietly.

"Pearl? I didn't hear the door open and close. Where's Aubrey?" she asked gazing around.

"I let myself in quickly, Mommy." I flashed a smile.

"I thought you would be coming home much later," she said stepping toward me.

"No, it didn't work out."

"So you didn't have any supper?" she asked. Her eyes, those Cajun searchlights, as Daddy sometimes called them, examined my face, gathering clues. I had to look away.

"I'm not that hungry yet. I'll eat something later," I said and flashed another quick smile before heading for the stairway.

"Pearl?"

"Yes, Mommy?"

She looked back toward the doorway of the sitting room. I realized Daddy was there, but hadn't heard our conversation; otherwise he would have surely come out to see me.

"Something's wrong. What is it, honey?"

My lips trembled. Tears burned behind my eyelids, then trickled down my cheeks. I shook my head and ran up the stairway. I hurried to my bedroom and fell face down on my bed, gulping back my sobs.

Moments later Mommy was there. She closed the door softly behind her, and I turned around. "What happened?" she asked firmly.

"Oh, Mommy. It wasn't something special."

"He didn't invite you up to his apartment to study as he had said," she remarked, nodding.

"No. We started to study, but he had chosen the topic as part of his elaborate plan to . . ."

"To what? What did he do?"

"I didn't let him do it, Mommy."

"Mon Dieu," she said, pressing her hand to her heart. "If your father finds out, he'll tear that man limb from limb."

"We better not tell him, Mommy. It was nothing. I can take care of it. In fact I did. He won't bother me anymore."

"What did he do?" Mommy asked, coming to sit on my bed.

I sat up and traced the threads in my skirt for a moment. "He said he had a young woman patient who had a problem making love. He called it the honeymoon injury and said he found out her problem was psychological. Then he started asking me personal questions, pretending he was just trying to learn about the problem."

"Go on," Mommy coaxed.

"He said I was frigid because I was too smart and I couldn't enjoy sex. He said he wanted to help me be sure I didn't have the honeymoon injury."

"Mon Dieu. This man should be brought up before the board of inquiry."

I shook my head. "I don't want to have to tell this story to anyone else, Mommy. Please."

"All right, honey. Don't worry. Of course," she said nodding, "you should have nothing more to do with him. If he so much as speaks to you—"

"He won't bother me," I said.

"I'm sorry you had such a terrible experience, Pearl."

"It won't be my last time, Mommy," I declared confidently.

Mommy stared at me a moment. "No, it probably won't. You're very wise to know that, Pearl."

"Did such a thing happen to you?"

"Yes. Worse," she added. "My grandfather tried to sell me to a man. He even chained me to a bed so I would be there when the man came."

"How horrible. How could your grandfather do such a thing?"

"He was an alcoholic. He would have sold his soul for money to buy whiskey. Grandmere Catherine believed he did."

"What happened to you?"

"I managed to escape, and that was when I came to New Orleans and met your father. So you see, every dark cloud does have a silver lining," she added, smiling. I smiled and nodded and then tightened my lips and looked down again. "What else happened, Pearl?"

"It's not that anything else happened. It's . . ."

"What honey?"

"It's what he said. I wonder if there is any truth to it. My school friends think so, and so do all my ex-boyfriends. Oh, Mommy, what if it's true? What if I can never relax with any boy? No one will ever fall in love with me," I moaned.

"I don't think it's true, and I know you don't have to sleep with the first man who propositions you, just to prove you're not frigid. I don't suppose there's an approach that hasn't been tried on some unsuspecting young woman, but for him to use his authority as a doctor . . . deplorable. There's nothing wrong with you, honey," she said, putting her arm around me. "I didn't sleep with every boy who wanted me to sleep with him."

"How many did you sleep with, Mommy?" I asked and then bit my tongue. Even though we were like sisters, I hated prying into such a personal part of her life.

She stared for a moment and then smiled. "I slept

only with your father. No one else mattered," she replied. "Maybe that sounds stupid to today's young people, sounds boring, but—"

"It doesn't sound stupid or boring to me, Mommy."

"When you find the right person, something precious and good will happen, and that will make you feel safe with him. When you feel safe, you won't hesitate to be a complete lover. I'm not one of these love experts who write columns in the newspapers, but I know what was true for me, and I feel sure it will be true for you as well. You think too much of yourself and you value your emotions too much to give anything away cheaply. That's good, and it doesn't make you a prude or frigid. It makes you wise." She smiled and laughed to herself.

"What?"

"I remember when I was a little girl, I was watching two larks flitting about madly, and I asked Grandmere Catherine what was wrong with them. She said they were doing a mating dance. The female was pretending not to be interested, which, Grandmere Catherine explained, made the male even more interested and guaranteed the female she wouldn't be disappointed. 'She just wants him to know she ain't no easy date,' Grandmere said."

We both laughed.

"You were so lucky to grow up in the bayou. I wish I had," I said.

"Oh, it was no picnic. We worked hard to have what we needed just for day-to-day living, but the mornings and the nights . . ."

"You still miss it, don't you, Mommy?"

"I do. Some."

"Why don't we go back? Why don't we all visit Cypress Woods?" I said excitedly.

"No, I don't think so, honey. Not just yet," she said

getting up, obviously uncomfortable with the idea. "Feeling better?"

"Yes, Mommy."

"Hungry?"

"A little."

"Then let's go downstairs. We'll pretend you just came in and we'll go get you something to eat. Daddy will want to hear every detail about your day at the hospital."

"I know. It's sad he never became a doctor."

"Life holds a surprise around every bend. Some good, some disappointment. The trick is to keep poling your canoe," she said.

"I've never even been in a pirogue. Why can't we go to the bayou?" I pleaded.

"We will. Someday," she said, but it was the same someday I had heard hundreds of times before. This one had no more ring of truth to it. But it did have a darker, deeper, and hollower resonance. It left me feeling uncertain, like someone grappling with the darkness, pressing her face into the night, waiting hopefully for the first star.

The past, our past, resembled the maze of canals that were woven through the bayou, some leading out, some leading farther and farther into the unknown. It would take courage to risk the trip, but I was confident that someday I would embark. Someday I would go back and discover the answers to the questions that lingered.

I only hoped, how I hoped, that I would have someone precious and loving alongside me when I pushed away from the shore and began the journey.

5

Is Love for Me?

Although I had assured Mommy I would have no trouble working in the hospital near Jack Weller, I couldn't help feeling as if my heart was wound in tight rubber bands when I stepped off the cable car and walked to the hospital the following day. The sky was heavily overcast and gray with rain only minutes away. In fact, the air was so humid I thought I saw drops forming right before my eyes. Sophie had already arrived. She had come early because she had a ride that brought her within a half dozen blocks and she could save the cable fare. Fortunately, Jack Weller wasn't coming on duty until midway through my shift, so for the first few hours at least I wouldn't have to confront him.

But when Sophie and I returned from lunch, Jack was standing in the hallway talking to one of the nurses. He gazed our way and smiled as if nothing at all had happened between us. I hadn't said a word about it to Sophie, so she thought Jack was just being his usual funny and flirtatious self. I went directly to the linen room. Sheila Delacrois, the young woman who I had thought had trouble with her gallbladder, did have a problem and had been taken upstairs for an operation. Afterward she would go to recovery and she wouldn't return to our floor, so I had to change her bed and prepare it for a new patient.

I was busy stacking the pillowcases and sheets when I heard the door of the linen closet close softly behind me. I spun around to discover Jack standing there, his back against the door, his hands behind him on the knob.

"Open the door," I demanded.

"I just want to talk to you privately for a moment," he replied.

"We have nothing to discuss. Just open the door," I insisted.

"Look, I want to apologize. Maybe I stepped over the line, went too far too quickly. Because of how intelligent you are, I thought you were more sophisticated. It was my mistake. I admit it. I just want to say it won't do either of us any good to talk about this to others."

"You don't have to worry. I won't say anything to anyone. However, I did tell my mother," I added.

"Your mother?" His eyebrows looked as if they might lift right off his face.

"Yes. I don't hide things from my mother. We're very close."

"What did she say?"

"She didn't want my father to know. She thought he would come here and break your neck," I said dryly. Jack Weller swallowed hard and nodded. "I don't know what sort of a doctor you're going to be," I added, hot tears in my eyes.

"Hey, one thing has nothing to do with another. When I'm on duty, I'm a true professional."

"If you're not sensitive to people's feelings, it doesn't matter how much you know or how professional you appear," I retorted.

He smirked and shook his head. "I've seen girls like you before. Actually, I ran into your type throughout college and med school. You're too smart for your own good, know-it-alls who won't admit to their own feelings. You could have had a good time yesterday if you had let down your hair."

"I can live with the disappointment," I remarked dryly. My hot tears evaporated, and the trembling left my body. It was quickly replaced by cold anger, my fury showing in my eyes, eyes that glared down Jack Weller's arrogant smirk.

He shrugged his shoulders. "Suit yourself." He opened the door. My heart was pounding and my hands were clenched into small fists. He paused in the open doorway, checking first to be sure no one was close enough to overhear his remarks. "I feel sorry for the poor jerk who makes love to you the first time. He'll probably feel as if he's just had a medical exam," Jack added and closed the door behind him.

The tears that had been kept in check under my eyelids poured free. How many men would accuse me of the same thing? I wondered. When would I find someone with whom I truly wanted to be affectionate and warm? Was I too cold, too impersonal, too analytical for my own good? Every boyfriend I'd had eventually deserted me, and now someone I thought was sophisticated and knowledgeable had accused me of the same crime, if it was a crime.

No matter how reassuring Mommy had been and would be, no matter how many books I read on the subject or how many other girls I questioned, I would always have these doubts about myself, I thought. Was I someone for whom the magic of love, the mystery of passion, would remain unattainable? Was it a curse or a blessing that I had what Claude had called X-ray eyes?

"Why is it," he had asked one time when he had tried to get me to make love with him and I retreated, "that I feel like you're looking at me and seeing spleens and kidneys and lungs and not me?"

Of course I told him he was wrong, but as we kissed and he pressed himself against me, I was thinking about his quickened breathing, his quick hardness, and the moist feel of his skin and wondering how the nervous system was triggered by sexual arousal and how different organs were affected. I guess I was some sort of brain monster.

The twins used to try to frighten me by bringing in worms and bugs, and they were always disappointed by my calmness. To satisfy them, I even tried to pretend to be as shocked as most girls my age would be if they found thick night crawlers in their sink or a daddy long legs in their face cream jar, but I had no problem picking them up and putting them outside.

Pierre and Jean actually complained to Mommy about it. "Pearl isn't afraid to pick up a frog or a big black beetle!"

Mommy smiled and told them I had probably inherited my grandmother's love of animals. Even though she had never known her mother, she told us her grandmere Catherine described her mother as someone who felt comfortable with alligators and whom all creatures trusted. Birds would light on her shoulder and feed out of her palm. "Pearl's got that in her," Mommy had explained.

But was it that, or was I so scientific that I lacked feminine qualities? Couldn't I be interested in science and still be a warm, loving person?

I wiped away the tears and took a deep breath. Then I returned to my work and kept my mind on the tasks I was assigned. A wall of impersonal professionalism fell between me and Jack Weller. He made no more attempts at small talk, and if I walked into a room where he was, he would merely glance at me and then return to whatever he was doing.

There were other doctors—older, more accomplished professionals—with whom I had some conversations. Once they learned of my ambitions they were eager to speak with me and give me advice. If I went into a patient's room to replace a water pitcher or to bring juice or toast and tea, and a doctor was speaking to the patient in the other bed, I would linger and listen, learning about the diagnosis and treatment.

In the evenings I would tell Daddy about these things. He would listen, his eyes bright with interest and his lips relaxed in a tiny smile. If Mommy was there, too, she would sit back, her eyes full of pride, and she and Daddy would exchange secret glances.

Pierre and Jean were interested only in gory details. Had I seen another dead person? Did I see a lot of blood and broken bones? Most of my days were quite routine without any real emergencies, and in the twins' eyes those days were boring. Of course they were enjoying their summer—swimming in our pool, having their friends over, playing Little League baseball, collecting insects in jars. I told them not to take these days for granted, that time would flow by quickly and before they knew it, they would have to bear down and work hard to become successful at something. Jean didn't want to hear such advice, but Pierre would nod and give me a knowing look.

In early July Mommy's new exhibition was ready. It was being held at one of the newer galleries in the French Quarter. The impressive guest list for the opening included high government officials, doctors and lawyers, big businessmen, and some entertainers. The twins hated having to dress up and keep themselves spotless on the day of the opening. Mommy insisted that they wear identical dark blue suits with silk ties. She bought them shiny new shoes and Daddy took them for haircuts. They did look handsome, if uncomfortable, confined in their new clothes and forbidden to do anything that would dirty their hands or faces or stain their suits.

Jean kept pulling on his collar and moaning that he was choking to death. "Dressing up is dumb, Pearl," he groaned. "You've got to worry about furniture being too dusty or about brushing up against something greasy, and boys have to wear these stupid ties."

"You look so handsome, Jean. Both of you do, and you're doing it for Mommy. You know how big a day this is for her," I explained. Jean nodded, reluctantly agreeing; but a few minutes later he was teasing Pierre by deliberately stepping on his shoes and messing up his hair, then running off through the house. Daddy had to pull them both aside and give them a stern lecture, after which they both sat waiting with their hands folded in their laps, looking glum.

For a while the music and the excitement at the exhibition kept them amused. Daddy had given them instructions about how they should behave at the gallery, but the moment we all arrived, Daddy and Mommy were surrounded by friends, guests, and the press. The twins slipped away from me and explored. Every once in a while I caught sight of them darting in and out among clusters of people, gobbling hot hors d'oeuvres, and even sneaking a sip of wine. I cornered them a few times and had them sit quietly, but moments later they were gone.

From the comments we were hearing, Mommy's exhibition was being well received. A number of her pictures were sold during the opening. Afterward a party was to be held at Antoine's, one of the French Quarter's oldest and most famous restaurants. We had our party in the private dining room known as the Dungeon and actually used as such during the Spanish period in New Orleans. My waiter, who lingered at my side for a few moments after he served something, was very proud of the restaurant and proud that his name was Antoine, too.

"Oysters rockefeller, one of our most famous dishes," he said placing them before me, "were not created for John D. Rockefeller, you know. They were so named because of the richness of the sauce, and since Mr. Rockefeller was America's richest person at the time . . ."

"Oh, I see," I said, smiling.

He nodded at a waiter across the table from us who was pouring expensive wine like water. "Our wine cellar contains over 25,000 bottles, the oldest wine dating back to 1884. We even have a brandy produced in 1811."

I tried to appear sufficiently impressed, which encouraged him to continue his explanations and boasting with every course he served.

"Princess Margaret called our crabmeat soufflé a poem."

The restaurant went all out to impress our guests and my parents. We were served chicken Rochambeau, crawfish cardinale, Brabant potatoes, and Antoine's famous creamed spinach. However, the twins went right to the desserts.

While we were having dinner, the first of the art reviews was brought in and read aloud because it was so favorable. Everyone applauded and Mommy stood up and thanked the guests. Then she and Daddy kissed.

Every time they kissed, it seemed to me as though they were kissing for the first time. Their faces always radiated excitement, and their eyes were full of the glitter of discovery. How was it possible for me to ever find such love and happiness? I wondered. Mommy, sensing my thoughts, gazed my way and smiled at me, her eyes saying, Don't worry, Pearl. There's someone like Daddy out there for you, too. I'm sure of it.

How I wished I could be as sure of it.

Right in the middle of all the excitement, while people were coming to our table to congratulate Mommy, while music was playing and the great meal was being served, I saw Mommy suddenly stop smiling and turn toward the doorway. Her face drained quickly and became white with concern. I gazed toward the doorway, too, and saw a tall, thin caramel-skinned woman wearing a red tingue. The maître d' went to greet her, and she nodded in Mommy's direction. He kept her from entering, but because she was so insistent, he brought a message to Mommy. I watched her read it and saw her face grow even paler. She leaned over to whisper in Daddy's ear, and he became visibly upset.

I got up quickly and went to her. "What's wrong, Mommy?"

"Oh, Pearl honey, this message is about Nina Jackson, my father's cook."

"What about her?" I looked toward the doorway but the mysterious woman was gone.

"She's dying and has asked for me. I've got to go to her at once, but Daddy doesn't think I should leave the party."

"It's your party, Mommy. How can you go? Is she going to die any moment?"

"I don't know, honey."

"Can't you go right afterward?"

"That's what Daddy wants me to do. We're having pictures taken in about a half hour. The mayor is supposed to be here."

"Then you have to stay, Mommy. But I'll go with you as soon as you can leave."

"Thank you, darling," she said, pressing my hands between hers. "I just feel I should get right up and go. Oh, dear."

I thought Mommy was upset enough to excuse herself and run out, but just at that moment the mayor of New Orleans made his entrance. There was applause and great excitement as he made his way through the party to greet Mommy and offer his congratulations. I went back to the twins and waited, knowing the turmoil Mommy was experiencing.

Finally, nearly an hour later, Mommy told Daddy she felt she had to go. Some people were already leaving. She asked Daddy to take the twins home. The twins and I were standing beside them while they discussed it.

"Pearl is going with me. We'll take a cab," Mommy told him.

Daddy looked troubled. "I don't like the idea of the two of you going places alone at night," he said.

"We'll be fine, Beau. We're just going from the cab into the house and back into the cab. I'll have the driver wait," she explained.

"I don't know what good it's going to do, your going," he muttered.

"She was very dear to me once and we remained friends for a long time after she left the House of Dumas, Beau. There was a time when Nina Jackson was practically the only one looking after me."

Daddy nodded and looked away. I imagined Mommy was referring to the time when he left her and went to Europe. "What am I to tell the rest of these people?" he asked under his breath.

"Tell them the truth, Beau. A dear friend is on her deathbed, and I went to her," she said.

"All right, all right. Be careful, will you?" He kissed her on the cheek.

"Take care of your mother, and make sure she doesn't do anything foolish," Daddy warned me.

"I will, Daddy," I promised.

"Let's go, honey," Mommy said.

"We want to go too," Jean whined.

"You two are going home with me," Daddy snapped. "You'll both need castor oil after hogging down all those pralines tonight and eating all that crème brûlée, I'm sure. Don't wander out of my sight," he advised. The two of them looking longingly at me.

"Be good boys," I said and nodded at Pierre, who I knew could make Jean behave. He grimaced with unhappiness, but led Jean to chairs where they would sit obediently and wait for Daddy.

Meanwhile Mommy had the restaurant hostess hail us a cab. "Quickly, honey," she told me. We rushed out.

"Where to?" the driver asked.

Mommy gave him the address.

"You sure you want to go there? That's not the safest part of town this time of the night," he said.

"We know where we want to go. Just get us there quickly," Mommy said. Her anxiety made her unusually firm and caustic. No one I knew spoke to servants and service people as kindly as Mommy usually did.

As we drove out of the Vieux Carré and toward a poorer section of the city, Mommy told me of the time Nina Jackson took her to see a voodoo mama so she could get a charm or learn a ritual to keep her sister Gisselle from being cruel to her. She described how she had cast a ribbon belonging to Gisselle into a box containing a snake.

"Not long after that, Gisselle was in the car accident," she said mournfully. "I always felt guilty."

"But, Mommy, you surely don't believe the ritual was the reason for the accident. You said her boyfriend had been smoking pot and driving recklessly."

"Still . . . the voodoo ceremony might have put her in the grip of danger. Afterward, I returned with Nina, and the mama made me reach into the box with the snake in it and take out the ribbon, but she wouldn't guarantee I could rescind the curse. She said once my anger was cast into the wind, the wind had control and I probably couldn't pull it back."

"But, Mommy . . ."

"I told Gisselle, you know."

"What did she say?"

"She just used the information to blackmail me into becoming her slave, but I deserved it. I should never have let my anger get the better of me. No one else knew about it but Nina. She was always burning candles to keep evil away from me and giving me good luck charms, like the dime you now wear," Mommy said, smiling.

We turned the corner and started down a long, dark street. The buildings looked no better than shacks. Despite the hour, I saw young children still playing on the stoops and on the scarred and bald front yards. Broken-down cars were parked along the sidewalks, and the streets were very dirty, the gutters full of cans, bottles, and paper.

We stopped at a shack that looked somewhat better than its neighbors. The yard and the sidewalk were clean, but I saw bones and feathers hanging above the front door.

"Wait here for us," Mommy ordered the driver.

"I won't wait long," he warned.

"I have your name and your license number," she told him. "You had better be here when I step out of that house with my daughter," Mommy countered. He grunted his reluctance, but sat back. Mommy took a deep breath and then found my hand. We walked to the stoop, and Mommy knocked on the door. A moment later a short black woman peered out at us. Her long gray hair hung down to the middle of her back, and she wore what looked like a potato sack and old sneakers without laces. Dangling from her earlobes were two small live lizards. They both held on for dear life.

"We're here to see Nina," Mommy said.

"Nina is not here," the small woman said.

Mommy glanced at the note she had been given. "I was told to come to this address. I was told Nina Jackson was very sick and dying in this house."

"That be told true, but Nina's gone. Zombie take her about an hour ago. She's in paradise."

"Oh, no. We're too late," Mommy moaned. I squeezed her hand, and she straightened her shoulders. "I want to see her anyway," she insisted.

The woman stepped back for us to enter. A sweet aroma flowed from the rear of the house. The old lady nodded toward the left, and we heard the monotonous rat-a-tat of a drum. Slowly Mommy and I walked toward the entrance to the rear room.

It was a small bedroom with the shades drawn. The bed took up most of the space. Around it nearly a hundred candles were burning. Another black woman, not much bigger than the one who had greeted us, sat very still beside the coffin. Across from her, an elderly man with a luminous white beard was tapping a drum made of thin cypress staves hooped with brass and topped with sheepskin. He didn't look our way or move his head an inch when we entered, but when the woman turned toward us, her large, sad eyes brightened with some recognition.

"You be Nina's Ruby," she said.

"Yes," Mommy said. "Are you Nina's sister?"

The woman nodded and glanced at the body of

Nina Jackson. Her face looked waxen, like a mask. I hadn't seen them at first, because my eyes were blinded by the glow of the candles, but at the foot of the bed were two cats, a black one and, on its left, a white. They were both dead, preserved by a taxidermist. Above the headboard dangled a black doll wearing a brightly colored dress and a necklace of snake vertebrae, from which hung an alligator's fang encased in silver.

"My sister couldn't wait no more," the woman said.

"I'm sorry," Mommy said, moving to the side of the bed. I was right beside her. "Poor Nina."

"She be rich Nina now," the sister said quickly. "She be with zombie."

"Yes," Mommy said, smiling. She sucked in her breath and sighed before reaching out to touch Nina's hand. She closed her eyes and said a silent prayer and then looked at Nina's sister. "Is there anything I can do for you?"

"No, madame. Nina called for you because she wanted to do something for you. Before he took her, zombie told her something. Before she go for good she say, go fetch Madame Andreas. Bring her to me. I got to tell her what zombie let me know. But you don't come, and she couldn't wait no longer, see?"

Mommy made a tiny cry. I took her hand. "Did she tell you anything?"

"No, no. Nina can tell such a thing only to you. All she do is tell me get you fast, and then she asked if you be here and I said no. A while later she asked again, and again I say no. Then I heard her mumble a prayer. I seen her take her last breath and when I look closely, I see she died with a tear in her eye. That bode no good omen.

"You go pray now, madame. You go pray for Nina's voice. Maybe best you go to cemetery at midnight.

Bring a black cat. Nina maybe speak from beyond through the cat's mouth."

The drumming got louder.

"Mommy, let's go," I whispered, feeling a chill in my spine. She looked transfixed, her eyes frozen in fear. "The taxi."

She took another deep breath and then opened her purse and took out some money. "Please, take this and buy what you need for Nina's burial," she said. Nina's sister took the money. Mommy looked at Nina again and turned to leave.

"You better go to the cemetery at midnight," Nina's sister called after us.

Mommy was silent most of the way home. She stared out the window until we were nearly there. Then she turned and mumbled, "I should have gone immediately. I knew it. I should have just gone to her."

"But, Mommy, how could you? All those people had come to see you."

"None of that mattered as much. I know Nina wouldn't have sent for me if it hadn't been important," she said, shaking her head.

"Mommy, you don't really believe all that; you don't really believe Nina went to the land of the dead and returned to tell you something, do you?"

She was silent.

"Mommy?"

"I remember once going with Grandmere Catherine to drive away a couchemal," she said, "an evil spirit that lurks about when an unbaptized baby dies. She was called to drive it away so it wouldn't bring the family bad luck."

"How did she do that?" I asked.

"She put a drop of holy water in every pot, every

107

cistern, anything that could hold water. We went around the house searching and while we she was depositing the holy water . . ."

"What?" I asked when she hesitated.

"I felt it. I felt the spirit," she whispered. "It flew past me, touched my face, and disappeared into the night."

I swallowed back my gasp.

"I don't mock anyone's beliefs," she said, "and I don't challenge the charms, the gris-gris, or the rituals. I don't want to believe in most of it, but sometimes . . . sometimes I can't help it. It fills my stomach with butterflies."

I embraced her; she was shivering. "Oh, Mommy, those are just foolish old superstitions. People make them up. You can't believe anything bad will happen because you didn't get to see Nina in time."

"I hope not," she said, shaking her head. "I hope not."

Daddy and the boys were home when we arrived. He had sent the twins to bed, but fifteen minutes later they were both complaining of stomachaches. "Which doesn't surprise me one bit, considering what they gobbled down tonight." He paused and looked hard at Mommy. "What's wrong? Nina died?"

"Yes, Beau. She died before I got there."

"I'm sorry," he said. "She was quite a character, Nina. I remember how well she dealt with Gisselle. She was the only one who could get her to do as she was told. I think Gisselle was a little afraid of Nina, even though she mocked her and her voodoo."

"Her sister said that Nina had something important to tell me, Beau."

Daddy looked at her. "Something about what?"

"Something she learned in the other world," Mommy blurted.

At first Daddy just stared. Then his mouth dropped. "You don't mean to tell me you believe Nina came back from the dead to tell you something?" Mommy nodded. *"Mon Dieu,* Ruby. A woman with your intelligence and—"

"It has nothing to do with intelligence, Beau."

Daddy clamped his lips shut. He and Mommy had had arguments about this before, and he knew how firmly she held on to her old beliefs.

"I'm tired," he said. "I'm going up to bed. Oh," he added turning at the stairway, "Bertrand from the gallery said seventy percent of your work has been sold—a record for an opening. Congratulations." He started up the stairs.

Mommy sighed. "What a night. I should be happy, but long ago I learned that for every ray of sunshine, there's a shadow lurking. We've just got to balance ourselves between them, I suppose." She smiled at me. "Thanks for being at my side and being my comfort."

We hugged.

"I better go up and see how the boys are doing. I might have to use one of Grandmere Catherine's herbal recipes," she said.

When the boys set eyes on her, they're begging for attention. "It's no use bawling them out tonight," Mommy said, coming out of their room. "They're both too green to hear a word."

Mommy went down to prepare the old tried and true remedy, and I went to bed. However, as soon as I closed my eyes, I saw the hundred candles and heard the dreary drumbeat. Later I had a horrible nightmare in which Nina sat up on her deathbed and turned to me. She opened her eyes, and they were yellow. Instead of tears, hot wax streamed from under her eyelids and hardened on her cheeks. When she opened

109

her mouth to speak, all I heard was Mommy's voice screaming "Noooo!" I woke with a start. I was about to get up for a drink of water when I heard footsteps and sobbing in the hallway. I waited and then peered out. Mommy was descending the stairway. I saw her go out a patio door. She appeared to be sleepwalking.

I put on my robe and followed. At first I didn't see her. Then I caught her silhouette in the garden shadows. "Mommy," I whispered, "why are you out here?"

She didn't hear me, so I drew closer and asked again.

"Oh, Pearl," she replied in a voice drawn from a well of sadness. "I was hoping Nina would speak to me in the darkness. Don't tell Daddy I came out here," she pleaded. I took her hand. Her skin felt clammy and cold.

"You better go back to bed, Mommy, and stop this worrying."

"I can't. Something's going to happen because of some bad luck my past actions have brought into our home. Nina wanted to warn me, I'm sure."

"That's silly, Mommy, and you know it is. Things happen for logical, natural reasons only."

She sighed deeply. "I don't know," she muttered. "I don't know."

"Well, I do," I said firmly. "Now come back in and go to bed or I will tell Daddy."

She started back to the house with me and then stopped and seized my hand in a desperate grip. "Did you hear that?" she asked, softly.

I listened, but heard nothing unusual. "Hear what, Mommy?"

"The sound of someone sobbing. I heard it before, too," she said.

"Wasn't that you?" I asked.

Her eyes widened. "Then you heard it too!" she said quickly.

"Stop it, Mommy. You're scaring me."

We both listened a moment longer.

"I don't hear anything," I declared.

She shook her head and walked back to the house with me. We both returned to our bedrooms, but I didn't fall asleep until nearly morning.

Mommy didn't come down to breakfast the next morning before I left for work. Daddy said she had spent a restless night and was still sound asleep. In fact, despite the wonderful reception her new works had received, Mommy remained in a melancholy state for days. The twins were usually there at the door complaining when I returned from work.

"Mommy's losing her hearing," Pierre concluded.

Jean, nodded worriedly. "She should go to an ear doctor."

"Maybe you can test her hearing, Pearl," Jean said.

"Why do you say she's losing her hearing?" I asked with a smile.

"If we ask her a question, we have to ask her twice, maybe three times," Pierre explained.

"Sometimes we have to shout!" Jean added.

"She's a bit distracted these days," I told them. "It's not her hearing. Just be patient."

They shook their heads skeptically and went back to their games. But the mood of despair that had laid itself over our home depressed them. They had no enthusiasm for their pranks. Daddy began to worry about Mommy, too. She wasn't working; she didn't visit with her friends or have any visitors, and she wasn't eating well. Finally, one night at dinner, my father thought he had a solution.

"Pearl has Monday and Tuesday off this next week and I'm due for a holiday. What say we go to the

111

château, this weekend, Ruby? The change of scenery will do you good. You can get some ideas for your work, and the boys and I can go fishing."

"Yeah!" Jean cried.

"I don't know," Mommy said. Daddy looked to me for help.

"I'd love a change of scenery, Mommy, and we haven't been to the château for quite a while," I said. "I can get some of my college preparatory reading done, too."

She looked at me and nodded. "I suppose we could go," she said.

The boys were cheered, and the packing and planning did add some brightness to what had otherwise been a dark time. Despite her initial reluctance, Mommy dived into the preparations. No one had to wake the boys the next morning. They were already dressed and ready by the time Mommy, Daddy, and I went downstairs for breakfast. They had packed their own suitcases, but when Mommy inspected them, she discovered they had included slingshots, baseballs, shedded snakeskins, marbles, and jackknives.

"You'll have plenty with which to occupy yourselves at the château," Mommy told them. "No need to bring all this junk."

Daddy packed the car immediately after breakfast. I think he was even more excited than the twins about taking the holiday. As usual the twins talked a blue streak during the drive, asking questions about practically everything in sight. What were people selling on the sides of the highway? How did they make those baskets and palmetto hats? Why were the shacks built on stilts? Mommy had little time to dwell on her dark thoughts, so even though Daddy normally would have asked the twins to take a break, he simply smiled at me, winked, and let the questions go on and on.

It was a beautiful summer day. Bringing Mommy

out to the rural world appeared to be the panacea Daddy and I were hoping for. The sight of her beloved Spanish moss draped from old cypress trees, the glistening goldenrod, the willows and cottonwoods, and here and there a pond covered with lilies and hyacinths filled her with pleasure and restored the glow to her eyes and cheeks. The twins loved to test her knowledge of birds, and she was more than eager to identify a grosbeak heron or a scarlet cardinal. They were fascinated by her description of a butcher bird and how it stored its food on thorns so it could eat the cured flesh during the winter. Everything about nature fascinated them. I decided they were the ones who had really inherited our grandmother's affinity for wild things.

"I hope we see snakes and alligators," Jean said as we drew closer to what had been the Dumas family's country home.

"Never mind about them," Mommy warned. "You two mustn't wander off exploring on your own. I want you close to the house except when Daddy takes you, hear?"

Reluctantly, they promised.

"There she blows," Daddy cried as we came around a turn and our country house came into view.

The building that my grandfather Dumas used to refer to as his ranch actually resembled a château. It had a steeply pitched hipped roof with spires, pinnacles, turrets, gables, and two oddly shaped chimneys. The metal cresting along the roof's ridges was elaborately ornamented. The windows and the doorway were arched. To the right were two small cottages for the servants and caretakers, and to the right, some thousand yards or so away, were the stables with the riding horses and a barn. The property had rambling fields with patches of wooded areas and a stream cutting across its north end.

Like some of the châteaux in the French country-side, it had beautiful gardens, and two gazebos stood on the front lawn, as did benches and chairs and stone fountains. When we arrived, the caretakers were busily trimming hedges and weeding.

"Can we go horseback riding right away, Daddy?" Jean cried.

"Let's settle in first, unpack, and get organized. Then we'll see about the recreational schedule," he said.

The twins put a cork in their overflowing bottle of excitement, but both looked as if they would burst as they feasted their eyes on our beautiful grounds, the ponds, the fields, and the stream that wove its way deep into the woods and promised adventures forever. They started to rush away as soon as Daddy stopped the car, but he hauled them back with a cry.

"You two help unload. Carry your own suitcases to your room. Come on. You're both big enough to take care of yourselves," he said.

They returned to the car and took their things, Jean proudly heaving his suitcase over his shoulder and helping Pierre unload his.

Mommy stood for a moment gazing around. Then she lifted her eyes to look at an upstairs window. Some memory brought shadows to her face. Daddy sensed her concern and moved quickly to her side.

"Let's have an enjoyable few days and let the past remain buried, Ruby. Please," he pleaded. She nodded, took a deep breath, and started for the front door.

Except for the inclusion of some of Mommy's paintings, my parents had done little to change the decor. The château had a short foyer decorated with drapes and large landscape paintings. The furnishings were a mixture of modern and the same French Provincial found in our New Orleans house.

After we all settled in, Daddy took the twins fishing, and Mommy and I went into the garden, where I read and Mommy set up her easel. Although we didn't converse much, we sensed and drew from each other's presence. Both reading and working on artistic projects required concentration and solitude. Mommy soon became lost in her project and I in my reading. Before either of us realized it, the afternoon had turned to dusk and we had to go in to prepare for dinner.

Daddy and the twins returned with their catch. The twins were so excited about the turtles and the other wildlife that they jabbered continuously through dinner. No one else had a chance to get in a word, but their excitement was infectious. All of us felt rejuvenated—Mommy especially. I took charge of getting the twins to bed and left Mommy and Daddy alone to enjoy the warm, star-blazing bayou evening. The twins reluctantly surrendered to sleep only when Daddy promised they could go horseback riding in the morning.

I enjoyed riding too, so the next morning Mommy went back to her painting while Daddy and I and the twins rode for nearly two hours. After lunch Daddy went up to his room to take a nap, and Mommy and I returned to the garden where she continued to paint and I continued to catch up on my college reading.

Toward the later part of the afternoon, a wave of dark clouds crept in from the east. The breeze kicked up, and Mommy decided to go inside. The wind played havoc with our hair, my pages, and Mommy's easel and canvas. We both laughed at our struggle to keep control of our possessions. As we packed up Mommy's brushes and paints, canvas, and easel, she suddenly paused, a half smile of confusion on her face. "What's that?" she asked.

I shook my head. "What's what, Mommy?"

"Didn't you hear it? It sounded like someone screaming." She turned slowly. Daddy had just stepped out of the house and was moving toward us when I heard the screams, too.

"Pierre," I whispered. I saw him flailing about as he struggled to run through the tall grass. He fell once, and Mommy cried out. Daddy started to run toward him.

"Pearl," Mommy moaned.

"It's probably nothing, Mommy," I said and started toward Pierre. But where was Jean? I wondered and felt my heart turn to cold stone when I heard Pierre cry out Jean's name and point to the wooded swamp area behind him. "Snakebite!"

His words were carried to us on the wind and reached Mommy who had followed behind me. She brought her hands to her cheeks and screamed at the fast-approaching storm clouds.

"Nina!"

I stepped back to embrace her just as her legs gave out.

The thunder seemed to come from both our hearts.

6

The Curse Strikes

The water moccasin is a large poisonous olive-brown viper. Folks in the South often call it a cottonmouth. It coils itself on the lower limbs of willow trees and when it lies in the water, it can look like a broken branch floating.

Jean had waded into a pond to catch a turtle sleeping between the lily pads. Pierre had warned him not to, but Jean was fascinated. I knew that when Jean fixed his mind on something, he was sometimes like someone hypnotized. He would turn off everything around him and concentrate on what he wanted to do or see or touch. Pierre had remained on the shore screaming at him, but Jean had ignored him.

When he got too close to the snake, it struck.

"I thought it was a branch, Daddy," Pierre moaned. It would be something he would chant in his own mind, for a long time: "I thought it was just a branch."

Jean was floating face down when Daddy lunged into the water to get to him. He scooped him up, lifting him over his head. I had just arrived at the clearing and saw him rushing from the water as if it

117

were boiling around him. There is nothing more frightening to me than the sound and the sight of a grown man screaming. Daddies aren't supposed to cry. There was no sight more heartrending and terrifying to me at the same time as the sight of my father, petrified at the prospect of losing his son, my brother. Daddy looked as if he had lost all sense of direction; he had lost his wits.

Daddy flooded Jean's face with kisses I knew he prayed would be magical; but the stitches that had drawn Jean's eyelids shut appeared unbreakable, and his beautiful little face, a face always animated, those blue eyes sweeping a room or a place to find something interesting, was already growing as pale as a faded water lily.

Daddy turned to me with eyes I shall never put to sleep in my memory, frantic eyes.

I hurried to his side.

"He's not breathing!" he said.

I had him put Jean on a patch of soft moss.

"Make him better, Pearl. Make him better," Pierre pleaded.

Jean had been bitten on the left wrist. It had swollen into a large lump, so I knew an adult viper had bitten him and he had taken a big dose of venom. The shock of the bite and its effect on his nervous system must have put him into a panic. He obviously fell into the water, but instead of heading for shore, he had floundered into deeper water. His wrist was surely burning; his heart pounding.

From a first aid course given by the fire department last year, I knew that when a person panics at the surface of water, his thrashing movements are incapable of keeping his body afloat. If they sink and begin to swallow water, initially, an automatic contraction of the muscle in the windpipe prevents water from entering the lungs and instead it enters the esophagus and stomach. However, the laryngeal reflex impairs breathing, which can quickly lead to the loss of consciousness even without the injection of lethal viper venom. This was surely what had happened to Jean.

Jean's lips had turned blue-gray. I couldn't hear his heartbeat or feel a pulse in his wrist, so I began CPR, never having dreamed when I learned it last year, that I would be practicing it for real on my own little brother. I kept reciting the instructions in my mind, shutting out Daddy's moans and Pierre's cajoling to make Jean better. Instead, I heard my instructor saying the rate of compression should be eighty per minute with two breaths given after every fifteen compressions. After what seemed like hours, but was really only two minutes, I looked up at Daddy.

"We've got to get him to the hospital."

He nodded and lifted Jean in his arms. Pierre and I followed him out of the woods and across the field. Mommy was seated on a bench, her face drained and white, her tears flowing, her lips quivering.

"We've got to rush to the hospital," Daddy shouted and headed for the car. Mommy shook her head violently, as if to drive off mosquitoes. I took Pierre's hand and we both helped her to her feet.

We all piled into the car. Mommy and I remained in the back with Jean. She kept his head on her lap and stroked his hair, her tears now falling on his face as well.

I don't remember the ride. Daddy had the car on two wheels around turns, his horn blaring at anything and anyone in our way, driving them off the road. We pulled into the hospital emergency lane, and Daddy scooped up Jean again. Mommy rose slowly to follow. All hope was gone from her. She was a shell of herself, drifting along with us.

A team of doctors and nurses worked on Jean. I sat

with Mommy in the lobby, holding her limp hand. Pierre sat beside me, stunned, his head against my shoulder, his hands clutching my other hand as if he hoped I could pull him up from the tragedy unfolding around us.

Mommy had been sitting there staring blankly at the wall, when suddenly she spoke: "If only I had left the party . . . if only I had spoken to Nina before she died."

"Stop that, Mommy. Nina had nothing to do with this."

She shook her head and sighed so deeply I thought I heard her chest shatter. She continued to stare ahead with vacant eyes, waiting.

In my mind I envisioned what they were trying to do with Jean. They were injecting the antivenom; they were defibrillating his heart; they were drawing the water from his lungs. Daddy was beside them watching, praying, a man turned to stone.

Time had no meaning, so I didn't know how long we actually waited before Daddy emerged, followed by some of the medical staff. There was no need for words. Everything was said in their faces.

Pierre, who had drawn even closer to me and put his arms around my waist, still clung desperately. The analytical part of me, incredibly detached emotionally, wondered when we as children first understood the finality of death. We are told that people who die go away forever to a place that is nicer, and that eases our confusion and the pain because we can imagine them even happier. It helps us to put them aside, to forget, to turn back to those who are still with us.

But later, at some fragile age, we suddenly realize that death is more than just a ticket on a train or a plane, and we understand the temporal nature of our own lives. Sometime, somewhere, somehow, we, too, will take that inevitable journey. But nothing is more unfair and unreasonable than when a child is made to go.

Maybe Jean wouldn't have become a doctor or a lawyer, but maybe he would have become a great athlete or a good businessman. He would have had his own family and his own children. He was still at the well of "maybes," there to draw from the dreams and possibilities. He was curious and alive and full to the brim with a desire to live every moment, to taste every cookie, drink every soda, laugh every laugh, run until his heart felt as if it would burst, climb trees and have a dog at his feet or a cat in his lap. He was Everyboy, our own Huckleberry Finn, more comfortable in a pair of torn jeans than in suit and tie, never annoyed by strands of hair over his forehead, eager to poke his finger into the pie or the cake icing.

And now he was no more.

"He's gone," Daddy said, and the stone face crumbled under the flow of his own cold tears.

Mommy raised her eyes toward the ceiling and screamed just before she collapsed into Daddy's arms. I was so shattered by her reaction that I never noticed Pierre had toppled back. But when I looked at him, I felt a second stab of ice through my heart. I realized he had fallen into a catatonic state, his eyes wide open.

Our tragedy was just getting under way.

To see Pierre without Jean at his side was like looking at someone who'd had a limb removed. He always looked incomplete; so it was understandable that he would fall into a state of shock, perhaps even deeper and more intense than the shock Mommy was feeling. The doctors examined him. They thought he would snap out of it after a while. They advised us to take him home and pay him as much attention as possible. Daddy had carried his one twin son into the hospital, and he had to carry the other out. We drove back to the château as if we were already in Jean's funeral procession. Mommy lay back, her head against the side of the car. I sat with my arm around Pierre, holding him beside me and whispering words of comfort in his ear. Daddy was mechanical, going through the motions of what had to be done. He carried Pierre into the château, and I helped Mommy. Daddy put Pierre to bed, but we weren't going to stay there. Daddy had the servants get our things together quickly, and he called ahead and had our doctor waiting at the New Orleans house. Then he made the arrangements for the transfer of Jean's body to the funeral parlor. I was at his side, ready to help him with anything, but he wanted me to concentrate on Pierre, who still hadn't snapped out of his semiconscious state. When it was time to leave, he had to be carried to the car, where he lay limp against me all the way to New Orleans. Mommy was collapsed in the front seat, her eyes shut to keep out the reality.

Nothing travels as fast as bad news. We weren't home an hour before the phones began to ring. Daddy had to call Europe to tell Grandpa and Grandma Andreas what had happened. As usual, they had gone to the Riviera for the summer. Grandma Andreas told Daddy that Grandpa was too sick to travel home for the funeral. He had suffered a stroke the year before.

The doctor had given Mommy a sedative. He examined Pierre and thought he would snap out of his shock soon. Following the doctor's orders, I tried to get him to eat something, drink something; but he wouldn't open his mouth. I began to fear that the doctors at the hospital and our doctor might have underestimated the intensity of his emotional trauma.

The air of gloom that had permeated our house before we went to the country was nothing compared to what followed. Death had made a camp in our dark corners; it moved proudly and freely through the corridors, dimming every light, fading every color, making every flower droop, and painting our windows with a gray tint so that no matter how much sunshine fell from the blue sky above, it looked like rain to us. People spoke only in whispers and lifted their feet so their footsteps were barely audible. The servants glided in and out of rooms to do their work and then hovered together in the kitchen or the pantry to console each other. The ticking of clocks began to sound like thunder.

Later in the day Daddy gathered all his inner strength to greet people in his study and finalize the arrangements for Jean's funeral. In the dim lamplight, he looked ashen and gray, like a man who had aged decades in minutes. Early in the evening, just after one of his business associates left, I entered his study. He was sitting back in his desk chair, staring blankly at the opposite wall. He didn't seem to notice me.

"Daddy," I said.

He turned to me as in a dream. His dark eyes shone, full of tears. "Yes, Pearl."

"It's about Pierre, Daddy. He's not improving. He hasn't eaten anything since . . . since the hospital. He won't even sip water."

"He's blaming himself," Daddy said, shaking his head. Then he pounded his chest with his closed fist so hard that I winced. "I am the one to blame," he declared.

I hurried to his side and put my hand on his shoulder. "Of course you're not, Daddy. No one's to blame."

"I wanted us to go there. I pushed for it," he moaned, his voice cracking.

"But, Daddy, sooner or later we would have gone there anyway. You can't blame yourself. It was a horrible, horrible accident."

"Accident," he said bitterly. His chin quivered. "I warned them; I told them not to wander off, didn't I?"

"Yes, Daddy. Stop blaming yourself. Mommy's upstairs wrenching her heart with blame, and Pierre has fallen into a serious coma because he blames himself. Jean simply shouldn't have gone into the water."

"He was just a young boy, still a child," Daddy protested. "It was my job to take care of him, watch over him, protect him. I failed. I failed miserably," he said and closed his eyes. He looked as if he might keep them shut forever.

"Daddy, I'm afraid for Pierre. We've got to do something. Call the doctor back."

Daddy opened his eyes slowly and stared at me as if my words were taking hours to enter his brain. "You think it's that serious?"

"He'll be dehydrated. I think he's even running a fever."

"Oh, no. I'll lose both of them," he said and stood up. He nodded after his own thoughts. "I'd better pay some attention to him and stop wallowing in my own tragedy," he added and started out. I followed him up the stairs to Pierre's room.

Pierre hadn't moved a muscle since I had last been beside him. His eyes were open, but so empty it was as if I could see through them, down the long corridor, into the blackness of his closed-down mind. Daddy went to the bed and sat beside Pierre, taking his hand into his.

"Pierre, you've got to snap out of this and help us, help Mommy. You must eat and drink something. It wasn't your fault. You tried to keep Jean from going into the water. Come on, Pierre," Daddy pleaded. Pierre didn't even blink. "Pierre." Daddy touched his cheek. "Come on, son. Please," he begged. Pierre's eyes remained turned inward. Suddenly he grimaced

124

as if in great pain. And then he made a horrible guttural noise that frightened Daddy and me. Daddy retreated with surprise and stood up. "What's wrong with him? Why is he doing that?"

"I think he's reliving the tragedy," I guessed.

"Pierre, stop it. Stop it," Daddy ordered. He shook him by the shoulders. Pierre's expression didn't change, but the horrible sound ended. Daddy released him and turned to me. "I'd better call the doctor, as you say, Pearl."

"Go on, Daddy. I'll stay with him," I said.

Daddy left the room.

I sat on the bed and took Pierre's hand in mine, stroking it gently.

"Poor Pierre," I said. "You had to see such a terrible thing, but you can't blame yourself. It wasn't your fault."

I lifted my eyes to his face and saw the beginning of a single tear as it crawled over his eyelid and made its slow zigzag journey down his cheek to his chin. Incredibly, that was it, only one tear; as if he had cried all the others inside and had nothing more left to show. I leaned over and wiped the solitary tear away.

"Won't you try to drink some water, Pierre? Please. For me. Please," I begged. His lips didn't move, and his eyes remained as cold and hard as chips of turquoise. I sighed and held his hand and spoke to him softly until I was exhausted with the effort. Then I heard the door open and saw Mommy standing there, her hair down, her face streaked with her own dried tears, her skin waxen. She was in her nightgown, but wore no slippers.

"What's wrong with him?" she asked in a voice stripped of emotion. She sounded like someone who had been mesmerized and was speaking under a spell, but she seemed finally to realize there was something the matter with Pierre.

"He won't drink or eat anything. His expression hasn't changed since we returned, nor has he moved. He's in a catatonic state, Mommy. I told Daddy to call the doctor."

"Mon Dieu," she said. "What have I done?"

"Mommy, please. It doesn't do anyone any good if you blame yourself. Look what it's doing to Pierre." I turned to him. "I'm sure he's blaming himself."

"My baby," she said and moved forward to embrace him. She sat on the bed and took him in her arms, but he was like a rag doll, his head wagging, his eyes frozen, his limbs lifeless. She rocked with him and tried to soothe him, but he didn't respond. The realization struck her, and she lowered him to the pillow, an expression of shock and fear in her face.

"What can we do, Pearl?" she cried.

"The doctor will be here any minute, Mommy, but I think Pierre's going to have to go to the hospital. They'll have to put him on an I.V. until he returns."

"Returns?" she asked. "From where?"

"From his own sanctuary, his place of escape, a place where what's happened is not a reality."

"How long could this last?" she asked, looking at him. I was afraid to tell her what I knew. I had read of people who had gone into a catatonic state for years because of some emotional trauma. Some of them never emerged, and some, when they emerged, were dramatically different because they had regressed into childhood.

"He'll snap out of it soon, Mommy, but he needs medical attention," I replied.

"Yes, of course, you're right." She put her hand on my cheek gently and smiled. "You're my big girl. I'm going to depend on you for so much now, Pearl. It's not fair, I know. You should be able to enjoy these years and not be weighed down by so much hardship and misery. I had hoped your life would be different from mine. I had hoped . . ." She paused, her lips quivering.

"I'll be all right, Mommy."

She looked at Pierre again. "The twins were so close. Even as babies when one would cry, the other would, too, and when one woke up, the other was soon to wake up as well. Jean started to walk before Pierre did, you know."

"I remember, Mommy."

"But even though he could, he still crawled because Pierre crawled. One never wanted to leave the other too far behind. Now . . ." She closed her eyes. I put my arm around her, and we cried and comforted each other for a few moments. Finally the doctor arrived, and Daddy brought him up to Pierre. We all stood back and watched him examine my brother, noting the way his pupils dilated, checking his pulse, listening to his heart and lungs.

"We should put him into the hospital, monsieur," he told Daddy. "I'd like him to be under the care of a psychiatrist too."

Daddy swallowed hard. Mommy started to sob softly.

"I'll make the arrangements," the doctor said. "If I may use the phone."

"Come down to my study," Daddy said.

"I'll get him ready," I offered quickly.

"He'll be so frightened," Mommy moaned.

I dressed Pierre in his bathrobe and slippers and put together some of the things I knew he would need, things I prayed he would soon need. Mommy went to get dressed. Soon afterward Daddy carried poor Pierre to the car again and we were off to put him in the hospital.

He looked so much smaller when he was dressed in a hospital gown and put in a hospital bed; and when they inserted the I.V. in his arm, the seriousness of

127

what was happening to him struck both Mommy and Daddy at the center of their hearts. Daddy embraced her, and they stood together watching as the nurse and the doctor attended to him.

Because the nurses knew me, they were more concerned and sympathetic. The psychiatrist who was called in was a Dr. LeFevre. She was in her early sixties with fading light brown hair. I knew of her, but I had rarely seen her and never talked to her before. She interviewed Daddy first to learn about the circumstances and then went in to examine Pierre. After her initial examination, she spoke to Daddy, Mommy, and me in the hallway. She was a soft-spoken woman, but her demeanor was authoritative and confident.

"Your son is suffering from post-traumatic stress disorder," she began. "After the experience you've described," she said to Daddy, "it's quite understandable. It's not unlike what some combat veterans experience. In the profession we sometimes refer to this as emotional anesthesia. He's turning himself off, in a sense, to keep from suffering."

"How long . . ."

"I think we'll bring him out of it soon, but I must warn you, he'll need serious therapy, maybe for some time. Something like this could leave him with severe depression and anxiety. We could find he experiences chronic headaches, has difficulty with his concentration . . . Of course, we have to wait and see. In the meantime, we'll see that he's well looked after." She turned to me. "Why do you look so familiar to me?"

"I work here," I said. "I'm a nurse's aide."

"Oh, yes. I've heard good things about you. Well, I'll examine Pierre again tomorrow. Call me in the late afternoon."

"Thank you, Doctor," Daddy said.

Mommy wanted to stay with Pierre a while longer.

Some of the friends I had made working at the hospital came over to speak to me and offer condolences when they heard what had happened. Jack Weller wasn't on duty. I was happy that I didn't have to confront him at this terribly emotional moment. Mommy just sat in a chair staring at Pierre. Finally Daddy forced her to get up to go home. We had hard days waiting for us. He knew she needed some rest.

"I'll be here with him every possible moment, Mommy," I promised. She smiled, looked back at Pierre's pathetic face, still frozen in a bland expression, and then she permitted Daddy to lead her out and to the car.

The house was too quiet that night. I slept in short cycles, waking with a start and listening, hoping for the sound of my brothers doing some mischief, hoping that all that had happened had been only a nightmare. But there was nothing but the ticking of my clock and the gong of the grandfather clock downstairs. It echoed through the hallways, telling me we were that much closer to Jean's funeral. I buried my face in my pillow to smother the tears, but every time I closed my eyes, I saw Jean's face, mischievous, happy, full of life and promise.

At the break of day, unable to sleep, I rose, dressed, and went downstairs to discover that Daddy had risen during the night. He had his head down on his desk and was asleep from emotional exhaustion. Beside him on his right was a recent picture of the twins, and on his left was a nearly empty bottle of bourbon. I didn't have the heart to wake him. I simply slipped out quietly and closed the door. Then I went to see about some breakfast for Mommy and the start of what I knew would be the worst week of our lives.

So many people attended Jean's funeral that the crowd of mourners spilled out of the church door and down the steps onto the sidewalk. A few of my school friends were there, but I didn't see Claude. I knew Catherine had gone on a holiday with her family and wouldn't find out about Jean until she returned. Mommy, somewhat sedated, moved in a dreamlike state, her face sculptured in a tight grimace that sometimes appeared like an angelic smile but told me of the deep pain she was feeling from her toes to her head and into the very essence of her soul. By now everyone knew how Pierre's condition compounded our tragedy. He was still hooked to an I.V., still catatonic.

After the church service, the procession wound its way to the cemetery. I recalled Jean's and Pierre's questions about the vaults—what we in New Orleans call the burial ovens—built above ground because of the water table. What had once been a place of intrigue and curiosity to Jean would now serve as his home and resting place.

Daddy and Mommy clung tightly to each other. Most of the time, Daddy was holding Mommy up, her legs moving like the legs of a marionette on a string. I remained as close to her as I could, ready to embrace her myself if she started to topple. At the gravesite, the three of us embraced. I don't think any of us actually heard the priest's words. There was just the morbid rhythm of his voice reciting the prayers. He showered the holy water on Jean's casket and finally said "Amen."

I barely had raised my eyes higher than Mommy's and Daddy's faces all day, so I wasn't aware of the blue sky. To me it was a totally overcast day with only a slight breeze.

As we turned to walk back to our limousine, I saw Sophie standing under a tree. She was grinding the tears out of her eyes with her small fist, but the sight of her gave me a boost and helped me manage the journey home.

Mommy went right to bed. Daddy sat on the sofa in the sitting room greeting people and sipping from a tumbler of bourbon. As soon as I had the opportunity, I called the hospital, hoping Pierre had begun his recovery. We so desperately needed a morsel of good news, but his condition remained unchanged.

I decided I had to go to him, that a full day without any of us at his side was unacceptable, even though it was Jean's funeral day. I whispered my intentions to Daddy, who just nodded. He was numb with grief and unaware of what was happening around him.

At the hospital I met Dr. LeFevre in the hallway. She had just been in to see Pierre. "I'm going to move Pierre to the psychiatric unit," she said. "His recovery is going to take longer than I first anticipated. The emotional wound goes deep. I gather he and Jean were very close."

"Inseparable," I said, "and very protective of each other."

"Well, I know it's a difficult time for you and your parents, but try to give him as much time as you can. Just hearing your voice, feeling you beside him, will help reassure him and make his recovery that much more likely," she added. I didn't like the way her eyes shifted away from me.

"Do you think he will recover? I mean, will he be all right?"

"We'll see," she said in a noncommittal tone and walked off.

I put my chair as close to Pierre's bed as I could and sat holding his free hand. He stared ahead, blinking, his lips slightly open. I stroked his hand and spoke softly to him.

"You've got to try to get better, Pierre. Mommy and

131

Daddy desperately need you to get better. I need you. Jean wouldn't want you to be like this. He would want you to help Mommy and Daddy. Please try, Pierre."

I sat there, waiting, watching. Except for the reflexive movement of his eyelids, he was like a statue made of human skin and bones. His ears and his eyes had brought him shocking, horrible information, and he had shut them down as a result, locking out any further details. Somewhere inside himself he was safe; he was playing with Jean; he could hear Jean's voice and see him. He didn't want to hear my voice, for my voice would shatter the illusion like thin china, and the shards would stab him in his heart forever and ever.

Sophie stopped in before going on duty, and I thanked her for coming to the funeral. She promised she would peek in on Pierre whenever she could and talk to him, too. I told her he would soon be moved to the psychiatric wing.

"That's all right. I'll get up there, too," she promised. We hugged, and she went to work. I remained as long as I could, talking to Pierre, pleading, soothing, cajoling him to return to us. Finally, exhausted myself, I went home.

All of the mourners had gone. The house was dead silent. Aubrey told me Daddy had retreated to his study. I found him sprawled on his leather sofa, mercifully asleep. I put a blanket over him and then went up to see Mommy.

At first I thought she was asleep too, but she turned her head slowly toward me and opened her eyes like someone who had risen from the grave. She reached out for me, and I hurried to her side and took her hand. We embraced, and then I sat beside her.

"Where's your father?" she asked.

"In his study, asleep."

"Did you go to see Pierre?"

I nodded. "The doctor wants to move him to the psychiatric ward so he can get the kind of treatment he needs," I told her.

"Then he's no better?"

"Not yet, Mommy. But he will be."

She shook her head and looked away. "Don't think your sins ever go away," she said. "You confess, you perform penance, you hope for forgiveness, but your sins are indelible. They hover like parasites, waiting for an opportunity to feed on your good fortune."

"You've got to stop doing this to yourself, Mommy."

"Listen to me, Pearl," she said tightening her grip on my hand. "You're brighter than I was at your age. You won't make the same mistakes, and you won't succumb to your weaknesses. You don't have the weaknesses I had. And that is good because you don't just hurt yourself, you hurt those you love and who love you."

"Mommy . . ."

"No. What could a free, innocent soul like Jean possibly have done to be so punished? This is not his doing. The weight of my sins was placed on him, and he suffered because of that, don't you see?

"Nina knew," she muttered. "Nina knew."

I sighed so deeply and loudly that she spun on me.

"A long time ago I did a bad thing, and I'm not referring to getting pregnant with you. You are too beautiful, too wonderful, to be anything but good; but after you were born, we were alone in the bayou."

"You told me this, Mommy. You don't have to explain."

"I want to explain. I need to explain. I didn't agree to marry your uncle Paul just because your father was off in Europe living the rich young man's life."

"But you thought he had become engaged and there was no hope of you two ever marrying," I reminded her.

"Yes, yes, but Paul was my half brother. True, we didn't learn that truth until we were both teenagers and after Paul had already fallen in love with me, but that didn't excuse it."

"Excuse what, Mommy? Look how we were living when you returned to the bayou. Why shouldn't you have agreed to live at Cyprus Woods? You said everyone thought I was his child anyway."

"Yes, they did, and he did little to convince them otherwise."

"Why are you telling me all this again?"

"Because I gave in to him and let him talk me into marrying him. We actually were married by a priest."

"But you told me that was just a marriage of convenience, that you and Paul were like roommates."

"Not always," she said. "There was a time when we pretended we were other people, people from the past, and . . . I sinned.

"I didn't do penance; I didn't ask forgiveness. I pretended it didn't happen, but the sin was part of my shadow and followed me from the bayou. Slowly that shadow moved over this house and this family until it claimed my poor Jean."

"Oh, Mommy, no," I said. I shook my head. It hurt me to learn this, but I couldn't believe God would punish Jean for Mommy's sin.

She closed her eyes. "I'm so tired, but I don't sleep. I see only Jean's face, see only Beau rushing from the swamp with him in his arms. And when I looked back, I saw that shadow smiling triumphantly at me."

She opened her eyes and seized my hand. "Jean is still here, still with us, still in this house. I want you to go back to Nina's house and see her sister. I want you to tell her what's happened and get her to bring the right charms here."

"Mommy, you're talking nonsense. Daddy wouldn't let us bring charms into this house anyway."

"You've got to do it, Pearl," she said, her eyes wide. "Will you promise?" she demanded. I saw she wouldn't rest until she had my word.

"Okay, Mommy. I promise."

"Good. Good," she said, releasing my hand and closing her eyes again. "Now I can sleep."

I sat there for a while staring at her until her breathing became slow and regular. Then I got up quietly and slipped from her room, thinking about the heavy burden of guilt Mommy had kept buried in the vault of her memory. Surely it had weighed down her heart before, but she had been able to pretend it had never happened. She had been lonely and afraid, I told myself. Everyone she loved but Paul had deserted her. I could never blame her for anything evil. Never.

Mommy was like an invalid for the next few days, never leaving her room, getting up only to bathe and change her nightgown. Daddy and I visited Pierre often in the psychiatric ward. Daddy did a little work, but by early evening, he was usually in his study drinking bourbon to help him sleep.

One afternoon about four days later, I went to the hospital first. I started talking to Pierre the same way I always did: first reviewing the things that had happened at the house, the people who called, the friends of Pierre's and Jean's who had asked about him. I talked and talked and stroked his hand and kissed his cheek and told him how much Mommy needed him. And then the nurse's aide brought in some juice and as usual, I tried to get Pierre to take something by mouth.

It looked as if I would fail as I had so many times before, when suddenly his lips opened and his clenched teeth unlocked. Excited, I started to feed him the juice in tiny increments. He took some on his tongue, and then he swallowed and took some more.

"That's good, Pierre. That's wonderful. We'll get you off this I.V."

I rushed out to tell the nurse, who called Dr. LeFevre. By the time Daddy arrived, Pierre had drunk most of the juice. He wasn't speaking and he wasn't moving, but at least there had been this small change.

Daddy was overjoyed. "We've got to get home to tell Ruby. Maybe now she'll get up and come to see him," he said.

We hurried home; a shaft of bright light and hope had finally pierced the dark clouds over us. When we pulled into our driveway, we saw a tall, slim black woman leaving the house. She wore a long red skirt, sandals, and a bone-white blouse. Her bracelets were made of animal bones, and her dangling earrings were silver embedded with what looked like cats' eyes. She glanced our way, but didn't pause. I saw she had a scar across her right cheek with a triangular cut at the top end of it right beneath her sharp cheekbone.

"Who the hell is that?" Daddy muttered.

The woman disappeared around our gate. We hurried inside and up the stairs. Mommy wasn't in the bedroom, but a can of brimstone was burning on each nightstand. The scent of sulfur permeated the air.

"What the . . ." Daddy snuffed them out quickly. "Where is she? What is she doing?"

"Don't yell at her, Daddy," I warned. "She's—"

"I know what she's doing. I know exactly what she's doing," he said and left the room. I followed him downstairs. Mommy wasn't in the sitting rooms, the study, or the kitchen. We finally found her in her studio. She was sketching on an easel, but on either side of her burned a blue candle.

"Ruby," Daddy said and she turned slowly.

"Hello, Beau."

"What was that woman doing here? Why were you burning that stuff in our bedroom? And what is this with these candles?"

"I had to get us some good gris-gris and fight back, Beau. Don't be angry. I feel safe again. I'll start to work, too." She smiled at me, but I thought it was a strange smile, the smile of someone who was under a spell. Like Daddy, I wondered what that voodoo woman had done.

"I can't believe this," Daddy said. "Stinking up our bedroom . . ." He shook his head and then remembered why we had rushed home. "Anyway, we've got some good news. Pearl got Pierre to drink some juice."

Mommy just stared at him, that same strange smile frozen on her lips.

"Didn't you hear what I said, Ruby? Pierre has drunk some juice. Perhaps he can be taken off the I.V. soon. There's light at the end of the tunnel," Daddy said, obviously annoyed that Mommy remained so unanimated.

"Of course there is, Beau," she finally said. "I knew it. It's because of what the voodoo mama did here. Don't you see? Nina's going to help us . . . from beyond." She lifted her eyes toward the ceiling. "She's going to help us."

"*Mon Dieu,*" Daddy said. "I can't believe this. Don't you want me to take you right over to see Pierre?"

"Not yet, Beau. I'm not ready yet. Soon."

"I give up." Daddy threw up his hands. "You talk to her, Pearl. Maybe you can get her to regain her senses so she can visit her son and not act like a lunatic," he cried and left the studio.

"Beau's always been so skeptical," Mommy said. "But he'll change." She turned back to her sketch.

"Mommy," I said, going to her. "You can't bury yourself in these rituals and charms now. You've got to come with me to see Pierre."

"Not yet," she said. "There are still some things to be done. Otherwise I'll only bring him bad luck. He'll understand. Later I'll make him understand. You see I'm right, don't you, honey?"

I said nothing. I gazed at the sketch Mommy was doing. She was drawing Jean floating in the swamp. "Mommy . . ."

She continued her work as if I weren't standing there. After a while I started to turn away, but she sensed it and reached for my hand. "You've got to do something with me, Pearl. We've got to do it tonight. Only you must not tell your father. I know he'll try to stop us; he just doesn't understand."

"What, Mommy?"

"We've got to go to the cemetery at midnight. Mama Leela will be there with a black cat. We will be able to speak to Nina and see what else we can do."

"Oh, Mommy, no. We can't do that."

"We must," she said, her eyes wild. She was digging her fingers into my skin.

"Okay, Mommy. Okay."

She relaxed. "Promise not to tell Daddy."

"I promise," I said. Now I was feeling as if I were making a deal with the devil.

"Good." She smiled and turned back to her painting.

I watched her for a moment and then left. I found Daddy sitting on the sofa in the office, sipping from his glass of bourbon.

"Can you believe your mother?" he asked as soon as I entered.

"She's having her own sort of nervous breakdown, Daddy. We've got to be sympathetic and indulge her for a while, until she returns to her senses," I added.

Pain flashed in his eyes. "I thought she would want to rush out to the hospital with me. Instead, she's burning candles, painting weird pictures, and mumbling about chants and gris-gris. I've got only one friend now," he said and lifted his glass.

"That's not any better than what Mommy's doing, Daddy. You've got to stop drinking," I warned.

"I know," he said. "Soon. Well, I have to attend to some business problems. We'll stop in on Pierre after dinner. Maybe Ruby will snap out of it and come with us."

I didn't want to discourage him, but I didn't think she would. "We'll see," I said.

Mommy wouldn't come with us to the hospital, of course.

The nurses told us Pierre had eaten some soft-boiled egg and drunk some milk. He still didn't speak or act as if he heard what anyone was saying, but we were all encouraged. It was enough to buoy Daddy's spirits. He was more talkative and energetic.

"You've got to come with us tomorrow, Ruby," he told Mommy when we returned home and found her in the sitting room listening to music and reading.

"All right, Beau," she said, giving me a conspiratorial glance. "I will."

"Good. Good," Daddy replied and looked at me. I could tell from his face that he thought things were finally turning around. "I'm going up to bed."

"I'll be right along, Beau," Mommy told him.

"Pierre has made good progress, Mommy, but he needs to see and to hear you now," I told her.

"I know, dear. And he will as long as you remember what you promised."

"Mommy . . ."

"I'll come by your room at eleven-thirty and knock softly. Be ready," she said.

I stared at her a moment. What was I going to do? Then I looked down at the book in her hands.

She was holding it upside down, just using it to stare at her own maddening thoughts.

"Mommy, it's too dangerous to go to the cemeteries at night. Daddy would be very, very angry at both of us, but especially at me. Please," I begged.

She gazed at me. "Okay, Pearl," she said. "If you don't want to do it, it's all right."

"But you're not going either, Mommy, right? Right?" I insisted.

"I won't go," she finally said, but I didn't believe her.

I pledged to stay awake and listen for her footsteps just in case.

7

Beyond the Grave

Despite my urgent and great desire to do so, I had trouble keeping myself awake. I tried reading, but my eyes were drifting off the page and my head was nodding more and more. I told myself it would be easier to just lie quietly in the dark, but almost immediately after I put out the lights and lowered my head to the pillow, my eyelids closed. The next thing I knew, I woke with a start and when I glanced at the clock, I saw it was nearly a quarter to midnight. If Mommy had come to my door to knock or if she had walked by, I hadn't heard her. I couldn't imagine her going out at night to a cemetery by herself. Confident I would find her still in her bed, I rose, put on my slippers and robe and tiptoed across the hallway to my parents' room.

The door was slightly ajar. I pushed it gently and peered in. The amber light of a half moon outlined the silhouettes of the dresser, lamps, chairs, and vanity table. I could see Daddy's head on the pillow, but when I looked closer, I did not see Mommy's. For a long moment panic nailed my feet to the floor. She must be in the bathroom, I told myself. I waited and listened, but there was no sign or any sound of her. I knocked gently on the door and waited for Daddy to lift his head. He didn't move.

I entered their bedroom and whispered loudly, "Daddy."

A heavy, resonant snore was his only response. I went to his side and touched his shoulder. I didn't want to wake him abruptly and frighten him. He might think the hospital had called about Pierre. But he wasn't responding.

"Daddy." I shook him. He moaned and turned over, still not opening his eyes.

The strong odor of bourbon reached me, and I saw the nearly empty tumbler on the nightstand. When I shook him again, more roughly, my father groaned and his eyelids fluttered but barely opened.

"Whaa," he said.

"Daddy, wake up. Where's Mommy?"

"Whaa." He closed his eyes and turned on his side. Frustrated but frantic about Mommy, I retreated from the bedroom and hurried down the stairway. I searched the rooms, all of which were dark, and then I peeked in the kitchen, hoping she had gone there to make herself some warm milk. But I found only the night-lights on and no one anywhere.

I thought for a moment and then hurried down to her studio. Even though it was dark, I could imagine her sitting there, so I flipped on the lights. My heart throbbed in triple time as I held my breath. She wasn't there, but her recent picture caught my attention. I drew closer to it and saw that she had added more detail.

It was a sketch of Jean's face on a ghostlike body floating out of the swamp, but vaguely suggested in the water below was the figure of a man, his eyes wide.

I studied the picture and then stepped back and gasped. This was the face I saw so often in my own nightmare; it was the face of Paul Tate, who was thought to have drowned himself out of grief when Mommy went to live with Daddy. It was a face that obviously haunted her as well.

I turned off the lights and hurried through the house to look in the garage, where my worst fear was confirmed. Mommy's car was gone; she had driven off to meet the voodoo mama in the cemetery in which Nina Jackson had been buried. Upstairs, Daddy was in a drunken stupor. What was I to do?

I dressed quickly and drove Daddy's car to the cemetery. In the glow of the moonlight the burial vaults took on a pale flaxen glow, and the shadows around them deepened, creating long corridors of darkness that wrapped themselves tightly around most of the ovens and permitted only the very tops of monuments to be seen. The darkness resembled a sea of ink.

I hesitated and then drove slowly around the cemetery. At first I saw nothing and hoped Mommy had gone someplace less ominous; but when I made a final turn, I saw her car near an entrance, and she wasn't in it.

My heart began to thump. I pulled up behind her car and reached into the glove compartment for the flashlight. Then I turned off the engine and the lights, allowing that sea of ink to rush in around me, too. A wave of anxiety washed over me and sent my throbbing heartbeat into my bones. My fingers trembled when I reached for the door handle and stepped out. For a moment it felt as if the ground beneath my feet had softened into quicksand. Every step toward the cemetery took great effort.

I turned on the flashlight and directed the beam

down the corridor ahead of me, not daring to look back or to my left or right. With my attention glued to the ray of light, I walked on, listening, hoping to find Mommy quickly and get her out of here and home.

Suddenly the screech of a cat sent sharp shivers through my chest and made my stomach do flip-flops. Blood drained down into my feet. I stopped and waved my flashlight over the ovens, cutting across the stone figures, the engraved words, and the embossed faces of the dead. A second screech was followed by a snarl, and then all went silent.

"Mommy!" I cried into the night and waited for her response, but I heard nothing except the drumming of my own heart in my ears. "Mommy, where are you?"

A shrill laugh pierced the silence. It didn't sound like Mommy, so it sent me retreating a few steps. I spun around when I heard loud whispering on my right.

"Mommy, it's me! Where are you?"

The whispering stopped. I waited and then turned down another corridor. A few moments later the voodoo mama whom Daddy and I had seen leaving our house the other day crossed in front of me. She had a black cat in her arms. She didn't look my way. She walked into the darkness as if she had flashlights for eyes, and just as quickly as she had appeared, she disappeared. A moment later Mommy stepped out of the darkness, cupping a white candle in her palms, walking as slowly as a somnambulist, the glow of the candle turning her eyes into pools of gray light and making her cheeks glitter.

"Mommy!" I cried and ran to her.

"Pearl. It's all right," she said softly, but she didn't look directly at me and she didn't pause. Her eyes were fixed on what she remembered rather than what she saw, and she kept walking. It was as if she thought

I too was an apparition. I seized her hand, and she turned to me, her eyes still full of the candlelight. "Nina has spoken to me," she said. "I know what I must do."

"Mommy, stop this. You're scaring me." I shook her hard, and the candle fell from her hands and was snuffed out as soon as it hit the ground.

"Oh, no!" she said, looking back into the darkness. "Quickly. We have to leave the cemetery. Quickly, Pearl." She grasped my hand desperately and pulled me forward. We ran down the dark corridors to the street. There she paused to catch her breath.

"Why did you do this, Mommy? Why did you come here by yourself?"

"I had to, Pearl. I had to. Let's go home now. It's all right. You didn't have to come looking for me."

"You told me you weren't going to do this. I fell asleep, and when I went to look for you, I saw you were gone and had taken your car. I tried to wake Daddy, but he's sound asleep," I said, eager to keep myself talking and hear the sound of my own voice. A thin wisp of a cloud had moved across the moon and weakened the little light there was around us. The silence in this dark cemetery was terrifying.

"It's all right," Mommy said. "It's going to be all right."

"Can you drive yourself home, Mommy?"

"Of course. Let's go. And, Pearl, there's no need to tell Daddy where we were."

"Let's just get home, Mommy. Quickly."

She got into her car, and I got into mine. She drove slowly but carefully, and we pulled into the driveway together. We put the cars in the garage and then went into the house and upstairs.

"What did you do there with that woman, Mommy?" I asked her outside my bedroom.

"I did what I had to do to speak with Nina."

"You spoke to her?" I was astonished that she could believe in such a thing.

"Yes, and then she spoke to me through the cat. I know what I must do."

"What, Mommy? What did she tell you to do?"

"It's not for me to tell anyone else, darling Pearl. Only know this: I love you and your father and your brother more than I love my own life."

"Mommy, what are you going to do? I'm frightened."

"There's nothing to be frightened of, not anymore," she said with a smile. Then she hugged me. "My sweet, darling Pearl," she said wiping strands of hair from my forehead. "You deserve better than to be born under so many dark clouds. But soon, soon, we'll have sunshine again. I promise."

"Mommy, you must tell me what you think you should do. Please. I won't tell Daddy."

"It will be all right. You have to have faith, Pearl. I know you have a scientific mind, but you must have faith in things that are beyond microscopes, beyond the laws of nature, too. You must believe in things you cannot see, for there is something behind the darkness, waiting, watching. Believe and do not be afraid," she said. Then she closed her eyes.

"Mommy . . ."

"I'm tired. Let's talk tomorrow. Okay? Now let me slip into bed without waking Daddy. Get some rest, honey. Go on," she prodded.

I bit down on my tongue to keep myself from asking more questions as I watched her cross to her bedroom. She seemed to float through the doorway and was gone.

My heart was beating fast, and it was difficult for me to breathe and not be drowned by everything that was happening so fast. I hated the thought of betraying Mommy, but I was convinced that I had to tell Daddy about this night and the things she had said. He had to take more interest in what she was thinking and doing and stop being so angry about it.

I spent a restless night, tossing and turning, waking and falling back into a deep sleep like drifting. Although I was exhausted, I welcomed the soft kiss of sunlight on my face and rose quickly to wash and dress so I could hear happy voices, and smell the scent of morning blossoms. The memories of last night felt so vague that I thought perhaps I had dreamed all of it; but when I looked at my sneakers, I saw the dirt from the cemetery and a chilling shiver ran down my spine.

To my surprise I discovered that Daddy had risen early and had already left the house to go to his office. Mommy hadn't come downstairs. I waited for her and finally went back upstairs to see how she was doing. I saw she was still fast asleep. Poor thing, I thought, tormenting herself so. I closed the door softly and returned to the dining room to eat my breakfast. Mommy still had her eyes closed when I looked in on her again, but I entered the bedroom and stood by her side, watching her chest rise and fall in a slow rhythm. As I turned to leave, she groaned, opened her eyes, and sat up.

"Good morning, Mommy," I said.

She raked the room with her eyes as if she had forgotten where she was. Before she responded, she rubbed her forehead vigorously as if to erase her lingering dreams. Then she took a deep breath and brushed back her hair. "Good morning, honey. What time is it? Oh, dear," she said, gazing at the clock on her nightstand. "I hope your father isn't waiting for me before he has his breakfast."

"No, he rose early and has already gone to work."

"Work?" She thought a moment and nodded.

"Good. That's what he needs to do . . . keep himself busy. You too, honey. I want you to go back to work at the hospital."

"Not yet, Mommy. I want to devote as much time as possible to Pierre."

"Don't worry about Pierre. He's going to be fine," she said with confidence and that strange half smile she had been wearing ever since Jean's funeral.

I returned to her bedside. "What did you mean last night when you told me you knew what had to be done now, Mommy? What exactly are you planning on doing? What did that voodoo lady tell you?"

"Oh, it's just some harmless chants and rituals, Pearl. You need not worry. Let me indulge myself in my old beliefs. It doesn't do anyone any harm and who knows . . . As I always told you, you shouldn't discount any one else's faith." She dropped her half smile and grew concerned. "You didn't tell your father about last night, did you, Pearl?"

"No, Mommy. He was already gone by the time I went downstairs this morning."

"Good. Please don't say anything, darling. He's so emotionally fragile as it is. One more thing could push him over the edge. You don't want that, do you?"

"But, Mommy, going to cemeteries at night . . ."

"I promise I won't go there again. Okay? Come here, honey," she said and reached out for me. I stepped closer, and she took my hand. "You and I have always had a deep bond between us, haven't we? We have always trusted each other entirely."

"Yes, Mommy."

"Trust me, then, Pearl. Please," she pleaded, her eyes soft and loving.

"All right, Mommy. As long as you don't go back there."

"I won't." She looked around. "Well, I guess I'll get up and have breakfast. I am hungry this morning."

"Will you go to the hospital with me today, Mommy?"

"I will," she said. "I have just a few things to do first. Why don't you go ahead and I'll join you later?"

"When?" I demanded.

"After lunch. Okay?"

"Maybe I should wait for you and we should go together," I said, not believing her.

"Now, Pearl, what did I just ask from you? I asked for a little trust between us, right? I'll be fine. Besides," she said, "by the time I arrive, Pierre will have begun a real recuperation. You'll see," she said. She rose and went into the bathroom. I lingered awhile, wondering if I shouldn't just call Daddy and tell him to rush right home.

But then I realized that Mommy was right. Daddy was fragile, too. If he was beginning to put himself together, I should let him do that unhampered. It had fallen to me to be the pillar of strength in our house, whether I wanted it or not. It was getting late anyway, and I didn't want Pierre to see so much of the day go by without any of us there.

When I arrived, however, I learned that Daddy had already visited with him. He had brought him his favorite comic books and some of his favorite pralines, but everything remained on the table where he had left it. Pierre was propped up comfortably in his bed, his hands folded in his lap, his eyes fixed on the wall, the lids blinking reflexively. His lips quivered slightly when I kissed his cheek and sat beside him, taking his left hand into mine.

"Mommy's coming to see you today, Pierre. Won't you try to speak just for her. She desperately needs to hear your voice."

His blinking continued in the same rhythm, and his eyes didn't shift. I looked down at his hand in mine. His fingers were curled inward and his palm was cool.

"We're all blaming ourselves, but it was no one's fault, Pierre, no one's," I murmured. Slowly his fingers began to straighten. I looked up and saw his eyes and then his face turn toward me. His lips began to stretch with his effort to open his mouth and then I saw his tongue lifting against his teeth. His eyes widened with the tremendous struggle to animate his face and produce an intelligible sound. I waited, holding my breath.

And then his lips moved up and down, followed by a clicking sound. I rose and stroked his forehead and his hair.

"Easy, Pierre. Easy. What do you want to say? I'm right here."

I kissed his cheek again. His lips moved faster, and a sound started in his throat. It formed itself into his first word since Jean's tragedy: "I . . ."

"Yes, Pierre," I said, my tears building. "Yes, honey."

"I . . . tha . . . tho . . . thought."

I brought my ear closer to his lips.

"Thought it was a branch," he said and closed his eyes.

"Oh, Pierre." I hugged him. "We know. We know, honey. No one blames you. No one," I said rocking back and forth with him in my arms. When I released him and sat back, however, he was staring at the wall again, his lips frozen, his eyelids blinking in that same rhythm.

"How are we doing?" I heard someone say. I turned to greet Dr. LeFevre.

"He spoke to me!" I said. "In a whisper, but he said a sentence."

"That's wonderful. His recovery has really begun. I am going to recommend that you and your family take him home. He'll need some nursing care, but he's off the I.V. and taking in food and water. The rest is just a matter of time and tender loving care. Afterward we'll see what sort of therapy is required."

"Oh, Pierre, do you hear that? You're going home. Isn't that wonderful?"

He didn't react, didn't change his expression, didn't move his lips.

Dr. Lefevre checked his blood pressure, then spoke to him. "Your family wants you home, Pierre. They need you to get well and be yourself again. But they can't do everything for you. You've got to want to help yourself. You've got to do what we talked about, okay?" she said, patting his hand. He didn't seem to hear her or see her. She smiled and winked at me. "It's going to take time," she said. "Time and patience."

"I'll call my father and tell him what you want us to do."

"Fine. I can recommend some nurses. Have him call my office in an hour or so," she added. Then she paused and led me away from the bed. "How is your mother doing? I've seen your father here, but not her."

"Up until now she hasn't been doing well. She blames herself too," I said.

"Of course. But she's made an improvement?"

"I think so."

"Taking care of Pierre will occupy her mind and end her self-condemnation. She won't have time for it," Dr. Lefevre assured me. "And you should come back to work, too," she added. "They miss you around here."

I smiled and thanked her, and then I hurried out into the corridor to call Daddy.

He was very excited. "Did you call your mother yet?"

"No. I thought I'd call you first so you could make the arrangements."

"Good. Okay, I'll get right on it. You call her. She

was so dead to the world when I rose that I didn't even speak to her," he said.

"I know." It was on the tip of my tongue to tell him why, but I thought Mommy would be devastated if I broke our pact. "I'll call her now."

I phoned and Aubrey answered.

"I have to speak to my mother right away, Aubrey," I said quickly.

"Madame has left the house," he said.

I glanced at my watch. She had said she wasn't coming to the hospital until after lunch. "Did she say where she was going?"

"No, mademoiselle. She just said good-bye to everyone and left."

"Said good-bye? How do you mean?"

"She made it a point to see every servant before leaving," he said, obviously confused by Mommy's behavior. My heart began to pitter-patter. Where had she gone? What was she doing? I was wrong to leave her and to make such promises, I told myself.

"Did she receive any phone calls this morning or any visitors, Aubrey?"

"None that I know of, mademoiselle."

"Did she take anything with her when she left?" He hesitated. I knew he didn't like reporting or seeming like a spy. "It's all right, Aubrey. Mommy has been troubled since Jean's passing and isn't herself. I have to know."

He was silent for a moment and then began. "The only reason I know this is because Margaret was confused and mentioned it to me, mademoiselle."

"You know what, Aubrey?" I demanded with impatience.

"Madame was searching for something in your brother Jean's dresser. She pulled all of the drawers out and spilled the contents on the floor, and then she

152

took down the picture of the twins that hung above Monsieur Andreas's desk and . . ." He paused.

"And?"

"She cut your brother Jean out of it and left the other half, and then she left the house with only a small satchel."

I sensed from the way his words hung in the air that there was something more. "What else Aubrey?" I asked, my teeth practically chattering in anticipation.

"She didn't take the car, mademoiselle. She simply walked away."

"No one came to pick her up, not a taxi, nothing?"

"Not that I saw, mademoiselle."

"You saw her walk away from the house?"

"Yes, mademoiselle. She never looked back. Is there something you wish me to do?"

"No, Aubrey. Nothing now," I said, the tears filling my eyes. "I'll be home soon." I said good-bye, then cradled the receiver and stood there, a stone-cold numbness creeping up my legs. Where was Mommy going? What strange ritual was she off to perform now? A chill embraced me, and I crossed my arms over my breasts.

"Hi, Pearl." I turned to see Sophie. "I just stopped at your brother's room, and the nurse told me you were still here. I heard the wonderful news. The doctor's sending him home, huh?"

"Yes," I said, trying to smile.

Sophie needed only one look at my eyes. "What's wrong?" she asked. "Why aren't you happy about it?"

"Oh, Sophie, it's not my brother; it's my mother," I cried and threw myself into her comforting arms.

After I calmed down, I tried to call Daddy, but he had already left his office. I went straight home, hoping Mommy had returned, but Aubrey shook his head glumly when I asked, his hazel eyes full of worry. He had instructed the maid to put Jean's room back in order and refold his clothing. The dresser drawers in her own room were still open and had also been rifled, but I could find no clues as to what she had taken, what she was up to, or where she had gone. The sight of the torn picture of the twins put a chill in my heart. She had ripped Jean away from Pierre just as death had, and although I knew that pictures couldn't change expression, Pierre seemed to be gazing out with forlorn eyes.

I wandered down to Mommy's studio and looked at the eerie picture she had been painting. It was completed now. To me it looked like Jean's soul was fleeing Uncle Paul's floating body. When I looked closely, I saw she had made Uncle Paul's body look like a snake's. Farther away in the canal, nearly hidden by the draping Spanish moss, was a tiny face that resembled Mommy's. Surely this whole scene had come right out of one of her horrid dreams, I thought. I covered the picture and returned to the sitting room. Aubrey came to tell me Daddy had arrived and had immediately gone upstairs, thinking I was in my room. I hurried up to him.

"Where's Ruby?" he asked emerging from the master bedroom.

"Oh, Daddy, didn't Aubrey say anything?"

"Say anything about what?"

"She's gone. She took something from Jean's dresser, tore off his picture from the portrait of the twins in your office, and left carrying a small satchel."

"Where did she go?"

"I don't know," I moaned and sat down on a hallway bench.

"What are you saying, Pearl? What's going on?"

"I didn't get a chance to tell you because you were gone by the time I went down to breakfast this morning, but Mommy left the house last night while you were asleep. She went to Nina Jackson's tomb, where she met with that voodoo lady. She had wanted me to go along with her, but I refused and got her to say she wasn't going. But she went anyway. I went looking for her and found her there."

"All this went on last night?" he cried in disbelief. "Why didn't I—"

"I tried to wake you, Daddy," I wailed.

He stared at me a moment and then shook his head.

"I'm sure you tried. I seem to be letting everyone down lately," he said.

"She made me promise not to tell you, but I was going to tell you anyway," I said and wiped away a fugitive tear. "Only I waited too long. I forgot about it when I arrived at the hospital and saw Pierre's progress and spoke with the doctor. I got so excited. I should have told you when we spoke."

"It's all right, Pearl," Daddy said, coming to me. "It's not your fault. I should have heard or seen her leave last night. I shouldn't have drunk myself to sleep. This hasn't been easy for any of us. I know she's been acting strange, those damn supernatural beliefs," he muttered. "I should be paying her more attention. Where do you think she's gone?"

I swallowed and thought. "Maybe back to Nina Jackson's sister's house. That's where it all started."

"Right. Do you remember the address?"

"Yes."

"Okay. Then we'd better go looking for her."

I nodded and took a deep breath. "What about Pierre?" I asked.

"I've already arranged for the nurse. She'll be here by five. We can pick Pierre up after we locate your mother. Let's go."

"I'll get something for Pierre to wear," I said. After I did so, we hurried down the stairs.

On the way to Nina Jackson's sister's house, I told Daddy about the ritual Mommy had performed the night before and how she kept saying she knew what she had to do now. "She claimed Nina had spoken to her through the black cat."

"These people should be arrested and shipped out of here," Daddy complained. "They cause more trouble . . . but then again, your mother was brought up believing in a lot of this—faith healers, evil spirits, protecting your home with candles and statues of saints. It's the age of interactive television, and these people are still living in the fifteenth century," he said shaking his head.

"Look at this place," he muttered when we arrived. "Who in her right mind would want to go in there: feathers dangling, bones clinking, powder on the steps to ward off evil. Are we in the twentieth century?" Daddy cried, his face crimson with anger and frustration.

I put my hand on his shoulder, and he took a deep breath and calmed down.

"Let's go get your mother and take her home," he said in a tired voice.

We went to the front door and knocked. Daddy's Rolls-Royce had drawn the attention of some neighbors who stood outside their homes watching. Daddy knocked again, more vigorously this time.

Nina Jackson's sister finally came to the door wearing a tattered robe. She was barefoot, and her hair was dripping wet. Daddy's mouth fell open.

"Hello," I said quickly. "We're sorry to bother you, but maybe you remember me. I'm—"

"You be Ruby's girl. You came here to see Nina."

"Yes," I said.

"Is my wife here?" Daddy demanded.

She shook her head.

"Are you sure?"

"No one be here. I be protecting myself against being crossed. I take a bath of garlic, sage, thyme, geranium water, dry basil, parsley, and five cents' worth of saltpeter," she explained proudly. Then she leaned toward me. "Since Nina's death, some folks think her spirit go haunting them, so they try to get even by putting a curse on my steps. But," she said, pulling her shoulders back, "I stop that."

"Have you seen my wife?" Daddy asked impatiently.

Nina's sister shook her head. "She be gone away?"

"Yes, and we're very worried about her," I said.

Nina's sister thought a moment. "If she run away, best you burn some of her clothes in gasoline with chicken droppings."

"Oh for God's sake," Daddy moaned, "let's get out of here."

"She went to the cemetery to speak with Nina last night," I said quickly. "Why would she go away today?"

"Oh. That be different. She must be carrying some kind of curse and Nina tell her how to fix it."

"But where would she go?" I said.

"Wherever she think the curse first start," Nina's sister replied. "She got to meet the devil man at the door and slam it shut in his face. That's what Nina would tell her."

"Satisfied?" Daddy said. "We're no better off than we were. Let's go, honey."

"Wait," Nina's sister said. "Don't you move your toes." She went into the house and quickly returned to press something in my hands.

"What is this?" I asked. It looked like a marble embedded in silver.

"Eye of a black cat killed at midnight. When you be lost in the dark, it will be your eye and show you the light," she said.

"A real eye?" I started to open my hand, but she closed my fingers over it again.

"Don't be 'fraid. Go on. Find your mother."

I swallowed back a throat lump and shoved the eye into my pocket. Then I thanked her, and Daddy and I returned to the car.

"Was this a wasted trip or what?" he said, pulling away.

"But where is she then, Daddy?"

"I don't know, but I'm sure she'll come home soon, and when she finds Pierre there, she'll be too busy to dwell on this stupidity," he said.

I hoped he was right, but I didn't have much faith.

We went directly to the hospital to take Pierre home. If he had any inkling he was being brought home, he didn't show it. He sat as stiff as always and stared blankly ahead. However, the nurse said he had eaten some more food and was sipping juice through a straw now.

"That's wonderful," Daddy said. He turned to Pierre. "Hey, buddy, ready to come home?"

Pierre blinked, but didn't respond. Daddy ran his hand through Pierre's hair the way he had so many times before, and then we got him dressed and transferred to a wheelchair. The nurse let me wheel him out and down to the door while Daddy signed all the papers. Daddy tried to get Pierre to stand, but his legs were like sticks of butter. He had to carry him to the car and slip him into the back seat. I sat beside Pierre and we headed for home.

"It will be good to be back in your own room, Pierre," I told him, "and eating Milly's cooking instead of hospital food."

"And you'll be able to go outside, too," Daddy added. "All of your buddies have been calling and asking about you, Pierre."

He didn't respond to any of this, but his eyes moved

158

from side to side, and I was sure he was wondering about Mommy.

"Mommy can't wait to see you, Pierre," I said. "She's out getting things for you."

Daddy said nothing.

When we arrived at the house, Aubrey came out to help and to introduce Pierre's nurse, Mrs. Hockingheimer, a short, stout woman of about fifty with light brown hair cut so straight it looked as if it had been ironed down to her jawbone and over the back of her neck. But she had pleasant green eyes and a soft, gentle smile that immediately put me at ease. As soon as we were all introduced, the first question on my lips for Aubrey was "Did Mommy return?"

Aubrey glanced quickly at Daddy and then shook his head.

"Did she call?"

"No, mademoiselle."

"Let's just get Pierre up to his room," Daddy said angrily. "Then we'll worry about your mother."

He carried Pierre into the house and up the stairs, with Mrs. Hockingheimer following. She got Pierre dressed in his pajamas and comfortably settled in his bed. She already had provided something cold for him to drink. Pierre must have felt comfortable with her, because he let her give him a glass with a straw in it and started to drink when she asked him to. His eyes continued to shift from our faces to the doorway, anticipating Mommy's entrance. Daddy and I looked at each other, and then he signaled for us to leave.

"We told her Pierre had made some improvements," he reminded me. "Why wasn't she at the hospital today instead of gallivanting about with these voodoo women? I'd better start making phone calls to see if any of her friends or acquaintances have seen her today," he said and went to his office.

Later he came to tell me no one had seen or heard

159

from her. "It's as if she stepped off the face of the earth," he added, now more concerned than angry. It was getting later and later, and the twilight was already turning the shadows in our gardens darker and making the streetlights come on.

"What should we do, Daddy? Should we call the police?"

"And tell them what? That my wife is out performing voodoo rituals somewhere? She's an adult, Pearl. I can't ask them to find her."

"But she's not thinking clearly, Daddy. Maybe she's wandering about confused."

He gazed out the window. Night was waving its wand of darkness over the world around us. "Maybe she'll come to her senses soon and return or at least call and tell us where she is," he said. He looked up at me with desperation and held out his arms. "I don't know what else to do, honey. We've got a little boy upstairs, who desperately needs his mother and she doesn't even know he's home from the hospital."

"Maybe that's where she'll go, Daddy," I said hopefully. "Then she'll come home quickly."

"Maybe, but she obviously hasn't gone there yet." He reached for his bottle of bourbon.

"Daddy, please don't drink too much tonight."

He hesitated and nodded. "You're right. I'd better stay alert. Who knows what will happen next?" he said, which put the pitter-patter in my chest and turned my legs to cold stone.

Another hour passed. Mrs. Hockingheimer tried to feed Pierre, but he was reluctant to open his mouth. I knew why. He wanted his mother. I stayed away from his room, not knowing what white lie to tell.

Daddy and I tried to eat a little, but neither of us had much of an appetite. We talked and waited and shifted our eyes from the clock to the door. Every gong of the grandfather clock was like a punch in the stomach. After dinner we went up to visit with Pierre. Mrs. Hockingheimer must have been wondering where Mommy was too, but she was too polite to inquire. She stepped out of the room while Daddy and I tried to talk to Pierre about everything else. Every once in a while, his eyes shifted back to the door until finally a single tear crawled over his right eyelid, and his lips began to move.

"Mom . . . Mommy . . ." he said.

"Mon Dieu," Daddy said, bouncing up. "I can't stand this any longer." He charged out of the room and down the stairs.

I turned back to Pierre and took his hand into mine. "Mommy's very troubled and confused by what has happened, Pierre. She's trying to find the answers, but she loves you very much and wants to do something to help make you better quickly. She'll be here as soon as she can. You'll see," I promised, and then I kissed his cheek.

"Mom . . . Mommy," he repeated. He closed his eyes.

Mrs. Hockingheimer returned and examined him when she saw the concern on my face. "He's just exhausted," she said. "For him in his fragile state, being brought out of the hospital and set up here was a major effort."

I nodded and rose as she helped Pierre lean back on his pillow. It looked as if he had fallen asleep. In this case, I thought, that was a blessing.

I went downstairs to look for Daddy and found him pacing back and forth in his study and gulping from a tumbler of bourbon. He was muttering to himself. "What right has she to do this? Why isn't she thinking of Pierre, if not of me? And Pearl. We have a family to protect, a little boy to heal. How could she do this?"

"Daddy, don't . . ."

He paused and looked at me, blinking madly.

Suddenly he tilted his head as if he had just heard something no one else could hear.

"Oh, Pearl," he said in a hoarse whisper.

"What is it, Daddy?"

"I don't think . . ."

"What, Daddy? What don't you think?"

"I don't think she's ever coming back," he said.

8

A Letter Comes

I sat by the front window and waited, my eyes constantly searching the street for signs of Mommy. Daddy's words had put butterflies in my stomach. They fluttered in a frenzy and crawled through my chest. My heart felt like a lead fist pounding my blood through my veins. The grandfather clock bonged; Aubrey turned down the lights and the traffic outside all but disappeared. Still there was no sign of Mommy. Daddy made a few more phone calls, all dead ends. He came to the doorway occasionally and we exchanged looks of futility.

"Did you look in on Pierre?" he asked after a deep and long sigh.

"Yes. He's asleep. He barely ate."

Daddy nodded, looked at his watch, and then returned to his study, where I knew he was drinking himself into a stupor.

Finally, a little after nine-thirty, I saw a figure cross the street and approach our gate. When she stepped into the light, however, I realized it wasn't Mommy. It was a very tall, thin black girl in a long black skirt and a gray sweatshirt. When she headed for our front door, I rose in anticipation, but Aubrey was there before me to answer the bell. I think he was just as nervous as I was about Mommy's disappearance. Daddy either hadn't heard the bell or was too unsteady now to come out to see who it was.

"Yes?" Aubrey asked.

"I have a letter to deliver, sir," the girl replied with a French accent. "I was told to put it directly into the hands of Mademoiselle Pearl or Monsieur Andreas," she added firmly.

"You can give it to me and I'll deliver it," Aubrey said, his hand out.

"I'm sorry, sir, but I cannot give it to anyone else," she insisted.

Aubrey was about to reply when I stepped closer. "It's all right, Aubrey. I'll look after this. I'm Mademoiselle Pearl. How can I help you?"

The tall girl studied me a moment and nodded. She didn't look more than fourteen or fifteen, but she had a strong and confident air about her that suggested she was older. She had a very smooth and shiny complexion with large ebony eyes, which captured the entryway light and sparkled like polished onyx. "I was asked to deliver this to you," she said handing me the letter.

I took it quickly. There was no name on the envelope and no return address. "Who sent this?"

"Everything is explained in the letter," she said. She didn't smile, but she fixed her eyes on me so intently that I felt as if she were delving into my very soul. Then she gave me a small, tight smile, turned, and walked out. I watched her step quickly over the tile patio and into the darkness from which she had so suddenly emerged.

Aubrey waited beside me, his face full of concern.

"It's all right, Aubrey," I said. He closed the door and returned to his quarters.

I looked at the envelope more closely and noticed some sort of red powder on the flap. I opened it quickly and saw it was addressed to Daddy and me and it was in Mommy's hand.

My heart stopped and then began beating madly. Without reading the first word, I pulled open the front door and lunged down the steps. I ran over the tile drive and into the street just as the tall, black girl turned the far corner. She was walking very quickly.

"Wait!" I screamed, but she didn't hear me. I ran up the street after her. When I turned the corner, she was heading toward the streetcar. "Wait!" I shouted. The streetcar rumbled down the tracks to the station. "Please, mademoiselle, wait."

I ran as fast as I could. She turned as she stepped up to the car and looked my way, but she didn't hesitate. She got in, and the car door closed just as I approached. I saw the girl take a seat by an open window in the rear. She gazed out at me. I waved the letter and ran alongside the car.

"Where is she? It's my mother! Where is she?" I cried.

The girl stared out at me without speaking.

"Please!" I cried as the car began to pull away from me. Suddenly the girl threw something out of the window. It bounced on the grass in front of me as the streetcar made a turn and disappeared. I stopped to catch my breath. My heart was a wild frantic animal in my chest, thudding so hard that my ribs felt as if they would burst. Gasping for air, I stepped forward until I found what she had thrown. Whatever it was, it was in a small cloth sack. I picked it up and undid the string, pausing to look in the direction of the streetcar. What could this have to do with Mommy?

I felt something hard in the bag and pulled it out carefully. The moment I set eyes on it, I screamed and dropped it. It was the head of a snake. My heart seemed to jump out of my chest and into my throat. I felt my face turn crimson, and for a moment it was as if I had stepped into a hot oven. People driving by slowed down to gaze at me. I'm sure I looked wild and hysterical, gasping, crying, shaking my head. Finally, after I got control of myself, I turned and hurried back to the house.

As soon as I entered, I hurried down the hallway to Daddy's study. He was seated behind his desk, but had turned his back to the door and was gazing up at a portrait of himself and Mommy, a portrait she had painted from a photograph. He had a tumbler of bourbon in his right hand.

"Daddy, Mommy has sent us a letter!" I declared.

He turned slowly. His face was streaked with tears. He wiped them away with the back of his hand quickly. "What's that? A letter?"

"Some girl just delivered it. I tried to run after her and question her, but she got on the streetcar before I could stop her. She threw something terrible out the window at me when I screamed for her to tell me where Mommy was."

"Terrible? What?"

"A sack containing the head of a snake," I said, crying.

"Head of a snake? How sick."

"And there's red powder on the envelope," I said, holding it up for him to see.

"Red powder. Another voodoo thing," he said with an expression of disgust. "Where is she? What does the letter say?"

"I don't know. I haven't read it yet."

"Well, read it," he ordered and sat forward. I turned on the lamp near me and opened the letter.

166

My precious husband Beau and my precious daughter Pearl,

By the time you read this, I will be long gone. I tell you that so you won't go searching wildly over the city to find me and bring me back. That's why I waited until now to write and deliver this letter.

I know that you do not believe as strongly as I do in the powers of the unknown, but the two of you were not brought up in a world in which such things dwelt. I am the granddaughter of a true traiteur, and as such I have some spiritual insight. I know that more than ever now.

Last night I spoke with the dead. Nina's voice was clear, and her spirit was in me. She regretted not having been able to speak with me before our tragedy. She thinks it might have been prevented.

"What a state of mind she is in," Daddy commented. "These people have poisoned Ruby's thoughts, taken advantage of her while she is in mourning, weak, and vulnerable. I'll have them all arrested," he raged.

"There's more, Daddy," I said, my fingers trembling as I held up the paper.

"Go ahead," he said, lowering his head like a flag of defeat.

Although I couldn't prevent what happened to Jean, I can prevent any further bad luck from entering our lives and hurting my loved ones. Nina has given me specific instructions to peel away the layer of evil that has been spread over our home and our lives, evil that was born out of my sins.

These instructions require my leaving our home, maybe forever. That's up to Fate, I suppose. I didn't want to leave so abruptly, but I knew if I told either of you any of this, you would try to stop me.

167

Already we have seen what these rituals can do for us. Pierre will mend as long as I continue to pursue the path I've been instructed to pursue.

I beg you both not to try to follow me or stop me, but I want to assure you both just how much I love you and how difficult this will be for me.

I am depending on you, Pearl, to be the strength I couldn't be. Stay by your brother and your father and help them.

Beau, my darling, please find it in your heart to forgive me and believe in me. If I have your trust, I will be that much stronger in the days to come and during the battle that is to follow. I will feel your faith in me.

I will not be able to talk to you or call you or even write to you again until I have completed my mission. It is painful for me to be away from the ones I love. I am doing it only because I love you all more than I love myself. My pain is nothing if it will buy happiness and health for my family.

I love you.

Ruby

I lowered my hands and gazed at Daddy. Hot tears were streaming freely down my cheeks and dripping from my chin.

He stared for a few moments and then sat back. "Well," he finally said, "there you have it. Just what I feared and suspected. Who knows where she's gone to or what she's going to do?"

"We've got to find her, Daddy, and bring her home."

"Find her," he said angrily. "Those people close around their own like clams. They won't talk to us; they won't tell us anything."

He reached for his nearly empty bottle of bourbon and poured himself another drink. "Maybe she'll come to her senses and call us or come home," he muttered.

"Daddy, we've got to call the police. She's not in her right mind after all this sadness and tragedy. They'll understand and they'll help us," I said.

He shook his head. "Waste of time."

"No, it isn't," I insisted. "I can't stand the thought of her under the influence of these people. If you don't call them, I will."

"What are you going to tell them? That your mother wandered off to practice voodoo rituals someplace?" he asked disdainfully.

"Yes."

"They won't take you seriously, Pearl. They have a great many more urgent problems to deal with in this city."

"It's worth a try, Daddy."

He took a long gulp of bourbon.

"Daddy! You can't just sit there all day and night and drink yourself to sleep," I cried.

"She's gone, run off, returned to her bizarre past, and my son is dead," he said. "My little boy is gone. My other little boy is catatonic. What did I do to deserve this?"

"Stop this self-pity, Daddy. Mommy needs us."

He lowered his chin to his chest. I felt heat crawling up my spine. What had happened to Daddy and Mommy was terrible. No parent should endure such tragedy, but if Daddy didn't find a well of strength from which to draw new energy and determination, more terrible things loomed over us. Mommy had asked me to be strong. If that meant being cruel first, so be it, I thought.

"Is this the way you handle all your crises, Daddy? You wallow in them?" I sneered. "Is this why you ran off to Europe when Mommy was pregnant with me?"

He looked up sharply, knitting his brows as if a

169

sharp pain had cut across his forehead, as if my words were tiny knives.

"No, I—"

"You left her alone to face the anger and the abuse. She gathered strength and returned to the bayou, and she managed to care for herself and for me while you were enjoying the most expensive restaurants and the wildest parties in Europe. Now, when she needs you again, you sit there gulping whiskey and moaning about what's happened to you."

"Pearl, please, that's not the way I was or the way I am," he argued.

"Then get ahold of yourself and let's go find her. Call the police," I demanded sharply, firing my words like bullets.

He nodded, sobering up quickly. "All right," he said. "Maybe you're right. We'll start with the police."

I straightened my shoulders and wiped away my tears with the back of my hand. "I'll look in on Pierre. We've got to find Mommy and bring her home for his sake most of all," I added. Daddy bit down on his lower lip and nodded. Pivoting on my heel, I marched out of the room and up the stairs quickly, so he wouldn't see how painful it was for me to treat him so harshly. I had to pause at the landing to catch my breath and slow my thumping heart.

Mrs. Hockingheimer was dozing in her chair in Pierre's room when I looked in on him. She heard me and looked up quickly.

"How is he doing?" I asked softly. His face was in repose, but his lips were crooked, reacting to some nightmare, no doubt, I thought.

"He's having a restless sleep," she said. "I couldn't get him to eat any more, but he did drink some water. He felt a little warm, but he has no fever."

"Okay," I said sadly.

"Mademoiselle," she called as I started to turn from the doorway. "He did mutter something."

"What?"

"He's calling for his mother," she said. "Where is your mother, if I may ask?"

Mrs. Hockingheimer wasn't being nosy. Anyone would have wondered why Pierre's mother wasn't at his side, I thought. "My mother is very troubled by what happened, the whole tragedy. She believes herself responsible, and she's disappeared. We've got to call the police and . . ." My lips started to quiver badly. It was as if my face had mutinied. I couldn't pronounce the words. They got choked up in my throat.

Mrs. Hockingheimer saw what was happening and rose quickly to come to me. "You poor dear. I didn't mean to upset you," she said and embraced me.

"No one has seen her. My father and I are at our wit's end. We're calling the police right now."

"I'm so sorry. There, there," she said, patting my hand. "You must remain strong. Don't worry about Pierre. I will watch him very closely."

"Thank you, Mrs. Hockingheimer." I took a deep breath.

Mrs. Hockingheimer dabbed away the tears that lingered on my cheeks and smiled. "You're a strong young woman. You'll find a way to help your mother," she assured me.

I thanked her again and went downstairs to be with Daddy when the police arrived.

A detective and two uniformed patrolmen came to our door. The detective introduced himself as Lieutenant Ribocheaux. He was about as tall as Daddy, but with much wider shoulders and a square jaw. He looked like an ex-football player. The patrolmen stood in the doorway of Daddy's study and listened with Lieutenant Ribocheaux as Daddy described the terrible events that had unfolded. Daddy showed him Mommy's letter, and I then told him about Mommy's visiting the cemetary. I hadn't spelled out the details before. Daddy's eyes went as wide and round as quarters when he heard me talk of the screeching, the black cat, Mommy's walking about with a candle, and the whispering.

"This young woman who came to your door with the letter," Lieutenant Ribocheaux asked me, "had you seen her before? Was she at the cemetery too or at this house where your mother went to see the dead lady?"

"No, sir."

"And when you ran after her, you say she threw a snake's head out of the streetcar window?"

"Yes. I dropped it. It's probably still there. I can show it to you."

"I imagine it's only one of those souvenirs that the tourists buy in the voodoo shops in the French Quarter," he said.

"Still, I couldn't bring it home."

"I understand," he said, smiling. He turned to the uniformed policemen. "Ted, you and Billy take a look. Maybe it's still there, and it might give us some clue," he said, but from the looks on their faces, I knew they were doing it only to placate me. I told them where it would be, and they left.

Lieutenant Ribocheaux turned back to Daddy. "Monsieur Andreas, was your wife under a doctor's care?"

"Not in the sense I believe you mean," Daddy replied, "but our physician had given her sedatives."

Lieutenant Ribocheaux took out his notepad. "You've called all her friends, people she might go see, I imagine?"

"Everyone we could think of," Daddy said. "No one has heard from her or seen her."

"Relatives?"

"We have none presently in New Orleans. My parents are in Europe for the summer."

"Well, where are your closest relatives?"

"My wife's family comes from the bayou, around Houma, but she wouldn't go to them," Daddy added. "We don't get along that well."

"Except with Aunt Jeanne," I reminded him.

"Yes, but I don't think she would have gone to Jeanne," Daddy said.

"Okay," Lieutenant Ribocheaux said. "Let me have the address of that house, the Jackson residence." I gave it to him, and he jotted it down quickly. "We'll pay them a visit," he promised. "In the meantime give us a recent picture of Madame Andreas, please. I'd like to speak with the butler, too, and get a description of what she was wearing when she was last seen here."

Daddy turned to me, and I went to fetch Aubrey. He was reluctant to tell the police any of the bizarre details about Mommy's behavior, but I urged him to be as forthcoming as possible. Lieutenant Ribocheaux took more notes.

The patrolmen returned. They had found the snake's head, but Lieutenant Ribocheaux said there was nothing remarkable about it. "As I suspected, it's no different from what you can buy at Marie Laveau's. Someone's having some fun with you," he added.

"If that's true, it's very cruel," I replied.

After the police left, I sat with Daddy in his study.

"I'm not optimistic about their finding her, Pearl. They'll send a patrol car around, all right, but unless Mommy is standing right in front of them . . . I know these voodoo people. They believe they are doing something spiritual and something good. They won't

173

want Mommy to be found and brought back. That might break some sort of spell."

"Maybe we should go to Nina's sister's house too, Daddy," I suggested, "and stay until she tells us the truth."

"We won't fare any better. At least the police carry some authority. Why don't you go up to bed, honey? No sense in both of us staying up and worrying all night. Besides, I need you strong and healthy for the days to come."

"You're not going to remain down here all night, are you, Daddy?" I gazed at the bottle of bourbon.

Daddy saw where my eyes were fixed. "I won't drink anymore," he promised. "I've got to stay alert in case we're needed."

I nodded, rose, and went to him. We hugged, and he held on to me for a few moments longer than usual before releasing me and sitting back.

"Good night, Daddy."

"Good night, princess. Thanks for making me come to my senses," he said, smiling. "For a moment there I thought I was looking at your mother when she was about your age."

I kissed him again and walked away. At the doorway I turned. He had already swung his chair around and was gazing up at his and Mommy's portrait again, wondering, I'm sure, how they would ever get back to the happy, wonderful time they had when the portrait was painted.

When I peeked in on Pierre, both he and Mrs. Hockingheimer were fast asleep, so I closed the door softly and went to my room. Just as I got into bed, Sophie called. I told her all that had happened, right up to the black girl throwing the snake's head out of the streetcar window.

"I don't know much about voodoo," she said, "but nana does. I could ask her if you want."

I thought about it. I was beginning to agree with Daddy. The more we involved ourselves with these things, the more twisted and confused we became. All it did was fill my head with bad thoughts and give me nightmares. "No, thanks. I'd rather not know."

"I can come over after work and help you go looking, if you want," she volunteered.

"Thank you, but I wouldn't even know where to start. We'll wait and see what the police say tomorrow."

"Maybe she'll come home tonight."

"Maybe."

"I'll say a prayer for you and your family," she said. How ironic, I thought. A few weeks ago Sophie had sat in the streetcar gazing out the window at the Garden District, her face full of envy as I waved good-bye and started for home. She would have given anything to trade places with me, I'm sure. Now I was the object of her pity and sympathy. Money makes people comfortable, but it doesn't guarantee happiness, I thought.

"Thank you, Sophie." It brought tears to my eyes to think that none of my so-called upper-class friends from school had called or visited, but my new friend, my poorest friend, cared enough to volunteer her time to help me.

After I hung up, I put my palms together under my chin, closed my eyes, and said my own prayer. I prayed for Mommy, I prayed for Pierre, I prayed for Daddy, and I prayed that I would have the strength to help everyone. Then I tried to fall asleep. I tossed and turned for hours before drifting off, but my sleep was restless and continually interrupted. I woke often with a start, listening hard for the sound of a door being opened or a phone ringing. I longed to hear Mommy's voice echoing through the hallway or up the stairs, but the dead silence of our morgue-like house was all I heard.

Daddy was disheveled and tattered-looking in the morning. No doubt he had stayed awake most of the night. He had slept on the sofa in his study when he did catch some sleep. I made sure he ate something substantial for breakfast and then persuaded him to take a shower. Mrs. Hockingheimer had Pierre up and washed. She got him to eat a portion of his breakfast, but he had the same empty look in his eyes, the same anticipation when I entered. I spoke to him for a while. His lips quivered and then formed the word "Mommy." It shattered the thin veneer on my heart and made me gulp back the tears.

I convinced Daddy that he should call Lieutenant Ribocheaux to see if they had any leads, but they didn't. Daddy hung up the phone and looked at me, his face lined with exhaustion and frustration.

"I told you it wouldn't do us any good to call the police," he said. "They don't take this voodoo thing seriously, and when an adult disappears, they're not really concerned. Of course, they promised to keep looking."

"I can't stand this waiting around, Daddy. We've got to do something."

"What, honey? Ride around the city?"

"I don't think she's in the city anymore," I said. "I think we should go to the bayou."

Daddy laughed. "A lot of good that would do—you and I, two city slickers trying to find someone in the swamps. If we have little hope of doing so here, where we are familiar with the territory, can you imagine how futile it would be for us to go out there? I wouldn't even know where to begin."

I thought for a moment, recalling Mommy's stories, and then looked up at him with bright, hopeful eyes. "We'll start at the shack," I said.

"Shack?"

"Her old shack, where she returned when she became pregnant with me. She believes in spirits; surely she hopes her grandmere Catherine's spirit will still be there, or even her mother's spirit."

Daddy said, "Let me look at the picture you said she painted."

We went to Mommy's studio, and he stood gazing thoughtfully at it for a while.

"What are you thinking, Daddy?"

"What was it that crazy old lady, Nina's sister, told us . . . that Ruby went to wherever the curse started. You might be right. In her mind that could very well mean the bayou. Especially when I look at this picture. I'll give Jeanne a call." He returned to his office to do so. I followed and waited at the door while he spoke to Uncle Paul's sister.

Aunt Jeanne hadn't heard about Jean's death. That news was devastating enough for her to digest. Then Daddy told her about Mommy's disappearance. I waited hopefully at his side, but it was clear from the rest of the conversation that she hadn't heard from or seen Mommy, nor had anyone she knew.

Daddy shook his head and cradled the receiver. "Well, we know she hasn't been to the bayou yet," he said and sat back.

"We should still go out there, Daddy."

"I don't know."

"It's better than just sitting here and staring at each other hopelessly. Please. Let's go there and search. She might have just arrived, or she could be somewhere the Tates wouldn't know about. They certainly don't go looking around the old shack."

He considered. "Okay," he said. "I suppose it's worth a try and you're right. Not doing anything but waiting for phones to ring is just eating away at both of us."

"I'll go up and tell Mrs. Hockingheimer and Pierre what we're doing so he won't miss us," I said.

"Good idea. I'll dig out my maps of the bayou. It's been a while since I drove there."

Having a strategy and something concrete to do put hope back into our hearts and renewed our energy. I hurried upstairs to change my clothes, and then I went to see Pierre.

"I was just about to go down to see you and Monsieur Andreas," Mrs. Hockingheimer said. "I don't like the way Pierre keeps drifting off, and now he's refusing to drink any water."

"Oh, Pierre," I said, sitting beside him on his bed and taking his hand into mine. His eyes remained fixed on the wall. "You can't do this to yourself any longer. You've got to get strong and well again. We need you to help with Mommy. Daddy and I are going to find her and bring her home to you, but you must eat and drink so you can be strong when she returns. Please," I begged. "Please try."

His blinking quickened, and he took a deep breath. I brushed back his hair. "Will you, try, Pierre? Will you?"

He didn't respond, but I thought there was more light and alertness in his eyes.

"We'll be gone most of the day, Mrs. Hockingheimer, but we'll phone you in a few hours."

"I'll ask the doctor to stop by later this afternoon," she promised.

"Fine."

"Good luck, my dear."

"Thank you." I gazed back at Pierre. His lips were moving, so I sat beside him again and brought my ear close to his mouth.

"Mommy . . . Mommy went to get Jean," he whispered.

His words put a block of ice in my chest where my

heart should have been. For a moment I couldn't speak or swallow.

"Oh, Pierre honey," I moaned. I embraced him and kissed him and rocked back and forth with him. Then I wiped away my tears and rushed from the room, hoping with all my soul that we would find Mommy and bring her home where she belonged.

9

My Cajun World

As Daddy and I headed out of the city toward Terrebonne Parish and Houma, the town from which Mommy had come, a kind of paralyzing numbness gripped me. I had not been back there since I was an infant. Our troubles with Uncle Paul's mother and father since the famous trial to determine who should have custody of me had created an almost impenetrable wall around that part of the bayou. The income from the oil well Uncle Paul had left in my name had built a substantial trust for me, but I had never seen the well, since it was at Cypress Woods and neither Daddy nor Mommy could ever find the courage to return. At least, not until now.

Legal wrangling over the property had kept everyone from enjoying it, although Daddy had vowed never to go back there anyway, and Mommy apparently had too many sad memories that would be revived in those grand rooms. What was true for them was apparently true for Octavius and Gladys Tate as well, for it was our understanding that they did nothing with the mansion. Aunt Jeanne said her mother wanted it kept like a monument to Paul's memory.

Mommy might have returned to the shack in which she and her grandmere Catherine had lived and where I was born, but as far as I knew, it had been years and years since her last visit. Whenever I asked her why, she said that none of Grandmere Catherine's friends were still alive, and there weren't many people she cared to see.

Whenever she talked of her past and told me stories, they were fascinating. So much of her background was interesting to me, and yet so much of it was obviously painful for her. I wondered just how hard it had been for her to make this trip now, if she had indeed made it. Even doing it under the advice of someone speaking from beyond the grave must have been very difficult for her.

For the first part of our journey, neither Daddy nor I spoke very much. We were both lost in our thoughts and our fears, I suppose. It was a partly cloudy day. Most of the clouds were long, wide fluffy ones and when one of them passed over the sun, the shadows thickened and stretched over the highway and the countryside before us. Soon the roadside restaurants, service stations, and fruit and vegetable stands were fewer and fewer. Snowy egrets and brown pelicans began to appear along the banks of the canals, and every once in a while I saw an old shrimp boat, rusting and rotting in the underbrush.

Soon the toothpick-legged houses began to appear more frequently, some with children playing in the yards, some with Cajun women sitting on their galleries talking as they shelled peas into black cast-iron pots or wove split oak baskets and palmetto hats to sell to tourists. They looked up as we motored by. Just ahead of us, three fisherman emerged from a swamp, their poles over their shoulders, their beards long and straggly.

And suddenly it occurred to me how different my mother's old world was from the world in which we now lived. How difficult and frightening it must have been for her at such a young age to leave this world on her own and enter a new world of rich people and sophistication. It must have been like going to another country. But she'd had no choice. She had fled from her drunken grandpere, hoping to be rescued.

Now she had fled back to that Cajun world, also hoping to be rescued, and we were rushing there, praying we could save her. Life seemed to be drawn in circles. I sighed deeply and turned to look at Daddy. He was smiling at me in the strangest way.

"Why are you smiling like that, Daddy?" I asked.

"I was just thinking how right your mother is about you. You've turned out to be quite a strong and amazing young woman," he said. "Other girls your age would probably wilt and moan at home, but not you. You probably get your grit from your mother's Cajun side."

"What about your family, Daddy?"

"My family? Well, my whole family was spoiled, and I was no better off for having been born with that silver spoon in my mouth. It would have been better if I'd been born a Cajun."

"When were you last here, Daddy?"

"During the trial for custody of you, I suppose. Before that, when your mother was living at Cypress Woods, I took a ride up there occasionally. It was a beautiful place. I was very jealous," he admitted. "And terrified."

"Terrified? Why?"

"I thought your mother had everything she could ever want. I would never win her back. She had that beautiful setting, that magnificent studio, a man who doted on her. And what did I have? I had Gisselle, complaining in one ear until that ear was red from listening, and then she would shift to my other." He laughed.

"What's so funny?"

"One time when Gisselle and I went to Cypress Woods, your uncle Paul took us all on a tour of the swamps. Gisselle had nightmares for weeks afterward."

"Why?"

"The alligators, the insects. Ruby and Gisselle were twins, of course, but one was night and the other was day," he said.

"It must have been hard for Mommy to pose as Gisselle if she was so different," I said. That part of our story had always intrigued me: Mommy's assuming her sister's identity after Gisselle contracted Saint Louis encephalitis and the switch was accomplished.

"And how. Talk about Dr. Jekyll and Mr. Hyde. Ruby had to sound like Gisselle, act like Gisselle. I had hired new servants so she could at least be herself when she was with the help. Gisselle was always nasty to those she considered underlings, and Ruby would have had to treat them just as poorly. I know your mother actually was relieved when the ruse was exposed and she could go back to being herself.

"Now let's see," he said as he studied the road ahead. "I know there's a turn coming up soon." He slowed down and stopped to gaze at his map.

We were deep in the bayou now. The vegetation was very thick on both sides of the road, and through the brush and cattails, I could see the ponds. When I rolled down my window, I could hear the symphony of cicadas and tree frogs in the marsh. I didn't see it at first, but as I studied the surroundings, a shack appeared behind a cluster of weeping willows. The dull wood-frame house was nearly hidden by banana trees. The yard, or what remained of it, was cluttered with automobile and machine parts. Beside the house, just off the bank, was a half-submerged pirogue. What had happened to the people who lived here? I wondered. Could they have been relatives of mine? Was there a girl my age who was just as curious about my life in New Orleans as I was about her life here?

"Okay, I remember now," Daddy said. "We go down the road to the left about a mile and then turn left again. The shack is another mile or so along that road. Ready?"

"Yes, Daddy." I had my fingers crossed.

We drove on. Through a break in the overgrown bushes and heavy foliage, I saw a young man poling a pirogue. He slipped into a large island of lily pads, and about a dozen sleeping bullfrogs sprang up and splashed around him, making the water pop like bursting bubbles. I had only a glimpse of him, but he looked statuesque and brown-skinned, with a smile of deep pleasure on his face.

We made the second left and Daddy announced, "There it is!"

My heart began to thump faster. Would we find Mommy sitting on the gallery or wandering about the shack or sitting inside? I hoped she would be surprised but happy we had come for her. We pulled up, and Daddy turned off the engine. For a long moment we both just sat there staring at the shack.

I wasn't prepared for what I was seeing. I suppose I had been romanticizing the shack in my mind for years. Most of my memories were vague, but whenever I thought about it, I conjured up a sweet little toothpick-legged house with a rug of fine grass and beautiful wildflowers. I envisioned it coated in fresh paint, its corrugated metal roof glimmering in the noonday sun. In my memories the canal ran clear behind the shack. Pelicans and egrets hovered; bream leaped out to catch insects for dinner and the heads of alligators with curious eyes popped up to look our way.

Instead, we confronted an overgrown front yard where even the weeds were choking to death. The gallery leaned to the right, and the shack leaned to the left. Some of the clapboard had torn loose, and all of the windows had been shattered, probably by young boys having rock-throwing contests.

Still, my infant memories were stirred. A vision of the gallery flashed in my mind, and in it I felt myself being rocked in a chair and listening to a radio playing zydeco music in the living room. The roadside stand where Mommy had sold her woven hats, baskets, jellies, jams, and gumbo lay broken in the tall grass.

"It doesn't look like anything on two legs was here recently," Daddy commented.

"We better look, Daddy," I said.

He nodded, squeezed my hand and opened the door. "Be careful," he said as I followed. We paused at the foot of the vague front pathway, however. It did look as if someone had traipsed through recently. Daddy and I glanced at each other and then moved faster toward the gallery. The short stairway creaked and groaned under our weight, as did the floorboards. Daddy tugged the front door open. It complained on rusted hinges and wobbled.

Something scurried away inside when we started to enter, and I jumped back with a cry.

"Could be a raccoon," Daddy whispered. My heart was drumming so hard I thought I would lose my breath. There was a dank stench and gobs and gobs of cobwebs on the ceiling and walls, but the old furniture was still there. Daddy and I paused and gazed around the living room. Then I looked down at the floor and pulled Daddy's sleeve.

"Someone was here recently, Daddy. See the footprints in the dust?"

He nodded, crouched, and studied them. "Small, like your mother's."

We continued through the house. The kitchen was a mess. What was left of the stove was badly rusted. The door of the old-fashioned icebox had been torn off one of its hinges, someone had been swinging on it. Drawers were pulled out, some of them smashed, and here and there were gaping holes in the floor. Daddy gazed at the stairway.

"Maybe you better wait down here," he suggested. "I don't know how safe that is."

He started up. The steps creaked, but held. I waited at the bottom while he searched the bedrooms and the loom room. He stayed up there awhile.

The shack seemed so tiny to me. It was hard to imagine that Mommy and I once lived here. And now that it was so wrecked, it was creepy. The walls creaked in the wind, and things scurried under the floorboards. There were stains that looked like dried blood on the chipped plank table. I had visions of my great grandpere drunk and raging. Despite the high humidity and heat, my thoughts gave me the chills. I embraced myself and looked up the stairway. I hadn't heard any movement for a while.

"Daddy?"

He didn't respond.

"Daddy?" I called, a bit more frantic. A few moments later he came down the stairs slowly. In his hands was the picture of Jean that Mommy had torn off the photograph of him and Pierre together. It looked as if candle wax had dripped over it.

"She was here," Daddy said in a hoarse whisper. "You were right."

Excited by the discovery, we searched the property for more evidence of Mommy's presence, but there was nothing else to be found and no trail to lead us anywhere. Most of the land around the property was heavily overgrown, and Daddy thought we weren't properly dressed to go traipsing through marshland.

"Too dangerous. She couldn't have gone that way anyhow," he said.

"Where should we look for her, then?"

"There's only one other place I know. Cypress Woods," he said with a deep sigh. "She's going back through her past, a journey I hoped we wouldn't have to make."

We returned to our car, and Daddy sat thinking a moment.

"Let's go into town and get something to eat first," he suggested. "Town's not far, but Cypress Woods is the other way. It might be hours and hours before we have another chance to get a bite or something to drink."

"All right, Daddy," I said. I wasn't as hungry as I was thirsty. Just walking through the shack and around it for a little while was enough to get us hot and sticky. Our clothes looked pasted on us. It was that humid.

Some of the other shacks we saw along the way toward the town also looked deserted, but most were well kept, the grounds trim. We pulled into the parking lot of the first restaurant we saw. It advertised crawfish, "All you can eat." Because it was summer, there were few tourists at the restaurant. Nearly all of the patrons paused and looked up from their large bowls of crawfish when we entered. Although they didn't appear unfriendly, they did study us with some suspicion. One woman with long black hair and dark eyes paused and craned her neck like a bird around the man sitting in front of her to gape at us. I smiled at her, and she nodded.

A group of men all dressed in jeans and T-shirts, some with their forearms streaked with grease and oil, rose from a table to our right and started out, laughing as they walked. They all wore high boots. Every one of them glanced at us, but the youngest-looking man flashed a warm, soft smile and fixed his dark eyes on me for a moment longer. He tipped his hat as he went by, hesitating as if he wanted to say something.

"Come along, Jack. That's too rich for your blood," one of the older men said. Embarrassed, he hurried out the door and into their laughter.

We took our seats and a young girl in a red apron with her hair tied in thick knots came to take our order. Daddy had a chicken and seafood gumbo and I ordered jambalaya.

I saw a poster advertising a fais-do-do on Saturday night with music by the Cajun Swamp Trio.

"What is that?" I asked. "Fais-do-do?"

"That's a dance and big feed," she said with her hand on her hip and her shoulder up. "You ain't ever been to one?"

"No."

"Where you from?"

"We're from New Orleans," Daddy said, smiling.

"Oh. Well, you should come," she said. "You can do the two-step." She leaned toward me and added, her eyes shifting toward the door, "I know some boys who'd like to see you there."

"We're not staying," I said quickly.

Daddy laughed. He ordered a mug of beer for himself and I had iced tea.

"So," he said. "What do you think of your mother's world so far? You don't remember much, obviously."

"It's interesting," I said in a loud whisper. "But so different."

Daddy nodded and smiled at a memory. "When I first set eyes on your mother, I thought she was Gisselle. It was during Mardi Gras, and we were all getting into our costumes. I met her in front of the house, thinking Gisselle had dressed up like a poor girl. I should have realized Gisselle would never do anything like that, even for a costume party. I kept insisting she was Gisselle because I didn't even know Gisselle had a twin. After your mother's continued protests, I realized she was someone else, and I looked at her more closely. She was so fresh and natural, timid, but not afraid to say what she thought. Sometimes," he said after a long pause, "I wonder if she wouldn't have been better off if she'd remained here in this world."

"But what about her grandfather, and the terrible thing he was doing, selling her to a man for his wife?" I reminded him.

"Yes, that's true. Every place has its problems, I guess."

"Daddy, don't you think we should call or go see Aunt Jeanne?"

"Maybe after we check Cypress Woods," he said. "I'm not anxious to run into Gladys Tate."

"Why does Aunt Jeanne's mother hate us so, Daddy? Is it just because of their losing the trial?"

"No. Gladys blamed your mother for what happened to her son Paul. After his death she started the custody battle even though she knew you weren't Paul's real daughter. She did it for revenge. She never wanted Paul to be with your mother, of course, and from what Ruby has told me, I understand she was never very pleasant to either of you after you moved to Cypress Woods."

"Aunt Jeanne told me her mother was crippled up with arthritis these days. She doesn't get around much."

"Yeah, well, hate twists and turns your insides until you become something even you despise," Daddy said. "It's best we avoid her."

So much of Mommy's past was dark and unhappy. I understood why she had resorted to voodoo rituals and good-luck charms and why she believed that old curses followed in her shadow. Poor Mommy, I thought. She was in such torment.

Our food was delicious, but neither Daddy nor I had the appetite we expected. We were both thinking only about Mommy now. I hoped we would find her soon.

The roof of the mansion my uncle Paul had named Cypress Woods rose over the sycamore and cypress trees, looming higher and higher as we approached from the long driveway. The once beautiful grounds were overgrown, the flower beds choked with weeds, the fountains dry and littered with discarded junk here and there, and the gazebos had grass growing through the floorboards, weeds invading everywhere.

Off to the right were the canals and the swamps. A pirogue, tied to the dock, dipped and fell with the water. A large egret stood on the bow, its chest out as if it claimed the canoe. To the west we saw the oil wells and the rigs, and immediately visions from my recurring nightmare flashed in my mind. To me it was a bad omen. I leaned down and touched the good-luck dime Mommy had given me.

"Are you all right?" Daddy asked. He knew the oil rigs were always in my nightmare.

"Yes," I said after taking a deep breath. I turned to the house. It resembled a Greek temple. Across the upstairs gallery ran a diamond-design iron railing. On both sides of the house, wings had been constructed to echo the predominant elements of the main building.

Daddy stopped at the front and we sat in the car staring up slate steps to the portico and lower gallery. The windows were boarded. The vines that ran along the scrolled gates had gone wild and crisscrossed themselves, choking out the weaker sections so that they draped brown and dead over the iron works.

"Doesn't look like anyone's been here for ages," Daddy said, discouraged.

We got out of the car and started up the steps. We walked between the great columns, and Daddy tried the front door. It wasn't locked, but it was warped, so he had to push hard to open it. We paused in the Spanish-tiled entryway. The foyer was designed to take away the breath of visitors the moment they set foot in this mansion, for it was not only vast and long but so high-ceilinged that our footsteps and our voices echoed.

Above us hung the once dazzling chandeliers, the teardrop bulbs now as dull as unpolished rock. The furniture had been covered but no one had cleaned or dusted for years. Great cobwebs sailed over us from every corner. Mirrors were caked with dust, and there were rodent droppings everywhere. The interior had a stale, musty odor, especially with the afternoon sun cooking the stagnant air.

Before us was the circular stairway, twice as wide and as elaborate at the one in the House of Dumas. We walked slowly down the corridor, looking through each doorway. All of the rooms in the mansion were vast, only now the drapes looked weighted with age and dirt.

"I had forgotten how big this house was," Daddy said in a whisper. "Anyone in here?" he called. His voice reverberated and died somewhere deep in the house, probably as far as the kitchen. We waited a moment, and then Daddy suggested we go upstairs.

There were birds in what had been Paul's bedroom. They had come through an open window and built nests over the headboard. When we entered, they fluttered about madly, worried about their eggs. We looked into the adjoining bedroom, the one that had been Mommy's, but there was no sign of her or of anyone being in there recently. Daddy and I checked the other rooms, pausing at the nursery. But again we saw no sign of Mommy.

"Do you recall this room?" Daddy asked.

"Not very well. But I remember there was a music box on the dresser with a ballerina twirling. Mommy or Uncle Paul always turned it on after I crawled into bed."

"I don't remember that. Must have been left here." He gazed around and then said, "There's only one other place to look."

I knew where he wanted to go. We went up the rear stairway to the enormous attic, with its hand-cut cypress structural beams, which had served as Mommy's studio. There were large windows looking out over the fields and canals, but none on the side that faced the oil rigs. Even now the great skylights provided illumination and made the studio bright and airy.

I knew that Daddy had put all of his hopes in this room. Surely we would find Mommy hiding here; but again we found nothing, no sign of her or of anyone else. Some of her tripods were up, but they looked as if they had been left that way for years.

"Where can she be, Daddy?" I moaned.

He shook his head. As he gazed around the studio, his eyes narrowed. Suddenly he had a faint smile on his lips.

"What is it, Daddy? Why are you smiling?"

"It seems like yesterday," he said.

"What does?"

"When Gisselle and I came to visit your mother, Ruby brought me up here. We realized how much we still loved each other, and we made plans to meet in New Orleans."

"Maybe she went back to New Orleans, Daddy. Maybe all she wanted to do was go to the shack and leave Jean's picture there," I suggested.

He nodded hopefully. "Maybe. I'll find a phone, and we'll call Jeanne. That's all I know to do around here."

I followed him out and down the stairs. Waiting for us at the bottom were two men. I recognized one of them as the young man who had looked at me so intensely back at the restaurant. The other was a much older, stouter man with large dark eyes and puffy red cheeks. The tip of his chin was red, too. He wore dark overalls and suspenders. Both men wore white helmets, only the younger man had his tilted back and to the side like a cowboy hat.

"Who the hell are you people?" the older man demanded.

"I'm Beau Andreas, and this is my daughter, Pearl," Daddy said quickly.

"Pearl!" the younger man exclaimed. "That's number twenty-two."

"What?"

"He means oil well number twenty-two. Are you the owner?" he asked me. "Pearl Andreas?"

"Yes," I said.

The younger man whistled, smiled, and stared at me. He was a few inches taller than his companion. He wore his hair long enough to cover his ears and the nape of his neck. Right now there was an impish twinkle in his dark eyes and a small, tight smile on his

193

lips. Although he looked strong, with his broad shoulders and muscular arms, there was a gentle quality in his face, a softness in his features that put me at ease.

"Well, this house here belongs to the Tate family," the older man said. "No one told me anyone would be coming around today. I didn't mean to scare you, but we kinda keep our eye on it for them."

"I understand," Daddy said. "We thought my wife might have come here."

"Your wife?" The older man looked at the younger one, who shrugged. "We ain't seen nobody but you two," he replied. "Right, Jack?"

"Nobody," the younger man said.

Daddy nodded. "I've got to get to a telephone," he said. "Where's the closest one?"

"You can come over to the trailer and use ours. My name's Bart. I'm the foreman." He extended his hand, and Daddy shook it. "This here is Jack Clovis. He's the one looks over number twenty-two." Daddy shook his hand too, but he turned back to me.

"It's nice to finally meet the owner," Jack said, nodding at me. "Hello." He held out his hand, and I took it quickly.

"Hi," I said. We shook. My hand felt so tiny in his strong fingers and thick palm.

"Well's still doin' real good," Jack said.

"I don't even know which one it is," I said.

"Really?" He looked amazed and turned to Bart.

"What she have to know which one it is for?" Bart said. "She just has to know where the money's kept."

When Jack looked at me again, I thought I saw disappointment in his eyes.

"I'd like to know," I said quickly.

Jack beamed a smile. "Glad to show you," he said.

I looked at Daddy, who seemed surprised at my sudden interest. Then he looked at Jack Clovis and smiled. "You can go look at it if you like, honey, while I go to the trailer to call Aunt Jeanne and home."

"I don't want to trouble anyone," I said.

"Oh, heck, it won't be any trouble," Jack said quickly.

Bart laughed. "Jack's been waiting for someone to talk to about his well for months now."

"It's Miss Andreas's well," Jack reminded him.

"Not the way you brag about it," Bart retorted. Jack's deep brown complexion took on a crimson tint.

"I'd love to see it," I said.

Jack straightened his shoulders. "Right this way, ma'am," he declared.

"I'll come and get you," Daddy said. He left the house with Bart, and I walked out with Jack, who pointed toward the rigs.

"Yours is fourth from the left there," he said. "You know anything about oil?"

"Just that it comes in a can," I said, and he laughed so hard I thought he would crack a rib.

"It doesn't come in a can, ma'am."

"Please, call me Ruby."

"Ruby. Oil starts as crude oil deep in the ground. It takes several million years to be formed," he said in a tone of almost religious respect. "You know what it comes from, right?"

I shook my head. It seemed as long as I was willing to listen about oil, Jack Clovis was willing to talk.

"Dead plants and animal material that lie buried in sedimentary rock. So," he said, smiling at me. "You can see why it takes a while to get into that can."

"Do all those rigs have oil?" I asked.

"All the ones you see here are called development wells because this is a known oil field," he continued. "Even so, some of them were dry. We call them dusters. There's one," he said pointing at one that

195

stood still. "Once the oil is pumped up," he continued, "we put it in a metal tank called a separator, to separate the oil from the natural gas and water. Then it's stored in those stock tanks. It gets shipped off to the refinery where it's turned into the product you buy."

"How long have you been doing this?" I asked.

"Since I was twelve. You live in New Orleans, right?"

"Yes."

"We heard talk about you and your family, but no one knew anything for sure," he said, shifting his eyes away quickly.

"What sort of talk?" I asked.

"That you once lived here with a woman who wasn't your mother and Mr. Tate, who wasn't your father, and that now you lived in a rich old mansion somewhere and sat back and counted your money," he replied.

"First," I began, "that woman *was* my mother."

"Oh. Well, everyone gets stuff wrong here."

"And second, we don't just sit around counting money. That's hardly us," I said sharply.

"No offense meant. You asked, so I told you," he said casually.

"My father works hard; my mother is an artist, and I'm about to go to college to become a doctor."

"A doctor? Wow!" He whistled. "Well, there she is. Your well," he said. I just stared. "You really didn't know which one it was?"

"I was very little when I lived in that house," I said, nodding toward the mansion, "and I was afraid of the oil machinery. They looked too much like mechanical monsters. If anyone took me close to them, I would scream."

Jack nodded, his face serious, thoughtful. "I can imagine how a little girl might look out at these babies and think they are some sort of creature. They're alive to me," he said.

"Like bees, sucking up the oil?"

"Not exactly," he said, laughing. "Was that your idea?"

"One of them, in nightmares."

"Oh. I'm sorry. It's really very interesting work, and I'm always fascinated by the idea that we're drilling deep into the earth and bringing up something that was formed so long ago, even before humans existed."

I saw he was sincere about his fascination.

"Of course," he said, lowering his voice, "I don't talk about the work like this with the other guys."

I smiled. "Is it ever dangerous?" I asked him.

"You don't want to be near the rig if there's a blowout."

"Blowout?"

"A pocket of high-pressure gas gets into the well and *boom!*" he said, throwing up his arms.

"Oh," I said stepping back.

"It's all right. Your well is tried and true and as sweet as . . . as you look," he said. Now it was my turn to blush. "So," he said, "why were you looking for your mother in the old house? No one uses it anymore, far as I know."

"We thought she might have come back here," I said. My chin quivered.

"Something's wrong?" he asked. "I don't mean to pry, but if there's anything I can do to help . . . I know it sounds crazy, but after looking after your well all this time, I sorta feel I know you."

I wiped the fugitive tears from my eyes with the back of my hand and sucked in my breath. "One of my twin brothers was bitten by a poisonous snake and died. My mother is still quite upset," I said. "She ran off."

"I'm sorry. That's terrible. But why would she come here?"

"She grew up in the bayou, and as I said, we once lived in the mansion. I don't know what she's looking for or what she hopes to do, but we know she's around here someplace. She's very confused; she could have gone anywhere. We're very worried about her."

"We haven't seen her, but I'll keep a watchful eye."

I opened my purse, took a picture of my mother and me out of my wallet, and handed it to him. "That's her," I said.

"Beautiful woman. You look just like her."

"If you do see her, will you call me?"

"Of course. Give me your number." He took a pencil out of his top pocket and wrote my telephone number on the inside of his hand. "I'll copy it onto a piece of paper later," he said smiling. "Or I might just never wash and leave it there forever." He smiled softly.

"Hey, Jack," one of the workers called out, "what are you doing, conducting private tours now?" He followed his question with a laugh. Jack glared at him furiously.

"I shouldn't be taking you away from your work," I said, backing away and turning toward the house.

"Oh, no. It's all right. I'm on a break. Don't mind him. These guys are great kidders, but there's no better group to be part of. Riggers stand by each other. We're tight."

We started walking back.

"Is your father still working, too?" I asked him.

"No. He retired, but he still lives in the bayou. He spends all his time in his pirogue, fishing. I've only been to New Orleans twice," he said. "Once when I was just twelve and then again on my twenty-first birthday five years ago. My whole family went—me, my parents, and my two sisters. City life is sure different. All that racket and straining your neck to see the sun and stars."

I laughed. "It's not that bad where we live."

"You live in a house as big as that?" he said nodding toward the mansion.

"No, but it's big," I admitted.

"My father says people who live in the city probably want big houses because they want to be inside most of the time rather than in the dirty streets."

I laughed again. "We have beautiful grounds. The area is called the Garden District, and it's not really city life."

"That's good, but I'd still miss the open skies, the animals, and all this nature," he said.

"It is beautiful here," I admitted. "I know my mother missed it."

Jack paused and put his hand over his eyes to shade them from the sunlight. "Looks like your father's waving for you," he said, pointing, and I looked toward the trailer where Daddy was standing. He appeared disturbed. Maybe he learned something about Mommy, I thought and hurried along.

"Jeanne hasn't seen or heard from her," he said. "We can't stay and look any longer. I called the house."

"And . . . ?"

"Pierre's gotten worse. The doctor wants him back in the hospital immediately."

"Oh, Daddy."

We hugged. I saw Jack standing to the side, his helmet in his hand, watching. "I'm sorry for your trouble," he said when I went to say good-bye.

"My other brother took the loss of his twin very hard. He's in a catatonic state and won't eat or drink."

"On top of all that, you have this problem with your mother. I wish I could do more."

"Keep an eye out for her," I whispered.

199

"I promise I will," he said. "Bye."

I joined Daddy at the car. He sat there for a moment looking at the mansion.

"Jeanne is right. It looks like a gigantic tomb," he muttered. "They should either fix it up or knock it down," he declared angrily. Then he started the car and backed up. As we drove down the long driveway, I gazed back and saw Jack Clovis still standing there watching us leave.

Off to the left, my well pumped on as if it had a heart and a life of its own. For the first time, I thought of the wells as something other than monsters. Maybe now the nightmare would end.

Was there another waiting to take its place?

10

A Candle
in the Wind

Daddy muttered to himself all the way back to New Orleans. He chanted his hope. Sometimes it sounded more like a prayer.

"Maybe she's back. Maybe she came up here just to put that picture in the shack for some reason—one of her rituals, right? I mean, for all we know, we could have passed her on her way back when we were coming into Houma. That's possible. And if she got home before us, she found out about Pierre and went with him to the hospital. She would, and that would help the little guy snap out of it, wouldn't it?"

"Yes, Daddy," I said when he paused for a breath. He was driving so fast now, it made my heart thunder like a train. I was worried because he seemed to be gazing at his thoughts and not at the road ahead of us.

"No one saw her up here, so she didn't go anywhere but the shack as far as we know. And she wasn't at the shack when we arrived. Right? Where would she go? Certainly not to see the Tates. She would only go home. Yes, that's it. She's home. She's snapped out of this insanity just in time. We'll be able to help Pierre now, won't we, Pearl?"

"Of course we will, Daddy. Don't you think you're driving too fast?"

"What?" He looked at me and then at the speedometer. "Oh. I didn't realize." He checked his rearview mirror. "Lucky we didn't get a ticket."

"Do you want me to drive, Daddy?"

"No, I'm fine. I'll watch what I'm doing." He lowered his shoulders and relaxed. "Terrible how they're letting that beautiful mansion rot in the swamps, isn't it? Terrible. Did you remember much?"

"No," I said. Mommy had once told me that Daddy would like to forget I had ever lived there. She kept very few pictures of us taken at Cypress Woods, and the ones she had were buried deep in drawers.

"Well, the oil wells are still going, making the Tates millionaires over and over. They were wealthy people before the wells. Money doesn't discriminate, unfortunately," he added bitterly. "I can't imagine what it's like working for Gladys Tate. But those oil riggers are something else, aren't they? A breed unto themselves, I hear."

"He seemed very nice," I said.

"Who? Oh. Oh, yes." Daddy smiled. "How did you like seeing your well? It must eat Gladys Tate's heart out that she can't stop you from collecting the income."

"It didn't look any different from the others, but Jack explained a lot about it to me."

Daddy smiled. "He was buttering up the boss, eh? Can't blame him. Especially when the boss is as pretty as you."

"He wasn't buttering me up, Daddy. He was just being polite and informative," I said. I turned away quickly so Daddy wouldn't see me blushing.

Jack's beautiful dark eyes flashed before me, and so

202

did his soft smile. I couldn't recall meeting a young man who radiated so firm a sense of strength and yet appeared so gentle and compassionate. I had felt comfortable and safe when I was beside him. He worked with his hands and his muscles, but there was something poetic about his love for his work.

"You've got to be careful about who you meet, Pearl," Daddy said, turning serious. "Once a young man learns how wealthy you are, his interest in you will grow; only that might not be the sort of interest you need. Do you understand what I'm trying to say? I'm not as good at this as your mother is, I know."

"I understand, Daddy."

"I bet you do; I bet you do. I'm not worried about you. No, sir, not you."

He was quiet again, and then he started to repeat the mumbling. "She has to be at home. Has to. She must have come to her senses by now. She loves her family too much to stay away."

As we drew closer to New Orleans, the clouds closed up the holes of blue between them until there was an ominous gray layer above us. The first drops hit the windshield as we went over the bridge and onto the city streets. The wind had kicked up as well. People were losing their umbrellas and rushing about to get to shelter. The downpour started before we reached the Garden District. It got so heavy that the windshield wipers couldn't clear a view.

"Damn this," Daddy moaned. He had to pull to the side for a few moments. The rain swept over us in sheets, pounding the roof and pounding at the windows.

But it was one of those quick summer storms. It slowed, and the wind calmed down. Daddy started for home again. By the time we reached our driveway, the sun had pierced the thin veil of trailing clouds and dropped rays of hope down over our camellias and magnolia trees. The cobblestone sidewalks glittered. It was as if Mother Nature had washed away the sadness staining our walls and grounds.

Daddy almost leaped out of the car before he brought it to a stop. I couldn't keep up with him. He rushed up the steps two at a time and to the front door. Aubrey was in the corridor speaking with one of our maids and turned with surprise as Daddy thrust the door open. I hurried behind him.

"Monsieur Andreas," Aubrey said, approaching.

"My wife. Has she returned?" Daddy demanded quickly.

"No, monsieur." He shook his head and with troubled eyes gazed at me and then back at the maid, who turned to busy herself.

"Has she phoned? Did someone tell her about Pierre?" Daddy asked and nodded, hoping for a yes. But Aubrey could only disappoint him.

"Not that I know, Monsieur."

"Where's Mrs. Hockingheimer?" Daddy glanced up the stairway.

"She went to the hospital with Pierre, monsieur. The ambulance took them both."

"Ambulance?" Daddy released a small moan. Then he turned to me. I shrank into a tighter ball when I looked at those pathetic, sad eyes that showed his suffering.

"Where is she? Where could she have gone?" he cried, turning back to the butler. Aubrey stared, not sure what else to say or do.

"Daddy?" I tugged on his sleeve. "Daddy."

"What? Oh. Yes. We had better go directly to the hospital. Call me if you hear from Madame Andreas, Aubrey. Call the hospital immediately."

"Yes, monsieur."

We charged out the front door and down the steps.

"Maybe she called the doctor first and went directly

to the hospital," he said, wishing aloud. My silence brought him back to reality.

In no time we were driving into the hospital parking lot. The elderly volunteer at the front desk moved too slowly for Daddy when he asked where Pierre Dumas had been taken. He slapped the counter as she fumbled with the patient register. "Hurry, madame, please."

"Yes, yes," she said when she finally found Pierre's name. "He was just admitted. He's in ICU."

"Intensive care?" Daddy grimaced.

"Probably just a precaution, Daddy," I said. It was more like a prayer, too.

He took a deep breath and we hurried to the elevator. When we got to the ICU visitors' lounge, Mrs. Hockingheimer came out quickly to greet us.

"Oh, monsieur," she said, "thank God you're here."

Daddy held his breath, the words cluttering on his tongue.

"What's wrong? What's happened to Pierre, Mrs. Hockingheimer?" I asked breathlessly.

"He's gone into a deeper coma. The psychiatrist is upset. She says Pierre has suffered a serious relapse."

"Relapse?" Daddy said. "Back to what he was?"

"Even worse than he was originally," she said and began to cry. Daddy's face turned ashen. I felt my heart stop and then pound. Panic nailed my feet to the floor. My legs felt so numb I didn't think I had the power to move one in front of the other.

"Where is Dr. LeFevre?" Daddy asked finally.

"She's inside with Pierre. She came out and just went back in with another doctor," Mrs. Hockingheimer said. "A urologist."

I tried to swallow, but couldn't. Daddy's shoulders drooped. Although I was really feeling sick, I managed to find my voice. "Let's go talk to the doctor, Daddy."

205

We started toward the ICU, both of us terrified at what we were going to discover. Before we reached it, the door opened and Dr. LeFevre stepped out. She gazed at us, her eyes filled with confusion and disappointment.

"What's happening to my boy?" Daddy asked softly.

"I have a specialist in there examining him, Monsieur Andreas. He's suffering renal failure."

"What does that mean?" Daddy asked, gazing at me first. I knew he understood, but for the moment he was so nervous and excited he couldn't think.

"It's his kidneys, Daddy," I said.

"His kidneys aren't filtering out the waste, monsieur. They have shut down."

"Why? How can this happen?"

"I have seen this happen to patients who suffer prolonged coma, much more severe than what Pierre suffered, but his situation, which we thought was improving, suddenly took a turn for the worse and he went deeper into himself. Psychologically, monsieur," she said after a long pause, "your son is trying to get back with his twin brother."

"Get back. But . . . Jean is dead," Daddy said in a low voice.

"I know, monsieur. And so does Pierre."

"But then he's . . ."

"Willing himself to die," she said.

Her words fell like thunder over us. Daddy stared in disbelief.

"But how can someone . . . Surely that's not possible, Doctor," Daddy said.

"The mind is far more powerful than one might imagine, monsieur. People develop psychosomatic illnesses. Some people are unable to see even though there is nothing physiologically wrong with their eyes; others are unable to walk, even though there is nothing wrong with their legs." She paused and looked behind us. "Excuse me, Monsieur Andreas, but where is your wife? Where is the boy's mother?"

Daddy shook his head, the tears streaming down his cheeks.

"My mother has run away, Doctor," I said. "She left the house and sent us a letter. She blames herself for what's happened. We thought she had returned to her bayou home and went looking for her. We found evidence that she had gone there, but we couldn't find her, and when we learned about Pierre, we hurried back."

"I see. Well, I can't be sure, of course, but the boy might be thinking his mother blames him for his brother's death. I know he blames himself, and now that his mother is gone when he needs her . . . well, you see how this complicates matters, monsieur."

"Yes, yes, I see. What can we do?"

"Let's see what sort of treatment Dr. Lasky is recommending first," she said as a short bald man emerged from the ICU. He was dressed in a suit and tie and looked more like a banker than a doctor. He had small features with dark brown beady eyes.

"This is the boy's father and sister," Dr. LeFevre said. "Dr. Lasky."

"How do you do, monsieur. I'm afraid your son is quite ill," he said getting right to the point. "He has produced less than fifty milliliters of urine during the last twenty-four hours, according to your nurse. This is anuria, which causes a serious buildup of waste. As I explained to Dr. LeFevre, he has acute renal failure, usually the result of a serious injury or some other underlying illness. She has explained the psychological problems to me, and I am in complete agreement with her diagnosis of the problem."

"What can we do?" Daddy asked quickly.

"Well, until the underlying cause is treated, we must

direct ourselves to the physical threat. I have pre-scribed a diuretic, but if there is no change soon, I think dialysis will be necessary. Let's wait and see. This might pass."

"Can we see him?" I asked.

"Yes, of course," he said.

"Will he be all right?" Daddy demanded.

"Most people with acute renal failure eventually make a full recovery, but this case is unusual because of the psychological implications, monsieur. I'm afraid I cannot make precise predictions."

"Meaning what?" Daddy asked.

"If he remains unresponsive and doesn't produce and dispose of urine, we will put him on dialysis. But if his mind can shut down one organ . . ."

"Surely he will come out of this coma," Daddy said to Dr. LeFevre. She didn't reply. "He'll snap out of it. Won't he, Pearl?"

"Yes, Daddy," I said, so choked up, I could barely get enough breath to pronounce the words. "Let's go see him."

"Right," he said and started toward the ICU with me, refusing to face the dire possibilities that both doctors were presenting, but Dr. LeFevre seized his wrist and stopped him.

"It would help if your wife returned soon, mon-sieur," she said.

Daddy nodded. When he turned back to me, he looked as if he had aged twenty years in a minute. We entered the ICU and were directed to Pierre. The I.V. bag dripped its solution through the tube and into his arm. His eyes were closed, and his complexion was waxen, his lips so dull they almost looked white. I saw his chest barely rise and fall under the sheet, which was drawn up to his chin.

Daddy gulped back a moan and reached for Pierre's hand. "Hey, buddy," he said. "We're back. We're with you, Pierre. Pearl is here beside me. Come on, Pierre. Open your eyes and look at us." He rubbed Pierre's hand gently and waited, but Pierre was like a solid wall, unmoving, unresponsive, not even a blink of an eyebrow.

"Why is this happening to us?" Daddy moaned, his head back. "Maybe Ruby is right. Maybe it is some sort of curse. One horrible thing after another, beating us into submission, destroying us for daring to be happy."

"You mustn't think like that, Daddy. You mustn't give up hope. If for no other reason, then for Pierre. He needs us to be strong now."

Daddy nodded, but not with conviction. He stared at Pierre, watching his chest rise and fall, and then he sighed, lowering his head. Finally he lifted his sad eyes, a shadow of gloom making them look even darker.

"I'm going to go get a cup of coffee," he said. "I'll be back in a moment. You want something?"

"No. I'm fine, Daddy. Go on."

He rose and walked out, his shoulders sagging as if the air above him weighed tons. I turned back to Pierre and took his hand in mine.

"Pierre," I began. "We need you desperately. Mommy blames herself for what's happened; she's run off, and she won't come back until you start getting better. Please help us," I pleaded. "Fight this urge to sleep away your life. Return to us, to Mommy. Think of what this will do to her. Please, Pierre," I said, the tears streaming down my cheeks. My heart felt like a lump of lead in my chest. I sat there holding his hand, praying.

If Mommy would only come walking through that door. Why couldn't the spirits that whispered in her ears tell her she needed to return? Unless of course, they were evil spirits.

The scream of another patient in pain across the room snapped me back to reality. I had no idea how long I had been sitting there, praying and dreaming.

"I'm sorry, my dear, but we have to keep our visits short in ICU," the nurse said when she came up beside me. "You and your father can return on the hour if you'd like."

I nodded and gazed at Pierre again, but just as I was about to get up and let go of his hand, I felt his forefinger twitch. It was like a sting of electricity up my arm.

"He moved!" I cried.

"What?" The nurse looked at Pierre whose eyes remained shut.

"His finger. It moved in my hand."

"Just a nerve reaction, perhaps," she said.

"No, no, he's reaching out, reaching back. Please, let me stay."

"But . . ."

"Please, a little while longer. I have to keep talking to him!"

"I must ask you to lower your voice," she said. "There are other patients, all critical, here."

"I'm sorry."

"The regulations for visiting in ICU are five to ten minutes for immediate family every hour on the hour," she repeated in an authoritative monotone.

"Go get the doctor," I demanded, spinning on her. "I definitely felt my brother's finger move, and it was no nerve reaction."

"But—"

"Get him!" I insisted. She saw the fire in my eyes and bit down on her lower lip. Furious herself, she pivoted and marched back to the nurses' station. I sat down again and immediately began to talk to Pierre.

"I know you can come back to us, Pierre. I know

you don't want to be in this horrible hospital room with these horrible people any longer than you have to. Listen to me. We need you. I want you to wake up so Mommy can come home. I promise you, as soon as I leave here, I'll try to find her if you'll open your eyes. Please do it, Pierre. Jean wants you to help Mommy too. I'm sure he does."

I stood up and leaned over the bed to wipe the strands of hair off his forehead the way Mommy always did. Then I brought my lips to his ear and softly sang the old Cajun lullaby Mommy had often sung to him and Jean when they were little. As I sang, I heard footsteps behind me.

"Mademoiselle?"

I turned to see Dr. Lasky.

"You will have to obey the hospital rules. You work here as a nurse's aide, I understand, so you should know how important it is that we all——"

"Pierre moved his finger, Doctor. I felt it. If I can stay with him longer . . ."

"We have to let the nurses do their work and——"

I felt Pierre's fingers move again and cried out. When I turned back to him, his eyelids fluttered.

"Pierre," I said. "Show them. Show them."

His lids fluttered harder and, like eyes that had been closed for centuries, slowly opened.

"Go get Dr. LeFevre," Dr. Lasky ordered the nurse. She hurried away.

I continued to stroke Pierre's hand, cajoling him. "Come on, Pierre. That's it. Try. Come back to us."

His eyes remained open.

"That's good," Dr. Lasky muttered behind me.

"Hello, Pierre," I said. "Are you feeling better? Do you want to go home soon?"

He turned his head slowly toward me. I saw his lips moving, so I bent down to bring my ear close. He was just putting out enough breath to be heard in a whisper.

"Get Mommy," he said. "Make her come home."

"Oh, yes, Pierre. Yes. I will." I hugged him. "He spoke to me, Doctor!"

"Excellent," Dr. Lasky said and turned to greet Dr. LeFevre, who was rushing toward us. I stepped back as the two of them examined Pierre, and then I decided to go out and get Daddy. I found him in the cafeteria, hovering over a cup of coffee. When I told him the news, his eyes brightened and his face regained some color. The two of us hurried back.

Afterward, outside in the corridor, with Daddy and Dr. Lasky at my side, Dr. LeFevre asked me to repeat what I had said and done to get Pierre's reaction. She nodded as she listened.

"You must get your mother home to him soon," she said. "If not, he could relapse again, and I'm afraid each time that happens, he will retreat deeper and deeper inside himself until he becomes irretrievable. Do you understand?"

"Yes," I said and looked at Daddy, who just nodded, a look of terror in his eyes.

"With the diuretic working, we've at least stemmed the threat of acute renal failure for the time being," Dr. Lasky said. "But what happened before can certainly happen again," he cautioned. Neither doctor wanted to leave us with false hope. Their words, although realistic, were as sharp as darts.

Daddy and I returned to Pierre to reassure him we were going to find Mommy and bring her to see him as soon as we could. He listened and then closed his eyes. He was just sleeping now. The great effort to claw his way up and out of the grave his mind was constructing around him had exhausted him. We left him resting comfortably.

212

"What if Ruby doesn't return, Pearl? What if she never returns?" Daddy asked as we drove home from the hospital.

"She'll come back. She has to."

"Why? She doesn't know what's happening. We can't find her; we can't get a message to her." He shook his head. "If she doesn't come back, poor Pierre . . ."

"We'll sit and we'll think of what else to do, Daddy. We'll find her," I promised, although for the moment I hadn't the slightest idea what we should do next.

The doctors' words lingered like bruised and angry clouds waiting to drop a storm over us. Pierre remained on the brink of oblivion, and we were helpless.

Mommy wasn't there when we returned home, and there had been no phone calls from her or from anyone in the bayou. Daddy phoned Aunt Jeanne and explained the situation. She promised to send out everyone she could and make as many phone calls as she could to people in the area. She said she would contact the police up there for us, too.

"If we don't hear anything tonight or tomorrow morning, we should search for her again, Daddy," I said.

"Search where? We went to the shack and to Cypress Woods. I have no idea where else she might go up there. That part of her life is like a fantasy to me. For all I know there are places and people she never mentioned or that she did mention but I don't remember. You know all of her grandmere's friends are gone. What can we do . . . ride around the back roads, searching the swamps?"

"That would be better than just sitting here, wouldn't it?"

"I don't know, Pearl." He shook his head. "I don't

know. What if we go up there, get lost on some back road, and she calls here? No, all we can do is wait."

Neither he nor I had much of an appetite for dinner, but we sat and nibbled. All of the servants were quiet, their faces worried. The house had a funereal atmosphere. No one closed a door hard; everyone tiptoed through the corridors and spoke in whispers. There was no music, no radio or television, just the constant ticking of the grandfather clock followed by its hollow, reverberating gong to announce the passage of time, the flow of minutes without any word from or of Mommy. When Daddy and I gazed at each other, we thought but didn't speak the same thought: back in the hospital, Pierre was waiting, teetering on a tightrope above the dark chasm of gloom that would swallow him and lock him up forever in unconsciousness and finally death. I felt sure that in his mind he saw death as a doorway beyond which Jean stood, waiting.

Neither Daddy nor I knew what we would do or say when we returned to him. He would open his eyes hopefully, expectantly, not see Mommy beside us, and close those eyes again, perhaps forever. We were both terrified of taking the chance, and yet it was hard to keep from visiting him. The longer we stayed away, the deeper his skepticism would become.

Daddy spent some of the evening in his office talking to friends, getting advice. None suggested anything more than what we had already done, and none could understand why Mommy would have run off; but of course few if any of them knew her background and why she had come to believe she was the cause of our trouble.

I wanted to stay awake as late as I could to hear the phone ring, hopefully with news of Mommy, and to keep Daddy company, but when I lowered my head on the sofa and closed my eyes, sleep seized me so quickly I could have been the one in a coma. The next thing I knew, I heard the bong of the grandfather clock declare it was three in the morning.

I sat up slowly, rubbed my eyes, and listened. The house was dead quiet. The lights in the corridors had been turned down low. I was surprised Daddy hadn't come in to wake me and send me up to my bed.

I rubbed the sleep out of my eyes and got up to check on Daddy. The desk lamp in his office was still on, but he wasn't there. I saw that he had done some drinking. The bottle of bourbon was open, and there was a partially filled glass beside it. Thinking he had gone up to bed, I climbed the stairs. My legs felt as if they were filled with water. Every step was an effort. When I got upstairs, I saw that Daddy's bedroom door was open, so I went to it and peeked in.

The bed was empty, the lamp beside it lit. The bathroom door was open, but the bathroom was dark.

"Daddy?" I called quietly. "Are you here?" I listened and heard nothing.

I checked the other bedrooms and didn't find him, so I went back downstairs. The cars were all there, and no one was in the kitchen. I walked through the house and went to Mommy's studio. There were no lights on, so I was going to go back upstairs, frightened now that Daddy might have fallen asleep or collapsed on the floor beside his bed. But as I turned, I caught a whiff of bourbon and paused, staring into the darkness of the studio. My eyes grew used to the absence of light until I saw his silhouette on a settee. I stepped farther into the studio, slowly approaching him.

Daddy was sprawled naked on the settee with just a small towel over his torso. He looked fast asleep. What was he doing? Why had he gotten undressed to lie in here? I debated waking him and then decided to let him rest. Just as I started to turn away again, I heard him cry out my mother's name.

"Ruby. Go on," he muttered. I drew closer again to listen. "Go on," he continued. "You're a professional. You should have no problem drawing me. I want you to do it. Go ahead," he challenged. Then he laughed. "Ready?" He pulled off his towel and cast it over the back of the settee. "Draw with passion, my darling. Draw."

I stood transfixed, unable and afraid to move. I knew if he discovered it was I and not my mother in the darkness, he would be horribly embarrassed. After a moment he lowered his head to the settee again and mumbled something I couldn't hear. He grew quiet, and I tiptoed out of the studio, closing the door softly behind me, leaving Daddy back there, reliving some intimate moment with my mother.

Troubled but exhausted, I put my head on my pillow and fell asleep in moments, glad my mind hadn't the energy to think one more thought.

I awoke with a start. A mourning dove was moaning her ominous, sad cry just under my window. The sky was heavily overcast, shutting out the always welcome rays of warm sunshine and leaving the world draped in a dull film of dreary darkness. Rain was imminent. I gazed at the clock and saw that I had slept until nearly nine. Recalling what had happened the night before, I rose quickly, washed, and dressed. When I descended, I found Daddy, up and dressed and in his office on the telephone. He was speaking to the police in Houma. I stood in the doorway listening.

"Then you have been to the shack and searched the surroundings thoroughly?" he asked, glancing at me cheerlessly. "I see. Yes. We do appreciate that. You have my number, and please, if there is any expense involved . . . I mean, if there's anything extra you can

216

do but can't afford it . . . of course. Thank you, monsieur. We're grateful."

He cradled the receiver and sat back. His hair was disheveled, his face unshaven and gray, and he was dressed in the wrinkled clothing he had worn yesterday. To me it looked as if he had woken in the studio, dressed, and come to his office.

"Nothing," he said. "Not even a footprint. Maybe she was swallowed by one of the alligators behind the shack."

"Don't say such a thing, Daddy!"

"What can I say?"

"Did you call the hospital?"

"Not yet." He sighed deeply. "What are we going to do, Pearl?"

"She'll come home or she'll call us," I said. "She will," I insisted when he didn't react. "Did you have breakfast?"

"Just coffee. I don't have an appetite. But you go on. Eat something. No sense in both of us suffering like this," he said. "I'll give Jeanne a call in about twenty minutes. Everyone's going to get annoyed with us for nagging them, of course."

"No, they won't. They'll understand."

"That's good, because I don't," he said bitterly. He was at it again, swimming in a pool of self-pity. I just didn't have the patience for it, so I went to get some breakfast. Afterward I decided we should go see Pierre.

"I can't," Daddy said. "I can't face him and continue to promise him something that I have no idea will happen."

"But we can't not go, Daddy. Our presence is all he has now. We have to go," I insisted. "Get up."

His eyes widened. "Okay," he said. After giving Aubrey detailed instructions about how to reach us should anyone call with any information, he reluctantly drove us to the hospital. We met Dr. LeFevre in the corridor just outside the ICU.

"No word of your wife yet, monsieur?" she asked when she saw it was just us again.

"I'm afraid not," Daddy said.

"How is Pierre doing, Doctor?" I asked.

"He's going in and out of consciousness. Each time he emerges, it's with the expectation he will have his mother at his bedside, and each time he sees she's not there, he retreats into his deep sleep. Have you no idea where she might be?" she asked.

"Some, but there's been no sign of her anywhere," Daddy moaned.

Dr. LeFevre didn't hide her dissatisfaction, which only made Daddy feel worse.

"We're trying to find her, Doctor," I said. "We have the police looking, and we have friends searching."

"Very well," she said. "We'll do what we can," she added with the definite tone that said it wouldn't be enough.

The entire time Daddy and I were at Pierre's bedside he remained asleep. He didn't even move his fingers when I held his hand. He was waiting to hear Mommy's voice, not ours. The sight and the silence drove Daddy mad. He couldn't stay long and left before I did. I found him pacing in the corridor.

"Let's go home," he said. "Maybe someone's called."

No one had. The day seemed to last forever. Every hour fell like another heavy stone on our hearts. Daddy ate a little lunch, but started to drink in the late afternoon. By early evening he was in his own comfortable stupor, and I was left waiting for the ringing of the phone or the buzz of the doorbell. Nothing brought any news.

And then, just before nine o'clock, the phone rang

and Aubrey came to the sitting room to inform me that a Monsieur Clovis was on the line waiting to speak with me.

"Clovis?" At first I couldn't recall who that might be.

"He said Jack Clovis, mademoiselle."

"Oh, Jack," I cried and hurried to the phone.

"Sorry if I'm calling too late," he began.

"No, it's fine, Jack. What is it?"

"I don't know if it's anything, Pearl, but just before I was about to leave the fields tonight, I saw a light in a window in the big house. I knew it couldn't be the reflection of a star or the moon, because we've got heavily overcast skies out here tonight," he explained. "To me it looked like a candle."

"Did you go look?"

"I did because of what you told me about your mother and all. I took a flashlight and went into the house. I listened, but I didn't hear anyone. I swear I saw candlelight, though. I didn't see it when I was in the house, and I don't see it now, but someone was walking through that house tonight. I'd swear on a stack of Bibles."

I thought a moment. It was nearly a two-hour drive, but this was the first sign of any hope.

"We'll be out there in two hours," I said.

"Really? I don't know if you should do that, Pearl. I haven't found anything. It might have been a prowler, of course. I can't say I saw a woman. I hate to have you drive out here in the middle of the night for nothing."

"It's not for nothing, Jack. We're coming. I don't expect you to wait around, though."

"Oh, no problem. I'll go sprawl out in the office trailer. If I fall asleep, just knock on the door. Boy, I sure hope you're not coming out here for nothing."

"Don't you worry about it," I assured him.

As soon as I hung up, I went looking for Daddy. To

219

my chagrin, I found him sprawled out on the sofa in his office, his arm dangling over the side, his hand clutching the neck of the bourbon bottle.

"Daddy!" I rushed to him and shook him. He groaned, opened his eyes, and then closed them. "Daddy, Jack called from Cypress Woods. Someone was in the house, walking with a candle. We've got to go up there. It might be Mommy." I shook him again. This time he released the bottle, and it fell to the floor, spilling its contents over the rug and splattering my feet. "Daddy!"

"Wha . . . Ruby?"

"Oh, Daddy, no!" I cried. I stared at him for a moment and, realizing he wouldn't be able to drive anyway, and would certainly sleep all the way there, I turned and went to the desk. I found a pen and wrote a quick note explaining what Jack had said and where I had gone. Then, to be sure he read it, I pinned it to his shirt and left him, sprawled out drunk in his office.

I had never driven the car for as long a journey as this one was going to be, and at night, too. The thought crossed my mind to call someone to accompany me. I considered Catherine, but remembered she was on holiday. I certainly didn't want to call Claude or any of his friends. No one would want to go traveling into the bayou this time of night anyway, I thought. I had to do this alone, and I had to do it now.

Thinking about some of those dark side roads put a tremor into my legs and made my fingers shake when I finally got behind the wheel and turned the key. I took a deep breath, checked to see that I had enough gas, and then pulled out of the driveway, turning slowly into the city streets and leaving Daddy and the house behind me.

Somewhere ahead of me in the night Mommy waited. At least, I prayed so. Whenever I had any doubts I just conjured up Pierre's image and the plea in his eyes.

"Get Mommy," he had asked. "Make her come home."

I sped onto the highway and into the night to do just that.

11

Kiss

Ten minutes out of the city, the sky that had looked heavy and forbidding delivered on its threat. The rain fell, driven by a furious wind that splattered the heavy drops like eggs against the car windshield. The wipers groaned with the effort to keep the window clear. Oncoming car headlights blurred. It was like a monsoon. My heart throbbed in triple time as I held my breath with every turn.

Suddenly I felt the car sliding, and I panicked, hitting the brakes too hard, which sent the vehicle sideways. I screamed as the car rammed into a tree and the rear end whipped out, leaving me facing the side of the road, my front wheels in a ditch. Other drivers, whizzing by, sounded their horns as if in anger, fearful I would back out onto the road again and into their path.

But all I could do was sit and cry, my hands frozen to the steering wheel. I couldn't move a muscle. My heart was a wild frantic animal in my chest, thudding hard against my ribs. Tears coursed down my face and dropped from my chin.

The wipers were still going, even though the engine had stalled. I sucked in my breath and tried desperately to calm down. The rain sounded like giant fingers drumming the roof. More horns blared, and then a pair of huge headlights came bearing down on me. It was a tractor trailer truck, and I thought it was going to plow right into me. But the driver brought it to a stop about a dozen feet away. I saw him get out and run over to open my door.

He was a lean man in a faded white T-shirt and jeans. He had a well-trimmed dark mustache and thin brown hair. "You all right?" he asked.

"I think so. Yes," I said wiping my tears away.

"Your rear end is sticking out in the highway. You're gonna get smacked for sure. Did you try to back up and straighten out?"

"No, sir."

He was getting soaked standing there in the rain, but he didn't seem to care.

"Well, go on, see if she'll start," he said. I turned the key. The engine turned over and over, but the car didn't start. "We might need a tow truck," he muttered.

"Oh, no. I've got to get to Houma tonight!"

He thought a moment.

"Let me come around and try it," he said. I slid over, and he got behind the wheel. "Might be flooded." He kept his foot down on the accelerator and turned the ignition. It churned and churned and then suddenly sputtered and started. "Let's see how bad you're hung up in this ditch," he said and put the car into reverse. Then he accelerated. The car lifted and fell, lifted and fell. He shook his head. "I don't know. We could rip something out if we force her."

"I've got to get to Houma, monsieur. It's a matter of life or death."

"Ain't it always?" he muttered and looked at me. "You sure you're old enough to be driving?"

"Oh, yes. I have my license right here," I said fumbling for my purse.

"That's all right. I ain't the police. Your folks know you're out in this weather?"

"I'm trying to get to my mother," I said.

He nodded. "All right. I'll try something. I got a chain in the truck. Give me a few minutes to hook it up to your car and I'll see if I can tug you over the ditch here."

"Thank you, monsieur. Thank you."

He smiled at me and shook his head. "Women drivers," he muttered and got out. I waited. The rain didn't ease a bit. I saw him working, seemingly oblivious to the downpour. I was sure he was soaked to the skin. Finally he tapped on my window.

"Just hold the steering wheel steady. If she comes up and out, turn to the right so you straighten up, okay? Got it?"

"Yes, monsieur. Thank you."

"Don't thank me yet," he said. He ran back to his truck. I waited, and then I heard the chain tighten and I felt the car move back a few inches at a time. As it lifted, I did what he told me to do, and moments later I was free. My heart beat with joy instead of fear.

"Okay," he said, returning to the window. "You're out. If you're going to continue driving in this storm, you had better keep it slow, understand?"

"Yes, monsieur. How can I repay you?"

"Send me a thank-you card," he said and rushed away.

"But, monsieur . . ."

I waited. He got into his truck and drove off, beeping his horn as he went by. I never even got to know his name.

Minutes later I was back on the highway, driving

with exaggerated care until the rain eased. It slowed to a drizzle, and then, just as suddenly as it had started, it stopped. I chanced accelerating, feeling more confident as I put more miles behind me and the road looked drier and drier. Even so, traveling along highways with trucks and cars whizzing by and so few lighted houses made me nervous. If something happened to me, Mommy would never know and Pierre would never get well, I thought. Daddy would be left alone and would surely die, too. Just the thought of all this tragedy brought stinging tears to my eyes.

A half hour or so later I saw the clouds had broken up. Stars were visible, blinking their promises. It warmed my heart, and I felt even more self-assured. The horrible accident that had begun my journey became just a memory. When I drew closer to Houma, however, I realized I had forgotten the exact side road Daddy had taken to bring us to Cypress Woods. I slowed down and studied the roads, but they all looked the same now. Desperate, I decided to stop at the first shack with lights on inside. This journey that was supposed to take me about two hours had already taken nearly three. A house appeared on my right, so I slowed down and turned into the driveway.

As soon as I got out of the car, two gray squirrels scampered up a nearby cypress tree, their sudden movement making me gasp. They peered down at me curiously from the branch over my head. I laughed at them and walked up a gravel path to the gallery of the shack.

It was a paintless wood-frame building with orange stained screens on the windows. Some windows had shutters, some didn't. The yard was cluttered with used automobiles, washing machines, and damaged pirogues. The gallery had square columns that were barely holding up the tin roof, and the first step on the short stairway was broken. I hadn't picked the best place to stop for directions, but I wasn't sure how far away the next one was and I didn't want to get any more lost than I was. So I drew closer.

Zydeco music was coming from inside, and through the opening in the batten plank shutter, I saw a man playing a harmonica, another playing a washboard, and a third playing a fiddle. There was the sound of a woman's laughter and then someone shouted, *"Laissez les bon temps rouler"*—let the good times roll. More shouting was followed by more laughter and the sound of someone dancing on the plank floor. This close I could smell the heavy aroma of a seafood gumbo.

I hesitated to interrupt the festivities, but when I turned around and looked at the dark surroundings, the trees with the Spanish moss draped like ghosts, the fireflies like sparks in the night, and the absence of any traffic or people, I felt I had no choice. I stepped up to the door and knocked, too softly at first and then hard enough for the people within to hear.

Someone shouted. The music stopped. I knocked again. Moments later a man in just a pair of pants and suspenders came to the door. He had a heavy thin line of hair running down the center of his chest, which was spotted with pale yellow freckles. He was barefoot with toes that looked as thick and as long as fingers. His black hair was disheveled, some strands so long they reached the tip of his nose. He looked as if he hadn't shaved for days and never shaved the hair on his neck that curled over his collarbone. He just stared out at me.

"Anyone there, Thomas?" A woman demanded.

"Yes," he said.

Suddenly there were two little girls behind him, both in sack dresses and both with hair that looked as if it had never been cut. It reached below their shoulders. They gazed at me with large, curious dark eyes. Another, shorter man appeared, smiling widely, and then a tall woman, stout with rolling pin arms, pushed in between them. She had a chubby face with a double chin and large dark eyes.

"Well, whaddaya lookin' at, you two? It's just a girl. Whatcha want, missy?"

"I'm lost and I was hoping I could get some directions, ma'am."

"Lost, huh? Lookie what we got here, Jimbo," she said, pushing the shorter man back so that an older man with bushy white hair could come to join the curious group. He was the one playing the washboard. "She says she's lost."

"Where you goin'?" he asked. There was gray stubble on his chin and a light gray mustache.

"I'm looking for a place called Cypress Woods," I said.

"Cypress Woods!" The first man smiled, revealing gaping holes where teeth should have been.

"You related to the Tates?" Jimbo asked.

"No, monsieur."

"Well, Cypress Woods is the Tates' place," he said with narrow, suspicious eyes. The woman nodded. The group was joined by two more men, another woman, three older girls about sixteen, and a boy a little younger.

"You lookin' for one of them oil riggers?" the woman asked in a disapproving tone. She folded her arms over her bosom and straightened her shoulders.

"Not exactly," I said.

"Not exactly? What's that supposed to mean? Not exactly?"

"I'm not coming here to meet a man," I added. "But someone who works with the oil riggers has information I need."

"That so?" She looked like she didn't believe me. Why was it so important for them to know every detail before they would give me directions?

"Tates don't live there, if you're looking for them," Jimbo said.

"I'm not looking for the Tates. Listen," I said with a deep, impatient sigh, "I lived there once." I realized if I didn't give them more information, I might not get any out of them. "But I'm not related to the Tates."

"Lived there?" He looked at the woman. "Don't say?"

She narrowed her eyes, too.

"You related to the old traiteur lady?" she asked.

"She's too young to be Catherine Landry's grand-daughter," Jimbo said shaking his head.

"You her great-granddaughter?"

"Yes, ma'am, I am," I said.

"Well, I'll be. Yeah, she looks somethin' like a Landry would, don't you think, Jimbo?"

"That she does. They was good-looking people. Buster be happy to hear about this. He's been bulling around about it for years now."

"Do you know how I can get to Cypress Woods?" I asked, not hiding my impatience now.

"Sure. You go down here about hundred yards, see, and then you make a left turn, hear? Then you follow the road to the first fork. Turn left and follow that. It will take you to Cypress Woods, hear?"

"Yes, monsieur. Thank you."

"Buster ain't gonna believe this," the woman said. "She looks like her mother, don't she?"

"Buster ain't gonna believe this," Jimbo agreed, nodding. They all just stared at me with big eyes, making me feel like a ghost.

"Thank you," I said and hurried back to the car. When I looked back, I saw they were all still standing there gaping out at me. I hoped their directions were accurate. I drove slowly. These side roads were even darker than the road that took me close to Houma. The cypress trees loomed tall and thick, their branches twisted and turned above me. The reflected illumination of my car headlights made some of them look like skeletons. Something furry ran across the road, and when I made the last turn, an owl swooped in front of me, its wingspan so large it took my breath away. With my heart pounding, I finally turned up the driveway toward Cypress Woods and the oil wells. It had been more than three and a half hours since I had spoken to Jack Clovis. I wondered if he was still here.

The great house rose out of the night as I drew closer and closer. Its windows were dark, but some of them were like mirrors reflecting the movement of trees and bushes. The building radiated its emptiness in the silence that surrounded it. Only the wind stirred the loose shutters and brushed the tops of the weeds and tall grasses that grew unchecked along the sides. It looked much more abandoned and forsaken without the sunlight glittering around it. Now it was a house occupied only by shadows. As the clouds passed over the stars, those shadows shifted and twisted behind the windows and over the gallery.

I had an empty feeling in my chest as I gazed at the great mansion that had once been filled with song and laughter, good food and good friends, a place of joy and life in which my mother had created wonderful works of art. Now it was a grand tomb without a body, all the voices long gone, their echoes absorbed by the vast space.

And all of my childhood fears suddenly swept over me. I was afraid to turn my head and look at the oil rigs. My heart skipped a beat and then raced. Something luminous in the darkness radiated in waves over the field between the house and the swamps, going in and out of focus. Maybe it was just a reflection, but to me, for the moment, it looked like the face in my nightmares. I gasped as it seemed to draw closer and closer, floating toward me. A flutter of panic made my heart skip.

"No!" I cried, shaking my head. I accelerated up the driveway and turned left toward the office trailer. A tiny light burned on the door, and I saw some dull illumination through the window. I pulled up quickly and got out, hugging myself. It was far from cold. If anything, the humid, hot air should have made me sweat, but I had a chill in my spine that put icicles over my heart. I hurried up the steps to the door and knocked. There was no answer.

Oh, no, I thought. Jack gave up on me. I'm out here all alone. Something croaked in the grass to my right. I heard scurrying along the gravel. When I looked back toward the house, I thought I saw a thin veil float down from the upstairs gallery. Whatever it was, it disappeared in moments. I knocked again, harder. When no one responded, I tried the doorknob and discovered it was unlocked.

I stepped into the trailer. There was a desk to the right covered with blueprints and other papers, a telephone, and a copy machine. Behind it was a small kitchen. To the left was the living area and there, sprawled out on the sofa, his feet dangling over the arm of it, was Jack Clovis, sound asleep. I closed the trailer door and stood there for a moment, embarrassed, not sure what I should do next. Fortunately, he finally sensed my presence. His eyelids fluttered and then opened. The moment he saw me, he shot into a sitting position and brushed back his hair.

"Oh, sorry," he said, rubbing his cheeks vigorously. "I guess I fell asleep."

"I'm the one who should be sorry," I said. "I took so long to get here, but I got into an accident just outside New Orleans, and then I got lost for a while."

"Accident? Are you all right?" He stood up and buttoned his shirt.

"Yes, I'm fine. I just slid off the road into a ditch, but a truck driver helped me."

"Oh. Good." He looked behind me. "Isn't your father here too?"

"No," I said. "I came by myself."

"Yourself? Oh," he said without asking any more questions.

"Have you seen anything since we spoke?" I asked quickly.

"No. I watched the house for an hour or so, too. There were no cars. I don't even know how anyone would get here, except . . ."

"Except what?" I said.

"Except through the canals, of course. It was too dark to go down there and check. You want something to drink—cold water, juice?" he offered moving toward the small kitchen.

"No. I'm fine. I'd like to go into the house immediately and look where you saw the light."

"Sure. Let me get us a couple of flashlights," he said and went to a cabinet. "I really didn't mean for you to come up here so late. Tomorrow would probably be just as good. Does your father know you've come?"

"He doesn't know yet, but I left him a note. It's all right."

Jack nodded, but he looked skeptical.

"It's very important that I find my mother quickly. My brother needs her desperately," I said.

He stared for a moment, his eyes softening. "I understand. Okay, let's go, then." He opened the door for me, and we stepped out. "Might as well drive over to the house," he said, nodding at my car. We got in and I drove over, describing how bad the rain had been at the start of my trip.

"Didn't get much here," he said. "That's the way

these summer storms are. Sometimes we get them bad and you don't and vice versa."

We got out of the car and walked up the steps to the gallery. He flipped on his flashlight and I did the same. Then, we entered the house. Please, I prayed, please let Mommy be here. If I found her, I would take her directly to the hospital. In hours we could be at Pierre's bedside.

The small amount of illumination our flashlights provided elongated the shadows and made the rooms and corridors look deeper than they were. Furniture draped in sheets resembled spirits waiting patiently to be reanimated, and the silhouettes created by our flashlights slid across the walls and ceilings like phantoms gathering around us. Our own footsteps made the floorboards creak. Our shoes clicked over the tiles, a small sound amplified in the emptiness.

"The light was upstairs," Jack said. "Be careful."

He led the way up the grand staircase. The steps groaned under our weight. It had been a long time since anyone had walked up or down regularly. I felt a rippling sensation on the back of my neck, as if someone had stepped up behind me. I paused and spun around. As we were moving forward, the darkness, pushed aside by our beams of light, was rushing back in behind us. I decided to stay as close to Jack as I could. When we reached the landing, he directed me to the right and we entered what I knew was Uncle Paul's bedroom.

"I might be wrong," Jack said. "But I'm pretty sure the light was in here. I counted the windows from the end of the house. If there was someone in this room, that person was standing about here." He moved to the window. "The light lingered awhile and then grew smaller. My guess is that the person moved deeper into the house, away from the window. I called and called, but no one responded. Could have been a prowler or a burglar, as I said," he added.

"There isn't much here for a burglar to steal, is there?" I asked.

"Well, there are good furnishings, works of art, bric-a-brac, kitchenware . . . sure, there's good loot, especially for some of these swamp pirates. We don't have urban crime, but we do have some lowlifes meandering about the canals, breaking into other people's shacks. This place is so far out that it's not easy to rob, but desperate people do desperate things."

Our flashlights were like candles. They threw a glow over our faces as we stood talking.

"Why would your mother come back here by herself in the middle of the night?" he asked. "You obviously thought she would or you wouldn't have come. I don't mean to poke my nose where it don't belong," he added quickly.

I shook my head and bit down on my lower lip. If Mommy was in the house, she would have heard us, but I couldn't be sure she would let us know she was here. I had no idea what state of mind she was in at this point.

"I told you about my brother's death and how upset my mother was, but I didn't tell you that my mother blamed herself for the tragedy. She went to a voodoo mama and was told to enact certain rituals. The next thing we knew, she had left to do something else mysterious. She sent a letter telling us she wouldn't be coming home for quite a while, if ever. We suspected she had returned to the bayou and found something she left in the shack where she and my great-grandmother lived when my mother was a little girl."

"And then she lived in this house after she married Paul Tate," he said.

"Yes."

"So you think she's coming back here to perform some voodoo ritual?"

"She's returning to wherever she thinks she did something that might have put a curse on us. I'm sure there's some ritual that has to do with driving away evil spirits," I told him.

"You don't believe in any of that, I take it," he said.

"No."

He nodded thoughtfully. "I'm really sorry for your troubles."

"It's gotten worse. My little brother, the one who's in a coma, has become very sick. The psychiatrist treating him thinks he believes my mother blames him for my other brother's death because she doesn't go to see him. He doesn't want to live anymore," I concluded sadly.

"That's terrible."

"So you see why it is so important for me to find my mother and get her to come home."

"Yes, I do. I'm sorry I didn't try harder to find whoever was here. You want to go through the rest of the house?"

"Yes," I said.

He reached for my hand. "We'd better be careful. This place has been deserted for a long time. I don't know what to expect."

I didn't hesitate to give him my hand. He grasped it firmly. It was reassuring to sense his strength. We started through the upstairs, going in and out of the rooms, checking closets and bathrooms, looking into every possible space. I called for Mommy. I begged her to reply if she was in the house.

"Pierre needs you desperately, Mommy. If you're here, please call to us. Please!"

There was only the echo of my voice followed by silence. We returned to what had been my mother's bedroom. The bed had no linen, but there were still pillows and a mattress. Both of us ran our light beams over the floors and walls, even under the bed, but we saw no one and no evidence of anyone having been here recently.

"Maybe I just imagined the candle," Jack said woefully, "and brought you up here on false hope. The swamps play havoc with your senses sometimes. You ever see a flash of swamp gas?"

"No."

"It ignites and rolls across the water's surface like balls of lightning," he said. "It happens so quickly you're not sure whether or not you imagined it."

"I think I saw something like that when I drove up to the house. I don't really remember much at all about the bayou; I was just a little girl when I left. It sounds fascinating."

"I wouldn't want to live anywhere else," he said. "Don't mean any disrespect, but as you know, I'm not one for city life."

I smiled for the first time in hours, but I wasn't sure he could see in the dark.

"Well," he said after a moment, "you're welcome to come back to the trailer with me. I can make us something cold to drink. I got some watermelon in the fridge, too," he added. "Unless you're too tired."

I had been so excited and nervous, I never realized the lateness of the hour or the weariness in my body. Now that we had paused for a while, my legs did feel heavy, and fatigue began to climb up as if I had stepped into a pool of it.

"I'm okay," I said. "Just a little tired."

"What are your plans?" he asked. "You don't want to just turn around and drive back, do you?"

"Oh, no. I'm going to stay here," I said, gazing around.

"Stay here? You mean, in the house?"

"Yes. If my mother was here, she might come back, and if she's hiding, she might finally show herself. I don't know what else to do."

"But this is an empty house. Don't you have any relatives or friends to stay with? I mean, there are probably all sorts of creatures living in here by now, including spiders and snakes and——"

"Don't!" I said. "You're scaring me, and I have to stay here."

"I'm sorry," he said, seeing my determination. "If you're positive you want to do this . . ."

"Yes."

"Okay. Let's go back to the trailer. I'll dig out some food and get us some blankets," he said.

"Us?"

"Well, you don't think I'm going to let you stay here by yourself, do you? I wouldn't catch a wink of sleep lying back there in my trailer, worrying about you here," he said. "I mean, that candle could have been used by a prowler."

"You don't have to stay here. I'll be all right," I said, but my legs were shaking and my knees knocking.

"I told you, I take care of your oil well, and I'll take care of you," he said firmly.

I smiled in the darkness, grateful for his generosity and concern. "Thank you," I said.

"No thanks required. Let's go get what we need," he said, and we left the house.

The cold watermelon was refreshing. After I had eaten some, I used the bathroom while Jack gathered the bedding and a kerosene lamp. Then we returned to the house.

"Where do you want to camp?" he asked after we entered and stood gazing into the dark.

"Upstairs," I said. "My mother's old bedroom."

The glow from the kerosene lamp cast pools of dull yellow light over the walls as we climbed the stairs.

236

Our shadows spilled behind us down the steps and over the entryway. Jack saw where my attention had gone and laughed. He lifted the lamp making the shadows change their shapes and sizes.

"We're gigantic," he said. "We'll scare away any ghosts that might dwell in these crannies."

"Do you believe in ghosts, Jack?" I asked him.

"Sure. I've seen them occasionally."

"Stop," I said.

"No. I have." He paused at the landing and turned to me. "In the swamp at night, floating over the water. Indian ghosts, I'm sure."

"Maybe it was just that swamp gas you described," I told him.

"You don't believe in spiritual things?"

"I believe in God, but not in goblins and ghosts and voodoo spirits. I'm a scientist," I said. "I believe there's a logical cause and a logical reason for everything. We might not know it yet, but there is."

"Okay," he said with a small, smug smile on his lips.

"You think I'll be proven wrong?"

"Don't know. I just know what I've seen," he said confidently and continued to the bedroom.

When we entered with the brighter light from the kerosene lamp, the room looked larger. When Jack started to put the lantern down on the vanity table, I spotted something on the bed.

"Wait!" I cried. "Bring the lantern closer to the bed."

He followed me. We both stared down between the two pillows.

"What the heck is that?" Jack asked. "I didn't see it before, did you?"

"No." I reached for it slowly. "It's a mojo," I said.

"A what?"

"The leg bone of a black cat that's been killed

237

exactly at midnight. Powerful gris-gris," I told him. "My mother was definitely here! Either we didn't see this when we were here before or she came back after we left to go to the trailer."

When I turned around, Jack was standing there with his mouth open. "Leg of a black cat?"

"My mother's old cook gave her this mojo. She was the woman who died and came back with the warning my mother never got because she was at a party celebrating her new art exhibit. That's one of the reasons she blames herself for what happened to Jean," I explained.

Jack gazed at me as if I were crazy. "This woman died and came back?"

"I don't really believe any of this," I said. "I told you my mother's having some sort of emotional breakdown."

He nodded and then looked around the room. "Sure you want to stay here?" he asked again, a little tremor in his voice now.

"Positive. My mother might return."

"But what if she's off doing something weird some-place else?" he asked.

"The only way to be sure is to stay here and wait," I said, more determined than ever. He sensed the resolution in my voice and stopped trying to talk me out of staying.

"Okay. You want to sleep on that mattress? It's a little dusty, but if I put this blanket over it and this one over the pillow . . ."

"That'll be fine," I said. "Thank you."

"I'll fix myself a spot over there," he said, nodding toward the settee.

He prepared my bed and then went to prepare his own, placing the kerosene lamp between us.

"You all right?" he asked, after sprawling out.

"Yes," I said. "It's really nice of you to help me like this."

"No problem."

"How old are your two sisters?" I asked. Now that I was lying down in Mommy's old bedroom in the empty mansion and the darkness had closed in around us, I felt the need to keep talking. Besides, I was interested in Jack's life.

"Daisy's twenty-two and Suzanne is twenty-nine. She's married with two kids, a boy three and a girl four. Her husband runs a canning plant."

"What's Daisy doing?"

"She just finished college in Baton Rouge and got engaged. She's getting married in two months to a fellow over in Prairie. His family has a furniture business. They met at college."

"Did you go to college?" I asked.

"Me? No," he said. "I barely finished high school before I went to work with my father on the rigs."

"You said you were working when you were twelve."

"I was, but I couldn't collect a salary yet. How did you remember I said that?"

"I just did," I said quickly, happy he couldn't see me blush.

"No, I got my schooling on the job," he said. "I read a lot, though. We have lots of time to ourselves."

"What do you like to read?"

"Mostly about nature. The other guys call me Einstein because I always have my nose in a fat book. I think it's great that you want to become a doctor. 'Course, I've never been to a real doctor, just a traiteur lady."

"My great-grandmother was a traiteur."

"I know. She's kind of a legend around here. You got magic in your hands, too? Oh, I forgot, you don't believe in anything that isn't logical." He laughed.

"Sometimes people get better because they believe so strongly in someone. That's logical," I said.

He was quiet a moment. "I guess it is. You're pretty smart, huh?"

"I get good grades."

"How good?"

"Good enough to be valedictorian of my class," I said.

"No! Really? I thought so," he said. "You just look smart, but I wasn't sure."

"Why not?" I asked laughing.

"Well," he said slowly, "the only smart girls I ever knew were . . ."

"Were what?"

"Not ugly, but not very pretty," he said.

There was a long moment of silence between us, neither of us knowing exactly what to say. Finally I spoke.

"That's silly, Jack. Looks have nothing to do with mental abilities."

"You're right," he said. "I'm just babbling. Tired, I suppose."

"We should sleep," I agreed. "Good night, Jack. Thanks again."

"Night," he said. "You want the lamp on or off?"

"On, I think."

He paused and then said, "Not logical."

I had to laugh aloud. "You're a very nice person, Jack. I'm glad you're the one who's looking after my well."

"Thanks," he said. "Pearl?"

"Yes?"

"What did you do with that cat bone?"

"It's still here on the bed," I said. "That's where my mother wanted it."

He was quiet. The wind wove its way through the openings in the house and in and out of rooms below

240

us, sometimes making a whistling sound. Walls creaked, and a loose shutter tapped monotonously against a window frame somewhere. I thought I heard the sound of flapping wings and imagined bats had inhabited the rafters, but I knew they weren't dangerous.

It had been a long, emotional night. Now that I was lying down, my body felt as if it would sink into the mattress. I tried to stay awake to listen for footsteps or the sound of my mother's voice, but before I knew it, I was in a deep sleep.

I sank into dreams filled with the faces of people I had met in the bayou. I imagined the people in the shack who gave me directions, and I dreamed they were outside. They had followed me to Cypress Woods and were muttering to themselves in the shadows. They drew closer and closer and entered the house. They were all coming up the stairs, the woman with the rolling pin arms leading them and the children all following behind. I saw them enter the bedroom and sensed them around me. Their eyes were big, and their faces were liquid, changing from round to oval to round again.

And then I felt a hand on my cheek. It was too real to be in a dream, but I couldn't open my eyes. I moaned and struggled against the invisible bonds that bound me. I tried to open my mouth, but my jaw was locked. I gagged on my tongue and exerted all my strength to get my mouth open. Finally my lips parted and I screamed.

Jack was at my side in moments. I sat up and threw my arms around him.

"What happened? What's wrong? Pearl?" He held me tightly, and I locked my arms over his strong, secure shoulders.

"Just hold me," I pleaded. "Just hold me."

"It's all right," he said, gently brushing my hair,

first with his hand and then with his lips. "You're safe. It's all right."

I tried to swallow. My heart was pounding so hard I was sure Jack felt the thump in his chest, too.

"You poor girl," he said. "Damn this bad luck. Damn it."

His lips moved to my forehead. I closed my eyes, welcoming the warm affection and comfort, bathing in his touch. He continued to kiss me, moving his lips down to my closed eyes and then my lips. I didn't resist. We kissed long, but gently. And then he pulled back.

"I'm sorry, I didn't mean . . ."

"It's all right," I said and sighed as he eased his embrace. I lay back.

"What happened?" he asked.

"I felt a hand on my cheek."

"Just a dream, I suppose. I was having nightmares myself," he added. He held my hand. "You all right now?"

"Yes, thank you."

"I don't want you to think I was taking advantage of you or anything. I . . ."

"I'm glad you kissed me, Jack."

"You are?"

"Yes. It was very comforting."

"Good," he said. "Well . . . should we try to sleep again?"

"I'm sorry. I know you have to get up early and work."

"I'll be fine," he said. He stared down at me a moment longer and then started to rise, but hesitated, turned, and leaned down to kiss me again. "Just to be sure," he whispered. I saw his small smile and felt the warmest tingle travel through my breasts to my heart.

I actually was sorry when he rose and returned to the settee. I heard him settle in, and then I turned to look at him. For a moment we just stared at each other through the dim light of the kerosene lamp.

"Night," he whispered.

"Good night."

I turned over and thought for a moment before I realized why I was suddenly anxious. I patted the bed and searched with my hand.

Jack heard me moving about. "What is it, Pearl?"

"Jack," I said. "The mojo."

"What about it?"

"It's gone!"

12

Hatred Is as Slow
as Poison

If Mommy was in the house during the night, she was gone or well hidden by morning. Jack and I searched the studio, the kitchen, and even the pantries more vigorously than we had the first time, but there was no sign of her, and she didn't respond to my continuous calling and pleading for her to show herself.

"She's just not here," Jack finally said. "She must have gone someplace else during the night. Do you have any other ideas where she might go?"

"The only people I know are my aunt Jeanne and uncle James. My mother likes Aunt Jeanne. They've stayed in touch all these years."

"Maybe she finally went there, then. We can call them," Jack suggested.

"I'll just go see them," I said. "But I do want to call Daddy first."

"And you should eat some breakfast. You're running on an empty tank."

"I'll go into town and—"

"No, you won't. Let's go to the trailer," he insisted.

Most of the other riggers had already arrived by the time we drove over to the trailer. Heads spun and eyes widened when we got out of my car.

"Pick up a new helper, Jack?" someone shouted, and the others laughed.

"Just ignore them," Jack mumbled, keeping his eyes straight ahead and his head stiff.

When we entered the trailer, Bart LaCroix, the foreman, looked up from the small kitchen table where he was having coffee and a cruller. There was another rigger with him, a man about his age, only taller with a full head of dark brown curly hair.

"What's this?" Bart asked, surprised to see me.

"Mademoiselle Andreas has returned to continue her search for her mother," Jack explained. "It looks as if her mother was here during the night."

"Don't say. During the night? This ain't a place to be wandering around during the night."

"No one's wandering around," Jack retorted.

Bart grunted, gulped some coffee, and gobbled the rest of his cruller. "Billy says we're having a problem with the pump jack on thirty-three. Stop by and give it a look-see, hear?"

"Right. How about some coffee, Pearl?" Jack asked.

"Thank you," I said. The taller man stood up and pulled a chair away from the table for me. "Thank you."

"Your father here, too?" Bart asked.

"No, monsieur."

Bart raised his eyebrows and then looked at the other man, who stood waiting for an introduction. "Oh, Lefty, this here is Mademoiselle Andreas. Pearl. Number twenty-two."

"Number twenty-two? Oh," Lefty said, impressed. I sat down.

"How about a cruller?" Bart offered. "Picked 'em

up fresh on the way in today. We got a pretty good baker here. Bet he compares favorably with your Café du Monde."

"Thank you," I said and tried one. I smiled and nodded. "He does compare favorably," I said.

"Well, we better get shaking, Lefty. We got oil to pump," he said eyeing Jack, who pretended not to hear as he poured thick, black Cajun coffee. Bart and Lefty put on their helmets and left the trailer.

"You like a little cream with that?" Jack asked nodding at my cup.

"Please. I didn't mean to cause you any embarrassment with your fellow workers," I said.

"Don't think a second time about it," he said firmly. "Most of them are just jealous. I can make you eggs, if you like."

"This is fine for now," I said. "It really is a good cruller."

"How about some orange juice or cereal? I got some cornflakes, I think."

"I'm fine, Jack. Really. Just sit down and drink your own coffee. I don't want to keep you from going to work one more minute," I said.

He smiled and sat down. "Coffee's pretty strong, I know. The men like it that way. Bart says it keeps the hair off his tongue. He used to work with my father," he explained. "He might sound and look gruff, but he's a pussycat. Thinks he has to look after me."

"It's nice having someone who cares about you," I said, which reminded me of what I had to do. "I have to call my father."

"Go on. Use the phone right there." Jack pointed.

Aubrey answered on the first ring, which immediately sent a chill up my spine. It was as if he'd been waiting right there for my call.

"Monsieur Andreas is asleep, mademoiselle," he said a low voice, obviously not wanting the other servants to overhear his conversation. "He had a slight accident late last night."

"What sort of accident, Aubrey? What happened?" Had Daddy come after me and cracked up his car in that torrential downpour?

"I don't know what time he started up the stairs last night, but he got dizzy and fell, and I'm afraid he broke his right leg just under the knee. It's a small fracture, but the doctor had to set it and apply a cast and give him a painkiller. That's why he's asleep, mademoiselle."

I knew Aubrey was being kind to say Daddy had gotten dizzy. Surely he had risen from the sofa in his office and, still quite drunk, started up the stairs. "Does he know where I am?"

"Yes, mademoiselle. He found the note you pinned to him. It was still on him when he fell down the stairs. I heard the commotion and found him there. We got the doctor immediately, and he decided it would be all right for monsieur to remain at home. I took the liberty of calling Mrs. Hockingheimer and she will attend to his needs. I expect her arrival at any moment."

"That's good, Aubrey. When my father wakes up, please tell him I called and I will call again later today. Tell him . . . tell him my mother is still here and I hope to find her soon. Then we'll both come home."

"Very good, mademoiselle."

"Bye, Aubrey." I cradled the receiver slowly.

"More problems?" Jack asked and I told him. He shook his head. "A lot has surely fallen on you, Pearl. Sure you want to stay here?"

"I've got to find my mother," I said and then thought I should call the hospital and ask after Pierre. The nurse at the ICU nurses' station was curt. My brother was still going in and out of a comatose sleep. His last sleep had lasted eight hours, and he had been

247

conscious for less than a half hour. The doctors hadn't seen him yet this morning. The nurse advised me to call back in the afternoon.

My face wrinkled with worry as I sat down again.

"Anything else I can do for you?" Jack asked after I gave him the hospital report.

"No. You'd better get back to work. I'll go visit my aunt Jeanne and then return." I told Jack where Aunt Jeanne lived, and he gave me directions and drew a small map on a napkin. Then he gave me the trailer telephone number.

"Just call here if you get into any trouble or need anything at all," he said.

"Thank you, Jack."

"You look like you could use a good hug," he said and did it before I could protest, not that I wanted to. He held me close and I laid my head on his shoulder. "Things will get better," he promised. "You'll see. And for good, logical reasons," he added with a smile. His words brought a desperately needed smile to my own lips, and then I left to see Aunt Jeanne.

Jack's directions were perfectly clear. I arrived at Aunt Jeanne's house a little over a half hour later. Aunt Jeanne's husband, James, was a successful attorney, but her family, the Tates, were one of the wealthiest in the bayou anyway. Her home, although not as large and grand as Cypress Woods, was impressive.

I entered the grounds through an avenue of large oaks and cedars, the canopy of thick leaves and branches casting long, cool shadows over the drive and giving me the feeling I was traveling through a tunnel into another world. Acres and acres of lawns and gardens surrounded the house. A small pond lay off to my left, the water now covered with an island of lily pads. The house itself was a long one-story structure with a gallery that ran across the entire front and one side of the house. French doors connected the front rooms to the gallery.

I parked my car and stepped out slowly. I heard the whir of lawn mowers trimming the grounds behind the house and saw a gardener pruning flowers in a garden on the far right. The flower beds were a-bloom with hibiscus and blue and pink hydrangeas. In the middle of the garden stood a three-tier fountain. Gray squirrels scurried around the gardener, some so close he could have reached out to pet them. He gazed up at me, but went right back to pruning as if an unseen overseer were scrutinizing his work.

The morning sky was streaked with long, thin clouds resembling mist floating over the light blue background, but I could see thunderheads off toward the Gulf, and I surmised that it was raining in New Orleans. As I stepped forward, a pair of cardinals paraded across the gallery roof and paused to look my way. Aunt Jeanne's home was certainly set in an idyllic location, magical and peaceful, I thought. I moved quickly up the steps and rapped on the door with the brass knocker. A moment later the butler greeted me.

"I'm here to see Mrs. Pitot," I said.

"And who should I say is calling, mademoiselle?" he asked. He was much younger than Aubrey, perhaps only thirty-five or forty, and had light brown hair and hazel eyes. He was slender with a pointed nose and pencil-thin lips drawn taut in anticipation of my response.

"Pearl Andreas," I said. He nodded and stepped back to permit me to entry. I paused after he closed the door behind me.

"One moment, *s'il vous plaît*," he said.

I gazed around the entryway. It was a bright house

with windows everywhere to let in the sunshine. It had beautiful cypress floors and eggshell white walls decorated with pastoral paintings and scenes of fishermen in the canals. A bleached oak grandfather clock stood just ahead of me, and across from it was a fan of ivory and gold leaf painted with senoritas in ball gowns.

A few moments later, in a bright pink robe and Japanese slippers, Aunt Jeanne came sweeping down the corridor, her face beaming. Her unpinned dark brown hair hung down over her shoulders.

"Pearl! What a wonderful surprise!" She held out her hands and when I took them, she drew me to her for a hug. "Is your father with you?"

"No, Aunt Jeanne," I said.

She grimaced with concern. "Your mother is still missing?" I nodded and she shook her head and sighed. "How dreadful for all of you on top of everything else that's happened. How is Pierre?"

"Not well. Very bad, in fact. It's why I'm here. I've got to find Mommy. Pierre needs her. I was hoping you might have heard from her."

"Not a word, not a syllable. I'm sorry. No one I've asked has seen or heard anything. But surely she'll turn up," she added. "Come," she said taking my hand again, "Mother and I were just having a late breakfast. Are you hungry?"

"No," I said. I hadn't expected to see Mrs. Tate. My legs began to tremble and my heart pound.

"How do you like our home?"

"It's beautiful and so peaceful," I said.

"Yes. I just love to share it with people I love. You must stay here tonight. Promise you will," she followed.

"I can't," I said. "But maybe another night," I added quickly when her smile faded.

"Well, if you promise that, I'll let you get away with

not staying tonight. Come meet Mother." As she pulled me along I gazed into the first room, a pleasant sitting room done in teacup blue.

"Many of our furnishings are antique," Aunt Jeanne explained. "James loves to buy and restore things. It's his hobby. He gets more excited over a valuable find in someone's old barn than he does over his law cases. You see that sofa?" she said, pointing. "It's upholstered with material from a homespun bedspread, and that chair beside it dates from the early 1800s. In his office James has an original French Creole plantation desk made of rosewood and walnut. And his walls are covered with knives and swords and helmets that date back to the Spanish occupation of Louisiana. Ooh," she said pausing to hug me again, "I'm so happy you're finally here. Even though it's under terrible circumstances."

"Thank you, Aunt Jeanne," I said and took a deep breath as we entered the dining room.

Mrs. Tate had her back to us. She was seated at the table in a wheelchair and chewing slowly on a piece of toast. Aunt Jeanne brought me around so Mrs. Tate didn't have to turn her head.

"Look who's here, Mother."

Gladys Tate's head seemed to have sunk back in her neck because of the arthritis. Her short gray hair was so thin that her scalp was visible in spots. Her face was etched with wrinkles on her forehead, along her chin, and around her dark, watery eyes. Her pink and blue robe made her look even more shriveled and thin. It hung off her small shoulders and dangled around her. My eyes were quickly drawn to her hands. The fingers were swollen at the knuckles and curled like claws. The obvious attention given to her nails seemed bizarre, as did the rest of her makeup. Her face powder had been dabbed on so heavily, and her lipstick was too thick, giving her a clownish appearance. Overkill to detract from her pasty pallor, I thought.

She didn't smile. Her stony eyes burned into mine, and then her lips quivered into a sardonic grin. She lowered the toast to her plate, swallowed some coffee, and nodded. "It's her, is it?" she finally said.

"Isn't she beautiful, Mother?"

Gladys Tate shot a reproachful look at Aunt Jeanne and then gazed at me again, her eyes scrutinizing me so closely, I felt like a specimen under a microscope.

"She has a nice face," she offered. "Looks more like her father than she does a Landry. Which is fortunate for you," she added, nodding at me.

"My mother is considered one of the most beautiful and talented women in New Orleans," I retorted, fixing my eyes on her as intently as she fixed hers on me. "I'd be proud and grateful to be considered like her in any way."

"Humph," she said and raised the toast to her mouth. I saw she couldn't quite close her fingers enough to keep it secure. She chewed slowly, each swallow an effort. Age looked more like a disease than a natural course of events in her case.

"Please sit down and eat something, Pearl," Aunt Jeanne insisted. I sat down and the maid quickly served a cup of coffee. "That's homemade jam," Aunt Jeanne said nodding toward the dish in the center of the table.

The small rolls beside it did look good. I thanked her and took one and dipped my butter knife into the jam. Aunt Jeanne asked more about Pierre. I explained his condition.

Mrs. Tate studied every word I said and every move I made. "How old are you now?" she snapped, obviously not interested in our tragedy.

"I'm almost eighteen, ma'am."

"She's just graduated from high school, remember, Mother? She was valedictorian, and she's going to go to college to become a doctor."

Mrs. Tate smirked, deepening the valleys of those wrinkles. "Your father was supposed to become a doctor, too," she said, and then quickly added, "Don't be surprised that I know a great deal about your parents. You were almost brought up here, you know. You should have been."

"Now, Mother, you promised not to talk about that anymore."

She glared back at Aunt Jeanne with her cold gray eyes shooting devilish electric sparks. "Promised. What good are promises? Do people keep promises? Promises are no more than elaborate lies," she declared. Perhaps she had recently had a minor stroke, I thought, noticing the way one corner of her mouth twisted while the other corner remained still. Her right eye was closed a little more than her left, too.

"I don't know what you think, Mrs. Tate," I said. "But I will become a doctor."

For a moment she seemed impressed. Then she nibbled on her toast. "You know," she said, "my son, Paul, would have been a good father to you. Of course, I didn't want him to be your father, but she put a spell on him."

"Mother!"

A white line was etched around Mrs. Tate's tight, hateful lips. "Don't tell me. I know about spells," she said. "Some of the people here think your great-grandmother was a healer, a spiritual person, but I know the truth. She was a witch. I told Paul. I begged him to stay away from that shack, that house of evil, but he was entranced, doomed."

"Mother, if you're going to continue like this, I'll have to take Pearl someplace else to eat. The past isn't her fault."

"Whose fault is it, then? Mine? Look at me," she said holding up her clawlike hands. "Look what that woman did to me. She cursed me. And for what? For trying to save my son. My son," she groaned.

"I'm sorry," Aunt Jeanne told me.

"It's all right. Pain distorts people's thinking," I said. "I'm sorry you're suffering with arthritis, Mrs. Tate, but it's not because of some curse. I imagine your doctor has diagnosed it as rheumatoid arthritis," I said. "Are you taking an anti-inflammatory drug?"

"Drug. I have cabinets filled with drugs. Not one of them does me any damn good," she muttered.

"Perhaps you should go to a specialist in New Orleans."

"I've been to specialists. None of them are worth a damn. It's a curse, I tell you. No medicine will help me."

"That's not true, Mrs. Tate. I think—"

"You think? Listen to her, Jeanne. She *thinks*. What arrogance. Are you a doctor already?"

"No, but . . ."

"But nothing," she said. "Jeanne, get me one of those pills. At least they keep me from suffering."

"Okay, Mother." Aunt Jeanne looked at me and then got up. The moment she left the room, Mrs. Tate seemed to have a surge of new energy. She leaned toward me, her eyes small dark beads. "Tell me about your mother. Quickly."

I explained again what had happened to Jean and why Mommy had returned to the bayou.

The story apparently pleased her. She smiled and sat back. "It's true," she said. "She is responsible, and more will happen until she . . ."

"Until she what?"

"Drowns, just as my son drowned," she said bitterly.

Before my eyes, her face seemed to shrivel and grow haggard with the impact of her hate. The sight of this transformation sent a hot flash through my spine. Bitterly I met her eyes. "That's a horrible thing to say. You're not just sick in your body; you're sick in your mind. Daddy was right. You're twisted up inside, and your hatred has turned you into this . . . creature!" I cried and got up.

"Pearl!" Aunt Jeanne said, returning. "What happened? Mother, what did you say?"

"Just the truth," she muttered. "Give me the pill."

I ran from the room, my heart thumping, my face burning with anger and fear.

Aunt Jeanne caught up with me on the gallery steps. "Pearl, wait! Please! You mustn't listen to her, Pearl. She's not well."

"No, she isn't. She's so full of meanness and hate, it's eating her alive," I said. "I was hoping, praying, that for some reason Mommy would have come to you. She always liked you, but I can see why she would stay away," I said looking back through the front door.

"She might still call me, Pearl."

"I'm returning to Cypress Woods," I said. "That's where she was last."

"Cypress Woods? Oh, dear. I hope she'll be all right. The poor thing. There's nothing worse than losing a child. Look what it did to my mother," she added and I softened. She was right. There was no excuse for Gladys Tate's viciousness, but it was understandable that she would think the world had been cruel to her.

"Come on back inside, Pearl. She'll calm down and go to sleep, and you and I will be able to visit."

"Thank you, Aunt Jeanne, but I would just be on pins and needles thinking about Pierre and Mommy and Daddy."

"But what can you do at Cypress Woods?"

"Wait, hope, keep searching," I said. "I'll drive by the shack again and see if she's gone back there, and then I'll return to Cypress Woods."

"I'd go searching with you, but I can't leave my mother just yet," she explained.

"I'll be all right, Aunt Jeanne."

"My mother's going to return to her own home tomorrow. Then you can come and stay with me, okay? If you want, I'll ride around with you, too."

"I'll see." I was praying that I wouldn't have to be here tomorrow. "Thank you." We hugged, and I went to my car. She stood on the gallery, her arms folded, smiling hopefully at me. I saw the butler approach her and heard him say, "Mrs. Tate wants to see you immediately, ma'am."

Aunt Jeanne waved, and I got into the car and drove away, understanding a little more about the turmoil and unhappiness my mother had endured while she was a part of the Tate family.

At first the shack didn't look any different. I thought the path through the overgrown weeds might be more trampled, but I couldn't be sure. The front door, however, was now dangling, the top hinge having been broken off, and when I entered the shack, I gasped in shock. The remaining old furniture had been over-turned and tossed about like toy furniture. The legs of the sofa were cracked, as were the arms of the rocker. There were marks on the wall where a chair had been slammed against it.

The kitchen was worse. The table had been over-turned, and the cypress floorboards were cracked and splintered. The woodstove had been pulled away from the wall and the shelves above it smashed.

The sight of such wild destruction put terror into my heart. I gazed up the stairway. Mommy couldn't have done this, I thought. Even in a mad rage, she wouldn't have this kind of strength. But who would do this? And why?

Hesitant but curious, I started up the stairway. The steps creaked so loudly that I feared I would fall through. I gazed through the doorway of the first room I came upon and gasped. Someone had sliced up the mattress; the stuffing was strewn everywhere. There were deep gashes in the walls, too.

Suddenly I heard a thud, and for a moment my heart seemed to have fallen into my stomach. My first impulse was to turn and run down those stairs, but panic held me motionless. The thud was repeated. It seemed to becoming from below and behind the house. I took a deep breath, turned, and descended the steps slowly, quietly, listening.

There were no more thuds, but I was sure I hadn't imagined them. The silence was more frightening. My heart pounding, I walked out of the shack and looked around the grounds. Across the way, perched on a thick sycamore, a marsh hawk gazed at me with what looked like suspicion. It moved its wings nervously and turned on the branch. Then it flew off, soaring above me and away. I took another deep breath and went around the shack. I heard something slither through the grass and paused when I saw a long cottonmouth coiled on a rock, sunning itself. I couldn't swallow. I was afraid to make another sound.

Then I heard something splash in the canal, and I moved quickly to the corner of the house, reaching it just in time to see someone disappear around the bend, poling a pirogue. I turned slowly to look at the rear of the shack and saw that someone had thrown gobs of mud against the shack. But why? What did all this rage and destruction mean? Was it just vandalism?

Tiptoeing over the narrow pathway back to the front of the house, I hurried to the car. I sat in it for a while, thinking. Then I decided to go into town before returning to Cypress Woods. My throat was so parched that it felt like sandpaper. I needed a cool drink. I stopped at a small restaurant simply called Grandmere's Kitchen. It had a white Formica counter with ten stools and about a dozen folding card tables with wooden chairs. The aroma of crawfish, jambalaya, and gumbo stirred my stomach juices, and I realized that this emotional roller coaster I had been riding had made me hungry.

A short, bald man stood behind the counter with a stout woman who had a pleasant smile, big brown eyes, and light brown hair pinned tightly in a bun behind her head. Both wore full white aprons labeled Grandmere's Kitchen, Houma, Louisiana. Three of the tables were occupied, one with a party of elderly women, all of whom gazed at me curiously.

"Hello dere," the stout woman said to me. "Comin' for lunch?"

A blackboard announced that today's special was stuffed crabs.

"Yes, thank you," I said and chose the closest table.

She came around the counter. "Well, we ain't got printed menus, but we always have crawfish pie, Po'boy sandwiches, and Billy's special jambalaya." The bald man nodded and smiled. "Everything's served with country dirty rice. Today we have stewed okra and tomatoes, too, if you like."

"I'll have a lemonade and the jambalaya, please," I said.

"You hear that, Billy?"

"Yep," he said and went to work.

"Just passing through?" she asked, still standing beside me.

"Yes," I said. She stared as if she sensed I had more to say. "My mother used to live here," I added. "She came back, and I'm . . . hoping to join her."

"I lived here all my life. What's your mother's name?"

"Ruby," I said.

"Ruby? Not Ruby Landry!" I nodded, and she got excited. "You're Ruby Landry's daughter?"

"Yes."

"Listen up here," she declared to the room at large. "This is Ruby Landry's daughter." Everyone stopped eating and looked at me. "I'm Ella Thibodeau," she said. "My grandmere was your great-grandmere's friend. Where is your mother? Boy, I'd like to see her. We went to school together. She coming in here soon?"

"I don't know," I said. "She doesn't know I've come after her."

"Oh." She smiled, but her eyes reflected her confusion. "Been a long time since Ruby was here. I hear she's a famous artist in New Orleans now. She come here to do some painting?"

"Yes," I lied. I shifted my eyes away quickly. Daddy always said my face was a book without a cover. Anyone could read my thoughts.

"Ruby must've gone up to Cypress Woods. Sad how that beautiful place has been left to rot. I hope she gets it back," she whispered. "Crazy Gladys Tate won't let anyone near it, even to fix a broken shutter. And those beautiful grounds . . ." She made a clicking sound with her tongue. "Sad. Tragedy. Poor Paul Tate. Every one of us girls had a crush on him, you know, but your mother was the only one he cared to look at, really. We knew Gladys Tate didn't like Ruby. Mrs. Tate always walked around with her nose in the clouds. No one was good enough for the Tates.

259

"Then, when Ruby and Paul ran off and got married, we was all so happy for them. You were like a little angel child. Your mother was some brave young woman livin' in that shack house by herself with you, struggling along. Took Paul long enough to own up to his responsibilities," she said, "but once he did, he built that palace for Ruby. Tragedy," she repeated. "Some old curse for sure. If your great-grandmere had been alive, none of that would have happened," she assured me. "She was a miracle maker, especially when it came to healing folks.

"I remember . . ."

"You're talking too much, Ella," Billy shouted. "Come get the lady's lemonade."

"Oh, hush your mouth," Ella snapped, but she brought my lemonade to the table. "What was I telling you? Oh, yeah. I remember once I had this terrible earache. Couldn't sleep on that side. I went to your great-grandmere Catherine, and she blowed smoke in my ear and covered it with her hand. Next day my earache was gone. Simple remedy, but only a real traiteur knew just how much smoke and just how to do it, hear?" she said. I smiled.

"That's what I've been told," I said.

"You go to school?"

"I'll start college in the fall."

"Oh, ain't that something," she said.

"Here's the lady's jambalaya. You want to give it to her before it gets ice cold?" Billy remarked.

Ella rolled her eyes and brought me my lunch. "Billy ain't from Houma. He's from Beaumont, Texas," she said, as if that explained everything.

"Did you visit my mother and me when we lived at Cypress Woods?" I asked as I began to eat.

"Me? No. Your mother stayed to herself most of the time in those days and rarely came into town. Paul did everything for her. No man was more devoted to any woman. Men from Beaumont," she added loud enough for Billy to hear, "could have learned something from him about taking care of their women."

"Get away from that girl and stop bending her ear out of shape," Billy told her.

"Of course, the custody trial was a shocker. To this day people still believe you were really Paul's daughter. I can tell you this," she said. "Every time I saw you in his arms, I felt my heart warm. Father or no father, he couldn't have loved you more. Tragedy," she said again. "Well, you get your mother to stop by and see me, hear? She shouldn't forget her old friends now that she's a famous New Orleans artist."

I nodded, and she returned to the counter. As I ate, I thought about the things Ella had said. For a time, life at Cypress Woods must have been idyllic for Mommy. She lived in a castle with a man who treated her like royalty. Her art was her only contact with the outside world.

The jambalaya was delicious, but my stomach felt so tight after I began to eat that I couldn't finish it all. After Ella cleared away the dishes, I called Daddy from the pay phone in the corner. This time he was awake.

"I've really gone and messed things up some more, haven't I?" he moaned. "I should be up there with you, looking for Ruby."

"I'm okay, Daddy. Are you in a lot of pain?"

"I deserve it," he replied. "Listen, Pearl, I don't want you wandering around up there by yourself. It's too dangerous. You better come home. After I recuperate another day or so, we'll figure something out."

"It's all right, Daddy. I know Mommy's here now. I can't leave without her. Jack Clovis is helping me."

"Oh. Well, at least someone is," he said, still

overwhelmed by waves of self-pity. "Call me and keep me up to date, will you?"

"I will. The moment I find Mommy, I'll call," I promised.

"Now I can't even get over to the hospital to see Pierre," he groaned. "I'm a mess," he added and started to sob. I attributed his tearful mood to the medicine and his condition. I tried to comfort him some more and then hung up and called the hospital. This time I got Dr. Lefevre.

"I'm afraid things are going badly," she said. "Dr. Lasky has Pierre on the dialysis machine. His periods of withdrawal are getting longer, and he is completely unresponsive to me. What have you learned about your mother?"

"I'm trying to find her. I'm in Houma."

"Time is not on our side," she told me. "Pierre's blood pressure is falling."

After I hung up, my worried expression drew Ella Thibodeau's attention. She came over to me quickly. "Is there trouble, sweetheart?" she asked.

I shook my head, but tears were streaming down my cheeks. "No, ma'am," I said, my voice cracking.

"Well, if you need anything, you call us. Cajun folks stick by each other."

I thanked her and paid my check. Then I left quickly to return to Cypress Woods.

As I drove there, I calmed down again. After speaking with Ella, I felt I had a better understanding of what life at Cypress Woods had been like. I wondered what Mommy had seen when she returned. Did it depress her even more, or did she look at her former home through rose-colored glasses? Did her memories take her back to the time when flowers were blooming and birds were singing, a time of music and beauty, comfort and safety? Considering all that had happened, it didn't surprise me now that she would flee to Cypress Woods and the world where she had once been protected by Paul's money and love and by Grandmere Catherine's magic.

Where was that magic now? I wondered. We need it so.

13

The Past Comes
A-courting

The thunderheads had been creeping along in our direction all day. By the time I returned to Cypress Woods, they were overhead, growling and heralding rain and wind. I drove directly to the house, but a cloud burst just as I stopped the car. I waited a moment. However, seeing it was only going to get worse before it got better, I pulled my jacket over my head, lunged from the car, and ran up the gallery steps. The wind whipped the heavy drops at me, soaking my face.

I stepped inside and closed the large door to keep the gusty air and the rain out, but I found myself standing in a very dark, dank entryway filled with stale air. A chill passed through me and settled like the cold palm of a large hand on the back of my neck. I shuddered and looked up the dark stairway.

"Mommy!" I yelled. "Are you here?"

My voice reverberated, and the echo sounded like someone tormenting me, imitating my desperation: "Mommy, are you here?"

Dead silence was followed by the heavy creaking of

the wood frame and floors. Shutters rattled. It began to rain harder. Was my mother wandering about out there? I wondered. The thought of her being caught in this storm terrified me. Tears streaked my face as much as the rain streaked the windowpane, mixing with the raindrops on my cheeks. Another chill shot through my chest, making my teeth chatter. I had to find a warmer place.

I hurried into the sitting room on my right and pulled the dustcover off the settee. Although it was dusty, I used it as a blanket and curled up against the arm of the settee, squeezing my legs up against my stomach and embracing them.

The wind seemed to be circling and embracing the house, seeking out every opening, no matter how small, and then threading itself through to whistle and whip about the rooms, making the long drapes move in a macabre dance and the chandeliers swing ominously above. The storm grew stronger. I had heard that summer storms in the bayou were often worse than they were in New Orleans. This one appeared to have the power to lift this enormous house from its foundation and carry it off into the swamp.

I groaned. "Mommy," I whispered, "where can you be in all this? Are you safe?" Maybe she was upstairs, cringing in a corner just as I was cringing on this settee. I looked up at the ceiling, wishing I could see through walls for just an instant.

A decorative plate shook loose from one of the shelves of the hutch on my left and shattered on the cypress-plank floor. The crash startled me and I cried out. The wind grew louder, angrier. The chandeliers were rattling like old bones. In another room down the corridor, another piece of glass or china fell, exploding like a gunshot. Raindrops pelted the windows, zigzagging like sharp fingernails scratching their way down the panes. The wind that passed freely through the house stirred up the dust. I coughed and buried my face in my hands as I began to alternate between feeling chilled and feeling feverish. The raging tempest blustered harder and harder. I thought it was never going to end. The very walls threatened to fall in, crushing me. It grew so dark I could barely see my hand, and then I heard the front door blow open.

But I heard it close, too.

"Pearl! Pearl, where are you?" Jack cried. Never was I so happy to hear another person's voice, especially his.

"In here, Jack!"

He came rushing in, dressed in a slick black raincoat and hat and knee-high boots. He carried a flashlight and had a bundle under his arm. "Are you all right?" he asked hurrying over. He put down the flashlight and swept his hat off. Then he brushed the rain off the back of his neck.

"This storm is so horrible and it came so fast," I complained through my chattering teeth.

"We had hurricane warnings coming in over the radio," he said. "The storm built up as it traveled inland." He took the bundle out from under his arm. It contained a blanket and a kerosene lamp, which he set on a table. "I saw you drive up and tried to get you to come to the trailer, but you didn't see me waving."

He took off his wet raincoat and put it on a chair just as a gust of wind slammed against the house. I released a small cry. Jack was at my side instantly. I welcomed his embrace and cuddled against the warm pocket between his arm and his chest.

"You poor thing. You're freezing," he said, rubbing my shoulders and arms vigorously.

My teeth stopped chattering. "Oh, Jack, what are we going to do?"

"We'll wait it out," he said. "But anything that's loose is going to fly away. Let me light the kerosene lamp." I lifted myself away so he could do so. Then he sat back and offered his arm again. I leaned into him. The illumination from the flickering lamp threw distorted shapes over the wall. They looked like the silhouettes of grotesque marionettes dangling on strings, moving to the rhythm of the wind.

"Warmer?" he asked.

"Yes, thank you. No one mentioned a hurricane," I said.

"Sometimes they creep up on us. Makes it exciting to live here," he added smiling.

"I think I can do without this sort of thrill."

He laughed. "Did your mother contact your aunt? She was obviously not there if you returned to Cypress Woods," he concluded.

"No. I'm sure she won't call or go there either. I met my aunt's mother," I said with a grimace.

"Gladys Tate?" I nodded. "I never saw her around here, but I heard she's a tough lady. Actually," he said after a moment, "the boys say she's the one who wears the pants in that family. Whenever Mr. Tate does come around here, he looks whipped. It's none of my business, so I don't pay much attention, as long as we all get what's coming to us when it's coming to us."

"I returned to my great-grandmere's old shack, and, Jack, someone has been there since Daddy and I were there. Whoever it was tore the place apart."

"Tore it apart? What do you mean?"

I described the furniture, the walls. "Why would someone do that to an old, deserted place?" I asked.

"I don't know," he said with a look of worry. "It's strange." He thought a moment and shrugged. "Did you have anything to eat, drink?"

"I went into town and had some lunch in a place called Grandmere's Kitchen."

"Ella's place? Food's great, isn't it?"

"She went to school with my mother. I didn't tell

267

her why I was really here," I said. "Nor did I say anything about the shack."

"Well, it won't take long for the truth to get out and around. My daddy says a phone's a waste of money in the bayou. One person tells another something, and it's passed on before the words die on the originator's lips."

"Cajun people are really close, aren't they?"

"One big family," he said proudly. "We have our feuds, though, same as any people."

"I'm half Cajun," I said, "but I feel as if I'm in another country."

"My grandmere used to say you can become Cajun only three ways: by the blood, by the ring, or by the back door. I tell you what," he added, gazing at me, "you got grit like a Cajun. Not many fancy New Orleans girls would come here all alone, I bet, no matter how important it was."

"I don't know what else to do. My mother's not home; my brother's getting worse and worse; Daddy's laid up with a broken leg . . ."

Jack nodded thoughtfully.

Suddenly I realized the storm had stopped. The house was cemetery quiet, and the air was still. "It's over," I said gratefully.

Jack shook his head. "The eye is passing over us. More to come," he predicted, and sure enough, moments later the wind began to whistle through the house again, the shutters slammed and pounded, and the rain splattered and drummed over the trembling windowpanes. Upstairs, a blast of air blew out a pane. We heard it shatter on the floor.

I cringed. Jack held me closer. My heart was pounding so hard I was sure he thought it was his own.

"It'll be all right," he said again. I felt his lips on my hair, his warm breath against my cheek. The terror of the hurricane, the long storm of sadness that had been

268

raining over us, and the desperation of our situation made me long for the calm and the security I found in Jack's arms. He was soft and loving and very sensitive.

I buried my face in his shoulder, unable to keep back the flood of tears. He held me tightly and comforted me as I sobbed. We hadn't known each other long, but his sincerity made that short period seem more like years. The wind howled, the rain stung the house, more things toppled and smashed, another window shattered. It seemed that the world was opening and we would fall into the gaping hole. The sky grew purplish and dark. The kerosene lamp flickered precariously.

"Wow," Jack whispered, and I knew that even he, someone who had been born and lived here all his life, was impressed with this particular storm. The house continued to shake. Everything on hinges was rattling. We clung to each other like two desperate swimmers clinging to a raft in a tossing sea. The wind rose and fell, sending wave after wave of rain against the house.

And then, as suddenly as it had begun, the storm ended. Mother Nature relaxed and stepped over us, the storm trailing after her as she made her way northward to remind someone else how powerful she could be and how much we should all respect her. Jack eased his tight embrace around me, and we both sighed with relief.

"Is it finally over?" I asked, still skeptical.

"Yes," he said. "It's over. I just hate to go out there in daylight tomorrow and see the mess. You all right?"

I nodded, but I didn't leave his side. My heartbeat had slowed, but the numbness I had felt earlier in my legs was still there. I didn't think I could stand up. Jack stroked my hair with his left hand.

"How many of these storms have you been through?" I asked.

"A few, but this was a humdinger."

"I was born during a storm," I told him. "My mother told me about it and how my uncle Paul was there to help with the delivery."

"So that explains it," Jack said.

"Explains what?"

"Where you get your grit . . . from the hurricane. It left its mark in your heart. I bet you're a terror when you're angry."

"No . . . well, maybe," I said.

He laughed. "I don't intend to find out. So," he said sitting back, "what do you plan to do now?"

"Nothing. I'm going to wait here," I said.

"You don't really think your mother's coming back, do you?"

"Yes," I said. "She knows I was here; she's got to come back."

Jack thought for a moment. "Okay," he said. "Let's go to my trailer and get some things, see how bad the storm was, and then we'll return."

"No," I said. "I want to stay here. I was going to go through the house just before the storm began. Maybe my mother's hiding someplace."

"You sure got a Cajun stubbornness. When your mind's made up, it's made up," he said. "All right. Wait for me here. We'll search the house again together. I'll go gather up some food for us so we can have dinner."

"I'm not hungry."

"You will be," he assured me. "I'll leave the lantern, but promise you will wait for me before you start trekking through the house again."

"I promise," I said.

He stared at me a moment and then smiled that soft, small smile I was beginning to crave. I smiled back and he leaned toward me as my lips opened slightly to invite his. We kissed.

"I'll be right back," he whispered and put on his slick raincoat and hat. "Don't move."

"Don't worry. I won't," I said.

He laughed and hurried out.

I gazed around the room. In the throes of the storm, I had run to the nearest safe harbor without really looking at my haven. Now, calmer, I looked up at the large oil painting of a cove in the swamps. Although it was too dark to see the details, I had a vision flash across my mind and I saw the grosbeak night heron swooping over the water.

Suddenly a parade of childhood memories began. I saw myself peering down the grand stairway, which to me had looked as deep as the Grand Canyon. I heard laughter in the hallway, the full melodic laugh of my uncle Paul, who beamed his sunny smile at me whenever he saw me. I felt him scoop me up and carry me through the house on his shoulders. Delicious aromas from the kitchen returned. I saw our cook working over the stoves and ordering her assistant to cut this and mix that. All the people in my memories were big, gigantic in word and deed.

As I recalled more and more, the house that was now so dark and dreary was resurrected in my memory. In my recollections it was bright and warm and full of life. Uncle Paul was hanging one of Mommy's new paintings, and I was standing beside her, holding her hand, marveling at the magic that came out of my mother's fingers. With a sweep of a brush, she could put life in a face or make birds fly and fish jump. I heard music and more laughter. There were people everywhere; not a room, not a corner, looked lonely or cold. And from a window, probably in my room, I saw the gardens, bright and lush with flowers in all of the colors of the rainbow.

It seemed to me my mother and I had fled from this house one day, and because the flight was so quick and

271

so complete, my memories had fallen deeper and deeper into the vaults of my mind. It was almost as if I was afraid to let them emerge, afraid that they would return with some horrid nightmare trailing behind them.

The oil wells drummed in the night. Creatures slid along the banks of the swamp, and the water turned inky, dreadful, hiding the face that was to appear on the surface in the yellow moonlight, a face I was yet to see.

I blinked, and the memories faded as quickly as they had come. I was here in the present again, in the dark, dank house, searching for Mommy and hoping to find her before it was too late for all of us.

I didn't move until Jack returned and when he saw that I had barely budged an inch, he laughed. He was carrying a carton filled with food and drink.

"It's too dark to see it all clearly," he said, "but there are trees down, branches scattered, water running every which way. The trailer made out all right, although the phone's dead. I won't be able to inspect the machinery until morning though. I'll set this down on the dining room table," he said, indicating the carton. "Take the lantern and lead the way."

I did so. The sky was still thickly overcast, so the house was very dark. The glow of the lantern cast a dim pool of illumination over the floors and walls, but as we walked through the corridor, darkness seemed to cling to us. Field mice scampered into holes no bigger than quarters. I could hear scratching and scurrying in other rooms, and I surmised that other animals had fled here from the storm.

The dining room table was hidden by a dustcover that had yellowed with time. I pulled it back, and Jack put the carton down. Turning with the lantern, I

272

looked at the walls and ceiling, the grand chandelier and the large windows. Vague images tickled my memory. This table had looked miles long and miles wide to me when I was an infant. The image of Uncle Paul seated at the head flashed in the darkness like a ghost, and I gasped.

"What's wrong?" Jack asked.

I shook my head. "Nothing. I'm fine."

"You want to go through the house again?"

"Please," I replied. He took my hand and the lantern and we checked the kitchen and the pantries and then the sitting rooms before ascending the stairway. Through a window at the end of the upstairs corridor, I saw lightning flash in the distance. I was holding tightly to Jack's hand, squeezing his fingers together, but he didn't appear to mind.

We checked my old nursery, even the closets, checked the guest rooms, Uncle Paul's room and Mommy's. There was no sign of her.

"Where could she be in such a storm?" I mused aloud.

"Maybe she's with someone she didn't talk about much. Maybe she found an old shack and camped out in it, or maybe she went to a motel. There's nothing much you can do tonight, Pearl, with the phones out and the roads closed here and there. Might as well relax as best you can."

"I suppose you're right," I said. I sighed and realized my throat was dry and my tongue felt like a slab of granite. "I'm very thirsty."

"I brought water and some homemade blueberry wine," he said, leading me back to the stairway. "Dinner will be last night's leftovers, but I made it myself."

I laughed at the pride he took in his cooking. "And what did you make last night?"

"A batch of poached blackfish. Bart and Lefty were supposed to eat with me, but they went to a fais-do-do and an all-you-can-eat crawfish party," he said as we descended the stairs.

"Why didn't you go with them?"

"Wasn't in the mood," he said.

"Don't you have a girl, Jack?" I asked. I couldn't see his face when he turned to me, but I suspected that he was smiling.

"I've had a few girlfriends, but no one serious."

"Why not?"

"That's just it," he said, "no one's serious. Most of the girls I've met are . . ."

"What?" I asked, intrigued.

"Airheads," he said, and I laughed.

"Bart says a woman doesn't need much in her head to get by with a man, but that's not the kind of woman I want," he continued.

We returned to the dining room, where he set down the lantern and began to unpack the carton. Everything was neatly wrapped in tinfoil. He poured me a glass of water.

"Thank you, Jack." The water was cold and very refreshing. I drank it quickly.

"More?"

"Not right now, thanks," I said. In the glow of the lantern, his face looked shiny but soft, and his eyes twinkled. "What kind of a woman do you want, Jack?"

"Someone who can talk to me about important things, a companion, not just a . . ."

"Just a what?"

"Just a woman," he replied, turning back to his carton. "I brought a little Sterno stove to warm up the sauce. My grandmere's recipe: three cups of homemade mayonnaise, six drops of Tabasco, four tablespoons of lemon juice, one-half cup of capers, one teaspoon of caper liquid, and two tablespoons of dry mustard."

"Sounds wonderful. I'm not much of a cook, I'm afraid. We have a cook at home, had a cook all my life." He didn't say anything. "Do you think I'm a spoiled rich girl, Jack?"

"You don't seem spoiled," he said. "I've met spoiled girls, spoiled airheads." He gazed at me and shook his head. "You're not like any of them."

"Thanks. Can I do anything?"

"You can. Here," he said taking out a tablecloth, napkins, and silverware. "Set the table."

"Yes, sir," I said.

Jack found a serving table on wheels and used it to prepare our food. He produced two light blue candles and candle holders. After placing them at the center of the table, he lit them. They didn't add that much light, but it was a warmer glow. I set out the plates and the glasses, and Jack took out his homemade wine.

"Okay, mademoiselle, you may sit down now." After I did so, he poured the wine. "I hope this meets mademoiselle's expectations. It's vintage 1950."

I laughed and tasted it. "Very good, monsieur. My compliments."

"*Merci,* mademoiselle. And now the star of our show." He took my plate and prepared my entrée. Then he prepared his own and sat down next to me.

"It looks fantastic," I said. He had served some green beans and corn with the fish.

"I'm sorry there's no bread."

"We'll make do," I replied.

He smiled and reached for his glass of wine. "Shall we make a toast?"

"Yes."

"To the storm."

"The storm?"

"Which caused us to dine together tonight." We

clinked glasses. "Which only proves the saying that out of something bad, something good must come to those who wait and endure."

I felt the warmth from the wine, but I also felt a warmth coming from my heart.

"Let's eat," he declared.

Maybe because of the circumstances, because the tension and excitement had been so draining, I had a ravenous appetite. It was the most delicious meal I had had in a long time. As we ate, Jack told me more about himself and his family. His mother had been sick most of her adult life, suffering from diabetes. So his grandmere did most of the cooking and housework. He had grown up in the bayou and rarely left, only to go to New Orleans and once to go to Dallas with the family to see relatives, and once on a family vacation to Clearwater, Florida.

"I suppose my life's been very simple compared to what you've done and seen," he said. "I'm not what you would call sophisticated."

"Your life might be simple, as you put it, but you're not simple, Jack. Most of the so-called sophisticated young men I've known couldn't hold a candle to you," I added, perhaps with more energy than I intended, but after my third glass of homemade wine, my tongue felt loose and my thoughts free. Even in the low candlelight, I could see Jack blush and look happy. He softly laughed and flashed me a pleased look.

We continued to eat slowly, and whenever I lifted my eyes, they met his. Sometimes those eyes seemed to have the candle flame burning within them.

"I'm sorry I have no coffee or dessert," he said in a voice close to a whisper.

"That's all right. I've eaten more than I thought I would."

"You have, haven't you?" he said, nodding at my

empty plate. I had scooped up even the last drop of sauce.

"Very unladylike," I said, shaking my head. "A proper young lady always leaves something on her plate."

"Oh, really? Well, I guess I ain't never met no proper young lady," he replied, imitating some swamp rat. "I've known women who ate the plate."

I threw my head back and laughed. Then I leaned forward. He was laughing, too, and he leaned toward me. We brought our foreheads together gently and Jack kissed the tip of my nose. Our eyes locked again. My heart beat softly, but I felt warm blood flood my cheeks and my neck. Was it the wine?

"Should we clean up?" I asked softly.

"Clean up. Oh, no, mademoiselle. We have servants to do that. Please. Let me escort you to the parlor," he said, standing and offering his arm. I rose. "Perhaps we should take along our homemade wine." He seized the neck of the bottle and our two glasses. Then he blew out the candles and I took the lantern. We returned to the sitting room.

Although the storm had passed, there was a lingering drizzle. It made a gentle pitter-patter on the pane. Lightning still flashed in the distance, each streak turning the pitch-black sky flame-red for a split second. I fixed my gaze on it while Jack poured us each another glass of wine.

"I hope everything's all right back in New Orleans," I said.

"Don't lose hope." Jack handed me my wine, and I sipped it slowly. Then I relaxed and let my head fall back against the settee. Jack stood there gazing down at me. When I looked up at him, I saw far more than simple concern and worry in his eyes. What I saw made my heart stir and then thump. Could it be that there really was something called love at first sight? His eyes were pools of desire, which made me aware of my own ravenous need for romantic fulfillment. These sensations made me feel guilty. I swallowed hard and closed my eyes. When I opened them, Jack was at my side, taking my hand.

"Are you okay?"

"Just tired, I guess," I replied.

He nodded. "Sure. Considering what you've been through, no wonder. Well," he added, "if you insist on staying here another night, I guess we can go upstairs. We still have the blankets I brought last night."

I nodded. He took my glass and set it on the table. Then he helped me up and took the lantern. We made our way through the darkness and ascended the stairs, neither of us saying much. He wrapped his right arm around me, and I laid my head against his shoulder and closed my eyes.

Suddenly I heard something below and stopped walking. "What was that?"

"What?"

"I heard something." I gazed into the darkness beneath us. "Mommy! Are you there?"

Silence.

"Might have been a mouse," Jack suggested. I continued to listen and then agreed. He continued to lead me up the stairs, my head against his shoulder.

"Here we are," he announced when we reached Mommy's old bedroom. Jack set the lantern down on the nightstand, and I took off my shoes and lay back. He stood there for a moment looking down at me. I reached up and he took my hand. He brought it to his lips. I said nothing. My heart was pounding. He waited a moment and then let go to turn away and go to the settee.

"Jack," I said. It was as if my voice had the power to

278

act at will. His name was on my lips so quickly that I didn't have a chance to think why or what I wanted. It didn't matter. He knew.

He returned to my side, knelt beside the bed to kiss my hand, and then leaned over to kiss my lips. "Pearl," he whispered.

I tried to reason, to think about what was happening, just the way I always had when I kissed a boy. But tonight my scientific appraisal never took hold; the part of me that questioned and analyzed every touch, every kiss, never showed its face; and it wasn't only because of the wine. In Jack's arms I felt secure; I felt his concern and his care. What he wanted to happen, he wanted for both of us.

His touch was gentle, unselfish. Instead of feeling anxious and fearful, I welcomed the whirl of emotions; I wanted to be engulfed in the tidal wave. I felt myself unlock every door, invite every kiss. I lifted my chin so his lips would fall against my neck, and I kissed his cheeks and his eyes. When he rose, I moved over to make a place for him.

"Pearl," he whispered. Never did my name sound so sweet.

His hands moved over my arms to my breasts. Our clothing seemed to peel away so our skin could touch. Every time he paused, a little hesitant, a little unsure, I kissed him harder, driving away any reluctance, assuring him I wanted to follow the trail we were both burning to my heart.

"Are you sure?" he whispered one final time.

"Yes, oh, yes, Jack," I replied.

With each touch of his lips, of his hands, I felt electrifying sensations. I realized I was not some scientific creature, after all. I was a woman.

We exploded against each other. I bit down on his ear so hard I thought I tasted blood, but he didn't complain. He held me tightly, his kisses winding down slowly as our hearts slowed. He held on to me like someone who never wanted to let go.

"Are you all right?" he asked when I didn't speak and practically held my breath.

I nodded and whispered yes. He released his hold on me and lay back beside me. Neither of us said a word for a long moment.

"Pearl," he finally began, "I don't want you to think that—"

"Don't." I pressed my finger to his lips. "Don't you dare explain anything."

I could see his look of surprise.

"*Je ne regret rien*. I regret nothing," I said quickly. He smiled and kissed me.

We made love passionately, both sure of what we wanted. Without timidity and hesitation, it was a long, flowing stream of passion that climbed higher and higher until it burst in a waterfall, pounding rocks below again and again and again, each time punctuated with a bigger, happier Yes.

Exhausted, we separated and lay next to each other, waiting for our breathing to slow, our hearts to stop pounding. I felt a warm glow over my body and closed my eyes.

Jack found my hand and held it. "You were born in a hurricane all right," he said, and I laughed.

As my passion receded, however, my reason and logic returned, bringing with it the baggage of guilt. What was wrong with me? How could I behave with such abandon? I knew if I said one word, Jack would be filled with guilt, too, and I didn't want that.

Yet in the midst of all this turmoil and unhappiness, I had found such pleasure. It wasn't right, was it? I turned my back to him and bit down on my lip.

Jack, as if he were listening to my thoughts, turned to me and whispered, "It's all right. It doesn't mean you care less about your family or you're not trying hard to help them. You can't drive yourself at top speed without taking a break to recharge your batteries. You're human, Pearl. I think maybe you forget that sometimes."

I turned to him slowly and smiled.

"I won't forget it anymore, Jack." He smiled, too. He kissed me again and then cradled me in his arms, and I closed my eyes.

Sleep came rushing in as hard and as fast as the winds of the hurricane. I could no more keep it away than I could the wind. In moments I was drifting.

When I opened my eyes again, sunlight was pouring through the windows. It was hard to believe we had endured such a vicious storm the night before. In fact, the whole night seemed like a dream. Had Jack and I really enjoyed a romantic dinner? Did we really make love? When I turned to him, I found he was already gone. He had scribbled out a note and left it on the pillow.

> Didn't have the heart to wake you. You looked like an angel asleep. I had to get up very early because of the storm. Come to the trailer when you get up, and I'll fix you breakfast Cajun style.
>
> Love,
> Jack

I sat up and looked at my watch. I had slept until almost ten. Panic seized me. I should have risen early and gotten to a telephone. I had to see how Pierre and Daddy were doing.

I rose quickly and tried the sink in the bathroom. To my happy surprise, after a flow of brown water, clean water appeared. I had no warm water, but I was able to wash my face and go to the bathroom. Afterward I dressed and went downstairs. Jack had cleaned everything up from our dinner, but I saw the results of the storm's invasion everywhere: shattered plates, broken windowpanes, soaked drapes and floors.

It was terrible of the Tates to let this beautiful mansion fall apart, I thought. Why was it that people who had everything could be so wasteful and vicious? What possible revenge did Gladys Tate enjoy from watching her son's pride and joy deteriorate? Did she just want to make sure no one else ever enjoyed the house? Even from the little I remembered about Uncle Paul and from what Mommy had told me, I knew he wouldn't have wanted this.

I started when I heard footsteps behind me.

"Jack? Is that you?" I called. There was no response, but a floorboard creaked in the corridor.

Slowly I turned. It's Mommy, I thought. She has finally returned. My heart pounding with expected joy, I hurried down the corridor toward the kitchen. I would surely find her sitting there, waiting for me.

"Mommy!" I cried as I burst through the doorway; but instead of Mommy, I found a tall giant of a man. His face was bloated so that his thick nose had nostrils big enough to inhale three times the air he needed. He had heavy jowls and a round chin with thick purple lips. He was unshaven, and his three- or four-day beard of gray and brown stubble was thicker under his lower lip. When he smiled, I saw he was missing a lower tooth and some back teeth. All the rest were nicotine-stained yellow.

He was dressed in knee-high boots and torn jeans with a T-shirt that had a tear in the shoulder and looked as if it had been washed in rusty water.

He smiled, the curve in his soft, thick lips cutting deep into those bloated cheeks and narrowing his dull brown eyes over which his thick, heavily wrinkled forehead protruded.

"Who are you?" I asked.

"It's true," he said. "You are Ruby's daughter, ain'tcha?"

"I am Ruby Dumas's daughter, yes. Who are you?" I demanded more fervently. He stopped smiling.

"Name's Trahaw, Buster Trahaw. I'm a friend of your mother's," he replied. "Friends of mine told me you was here lookin' for her, so I come to see for myself."

"Have you seen my mother?" I asked. I didn't remember her mentioning a Trahaw, and I couldn't imagine why she would ever be friends with someone who looked like this, but as Jack had said last night, there were people I never knew and Mommy could have gone to see them or stayed in their homes while she was here, especially if she had gotten caught in the storm.

"Sure, I seen her," he said. "Why do you think I'm here?"

"Where is she? How is she?" I asked quickly.

"She . . . she ain't well," he said. "She's sick as a dog. When they told me you was here, she said, 'Go fetch her quickly.' So I come."

"Where is she?"

"She's at my mother's house," he said. "My mother's a traiteur."

"Oh," I said. It made sense. "Will you take me to her please?"

"Sure," he said. "Only we got to go quick. I got work to do and I can't be wandering about long."

"Okay. Let's go," I said, turning. "My car's out front."

"We can't go in no car," he said, not moving. "My mother's house is in the swamp. I come here in a pirogue to fetch you. This way . . ." He headed toward the rear door.

"But . . ."

"You coming or what, missy? I told you, I got work."

I hesitated. I should tell Jack, I thought. I took out his note and turned it over to scribble my own on the back.

> Dear Jack,
>   Went with Buster Trahaw, who said my mother was at his house. Be back soon.
>
> > Love,
> > Pearl

I left the note on the counter and hurried after Buster Trahaw, who had already stepped out of the house.

He nodded toward the dock. "My pirogue's just down here."

I followed along, looking back only once and regretting that I couldn't have the time to see Jack. But maybe I would get to my mother and bring her back before Jack even found my note. Full of hope, I hurried along. Buster Trahaw didn't wait for me. He practically ran to the dock and got into his pirogue. I hesitated. I couldn't recall the last time I had been in one, or the last time I had gone into the canals.

He reached up finally to help me, and I stepped into the canoe.

"Good," he said. "Finally."

He smiled, dipped his pole into the water, and pushed us away from the dock and into the swamps. I sat down hard and watched him anxiously. He never took his eyes off me, and he never stopped smiling.

14

Great Grandpere's Debt
Must Be Paid

Buster Trahaw's pirogue was so old and rotten that I was afraid it would simply come apart and dump us into the swamp water, which became the color of dark tea as we left the dock. Buster groaned and grunted as he pushed down on his pole. Soon beads of sweat as big as small marbles were breaking out over his forehead and rolling over his rough skin to drip off his chin and jawbone.

"How far do we have to go?" I asked nervously. Pieces of sun-dried bait and worms littered the canoe floor, as did cigarette butts, empty beer bottles, and crushed tin cans.

"Not far, not-far," he said quickly.

Instinctively I looked back toward the dock. I had a strong urge to ask him to return me there, but I couldn't help being afraid he was telling the truth and Mommy really needed me. I would have felt so much safer and reassured if I had seen Jack before I left. Who knew how long it would be before he found my note, and what if he didn't find it? I shouldn't have run off like that, I told myself.

"Don't worry," Buster said, still smiling. "We gonna be there soon. No one poles a pirogue faster than Buster Trahaw in these here canals."

I sat back. I really couldn't recall being in a pirogue when I was just a little girl, but certain visual memories returned when I saw things that were once familiar. Off to my right, among the lily pads and cattails, bream were feeding on the insects that circled just above the water. It looked like bubbles popping. Sheets of Spanish moss draped over cypress branches rose and fell with the breeze. Dragonflies hovered inches above the canal until something triggered them to veer right or left and hover over another area. They moved like dots merging into one large fly.

Buster turned the pirogue a bit to the left, and we entered a narrower canal, passing first under a canopy of willow branches. When I looked back, it was as if a green door had been slammed closed behind us. As we continued into the canal, the overgrowth became thicker. At times the canopy of cypress over the water was so dense it nearly blocked out the sun. I saw an alligator sleeping under a fallen, rotting tree trunk and then another floated past us, its eyes glaring with suspicion or anticipation.

Buster laughed when I cringed. "Ain't nothin' to worry 'bout," he said. "I wrestle gators for fun." He followed that with a cackle that echoed in the bush. "You're a fancy lady now, ain'tcha? Betcha don't even remember livin' here, huh?"

"No. But I'm not a fancy lady," I replied. "Just where is this place?"

"Yonder, 'round the bend." He jerked his head to the left.

I shaded my eyes and gazed in that direction. Flowering honeysuckle covered the far bank. Two snowy egrets paraded on a rock while bullfrogs leaped around them, but I saw no shack and no other human beings.

The stillness got to me. Except for the sound of a dove or the cry of a marsh hawk, all I heard was Buster's grunt and the rhythmic dipping of his pole. Along a nearby bank, I saw a couple of nutrias dash into their dried domes of grass and then a white-tailed deer lifted its head, gazed our way, and turned to trot off. It was as if everything in nature knew to be wary of Buster Trahaw.

"What do you do?" I asked him. He had made little or no effort to start a conversation and had really volunteered nothing about himself.

"Whatcha mean, do?"

"Are you an oyster fisherman or a carpenter?"

"I ain't a lawyer," he said and laughed. "I fish some. I hunt some. I sell Spanish moss to the furniture people to stuff them chairs and sofas, and I do odd jobs when I got to," he said. "My daddy left me a little money, too. 'Course, most of its gone down the gullet," he added and cackled again, his Adam's apple bouncing against his sandpaper skin.

As we made the turn around the bend, Buster poled as hard as someone being chased.

"How did my mother get out here?" I asked suspiciously.

"She come from the other end," he said quickly.

"What other end?" I asked.

"Stop asking so many questions," he snapped. "I can't pole this pirogue and talk at the same time."

I felt my heart begin to thump. I spun around and gazed back. Cypress Woods was miles behind us. We entered another, even narrower canal. At times I could almost stretch out my arms and touch both sides. The mosquitoes looked bigger, and the clouds of them were thicker. The water was darker, too. Something slithered off a rock and slipped into the water just ahead of us. I cringed again.

"I don't like this," I said. "We're not getting anywhere. Take me back. I'll get someone to drive me to the other end," I said, but Buster didn't look at me, nor did he slow down. "Mr. Trahaw, I said . . ."

He turned and looked behind him.

"There it is," he announced as we broke out of the narrow canal and into a pond.

I saw a trapper's shack ahead. It sat about six feet off the marsh on pilings lined up in rows. The planks appeared to have been slapped together with chewing gum. Some dangled precariously over the windows. The railing of the gallery was cracked on the far end, and even from this distance I could see there were gaping holes in the floor. How could my mother ever go to such a place?

"My mother wouldn't be there," I declared.

"Why not? You know whose place that was?" he said with his lips in a tight smile. "That there was your great-grandpere's shack, missy. That's where the likes of you come from, so don't sit up so high and mighty, hear?"

"My great-grandpere's?"

"That's right. Jack Landry. He was a trapper and the best hunting guide in these parts. 'Course, now I am," he added. He poled faster, and I strained to see signs of Mommy.

"Where is she?"

"Lying on the cot inside, sick as a dog, I told ya. Happy you come now?"

I didn't reply. Cautiously I sat back and waited for him to reach the dock and tie up the pirogue. There was a very shaky stairway up to the gallery. He planted his foot against one step and reached for me.

"Come on. I'll help you up," he said. I stood up slowly, but the pirogue rocked and I nearly fell overboard. I cried out, and he laughed. "Reach out," he demanded. Reluctantly, I did so, and the moment his hand found mine, he pulled me forward with such force that I lost my footing and fell into his huge arms. He laughed again, held me there a moment and then lifted me out of the pirogue as if I weighed no more than a baby. I found as firm a footing as I could on the stairway and walked up to the gallery. He followed close behind.

Scattered over the gallery in a disorganized fashion were nets for oyster fishing, piles of Spanish moss, empty beer bottles, dirty bowls crusted with dried gumbo, and the only piece of furniture, a rocking chair tipped over on its side, the right arm snapped off. I paused. The planks dipped. I was sure I would step through one.

"It's all right. Go on inside," he said, waving toward the door. I walked forward slowly and entered what he said was once my great-grandpere's shack.

It was only one room. There was a plank table directly in front of us, covered with old dishes and empty beer and whiskey bottles. To the right was a cot, the stained gray blanket dumped beside it, the sheet brown stained and torn. Skins and furs dangled off nails along the walls. On a long shelf near the table were jars of pickled frogs, snakes, and the ugliest water insects I had ever seen. Everywhere I looked, I saw strewn clothing and sacks. The two windows were both caked with grime so thick the light was practically kept out.

"Where's my mother?" I asked.

"Well, I'll be," Buster said. "Looks like she just up and left and didn't clean up after herself neither." He laughed, and I turned when I heard something rattle. He was standing in the doorway behind me, a long metal chain in his hand.

"I want to go back immediately," I demanded.

"Well, that ain't very friendly, now, is it? And after all I done for your mother?" He laughed again.

"Right now," I said and started toward the door. He laughed again and wrapped his arms around me, lifting me up and carrying me to the cot while I screamed. He slapped me down hard, wrapped the chain around my right ankle, and snapped a padlock before I had a chance to resist.

"And the key's right here," he said, showing it to me before putting it in his right pants pocket. When I sat up to protest, he lifted his enormous right palm and threatened to slap me down. I took one look at the callused dirty fingers and that thick wrist and recoiled.

"What are you doing?" I cried.

"Getting what's coming to me," he said and backed away holding the other end of the chain. He ran it to a big metal pin that looked like a railroad spike embedded in a floor beam and locked that end with a padlock, too.

"What's coming to you?" I asked, terrified.

"A wife, that's what. I paid for a Landry some years back, and she run off. Then, when she returned and I went to claim what was legally mine, she had me arrested. I spent some time in the clink 'cause of her, but Buster Trahaw never forgets a debt owed him. No, ma'am. Relatives of mine," he continued, reaching for a bottle that had an inch or so of beer left in it, "told me you was here, so I come lookin', and sure enough, there you was. Well, I ain't particular which Landry I get, long as I get one that's been owed." He brought the neck of the bottle to his thick lips and sucked out the remaining beer, his throat contorting like the body of a snake. Then he flung the bottle across the room. It didn't shatter, but it bounced off the wall and fell to the floor.

"I figured since I was cheated, I could claim this

shack, but it ain't nothin' near the payment owed me." He smiled. "You make up the rest."

"What do you want from me?"

"Want?" He looked confused for a moment. "Why, I want a wife. You do what a wife supposed to do is what I want. First thing, you clean up this place. I give you enough lead on this chain so you can get around the shack. Right there," he said pointing to a rusty pot in the right corner, "is the diddly. You can use them old newspapers I got piled next to it."

"You can't do this," I cried. "This is kidnapping."

"'Course I can do it. It's what's owed, and out here in the swamps, a debt is a debt, hear?"

I started to cry. He stared at me a moment and then stepped toward me ominously. I cringed against the shack wall.

"I don't want to hear cryin'; I don't want to hear yellin'. I want a quiet, obedient woman, just like my daddy had twice. Now I got you somethin' to wear, somethin' that ain't fancy. You're a swamp woman now." He dug under the cot and came out with what looked like another sack. "Put this here on. Now!" he shouted, some spittle raining over me.

My body was shaking; I couldn't move. He reached down and grabbed my left arm just below the elbow, squeezing so hard, I screamed. Then his left hand cracked across my right cheek, snapping my head back. The shock of it was worse than the pain that followed. I couldn't speak or swallow down the throat lump. He dug his fingers into the top of my head and gathered a clump of my hair, pulling me to my feet. I was sobbing silently, my chest feeling as if it would burst.

"Get them fancy rags off now," he ordered. "Do it!"

My hands shaking, I began to unbutton my blouse. I was crying and shaking the whole time. When I slipped off my skirt, he smiled with satisfaction.

291

"You take all of that off," he ordered. "Even them store-bought underwear. Do it. I got to see what I got."

I thought I would faint first. The air in the shack was stifling. My skin was crimson from the heat of fear passing through my body. When I didn't move, he turned, found a wide, black leather belt in the pile of clothing, and wrapped one end of it around his wrist and hand. My eyes widened as he approached, lifting his arm. I raised my arms to protect myself, and he swung the belt and slapped me across the thigh. The blow took my breath away.

Instead of lifting me by my hair this time, he dug his fingers under my bra and pulled with such force that the hooks gave way and the bra was torn from my body. He tossed it over his shoulder. I fell back against the cot, screaming. He hit me again, this time on the other leg. I felt my eyes roll back, and then all was dark.

When I opened my eyes again, I was on my back on the cot, wearing the sack dress with nothing underneath. I didn't move. The pain along my thighs reminded me vividly of what had happened. I saw that my lucky dime was gone, too. At first I was afraid to turn to the right or the left, but when I did look, I saw he wasn't there. I took a deep breath and sat up to be sure he wasn't in a corner or below me on the floor. The shack was empty.

Encouraged and hopeful, I stood up, but realized I still had that chain locked around my ankle. I tried to slip it over my ankle bone, but it was too tight. Maybe I could get the other end loose, I thought. If I had to, I'd carry that chain for miles to escape.

As I started across the shack, I saw a large note pinned to the closed front door. It had apparently been written with a burned piece of wood: "I went to get some whiskey and food for you to cook. Clean up fore I get back. Your husband Buster."

Panicking, I hurried over to the railroad spike and tried to get that end of the chain loose, but it was just as tightly wrapped and locked.

I opened the front door and stepped out on the gallery. I realized Buster had taken my watch, but I knew I had been here for some time because the sun was down over the cypress trees, casting long, dark shadows over the canal. Buster wasn't in sight, but neither was anyone else. Even so, I yelled, "Anyone, please help me! Please, anyone!"

I waited. My voice echoed over the water and died in the swamp. An egret flew out of the trees, soared over the water, and disappeared down the canal. When I looked off the left side of the gallery, I saw that the sky was growing overcast. A thick bed of ash-gray clouds was sliding in over the turquoise background, and the wind had begun to blow through the swamp. Then I turned to the right side of the gallery and saw a cottonmouth snake that had woven its body through the slats. It tightened its coil when it saw me. I couldn't breathe. Slowly I made my way back to the shack doorway and then stepped in and slammed it shut.

Buster Trahaw could leave at will without worrying about my escaping. I was chained inside and guarded by every creature that lived in the swamp, I thought. What was I going to do? Afraid of what Buster would do if he returned and I hadn't cleaned, I started to straighten up the shack. I picked up and folded all the clothing, most of it filthy. I gathered the dishes and pans and put them in the sink. The water was rust brown, but I washed the dishes as best I could. When that was done, I scrubbed the plank table, straightened up what little furniture there was, and made the cot bed. I found a broom in the corner. Half of it was gone, but there was enough for me to sweep the plank floor. I took a wet rag and cleaned the windows. I looked everywhere for my clothes, but I couldn't find them. I guessed he had thrown them into the swamp along with my watch and bracelet.

There was a small wooden box in the far right corner. I was hoping there was something in it, perhaps a tool that I could use to tear off this lock and chain, even though I didn't know what I would do once I was free of it. There was no other canoe outside, and I certainly couldn't swim in the canal with alligators and snakes just waiting. I had no shoes either, so even if I made it to the marsh, I would be terrified stepping through the tall grass.

There were no tools in the box, just a pretty linen tablecloth with hand-embroidered birds; but under the tablecloth I found some old sepia-tinted photographs. They were pictures of a pretty young woman standing barefoot on the grass in front of my great-grandmere Catherine's shack. When I studied the face, I realized the woman resembled Mommy. Buster had claimed this was my great-grandpere Jack's trapper shack. I guess it was and this was my grandmere, Gabriel.

If only her spirit were here now, I thought, hoping for the only thing that could help me . . . a miracle. There were pictures of an older couple who I imagined were my great-grandmere Catherine and my great-grandpere Jack. In one of them, Great-Grandmere Catherine was holding a baby, who I imagined had to be Mommy. Seeing their faces and realizing who they were gave me some comfort and for the moment I felt a warmth and a sense of hope. Somehow, some way, I would get out of this horrible situation.

I put the pictures back and closed the wooden box. Then I stood up and gazed about the shack. Where could I hide? What could I use to defend myself? A trapper's long knife hung on the wall. I seized it. I had never imagined myself stabbing anyone, even the likes of Buster Trahaw, but when someone was desperate, even someone like me, she could reach down into places she never thought existed within herself and find the strength. I was sure of it.

Suddenly I heard his thin laugh. Then Buster shouted for his wife to come to the door. I put the knife back, intending to use it when I had the best opportunity, and then I tiptoed to the door and opened it just enough to peer out. I saw him poling up the swamp toward the shack, pausing every few moments to take a swig from his jug.

"Wife! Get out on the gallery and greet your husband!" he screamed. "Get your rump out there or I'll beat it till the skin comes off! Hear? Get out!"

Terrified to disobey, I stepped out on the gallery. Even the cottonmouth must have heard him and fled, for it wasn't there.

"Now, that's more like it," he cried. "Wave. Go on. Wave."

I lifted my hand and limply did so. He laughed again and poled harder until he reached the dock. The whole shack seemed to shake when he stepped up. He staggered for a moment and then smiled and handed me a bag of groceries.

"Got us our wedding dinner," he said. "And lots to drink. Buster's finally going to celebrate his marriage. Take it." I moved quickly and did so. Then I turned and went into the shack. He came in and stood gaping.

"Well, now, this is a wife. I knew it. I knew a Landry wouldn't let me down. Good woman. We gonna have a good life together."

"What is this?" I asked timidly when I took out what was in the bag and unwrapped some of it.

"Pig's feet and gizzards and all the fixin's for a

gumbo. Don't you know how to make a roux?" I shook my head. "What! Sure you do, woman. You just stand there and work until you get it right, hear? I'll just sit back here, drink a little rotgut, and watch my good woman work. Go on. Do it! And if it ain't good, I'll take it out on your hide. You got one nice hide, too." He put his large hand on my back and slid it down over my buttocks and squeezed until I cried out, which only made him laugh harder.

"First we eat; then we consummate the marriage," he said in a hoarse whisper. His lips were beside my ear, and his breath smelled like a dead rat. My stomach churned, and my legs felt as if they would crumble, but I closed my eyes and held myself up, fearing that if I did faint, it would only be worse.

Fumbling with the ingredients, I tried desperately to remember what our cook did. I had watched her work a few times. A roux was only a brown sauce, but every Cajun cook did something different to make it special. My hope was that Buster would be too drunk to know what anything really tasted like. For the time being, I had to pretend I knew what I was doing. And so I started to prepare the meal, which to Buster Trahaw was a celebration but to me was more like a last supper.

Buster sprawled on the cot as I worked, and after a while, when I turned to look at him, I saw he was asleep. I gazed up at the knife. I could get it off the wall quietly, tiptoe over to him and . . . Could I do it? Of course. I had dissected frogs and worms. I knew where the blade should go, but I had never deliberately killed anything. I cried if I accidentally stepped on a grasshopper. I knew, however, that if I didn't do something, Buster would have his way with me.

Maybe I could just frighten him into giving me the key to the lock, I thought. I could put the knife to his throat and tell him to get the key out of his pocket, or maybe I should just hit him hard over the head with the cast-iron frying pan. My body was shaking with all these choices.

I heard him grunt and then snore. His eyes were closed, and his head was turned to the wall. This was my chance to get the knife. I put down the mixing spoon gently and just as gently started toward the knife, holding the chain as I moved so it wouldn't rattle over the floor.

Buster grunted again and I paused, holding my breath. He blew air through his thick lips, snorted, and then began to snore again. I tiptoed closer to the knife, reached for it, nearly dropped it, and then clutched it to my bosom. I turned slowly and just as carefully made my way back. When I was only a foot or so from him, I closed my eyes and prayed for the strength.

Mommy could do this if she had to, I told myself. My father and poor Pierre were waiting for me to find Mommy and bring her home. I couldn't remain a prisoner in this shack much longer, and all that was standing between me and my freedom was this cruel man who didn't deserve an ounce of mercy. I stood there, hardening my heart against him until I was convinced I had the courage to do what had to be done. Then I stepped forward, raised the knife, and pressed the blade against his ugly Adam's apple, which resembled a small rodent under his skin.

I pressed it quickly, and his eyes snapped open.

"Wha . . ."

"Don't move a muscle," I said, "or I'll slice your throat the way you slice a pig's." I pressed the blade tighter.

"Hold on, now, hear?" he said. "That's a sharp knife."

"Then don't move until I tell you to move," I said.

"I ain't movin'. Damn," he said, sobering up quickly. "This ain't no way for a man's wife to behave."

"I am not your wife and I never will be," I said. "I'd rather be dead, so don't think I won't cut your throat," I warned. I was surprised at the fury and the determination in my voice. "I have this knife right up to your jugular. Your blood will spray all over that wall you're staring at," I warned him. I could see his eyes widen and bulge with the imagined sight.

"Easy, now," he said. "I'm not going to hurt you. You be my wife."

"I told you. I'm not your wife. Now reach slowly into your pocket and take out the key to this lock you have around my ankle. Go ahead, but slowly. Slowly!" I cried, pressing the blade against his throat again.

"I'm movin' easy," he cried. He slipped in his hand into his pocket and came up with the key. I took it quickly.

"Don't move. Put your hand back into your pocket," I ordered. "Go on." He did so.

It was a bit of a contortion for me, but I lifted my foot up to the cot, threaded the key into the lock and turned it. It snapped open, and I took it off, loosening the chain so I could slip my foot free.

Now my problems were just starting, I thought. Once I took the knife from his throat, what was to prevent him from turning on me and attacking me again? Thinking quickly, I realized I could just duplicate what he had done. I picked up the chain and put it over his leg.

"Whatcha doin'?"

"Lift this leg. Lift it!" I screamed, keeping the knife pressed tightly to his throat. He did so and I pulled the chain under and around, threaded the lock through the links just the way he had done to tighten the chain, and snapped it shut. Then I took a deep breath to try to slow my heartbeat.

"You're crazy, woman. You can't do this to Buster Trahaw."

I counted to three and pulled the knife away and stepped back just a second before he took his hand out of his pocket and reached out to grab my wrist. Only an inch of space fell between us, but it was enough. I ran for the door as he turned on the cot and lunged.

He had enough chain to reach a foot or so out the front door, so I had to get out and to the pirogue before he reached that point. I nearly slipped and fell into the water when I hurried down the steps. I grabbed the railing. It cracked, but held my weight and I swung around to get my footing again.

Buster was out the door, waving his mallet-sized fist in the air and cursing. "You git back here and unlock this chain, hear? Git back here!"

I flung the key into the air and it plopped into the water. Buster's eyes bulged with fury. His face was cherry red; he looked as if the blood vessels in his cheeks and forehead would burst. He was so shocked and angry he couldn't form sensible words. He stuttered and stammered and waved his fist wildly, pounding his own thigh. Then he jerked on the chain, straining so hard the veins in his neck popped against the skin. Fortunately, he couldn't get the chain over his knee. However, the effort and the pain filled him with even greater frustration.

I didn't wait to see what he would do next. I stepped into the pirogue, untied it, and took the pole into my hands the way I had seen him do it. I pushed away from the dock.

"Don't you dare leave Buster Trahaw!" he screamed. "Don't you dare!"

I pushed down. The pole went so deep, I thought I would never reach bottom. I nearly fell over with the attempt and my effort to steady myself. The pirogue started rocking precariously. Terrified of falling into

299

the murky canal water, I sat down hard and waited for the canoe to steady itself. Buster continued to scream, his voice driving birds out of the branches. I think even the fish swam away.

I rose again and, more carefully this time, stuck the pole into the water until I found something solid. I pushed and the momentum sent the canoe forward. Another thrust moved it faster. I felt more confident and did it again. When I turned, however, I saw that I was driving the canoe toward a pile of fallen cypress trees. I switched sides quickly and poled to the opposite direction. Then I looked back at the shack. Buster had been quiet for a moment. He was staring at me, disbelieving; but when he saw I was making headway, his anger rushed back in an even greater wave of rage. He stepped back into the shack and then charged forward, tearing the spike from the floor and freeing the chain.

His momentum carried him over the railing and into the swamp. He fell with a gigantic splash. For a moment I just stood there watching, and then I saw him pop up. Chain and all, he started to swim after me. I dug the pole in frantically, my fear making my efforts clumsy. The canoe went too far to the right, hit a rock, bounced, then went too far to the left and almost got caught up in weeds. I pushed and tugged.

Buster drew closer and closer. His powerful body cut through the swamp water almost as quickly as an alligator. I could see his red face drawing nearer. I cried and dug the pole down, pushed and pushed, sobbing as I struggled to stay a few feet ahead of him.

"I'll get you and whip you good!" he vowed. "Stop that canoe." He paused to wave his fist at me, and I dug in again so I could make the turn and pass through the narrow opening to enter the wider canal. For a moment he was gone from sight. I developed a smoother rhythm and pushed with more accuracy, but

I hadn't realized that the canal was shallow at the turn. When Buster reached it, he gathered the chain in his hands and walked over the mound. Just when I thought I might have put enough distance between us to make his catching up with me impossible, he appeared only a half dozen feet away on the shore.

I pushed harder. Desperation gave me needed strength. He scampered through the narrow water and then dived in again, holding the chain with one arm for a moment, like a lifeguard saving a drowning swimmer. His power and determination were overwhelming. Surely he could catch me soon, I thought, and I would be doomed to a terrible punishment.

When the water grew deeper, he released the chain and began to swim with both arms. Now he was less than a half dozen feet from the canoe. I was only going to have a few more moments of freedom, I thought, and I contemplated diving into the swamp myself if he seized the canoe in those big hands of his. He might very well pull it over anyway, spilling me into the canal.

I was so tired. My thrusts grew shorter and the length of time between them longer. My hands were stinging with the effort, the skin on my palms blistered and bleeding. My shoulders ached, and my chest felt as if I had swallowed a rock which lay there, just under my pounding heart.

"Leave me alone!" I cried when he drew close enough for me to see his clenched teeth and snarling lips.

He dug his arms into the water with more determination, and then suddenly he stopped with a jerk.

"What the . . ." he cried with surprise. I saw him duck down and pull on the chain. "I'm caught on somethin'," he yelled. He treaded water as he struggled to free the chain.

I hesitated, held the pole, and let the canoe drift on

301

its own for a moment. He could be faking it, I thought, but he did look as if he had been surprised.

"Help me!" he called. "Don't leave me out here like this. Get back here."

Something splashed on my right.

"Alligator!" he yelled.

What was I going to do? If I went back and saved him, he would surely hurt me, but . . . to leave him there, helpless . . .

Maybe he would be grateful and too tired to take any revenge, I thought. I just couldn't leave him. A side of me was shouting warnings as I attempted to stop the pirogue and turn it back toward him. It took more effort than I imagined, but the canoe finally stopped its forward motion. He was waving and shouting. A good distance had developed between us.

I dug the pole in and pushed, using all my weight to start the canoe back. It inched forward and then picked up some momentum.

"That's a good woman," he cried. "That's a good wife. Buster ain't goin' to hurt you anymore. You can do what you want. Just get me out of the water fast. Come on, push on that pole. Good."

I pushed again and then I heard him splashing water and screaming at something. "Get out of here, go on, git."

I looked back and saw Buster lift a long, green snake out of the water and fling it. Then he shouted again, his voice far more shrill. The reason showed itself in the form of an alligator tail slapping the water nearby and then another one and another one. Buster was spinning around, fighting them off, but suddenly his head bobbed.

"Oh, my God," I muttered.

His head emerged. I saw him gasp for air and then go down again. He rose once more, but this time his body was limp and his arms weren't swinging. He floated there a moment and then went under. Bubbles formed where his head had been, and then they popped and all was still. I waited and watched. My stomach churned. I had to sit down because I started to dry-heave. I gasped and held my breath and then gasped. Every time I looked back at where he had been, I felt nauseated. Finally, that feeling subsided, but it was followed by a wave of fatigue that made my legs feel as if they were made of cement.

I gazed at my torn up hands, felt the aches in my arms and shoulders, but stood up and began to pole again anyway. I did so slowly, methodically, realizing I was slipping into a state of shock. I was terrified of what would happen to me if I passed out in the swamp.

When I looked ahead, I realized I was going through a canal, but there were other openings along the way. Which one would take me back to Cypress Woods? Should I turn right or left, take the first or second? All of the canals looked the same right now; the vegetation, rocks, and fallen cypresses resembled the ones I had seen when Buster poled the pirogue to the shack. Panicking, I made a choice, only to discover it led to a shallow, brackish cove with no other outlet. I had to turn about and pole back.

My stomach ached with an emptiness that made me feel light-headed. Here I was, a girl who had grown up in the Garden District of New Orleans, living in the finest home, catered to, spoiled, dainty, now dressed in a potato sack, poling a half-rotted canoe through a swamp filled with insects, alligators, snakes, and snapping turtles. And I was lost!

I started to laugh. I knew it was a hysterical reaction, but I couldn't help it. My laughter echoed around me and soon turned to sobs. When I succeeded in getting the canoe into another, wider canal, I paused and sat down. My throat was so dry I couldn't swallow and my tongue felt like a lump of sand. I gazed about helplessly, looking for some sign, some indication of direction. How could the bayou people make their way through these swamps? I wondered.

Exhausted and defeated, I lay back. The pirogue rocked with the movement of the water. Two egrets flew over me and peered down curiously but cautiously before flying off. They were followed by a more courageous cardinal who landed on the bow of the pirogue and did a small tap dance with its eyes on me.

"Do you know how to get out of here?" I asked.

The cardinal lifted his wings as if to shrug and then flew off after the egrets. I closed my eyes again and settled back, too tired to think. I must have fallen asleep for a few moments and drifted, for when I opened my eyes again, I was bouncing gently against a fallen cypress tree. A family of muskrats had trekked up to sniff and study me, but when I moved, they all scurried into the bush. I sat up, dipped my hand into the water, and scrubbed my face to wake myself up. Then I stood up and pushed the canoe away from the tree.

Just as I started to thrust the pole into the water, I heard the hum of a motorboat. It was hard to tell from which direction it was coming, but I waited. It grew louder, and I realized it was coming from my right. I poled the canoe in that direction. A moment later the boat appeared. It was just a small dinghy, but I saw Jack sitting in it. No sight ever looked better.

"Jack!" I shouted.

The sound of the motor kept him from hearing my shout as he went past. I screamed again, but he disappeared around a bend. Frustrated, I poled the canoe in his direction, but what chance did I have to catch up with a motorboat? I eventually stopped and sat down again, feeling an overwhelming sense of defeat. The water lapped against the canoe. I glanced upward at a sky turned stormy and forbidding, heralding rain and wind. What if there was another hurricane?

I put my stinging palms together under my chin, closed my eyes and prayed.

"Dear God," I said. "I know I haven't been as religious as I should be, and I know I have a scientist's skepticism about miracles, but I hope you will hear me and have mercy on me."

I rocked back and forth and started to sing a hymn. Then I closed my eyes and lay back again. Perhaps there was such a thing as destiny, I thought. Perhaps Mommy's faith in the inevitability of fate existed. Somehow, for reasons that would always remain mysterious, it was determined that I would be brought back to these swamps and they would claim me. Maybe all my efforts to become a doctor, to be someone else, were foolish vain efforts after all. Someone with stronger gris-gris had put a curse on our family, and we couldn't overcome it. I began to understand why Mommy felt she had to run away, to find some way to save her family from what she believed was inevitable disaster.

I was even too tired to cry. All I could do was lie there and wait for something terrible to happen. And then I heard the distant murmur of the dinghy motor again. It grew louder. I sat up and waited. Moments later the dinghy appeared. Jack saw me and steered in my direction. He cut his engine and brought the dinghy up beside my canoe. He was too shocked to speak; he just stared for a moment. I stared back, not sure if he was an illusion or real.

"Pearl, I've been frantic, searching for you. What are you doing in that canoe? And why are you dressed in a . . . a sack?"

Instead of answering, I started to cry. He moved quickly to get me safely into his dinghy.

"Look at you; look at your hands. What happened?"

"Oh, Jack," I said, "Buster Trahaw . . . tricked me into going with him. He took me to a shack, where he chained me up and said I was his wife. I escaped, but he came after me. Then he drowned or was eaten by alligators, and . . ." I was too exhausted to continue.

"Mon Dieu." He kissed my cheek and held me. "Don't worry. You're safe now. I won't let anything else happen to you. Let me get you back to Cypress Woods."

He started the motor, and we were off.

I looked back once at the pirogue bobbing in the swamp water. It had taken me to hell and back.

15

Eye of the Storm

When we arrived at the dock, Jack helped me out of the dinghy. My legs wobbled, and I had to lean against him for a moment. The full impact of what had happened to me and what I had gone through hit me the moment I set foot on safe soil. The rain had started again, too, but the two of us barely noticed. Jack scooped me up into his strong arms, lifting me like a baby.

"Jack, you don't have to carry me," I protested.

"I got grease cans that weigh more than you," he said, smiling. It did seem effortless for him to march up the pathway with me in his arms. He carried me all the way to his trailer. I realized that both of us were soaked to the skin—me especially, in the poor excuse for a dress Buster had forced me to wear. Some of the other riggers came running over to see what had happened, but Jack didn't stop to explain. He didn't put me down until we were inside.

"At least you can take a hot shower here. Get that sack off your body. I'll find something for you to wear.

307

Then we'll call the police and tell them what happened."

"I'd better call home, too, and see how Daddy's doing," I said, wiping the matted hair from my forehead and eyes. A small puddle had formed at my feet. "I'm making a mess."

"Don't worry."

Jack saw the welts on my legs that had resulted from Buster's whipping me with his leather belt.

"Maybe I should get you to a doctor or a traiteur," he suggested. "That doesn't look so good."

"It's all right. The skin wasn't broken. I'll put some ice on the bumps afterward."

"I forgot," he said smiling. "You're on your way to becoming a doctor. Comes in handy having you around."

I felt so dirty after what I had been through that I stayed in the shower until Jack knocked on the door to see if I was all right.

"Pearl!"

"I'm okay," I cried. I just stood there enjoying the warm water in my hair. I heard him open the door.

"I'll leave the clothing here," he shouted. I turned off the water and pulled back the curtain to peer out. He had given me a pair of his dungarees, one of his plaid shirts, and a pair of his slippers and socks.

"You can keep the pants on with this piece of rope," he said when I laughed. "I'm sorry I don't have any skirts."

"It'll do for now. Thanks."

"You okay?"

"I am now," I said. He beamed.

"I made some hot tea, and I've got biscuits and jam waiting."

"Thanks, Jack."

After I dried myself and put on his clothes, I

wrapped the towel around my hair. He looked up from the stove when I emerged.

"I feel like a new person, especially in these clothes," I said. I had rolled up the legs on the dungarees to make them shorter, but they were still much too large for me, as was Jack's shirt. "I guess I'm a pretty funny sight, huh?"

"You look great to me. Never knew my clothes would look that good on anyone." He smiled and then his smile turned quickly into a stern expression. "Now sit yourself down," he said, pointing to the chair.

His anger took me by surprise, and I sat down quickly. "What's wrong?"

He folded his arms across his chest and straightened his shoulders.

"How dare you go off with someone like that and just leave me a note? Do you know I came this close," he said, pinching his thumb and forefinger together, "to missing it? And when I read the name Trahaw, I almost had heart failure. I still can't believe you went into the swamp with that low-life scum."

"Jack, he said he knew where my mother was so I—"

"For a woman who is supposedly so intelligent, you sure do dumb things."

I looked down, my chin quivering.

"I'm sorry I'm bawling you out, Pearl, but when I saw you were gone and I realized you had gone into the swamp with that guy, I felt about as low as I ever felt in my life. I thought for sure I was never going to see you again."

I lifted my tear-filled eyes to him and saw he was very sincere.

"I'm sorry, Jack. It was stupid of me. I should have talked with you first."

"Yeah, well, maybe. He probably would have tried to stop you, though, and that might have even been worse," he offered in a compromising tone.

"I can't imagine it being worse than it was, Jack," I said.

He nodded and then turned when the teakettle whistled. He prepared me a cup of tea and gave me the biscuits and jam.

"Thank you." I didn't think I was hungry, but I devoured the biscuit and then ate a second one.

Jack laughed.

"I'll bring you some more," he said. "I don't want you taking bites out of the table."

"I guess I didn't realize how much energy I used poling that pirogue."

"Okay," he said bringing me another biscuit. "Tell me all about it now."

Jack sat across from me and listened to my description of what had happened in the shack and how I had escaped. After I was finished, he nodded his head, his eyes fixed firmly on me, a new look of appreciation in them.

"I take back what I said before. All of that was pretty fast thinking, even for a city girl," he said.

Jack had a smile that beamed so much warmth that I thought I could remain forever in the glow. His eyes and his gentle lips made me feel more than just safe. I was where I belonged, where I was meant to be. I used to question Mommy all the time about the magic of love, wondering if there really was such a thing as two people being drawn to each other by mystical forces not explained in laboratories. I wanted to believe in it, but since it had never happened to me, I was skeptical. Then all of my cynicism melted away under the heat of Jack's warm eyes.

"I'd better call home and see how Daddy is," I said softly.

Jack nodded. "Then I'll call the police. You'll have to tell them what happened and about where you think Buster went down."

"I don't know that, Jack. Everywhere in the swamp looks the same to me."

"Don't worry about it," he said. "My guess is no one's going to miss the likes of Buster Trahaw anyway."

Aubrey answered when I called home and told me Daddy was asleep. "He's asked after you a number of times, however, mademoiselle."

"Tell him I'll phone again as soon as I can, Aubrey. Tell him I'm all right, and tell him . . ."

"Yes, mademoiselle?"

"Nothing, Aubrey. I'll call later," I added. Why give Daddy the bad news now? I thought. I hadn't found Mommy. I had almost gotten myself trapped and maybe even killed, and I could do nothing to help Pierre.

"Don't drop the potato," Jack advised when I cradled the receiver and he saw the look of dismay on my face.

I smiled, remembering how Mommy often used that Cajun expression. "We're not licked yet," Jack added with steely, determined eyes.

I flashed another grateful smile, but in my heart I had given up hope. After all, there was nothing more to do here. I might as well head home.

Jack called the police, and a little while later a patrol car arrived with two officers. They listened to my tale, shaking their heads in disbelief.

"We'll get a couple of patrol boats into the canal and see if there's anything left of him," one of the policemen told me. "We know that your mother is missing. Your father called our station and spoke to the chief, and Mrs. Pitot has called a few times, too.

311

We've got your mother's description and we're keeping our eyes open."

I thanked him, and then Jack followed the two policemen outside to finish talking to them where I couldn't hear. When I looked out the window, I saw them shaking their heads with even more pity in their eyes. Jack shook their hands and they left, but almost as soon as they had, the other riggers gathered around to hear the story. Reluctantly, Jack described the events. Then they called to me and I stepped into the open doorway to hear their anger over what had occurred.

Everyone then volunteered to do something for me. One wanted to drive into Houma and buy me some new clothes. The others wanted to form a search party and traipse through the swamps searching for Mommy, but Jack explained why he didn't think that would do any good.

"Don't you worry, mademoiselle," they declared. "None of the Trahaws will ever set foot on this property again."

"You mean there are more of them?" I asked Jack.

"Cousins, but they don't live near here," he said, glaring angrily. I knew he was just trying to ease my fears.

"She'll be all right," he assured the other riggers. "Go on back to work." He came inside.

"I guess I had better think about going back to New Orleans before it gets too late, Jack."

"I hate to see you make that trip after what you've been through. Can't you stay one more night, rest up, and then go home? What difference will a few more hours make? You need some rest, Pearl. Just sprawl out on the sofa there and take a nap. I'll finish up what I have to do at the well and then make us a good dinner."

"I don't know. I should get home, Jack. Daddy needs me, and I've been away from Pierre too long."

"All right," he said after a moment's thought. "You'll rest and have dinner, and then I'll drive back to New Orleans with you. Bart can have Jimmy Wilson take over my work tomorrow. I'll catch a bus back."

"I can't ask you to do that for me, Jack," I protested.

"You're not asking. I'm telling you," he said. "You're in Cajun country now, and when a Cajun man speaks . . ."

"Yes?" I said, smiling.

"*Sometimes* a Cajun woman listens," he replied and we both laughed. The fatigue he'd predicted struck me. I yawned and fought to keep my eyes open.

"Just get over there and lie down for a while, hear?" he ordered.

"Yes, sir," I said, saluting. But I did what he said and sprawled on the sofa. I closed my eyes, vaguely listening to him clean up the cups and dishes. Before he left the trailer to check on his work, I was asleep, and I didn't wake up again until long after he had returned, made dinner, and set the table for us. It was already quite dark outside. I was shocked at how long I had slept. Jack didn't know I was awake. He lit a candle and stood there for a moment gazing down at the small flame. The illumination threw a soft glow over his face, and when he turned, the candlelight was reflected in his eyes.

"Hey, how are you?" he asked.

"A little groggy. How long did I sleep?"

"A while," he said coming over to me. He sat beside me and took my hand.

"I guess you were right. I was a lot more tired than I thought."

313

"Hungry?"

I nodded. The aroma of the food churned my empty stomach.

"Good. Tonight I have a real Cajun feast: baked stuffed red snapper with brown oyster sauce," he bragged.

"How did you learn to be such a good cook?" I asked, amazed.

"What are you talking about? I'm a Cajun," he replied as if that explained it. "Don't you know people say Cajuns can eat anything they catch and make it taste good?"

"I've heard that said, yes. What can I do to help?"

"You can sit down and eat. Everything's done," he said. I got up, washed my face, and joined him at the table. He poured us some white wine, and then I ate ravenously again. Jack sat there watching me gobble down his delicious dinner, a small, tight smile on his lips.

"Jack Clovis," I said pausing between bites, "this is delicious. Did you really prepare all this?"

"Well . . ."

"I thought so," I said. "Where did you get it?"

"I picked it up at a restaurant," he confessed, "and just warmed it up. But I had you convinced, didn't I?"

"That's because I trusted you," I said.

He stopped smiling and reached for my hand. "If I ever tell you a lie, Pearl, I'll tell you the truth in the next breath, and I'll never tell you a lie that could hurt you," he promised.

"It's all right, Jack. I'm not angry. I'm too hungry," I said, and he laughed.

He put on some zydeco music, and we finished our dinner with rich Cajun coffee and strawberry shortcake. I was so stuffed I couldn't move, but I felt content and well rested.

"Now are you going to listen to me and stay overnight?" he asked.

The thought of the long ride back and in the dark was overwhelming. "I guess," I said. "But I'll have to leave right after I wake up."

"Deal," Jack declared.

"I'm helping with the dishes," I insisted.

"I'm not stopping you," he replied. I poked him in the shoulder and he pretended to poke me back. We giggled and hugged. It felt so good to be light and carefree after what I had experienced. Just being with Jack put me at ease. While I was washing and rinsing the dishes, he came up behind me and kissed me softly on the back of my neck. I paused and felt his arms around my waist. I leaned back against him, closed my eyes, and invited more of his kisses on my cheeks, my neck, and finally, when I turned to him, my lips.

"You can leave those dishes," he whispered and once again lifted me into his arms. He carried me through the trailer to his bedroom and set me down gently. It was dark, but the clouds had broken and the rain was long gone. Shards of moonlight sliced through the darkness and through the trailer window to illuminate our silhouettes. Quietly, neither of us saying a word, we undressed. Naked, beneath the blanket, we kissed again, and I felt myself slip softly, comfortably, perfectly into his embrace.

Jack was very gentle. His lips were as soft as feathers, trailing down to my stomach and then up to lift and caress my breasts again. My moans were small whimpers that accompanied my quickened breathing. Even after he entered me, our movements remained graceful and gentle, building slowly to each crescendo and then building on that crescendo to reach greater heights each time, taking my breath away. Soon I was spinning, but it was a pleasant vertigo, a light-headed feeling that made me giddy. I felt as if I were falling back, but I didn't feel endangered. It was a wonderful free fall, a flight through ecstasy.

Jack's whispered words of love filled my ears along with the pounding of my own heart. I couldn't stop myself from telling him how much I loved him, too. The flood of emotion that had been damned up behind my wall of skepticism and fear broke free, and the rush of passion that followed threatened to drown us both. I clung to him; I demanded more and returned his kisses with more intensity.

Once I had feared I could never be a lover, but Jack's surprised laughter and plea to let him catch his breath made me realize those fears were foolish. I was the lightning that needed the right marriage of elements to fire up the night sky, and the right elements were someone who really loved me and someone I really loved.

Finally he turned over on his back and cried, "Mercy!"

I laughed and we held hands and waited for our hearts to stop pounding and our breathing to slow down. Then he lifted my hand to his lips and kissed my fingers. He put my hand over his heart.

"Feel how content my heart is now," he said. "Feel how it beats for you."

"And mine too, Jack," I said bringing his hand to my breast. We lay beside each other quietly, astounded by how hard and how deeply we loved. I realized this was like the eye of the storm, the quiet that came in the midst of turmoil. Jack told me the hurricane was in me because I had been born in one. Maybe he was right. In the throes of all this disaster and tragedy, I had found him waiting to embrace me; I'd found his love, and with it I'd found the strength to battle the storm to follow.

I closed my eyes and drifted into a soft, pleasing

sleep, but sometime in the night, as if I had been nudged, I woke. My eyelids fluttered. For a moment I had forgotten where I was. Then I heard Jack's soft breathing beside me, and I relaxed. Then I turned and gazed out the window that faced Cypress Woods. Immediately my heart began to pound, and I sprang up as if I had a coil in my spine.

"Jack!"

"Wha . . . what is it?"

"Look." I pointed at the house. Just barely visible in a corner window of my mother's art studio was the glow of candlelight.

Jack sat up and studied the great house looming against the purple night sky. His eyes narrowed and he turned to me slowly. In a whisper he said, "Someone's up there all right."

Quickly we dressed. Jack grabbed a flashlight and a shotgun.

"It could be burglars," he explained when he saw my surprise.

I was hoping beyond hope that it was my mother, but another possibility occurred to me. "Or Buster Trahaw's cousins?" I asked.

Jack grimaced, but he didn't deny the possibility. Instead, he reached into the drawer and took out another handful of shotgun shells.

We got into my car and drove up to the mansion. The night sky was an eerie purple with the cloud cover broken here and there to permit some stars to twinkle. The strong breeze made the willows and cypresses sway ominously. Shadows seemed to float and twist over the grounds. When we stepped out of the car, I heard the cry of a night heron and then saw it flap its wings and sail over the field and toward the marsh.

I looked up at the mansion. The candlelight was still glowing in the window.

Jack took my hand and walked quickly to the side stairway. He paused at the first step. "Let me lead the way," he whispered. "And let's go up as quietly as we can."

I tried to swallow, but couldn't. My heart was thumping so loud I was sure that if it was a burglar, he would hear it. I was afraid to breathe. Slowly, cautiously, we mounted the steps that would take us to the studio. I thought they creaked enough to announce our approach. I tried to be as light-footed as possible. Once upstairs, Jack hesitated, checked his shotgun, and then, keeping me behind him, opened the door with a strong, quick thrust.

At first neither of us saw anyone. A few white candles were burning around an easel upon which there was a blank canvas. Then she stepped out of the shadows, resembling a shadow herself. It was Mommy, finally.

"Mommy!" I cried with joy. Jack lowered his shotgun as I hurried past him, but I stopped short midway.

Mommy was behaving as if she didn't hear us or see us. She wore a slight smile and moved as if she were sleepwalking. Her hair was disheveled, strands curling every which way. Her face was streaked with grime, a dark blotch on her chin, and her dress was creased and crinkled, spotted and stained, suggesting she had slept in it the whole time she had been away, and slept outside, too! In her hands she clutched some charcoal pens and a rag.

"Mommy, it's me, Pearl," I said and waited. She turned her back to me and stared at the blank canvas, which was caked with dust. Jack stood beside me, gazing at her curiously, too. "Mommy? Don't you hear me?" I asked. She didn't turn. "Jack, what's wrong with her?"

"She's in some sort of daze," he said. "Careful."

We drew closer. I reached out and touched her shoulder. She put her hand over mine and patted it.

"It's all right," she said in a loud whisper that sent chills along my spine. "All I have to do is draw his face the way I last remember it, the way it was in my heart. He's trapped, you see, because of what he did.

"But you shouldn't blame him. No one should blame him, not even the church. He was very distraught. I should have realized he would be; I shouldn't have accepted his sacrifice so readily. We were all he had, really.

"Oh, he had this great house and all these grounds with their rich oil wells, but money had no meaning to him if he didn't have the people he loved around him, people on whom to spend the money.

"How he suffered," she continued, "until he could stand the suffering no more. He went out to the swamps to remember us, to recall those youthful days when we were always together, innocent and loving, believing in the promise of tomorrow and never dreaming there were monsters looming all around us, even in our very hearts.

"He went through great turmoil, drinking and crying and bemoaning his fate, and then he decided he could not survive with half a life, and he cast his measly existence to the wind. He dived into the water and swam in circles until he could swim no more. Then, choking, filling his lungs with the swamp water, he dragged his poor body to the shore and perished under the stars that had once looked so dazzling and promising to him.

"And it was largely my fault. Selfishly I had accepted his love and his help, and then, when my true love was available to me once again, I deliberately closed my eyes to Paul's suffering and accepted his generosity once more. I had a new existence; I was with the one I loved, beside him every night, while

Paul was beside an empty space he could fill only with his dreams. It wasn't enough.

"I put him through such torment. I pretended to oppose his every offer. I put up an argument to dissuade him, but I gave in to his arguments. I let him fool himself. Worst of all, perhaps, I let him love Pearl as if she were his daughter. I let him pretend to be her father; I let him have that illusion, and then I swept it out of his hands and his heart.

"He had lost everything that mattered, you see, and I had been a party to all that pain."

"Mommy . . ." Tears were streaming down my cheeks, tears that burned into my heart because I felt her suffering so strongly.

She patted my hand again, but kept her eyes fixed on the blank canvas. "No, no, there's no use pretending any more or denying. Grandmere Catherine told me: every time we incubate an evil thought or commit an evil act, another evil spirit is set loose in the world to do battle with the good. The evil spirits I set loose have finally come to roost. They found their way to my home. I must do what I must do," she said softly.

"What must you do, Mommy?" I asked, terrified of the answer.

"Grandmere Catherine's spirit told me. I slept on her grave last night and waited for her words of wisdom to seep into my brain. I must put the face of Paul that is in my heart on this canvas."

She took a rag and wiped away the dust. "And then I must bring it to his grave and set it afire so his troubled spirit can return to him and he can escape from limbo."

"Mommy, you've got to come home with me," I said through my tears. "I'm here now, with you. It's me, Pearl. Please. Look at me. Listen to me. We need you. Pierre needs you. Daddy needs you."

She didn't turn around. She raised her charcoal pencil to the canvas and began to draw a face.

"Mommy!"

"Wait," Jack said, putting his hands on my shoulders. "Let her do this first."

"Do this? But she's gone mad, Jack. I've got to make her snap out of it!" I cried.

"You won't succeed, and she won't be any good to you or to your brother. I've seen people like this before," he confessed. "At religious gatherings where a traiteur has conducted a ceremony to drive away a mental problem. Sometimes it worked, sometimes not, but you've got to let her do what she thinks she's been told to do."

"This is like black magic, voodoo. Jack, it's a waste of time."

"That's not for you to decide, Pearl. The important thing is, she believes it. You don't have to believe it. I'm not a psychiatrist, but I know the power of the mind when it comes to these things. You weren't brought up in the bayou where religion and superstitions are married to form a different set of beliefs, but your mother was. Leave her alone for a while," he insisted.

I looked back at Mommy. She had already shaped the face and was working on the eyes and the nose. As she worked, she began to hum softly. I had never heard the tune, but I saw how it brought a gentle smile to her face, a smile that suggested she was enjoying some memory.

The miracle in Mommy's fingers was never as evident as it was now. In minutes she brought the face on the dirty old canvas to life. I saw a glint in the eyes, felt the twisted movement in the mouth, and easily imagined a breath. Her hands flew over the canvas as if they had a mind of their own, as if the picture were flowing out through her fingers. There was enough detail in it for me to recognize Uncle Paul, but the expression on his face was frightening. I had seen it a hundred times. It was the face of the man in the water.

I gasped and backed into Jack's arms. "She's drawing him the way I've seen him in countless nightmares."

"It must be her nightmare too, then," he said.

Finally she lowered her arms and took a small step back. She looked at the picture and whispered, "I'm sorry."

She then dropped the charcoal and started to lift the canvas.

Jack stepped forward quickly. "Let me help you, Madame Andreas," he said.

She looked at him, smiled softly, and nodded. He lifted the canvas from the easel.

"What are we going to do now, Jack?" I asked.

"We'll do what she wants," he replied. "Go on. Help her along."

I took Mommy's elbow and gently turned her toward the doorway.

"Thank you, dear," she said, but kept her eyes forward as we followed Jack out of the studio, down the stairs, and out of the house, moving with funereal slowness.

"I know where Paul Tate is buried," Jack told me. We continued around the side of the house. Jack held the flashlight so the beam parted the darkness and provided a path for us to the iron-gated cemetery that contained a single tomb. In the glow of Jack's flashlight, it looked ghoulishly yellow instead of gray. Uncle Paul's name and dates were engraved on the granite, as was his epitaph: "Tragically lost but not forgotten."

Mommy paused at the entrance and turned to Jack

and me. "Thank you," she said. "But I must be alone now."

"I understand, madame," Jack said and handed her the canvas. I was deeply impressed with his understanding and sensitivity.

My mother took the canvas and entered the small graveyard.

Jack stepped back and reached for my hand. We waited and watched.

Mommy knelt at the tomb and lowered her head. She said a silent prayer and then laid the canvas against the stone. She looked up at the stars. Her shoulders shook with her sobs, and then she seemed to gather new strength before producing a book of matches.

Carefully she lit one and held it to the corner of the canvas. It took a while, but the flame finally leaped from the match to the dried material. The flame grew, consuming the canvas, traveling up toward the picture of Uncle Paul. Mommy remained there, staring into the flames. The smoke curled upward until it was caught by a breeze and carried into the night. Soon the canvas was burning fully, the flames so bright they illuminated the tomb and its surroundings. Mommy looked like part of the fire for a moment, and then, as quickly as it had exploded into a small conflagration, it began to dwindle. The canvas collapsed into ashes and sparks near the stone tomb. When it looked nearly burned out, Jack released my hand and stepped into the fenced graveyard. I followed.

He knelt down to take my mother's arms and help her to her feet.

"It's time to go now, madame," Jack said. "It's over."

"Yes," she whispered. "Yes. It's over."

"Mommy?"

Slowly she turned and, like one emerging from a deep sleep, gazed at me and realized who I was. Her face softened into a happy smile. "Pearl, my darling, Pearl."

"Mommy," I cried and embraced her. We held each other for a long moment. My body shook with sobs against her, and she stroked my hair gently, kissing my forehead. I straightened up and wiped the tears from my eyes and cheeks, smiling. "Are you all right?"

"Yes, dear. I'm all right."

"We've got to go home, Mommy. We've got to get back to Daddy and Pierre. Pierre needs you desperately. He thinks you blame him for what happened to Jean, and the doctors say that's why he won't come out of his catatonic state."

She nodded, thoughtful. And then she looked at Jack, really noticing him for the first time.

"This is Jack Clovis, Mommy. He's helped me, helped us."

She smiled at him. "Thank you," she said.

Jack nodded. "Let me continue to help you, madame. Come to my trailer and freshen up for your journey home," he suggested.

"That's very kind of you, monsieur." She gazed back at the tomb where the sparks continued to die. She sighed deeply, took one step forward, a contented smile on her face, and then collapsed into Jack's quick arms.

I gasped. He lifted her as easily as he had lifted me. "She's all right," he said. "She's just exhausted. Let's get her to the trailer."

He carried her to the car and put her in the front seat. I sat beside her, keeping her head on my shoulder until we reached the trailer. She was already regaining consciousness when we brought her in and set her down on the sofa. I put a cold washcloth over her forehead, and Jack got her some cold water. Her eyes continued to flutter and close, flutter and close. Finally, they remained open, but she looked very confused.

"You're all right, Mommy. You're safe now."

"Where am I?" she asked gazing around.

I explained and she drank some water.

"I don't even know what day it is," she said. "I've lost all track of time."

"When did you last eat, Madame Andreas?" Jack asked her. She couldn't recall, so he made her some tea and toast. As she ate and drank, her strength began to return and, with it, her memory.

"I knew you had come to fetch me," she said. "I saw you in the mansion one night, but I couldn't let you find me yet. I still hadn't gotten the answer from Grandmere Catherine."

"Where did you stay all this time, Mommy? We searched and searched for you."

"In the beginning, I was here," she said, and I realized that was when Jack had seen the candlelight. "I spent some time in the old shack, too, but one day, a dreadful man came after me, as if he knew I had come home. I hid from him, but he went on a rampage and wrecked the shack, so I fled to another empty shack."

"It was Buster Trahaw."

"Yes," she said. "How did you know?"

I told her some of what had happened, leaving out the most gruesome details, but she was very troubled.

"I was the cause of so much torment and agony," she said, her lips quivering.

"No, you weren't, Mommy. It's not your fault, if the evil intention isn't in your heart. You can't keep the evil out of everyone else's heart. Buster Trahaw was a horrible person and would have tormented someone else if he'd had the chance."

"He probably did," Jack suggested. "Many times before."

"Even so," Mommy said. "If I hadn't run off and you hadn't had to come after me . . ."

"It's over and done, Mommy. Let's not dwell on the past. We have bigger problems facing us," I said and told her more about Pierre's condition and how Daddy had broken his leg and was laid up in the house.

"We should get started right away," she said struggling to sit up. "They need us."

"I think you should get some sleep, madame. Morning's not far off and you can leave as soon as you wake," Jack said. "You won't do anyone any good if you're exhausted," he added.

Mommy smiled. "You have found a very sensible young man, Pearl," she said.

I looked at Jack and smiled. "I know."

Mommy's eyes were filled with awareness when I looked at her. She turned from me to Jack and then to me again. Then she nodded softly, closed her eyes, and lowered her head to the pillow. A few moments later she was in a deep sleep. I rose from the sofa and Jack came over to put his arm around me as we gazed down at her.

"I think the worst is over for her," he said. "The past is finally buried."

"But what about the future, Jack?"

"I don't know. No one does. You will just do the best you can and hope," he said.

I lowered my head to his shoulder. "I couldn't have done this without you. Thank you."

He kissed the tip of my nose, and I opened my eyes to gaze into his.

"You don't need to thank me," he said. "Let's go back to sleep so we can be of some use tomorrow."

After I made sure Mommy was comfortable and snug, Jack and I returned to bed, and I snuggled up in his arms.

"Jack," I said after a long, quiet moment.

"Yes?"

"Do you believe in the things my mother believes in? Do you think she heard my great-grandmere's voice at her grave?"

"I know I risk your thinking less of me," he replied, "but yes, I do."

I thought for a moment. "I don't think less of you, Jack."

"That's good. And I don't think less of you if you don't," he added. I laughed.

Then I thought about it and said, "I wouldn't be happy if you did." He held me tighter.

We didn't have to say anymore. Our bodies and our minds spoke silently to each other. I closed my eyes, upset that I wouldn't be secure in his arms again tomorrow and fearful of what the next day in New Orleans would bring.

I doubted that the worst was over.

16

The Real Thing

Despite her fatigue, Mommy rose before either Jack or I did. We heard her moving about, and then I heard her call for me. I got up quickly and rushed out to her. She wore a distraught and confused expression.

"It all seems like one long nightmare," she said and then, like one who had woken from more than just a night's sleep, she firmly added, "We must get home."

"Good morning, Madame Andreas," Jack said, emerging from the bedroom. Mommy glanced at me oddly for a moment.

"You remember Jack, Mommy."

"Yes. I'm sorry. I'm just so mixed up this morning. Good morning," she said.

"Did you sleep all right on that sofa? It's very comfortable. I've fallen asleep on it often," he said, smiling.

Mommy's lips relaxed. "I slept in places a lot less comfortable in the last few days," she said.

"How about some breakfast? I'll make coffee," Jack suggested.

"We've got to go," Mommy said, almost in a whisper to me.

"First, put something in your stomach, Madame Andreas. You'll need your strength," Jack insisted.

"Yes," Mommy said. "We will."

She was very quiet while we drank coffee and ate fruit and toast, but her eyes kept shifting from Jack to me. She watched his every move and seemed to have her eyes on us whenever Jack and I gazed at each other.

"Shouldn't we call Daddy and tell him you're on the way home, Mommy?" I asked.

"What? Oh, yes, of course," she said, still acting a bit dazed. "I'm just not thinking too straight yet. My head feels stuffed with clouds."

I called home. Aubrey got Daddy on the phone immediately when he heard I had Mommy waiting to speak to him.

"You found her!" Daddy cried. "Oh, thank God. And thank *you*, Pearl. Please let me speak to her."

I handed Mommy the phone.

"Hello, Beau. . . . I'm fine now. We'll soon be on our way home." She listened and then started to cry softly. "I'm sorry," she said in a cracked voice. "I'm very sorry." She couldn't say another word. Instead, she shook her head and handed me the phone.

"Ruby, Ruby?" Daddy was calling.

"She's all right, Daddy. She's just overwrought right now. We'll just finish our breakfast and then we'll be on our way."

"Hurry, but drive carefully," he said.

Mommy had sat down again. I asked Daddy softly if he had heard anything new from the hospital.

"No. No change," he replied.

"See you soon, Daddy," I told him and cradled the receiver. I went to Mommy and put my arm around her.

She cried softly. "No matter . . . what I do, I make more trouble," she said with a sigh.

"It's not your fault. You've got to stop blaming yourself for things. All of us bear some responsibility for our own actions. The blame can't all fall on your shoulders."

"Let's go," she said pushing away her cup and plate. "I can't eat another thing."

I helped her up.

"You sure you can make this drive yourselves?" Jack asked me.

"I'm fine, Jack. We'll be all right once we get started," I said.

He followed us out and helped Mommy get into the car. "Take care of yourself, Madame Andreas. I will say a prayer for you."

"Thank you." She looked surprised as she gazed at him.

Jack came around the car to say good-bye to me. We stood outside, the car door still closed.

"I'll be coming for my clothes," he kidded.

"Maybe I won't want to give them back. I've grown quite fond of them."

"Then I'll leave without them, but at least I'll have seen you."

"You know what this means, don't you? You'll be forced to come into the city where you have to strain your neck to see the sun."

He laughed. Then his face turned very serious, his eyes fixed firmly on mine. "I wouldn't be afraid to live in total darkness if you were with me, Pearl. You would bring me my sunlight."

His words brought tears of joy to my eyes, and then he glanced quickly at Mommy before chancing a good-bye kiss. His lips only grazed mine, but I closed my eyes and savored the instant, embossing it on my memory.

"Please be careful," he said squeezing my hand. "I'll call you later today."

"Good-bye Jack." I opened the door. "Thanks for all you've done."

I got into the car and started the engine. Mommy was biting down on her lower lip and holding back her tears. We drove off slowly. In my rearview mirror, I saw Jack watching us. The other riggers were starting to arrive. Some beeped their horns and waved.

"Everyone seems to know you," Mommy said, amazed.

"Oil riggers are a tight group," I replied, remembering how Jack had described them. "They help each other and anyone each of them cares about. Once they heard what had happened to me, they volunteered to do all sorts of things for Jack and me."

As we made the turn away from his trailer, and as the house began to disappear behind us, a soft smile couched itself on my lips.

Mommy noticed. "How did you meet this young man?"

"We met when Daddy and I first came to Cypress Woods looking for you. He takes care of my well, number twenty-two," I said proudly.

"Your well? Oh. Paul's legacy to you." She grew sad again. "He was so fond of you."

"It's horrible how the Tates are permitting the house to fall apart, isn't it, Mommy?"

"Yes. It was once the most beautiful home in the bayou. Paul was so proud of it and everything in it. I remember the day he brought you and me to see it completed. He couldn't stop bragging about his special windows and his chandeliers," she said.

"I met Uncle Paul's mother," I said and described my visit to Aunt Jeanne's home.

Mommy listened as I told her the things Gladys Tate had said, but she didn't seem angry. "She put us

331

through hell, but I can understand her terrible loss now and why she wanted to hurt us. Of course, hate poisons after a while, and that's the second tragedy," she added.

"But from what you've told me and from what I could see, Gladys Tate wasn't a happy woman even before all this happened."

"No. She had many crosses to bear. She made herself believe she was Paul's natural mother for her own sake as well as for his. I do believe she loved him as much as a natural mother could love a son. But she was possessive and always very angry. She had a bad marriage. Octavius was a ladies' man from the start and strayed often from their marriage bed. My mother wasn't his only conquest," she muttered. "Grandmere Catherine used to say unhappiness was a hungry snake that fed upon itself until it swallowed itself. The more miserable their marriage was, the more he wandered, and the more he wandered, the more miserable Gladys became. She's to be pitied now."

"I wonder why Gladys and Octavius got married, then," I said.

"Sometimes people get married for all the wrong reasons, but don't realize it until it's too late," Mommy explained. "The Tate fortune, the factory— all of it was in Gladys Tate's family, not Octavius's. He was a handsome, debonair man who chained himself to a woman for the money and property she possessed. I'm sure he said all the right things to her. Perhaps he didn't convince her he was in love with her; perhaps she convinced herself because she wanted to believe it, but the effect was the same. They started building a life on a foundation of lies, made promises they knew in their hearts they would never keep, and kept adding to the illusion until the devil came knocking and Octavius answered the door.

"So you see, you have to be careful, Pearl," Mommy

332

said sharply, turning to me. "You have to avoid the swamp of illusions and false promises. They dangle words in front of you, words that sparkle like diamonds, but when you reach out for them, you find they are only flecks of glass that shatters in your fingers and falls into dust at your feet.

"Sometimes they don't even mean to be false to us. Sometimes they believe their own false promises; they swallow their own illusions, too. But that's even worse, for when they are sincere, you accept and believe and give yourself completely to the dreams. You float higher and higher, and the fall is that much more severe. Believe me, I know.

"This young man," she said jerking her head toward the rear, "how involved have you become with him?"

"His name is Jack, Mommy, Jack Clovis. He's not just another young man."

"Jack," she said. "You were sleeping with him last night, weren't you?"

"Jack is the first man I've met who I felt was real, Mommy. He's sincere, and he doesn't make promises he can't keep. His feet are set solidly in reality. He's not a dreamer," I told her.

She shook her head skeptically. "What I've been trying to tell you, to show you with my own tragic background, is that you have to be extra careful. For some reason the Landry line was born to hoe a harder field, a field filled with sharp rocks and webs of stubborn weeds."

"I am extra careful, Mommy. I've always been. You know that."

"I know, but when you came up here looking for me, you were emotionally distraught. You have to be sure that what you see in this man and what he says to you isn't colored by your own vulnerability. He must have seemed like a guardian angel to you."

"He did," I declared. "And rightly so."

"I'm afraid for you," she said, her chin quivering. "Don't make the mistakes I did. Take your time, and when your heart is pounding and your body is demanding that you give yourself completely, step back and think of me.

"When you make a mistake, you hurt not only yourself but also the people you love.

"When I was living in the bayou with you, and Gisselle wrote me that your father was going to marry someone else, I thought I'd go mad. He had given me up for dead. Here I was a young woman with a baby, so I gave in to the illusions and the promises and the hope that Paul offered. I wanted to believe I could live in a magical world where we would be forever safe and protected. But that's when all the tragedy had its ugly start." She began to cry softly again.

"It's all right, Mommy. Please don't cry." I reached for her hand.

"Poor Jean," she muttered. "My poor baby. He's gone, gone . . ."

The pain in my heart was so heavy I thought I wouldn't be able to keep driving. I took deep breaths while Mommy whimpered softly. Finally she stopped, closed her eyes, and fell asleep against the window. When I gazed at her, she looked as if she had aged years. The sight of her brought the stinging, hot tears to my eyes and clouded my vision. It was as if it was raining.

It looked as if it might storm anyway. The sky was heavily overcast with some bruised, dark clouds rolling in from the southwest.

When I pulled onto the main highway, the bayou began to drop behind me, flowing back as if it had all turned liquid and was pouring down a drain. The toothpick-legged shacks were still visible here and there, and I saw oyster fishermen and Cajun women and children harvesting Spanish moss. We passed a few roadside stands, and then the road became relatively deserted for a while.

I thought about Jack and the things Mommy had said. Maybe she was right; maybe I was in a weak and vulnerable state when we met, but why did that have to mean what we felt for each other was just illusion? And why did that have to mean that Jack was less sincere than I thought he was? Sometimes tragic and difficult times bring together people who are meant to be together, I reasoned. Mommy was understandably wary, but I needn't live like that, too.

I didn't regret anything that had happened between Jack and me. Our loving remained an oasis of happiness in a sea of turmoil and pain. Everyone was always warning me about the dangers inherent in first love. It was better to be cautious, modest, reasonable, everyone said.

But I was convinced that what I felt in my heart now for Jack was more than just a young girl's first infatuation. He and I had found depths of feelings together that were beyond the reach of mere girlish crushes.

No, Mommy, I thought. Don't worry about my relationship with Jack. It's built on solid ground, not swampland, and the only illusion for us was the idea that we could ever forget each other and what we had come to mean to each other.

I sped up. The rain started just before we reached New Orleans, but it was a slow, steady drizzle rather than a blinding downpour. Mommy woke up after we crossed the bridge and started down the city streets toward the Garden District. In the gray light of morning, the city looked tired, worn. Without the glow of neon signs, the rainbow colors of costumes, and the sound of music, New Orleans in the morning resembled an aging woman caught without her makeup. Street cleaners were still trying to remove the debris cast about by frenzied partygoers. Sleepy store owners opened their doors and squinted at the daylight.

The rain slowed to a sprinkle, but the air was so hot and humid already that the sidewalks looked steamy.

"Are you all right, Mommy?" I asked.

She flashed a smile and nodded. "There were moments when I thought I would never set eyes on this city again," she said. "But that's over." She squeezed my hand. "Let's get Daddy and go to Pierre."

The rain came to a complete stop when we reached the Garden District. I pulled into our driveway, and we hurried up the steps to the front door. Aubrey, who knew we were on our way, must have been waiting by the window, for the door was thrust open before we reached it.

"Welcome home, madame," he said quickly. The warmth in his moist eyes was as much emotion as Aubrey had ever shown.

Mommy surprised him with a quick embrace. "Where's Monsieur Andreas?" she asked.

Aubrey was flustered for a moment. "Monsieur Andreas . . . oh, upstairs. I helped him dress. He's practicing with the crutches."

We charged up the stairway. When we reached the open door to Mommy and Daddy's suite, I stepped back. Daddy was up, leaning on his crutches, his leg in a cast. He stopped and looked at Mommy for a moment. "Ruby," he said, teetering.

She rushed forward, and he embraced her, the crutches falling to the floor. She held him firmly, and they stood there clinging to each other for a long moment. Their embrace sent my fugitive tears flowing freely down my cheeks. After another moment I picked up Daddy's crutches and held them out to him.

"What are you wearing?" he asked me with a quizzical smile.

"These are Jack's clothes, Daddy."

"Why?" He looked at Mommy.

"It's a bit of a horror tale," she said. "Let her shower and change. I need to shower, too. Then we'll go to the hospital, and Pearl will tell you all of it."

"But where have you been, Ruby? What have you been doing?"

"I'll tell you everything, too, Beau. Just give me a chance to catch my breath."

"Are you in any pain, Daddy?" I asked.

"Nothing I can't endure now," he said, shifting his eyes away shamefully. He knew I was aware of what had happened, but this wasn't the time or the place to blame anyone for anything. None of that seemed important anyway.

I kissed him quickly on the cheek and hurried to shower and dress, praying that it wasn't too late to help Pierre.

Mommy wasn't prepared for the sight she would see in the ICU. Even I, who had seen Pierre here before, was frightened by the pallid skin and the way his ashen complexion almost turned his hair gray. His lips were colorless. The skin on the back of his hands looked wrinkled. He lay so still he resembled a mannequin. The nurse explained that he had just had a dialysis treatment.

Mommy stood staring at Pierre. She was a few feet from the bed. It was as if the last twenty or thirty inches were impassable after the emotional journey she had just taken. Daddy stood beside her, leaning on his crutches.

"He looks as if he's shrinking," Mommy moaned. "I don't remember him being so small."

"It's just because he's in such a big bed, Mommy," I said. "Come, talk to him. I'm sure he'll hear you."

She nodded and finally stepped up to the bed. I got her a chair and she sat down, holding Pierre's hand in hers.

"Pierre, my darling. My sweet baby, please get well. I'm here now, here to help you," she said. "We need you to get well, Pierre. Please try."

The tears were streaming down her cheeks. She leaned over and kissed Pierre's cheek, but it must have been like kissing a corpse. His eyelids didn't flutter; his lips didn't move. All we heard was the beep, beep, beep of heart monitors and other hospital machinery.

Mommy turned desperately to Daddy. He bit down on his lower lip and shook his head.

"Where's the doctor?" Mommy asked me.

"I'll go see." I went to the nurses' station. Dr. LeFevre wasn't expected until midafternoon, but Dr. Lasky expected to visit his patients in about an hour.

"We can go downstairs to the hospital cafeteria and have something to eat while we wait, Mommy," I told her. She was just staring at Pierre.

"No, you go ahead, dear," she said. "Take Daddy. I must stay here now."

I thought the nurse might not like it, but this ICU nurse was more compassionate and understanding. She just nodded. Daddy and I went to the cafeteria. After I got us some sandwiches and drinks and brought them to the table, I began to tell Daddy about my near tragedy in the bayou and what had happened to Buster Trahaw.

Daddy sat listening with his mouth open. "I let you down," he said. "I let everyone down by drinking myself into a stupor and falling down the stairs, breaking my leg. There you were, doing the things I should have been doing and endangering yourself,

338

while I lay in a stupor. I don't deserve any good luck or happiness."

It was as if a transfusion of iron had been shot through my veins and into my spine. I straightened up quickly and snapped at him. "Stop this right now, Daddy. I don't want to hear another note of self-pity from your lips. Mommy desperately needs us to be strong for her, and Pierre will need us more than ever. There isn't any time to sit around bemoaning all the tragedy."

He looked up, surprised at my harsh tone, but I couldn't help speaking to him that way.

"When I was alone in that canoe, drifting from one canal to the other, lost and exhausted, I could think of only one terrible thing: I had let you and Pierre and Mommy down. If we just dwell on ourselves, we will become pitiful, and whatever evil looms around us will have its day with us," I concluded sternly.

"You, Pearl?" Daddy said, starting to smile. *"You* have come to believe in the power of spirits?"

"I believe in the power of the soul, yes. I believe we can do battle with what seems to be our destiny. If you don't try, you will be carried away by the winds of darkness. I don't believe in voodoo rituals or have faith in good-luck charms, but at least the people who do have faith in these things believe they can change their destiny. They have some grit," I added, and Daddy laughed.

Then he grew dark and serious.

"You seem to have grown years older in just a few days, Pearl. I sense a greater maturity in you. It's as if you have leaped over time." He sat back and stared at me a moment. "This Jack Clovis, he was a great help?"

"Yes," I said.

"You've become very fond of him?"

"Yes," I admitted. "And in a mature way," I added.

Daddy nodded. He looked very sad again for a moment and then sighed. "It's not easy to see your little girl become a woman. Goodness knows, no one knows the dangers that befall young people better than we now know them, but there's a wall of innocence around a young girl. Her pains and disappointments are all small compared to what she can endure later: a boy she likes doesn't ask her to the prom, her hair isn't as soft or as stylish as she would like, she has a pimple on her chin.

"I bet you've forgotten the time when you were in third grade and some boy said your head was far too big for the rest of you. You came running home crying that day, and Mommy was out visiting an art gallery where one of her exhibitions was being staged. I was in the office, and you came to my door in tears. I had to run a tape measure around your head and then work out the proportions to prove you weren't a freak. How easy it was to drive the demons away from you then. How hard it becomes now."

"Why must there be any demons, Daddy?"

"It just seems there always are," he said. "But I suppose if you find the right man he will have the weapons with which to protect you. I hope you will find a man who can do better for the woman he loves than I have."

"Stop it, Daddy!" I ordered.

"Okay, okay," he said, raising his hands. "I'll be the man you think I am." He straightened up. "You're right. There isn't any time for self-pity." He bit into his sandwich. "Tell me more about this Jack Clovis."

I didn't mind. I could have talked about Jack for hours. Daddy listened and nodded as we finished our lunch. He enjoyed teasing me about Jack, but I was so sad about leaving him that I welcomed even Daddy's joking.

Mommy was sitting right where we left her, holding

Pierre's hand and staring at his quiet face. I had brought her a cold drink, and she sipped it through a straw, but she insisted she wasn't hungry.

Dr. Lasky arrived and examined Pierre. Then he met with us outside. "Physically, he's slipping," he said bluntly. "His kidneys remain shut down; his blood pressure is too low. Despite his youth, I am worried about pneumonia. I am sorry, monsieur," he said directing himself to Daddy because Mommy stood with her head bowed while he spoke. "I wish I could give you a better report."

Daddy thanked him, and then we all sat down in the waiting room. Mommy laid her head on Daddy's shoulder. No one spoke for the longest time. Our thoughts and prayers were with Pierre. Looking through the windows toward the northwest, I saw that the layer of thick gray clouds was beginning to break apart. I thought to myself that Jack was gazing up at blue sky now, and I wondered how often he had thought about me since Mommy and I had left.

A short time later Dr. LeFevre arrived and Daddy introduced her to Mommy. I sensed her disapproval and anger when she spoke to Mommy. Her tone was coldly correct and firm, but Mommy didn't get upset with her.

"Of course, it would have been much more to Pierre's advantage had you been here sooner, Madame Andreas," she pointed out sharply, "but we must make the best of your presence now. I have spoken with Dr. Lasky and he agrees. We will move Pierre to a private room so you can spend longer periods of time with him uninterrupted. Of course you will need a private nurse around the clock," she told Daddy. "If you like, I will arrange for that."

"Please do, Doctor. What do you think of his chances?" Daddy asked and reached for Mommy's hand.

Dr. LeFevre thought a moment. She was careful when she spoke. "As I explained, each time your son fell back into a comatose state, he fell deeper and deeper and took longer and longer to emerge, and each time he regained consciousness, it was for a shorter period. Little by little, he's drifting away, almost like someone drowning, coming up occasionally for air, and sinking under again." She couldn't have chosen a more horrible comparison for my mother and me.

Mommy's face contorted. She groaned, and then her eyes rolled back in her head. I cried out as Daddy struggled to keep her standing despite his being on crutches. Dr. LeFevre helped us get Mommy to the sofa. I ran for a cup of cold water, and she was revived.

"I'm sorry," she said after swallowing some water.

"It's all right, madame," Dr. LeFevre said, with more compassion now. "Such news comes like a punch in the stomach, I know."

Mommy gazed at her with an expression that said, "You don't know. You couldn't even imagine."

"If you're all right, I'll see to the arrangements for moving Pierre," Dr. LeFevre said.

"Thank you," Daddy told her, and she left us. The three of us sat there, Daddy and I with our arms around Mommy.

"It's as if the snake had bitten both of the boys," she muttered. "As if the poison had traveled through Jean into Pierre. It's how they always were, remember, Beau? Once one got sick, the other followed soon after."

"Pierre is going to get better, Mommy," I insisted.

She turned to me with wet eyes, smiling at me as if I were so innocent and foolish. "He doesn't want to get better, Pearl. That's the problem now," she said.

"Then we have to make him want to," I insisted. "I will not let him drown."

I got up and ran from the lounge, my own tears flying from my cheeks, my heart pounding. I charged out into the corridor, not thinking about where I was headed, and just marched quickly past the rooms, past patients in wheelchairs, past nurses and doctors. I stopped when I realized I had walked to the linen closet. The door opened and Sophie emerged. Her eyes widened with happiness when she saw me.

"Pearl! How you been? *Where* you been? How's your brother?" she asked. Her arms were filled with sheets and pillowcases.

"Sophie. Oh, Sophie," I said, and the dam holding back my tears broke.

She dropped her pile of linens and embraced me. "You come in here," she said and led me back into the linen room. "Sit down," she ordered, forcing me to sit on a carton. "Now stop wailing and tell me what happened."

"Pierre's very bad," I said after a deep breath. "The doctor's aren't very encouraging."

"Well, the doctors don't know everything, Pearl. I've seen old people on their deathbed snap their eyes open and start yelling at me for not bringing them their juice or tea fast enough. Why, once they pronounced a man dead and he got up and left the hospital, he was so mad."

"No, they didn't," I said, smiling through my tears.

"I swear," she said holding up her hand. Then she laughed. "I missed you, and a lot's happened here since you've been gone."

"What's happened?" I wiped away the tears with the back of my hand.

"Dr. Weller was asked to leave," she said in a hoarse whisper. "He done something a doctor ain't supposed to do with a young lady patient. There was a big hullabaloo, but everyone tried to keep it squashed. Next thing I heard, he wasn't a doctor here no more."

343

"What did he do to her?" I asked, holding my breath.

"Nothing much, except make her pregnant," she said, and then her eyes widened. "There's talk the hospital might be sued, too. Guess you're lucky you didn't become his study partner, huh?"

"Yes," I said. "But it's tragic for everyone."

"My mama says you play, you pay. Just remember, I told her, I'm not getting pregnant until I'm married. You want to come with me and get some coffee or tea or juice?" she asked.

"No," I said, standing. "I'd better get back. My mother and father are going to need me more than ever," I said. "Pierre's going into a private room with private nurses."

"I'll look in on him, too," she said. "And I'll say prayers for him and give a donation at the church."

"Thank you, Sophie."

We hugged, and I returned to the lounge where Mommy and Daddy were still waiting for Pierre to be moved. We saw him settled comfortably in his new bed, and Daddy and Mommy spoke with the private nurse who was going to take the first shift. Mommy insisted on remaining at Pierre's bedside for the remainder of the afternoon and relented only when Daddy said he was in too much pain to remain at the hospital.

"We all need some rest now, Ruby," he said. "Otherwise we won't be able to be with Pierre as much as we like."

Reluctantly she agreed, and we went home. Mommy went right up to bed. She and Daddy had a light supper in their room. While I was eating, Aubrey came to tell me I had a phone call from a Monsieur Clovis. I left the table quickly.

"Jack!"

"I didn't want to call too soon. How are things?"

"Not good, Jack. Pierre is in a deep coma again, and the doctors are very pessimistic. They're not saying this in so many words, but I think it would take a miracle for him to recover."

"I'm sorry. I'd like to come to New Orleans, but I don't want to come at the wrong time."

"Any time you come will be the right time, Jack."

"All right," he said. "I'll be there day after tomorrow. Can you recommend an inexpensive hotel?"

"You'll stay here, Jack."

"I can't do that."

"Of course you can, and of course you will," I insisted. "We have more room than we need. If I'm not at the house, I'll be at the hospital," I said. There was a little pause before he spoke again.

"This may not be the proper time for me to say it," he told me, "but I miss you."

"I miss you, too."

I felt guilty being happy when my parents were so sad, but I couldn't help feeling a surge of excitement when I thought about Jack coming to New Orleans. I had a better appetite when I returned to the dinner table and finished my supper. Afterward I thought about watching television or listening to some music, but decided instead to go up to my room to read for a while before going to sleep.

The lights were out in Mommy and Daddy's room, so I didn't bother them, but a little less than an hour after I had put out my own lights, I heard Mommy scream. I got up and rushed across the corridor. The lights were on, and they were both sitting up in bed. Daddy was embracing Mommy.

"What is it?" I asked, my heart pounding. I hadn't heard the phone ring, but it could have. Was there bad news from the hospital?

"Your mother had a nightmare; it's all right," Daddy said.

"No," she cried pulling away from him. "It's not all right."

"Ruby!"

She shook her head vehemently and started to get out of bed.

"Where are you going, Mommy?" I asked as she reached for her clothing.

"I've got to go to Jean's grave," she said.

"Now?" Daddy said, amazed. "But it's nearly midnight, Ruby, and—"

"I have to be there at midnight," she declared. "My dream told me so."

"You can't go to the cemetery now, Ruby," Daddy said. "Be reasonable."

"Don't worry, Daddy," I said. "I'll go with her."

"But, Ruby, it's so late, and you know there are thugs loitering around the cemeteries."

Mommy continued to dress. Daddy grimaced and struggled to get his leg over the edge of the bed so he could reach for his crutches.

"What are you doing, Daddy?"

"If she insists on going, I'm going too," he declared.

I turned and ran back to my room to put my clothes on.

"At least wait for me," I heard Daddy cry. Mommy charged out of the bedroom and down the stairs. Her face was like a mask, her eyes fixed and cold as she hurried by.

"Mommy, wait," I called.

"See to your father," she replied.

Daddy emerged on his crutches, moving as quickly as he could. I went to help him, but by the time we got downstairs, Mommy had already driven off.

"She's gone mad again," Daddy declared. He and I got into his car and followed. I drove. Mommy had

346

already parked her car and gone into the cemetery when we pulled up behind her.

"What is she doing?" Daddy mumbled. I helped him out. We had a flashlight in the glove compartment, but we were fortunate in that the moon was nearly full and there were only a few small clouds. The moonlight made the tombs and vaults gleam. The polished stone looked bone-white against the darkness. I stayed right next to Daddy as he hobbled along the pathway toward my brother's grave. Mommy had lit a candle beside the vault and then had knelt and pressed her forehead to the stone. Her shoulders lifted and fell with her sobs. I left Daddy's side and hurried to her.

"Mommy." I hugged her.

"I begged him," she whispered in my ear. "He was lonely without Pierre, but I begged him to let Pierre come back." Daddy leaned on his crutches as Mommy lifted her head from my shoulders and looked up at him. "I had to be here at midnight, Beau. It's the time when the door between the two worlds opens just enough for my words to follow the candle smoke through."

Daddy leaned on his crutches and shook his head. "You're driving us all mad now, Ruby. You've got to stop. Come home and go to sleep."

"I couldn't sleep. That's why I came here," she said. "You see that now, don't you, sweetheart?" she asked me.

"Yes, Mommy."

She touched the stone of Jean's vault lovingly and smiled. "He heard me. He won't let Pierre leave us. Jean is a good boy, a good boy."

"Come home now, Mommy. Please." I helped her to her feet. She looked at Jean's tomb again, and then the three of us, crippled by our tragedy, hobbled along the pathway past other vaults and other scenes of sadness where the ground was soaked with similar tears.

I gazed back once and shuddered with the horrible vision of a second vault, twin to Jean's.

"Please, God," I murmured, too low for Daddy or Mommy to hear, "please help us."

17

Please Wake Up

Despite being exhausted by the time we all returned home and to bed, I tossed and turned, slipping in and out of nightmares. When I woke, I welcomed the morning sunlight, but I felt as if I had just run a marathon in the middle of the summer. My sheet and blanket were drenched with perspiration, and when I sat up, my legs and my back ached from the twisting and turning I had done in my sleep.

I was the first to rise, wash, and dress. Both Mommy and Daddy looked as if they had been through the same wringer of horrors when they entered the dining room and sat down to breakfast. Mommy had already phoned the hospital and spoken to Pierre's nurse, who told her there was no change.

"At least he's not getting worse," I said, hoping to find a ray of sunshine in all this gloom.

"Yes, but he's not getting better," Mommy replied in a voice that was totally devoid of energy and expression. She ate mechanically, her eyes fixed on nothing. Daddy reached across the table and took her hand. She smiled weakly at him and then turned and chewed and stared. Daddy flashed a sad look at me, and I could tell that he was at his wit's end.

"Jack's coming tomorrow," I announced, deciding that a change of subject might be the best antidote to our depression. Mommy's eyes widened with some interest, and Daddy looked impressed. "Is that all right?"

"He's coming here?" Mommy asked.

"Yes. I invited him to stay."

Mommy looked at Daddy, who shrugged.

"From what I hear, we owe this young man a great deal," Daddy said. "The least we can do is offer him hospitality."

"I don't think I'm up to being a hostess," Mommy said.

"Jack won't expect anything special, Mommy. He's here to be at my side and offer his comfort."

"He sounds like a special young man," Daddy said.

Mommy sighed deeply. I knew there was no room in her heart and mind for anything but sadness right now, but I also knew we had to dwell on hope and find new strength.

While Mommy got ready to return to the hospital, Daddy returned the phone calls of friends and business acquaintances who had been inquiring about Pierre's condition. Afterward we drove to the hospital.

The three of us stood around Pierre's bed gazing down at him in silence. Mommy choked back a sob and sat beside the bed to hold his hand and talk to him softly. She left his bedside only to eat some lunch, and only at Daddy's and my insistence.

There was a great deal of pressure building on Daddy, too. He had business problems and tried to handle them over the telephone, but some things required his presence. I told him it made no sense for all three of us to hover around Pierre's bed. He finally agreed and had a driver pick him up in a limousine to take him to some business meetings. I sat with Mommy and spoke with Pierre's nurse, Mrs. Lochet, a pleasant woman in her late fifties with short, thick gray hair and light blue eyes. Afterward I met Sophie for coffee in the cafeteria. I told her I had informed the hospital I wouldn't be able to return to work.

"My parents need me at home right now," I explained. She was sad about it, but I assured her we would always be friends.

"Maybe when you become a doctor, I can come work for you," she suggested.

"There's no one I'd rather have at my side while I tend to patients," I told her.

When I went back to Pierre's room, I found that Mommy had fallen asleep in her chair. The nurse and I gazed at each other and stepped outside the room to talk so Mommy could sleep.

"Have you ever seen a patient like Pierre improve?" I asked her.

"Well," she said hesitantly, "this is my first case where the patient has gone into a coma from psychological reasons. I have had comatose patients who were injured and who improved. I even had a young man who was shot by a mugger and who went into a deep coma and later improved. You can't give up hope," she added, but I didn't see any optimism in her eyes, and she did shift them away from me quickly.

Dr. LeFevre visited and merely said, "We'll see," when I asked her for an opinion.

Daddy returned to take us to dinner, but Mommy was so tired that we decided it would be better to just go home. Sitting in a chair and talking to Pierre all day didn't require much energy, but it was emotionally draining for my mother. She looked so bad, my heart cried for her. Her eyelids drooped, her lips trembled, her complexion was pallid, and she walked with stooped shoulders.

When we arrived home, Mommy decided to lie down. Her supper would be brought to her room, but she insisted Daddy and I eat in the dining room. We did, but we weren't very talkative. It was as though Pierre's funeral had begun.

"The doctor told me Pierre could go on like this for months and months," Daddy finally said. "I don't see how your mother is going to last. She was convinced her rituals and appeals to various spirits would help. Now that all of this mystical business has failed, she's at the lowest point I've ever seen her. I'm afraid we'll be visiting her in a hospital soon, too."

I tried to sound hopeful, to find the words that would restore faith and hope to him as well as to myself, but my well of optimism had run dry. All I could do was shake my head and mutter, "She'll be all right. Everything will be all right."

Daddy smiled. "You can't let any of this get in your way, Pearl. I know you are not a self-centered person by nature, but I don't want to hear any talk of you postponing your college education," he said firmly. "It's enough you had to quit your job at the hospital."

"But—"

"Pearl, promise me," he insisted. When I didn't respond immediately, he looked as if he might burst into tears, but he raised one arm and added, "We can't lose everything, even our dream for you."

"Okay, Daddy. I promise," I said. My chest ached. I knew if I didn't get up and go upstairs soon, I would sob openly and only make things harder for him. I forced a smile and excused myself.

When I looked in on Mommy, I saw she was asleep. I started for my room, but something drew me to the twins' room instead. I opened the door that had been kept shut tight since Jean's death and Pierre's transfer to the hospital, and I stood there gazing at their toys—Jean's frog and insect specimens on the shelf, his model airplanes and cars, their bookcase filled with adventure stories and books on animals and soldiers. How many times had I looked in and pleaded with the two of them to straighten up their things before Mommy saw the mess?

I smiled, remembering Jean's impish grin and Pierre's serious concern. I recalled them playing checkers, each of them looking into the other's identical face after every move in search of a reaction. Usually, Pierre won, and when Jean did win, I had the feeling Pierre was letting him win.

They were both hoarders, refusing to throw anything away. Their toy chest was filled to the brim, and in their closets were cartons of older toys and books. It was as if they wanted to mark and save every stage of their development, every moment of pleasure, every new discovery. Mommy was always pleading with them to sort out the things they would never use again, but how do you throw away a memory?

What would become of all this now? I wondered. Would Daddy see that it was discarded or given to poor children, or would it be stuffed in some attic corner and left to gather dust and cobwebs?

I stood in the doorway until I realized the tears were streaming down my face so fast and so hard they were dripping off my chin. Then I closed the door softly and went to my room to read myself to sleep.

I did fall asleep with a book in my hands. I never heard Daddy come upstairs, and later, much later, I never heard Mommy sneak out. She didn't go to the cemetery this time, nor did she go to see some voodoo mama. She returned to the hospital and to Pierre's bedside. Later she would tell me she heard his voice; she heard him calling for her in her sleep.

Well after three in the morning, when everything in

the world seemed to be slumbering, when even the stars blinked like tired eyes, I woke to the sound of the phone ringing. It rang and rang until someone answered it. When I realized what time it was, my heart thumped with a deep, hard pounding that took my breath away. I held my breath anyway, listening hard for the sounds I feared most—the sound of wailing, the sound of sobbing, the sound of death.

I heard a door open, and then I heard the tap-tap of Daddy's crutches. He came to my door. My reading light was still on, and I was still dressed, my book open on my lap. I sat up slowly. He looked confused, just woken from a deep sleep.

"What is it, Daddy?" I asked in a small voice.

"Your mother got up and left the house without my knowing," he said. "I never heard her. She must have walked on air."

"Where did she go?"

"To the hospital," he said. "She just phoned."

I brought my fist to my lips.

"She said Pierre . . . Pierre just spoke to her."

As soon as the words registered, I leaped from my bed and ran to him. We embraced, both of us crying so hard from happiness that neither of us could catch enough breath to tell the other to stop. He was kissing my hair, and I was holding him so tightly I was sure I was crushing his ribs.

Then he started to laugh through his tears, and I smiled and wiped mine away as quickly as they emerged.

"I'll throw something on," he said, "and we'll rush right over. My boy, my boy is coming home," he cried happily.

It was enough to turn even the most skeptical person into a believer. When we arrived at Pierre's room, we found him sitting up and sipping warm tea

354

through a straw. Mommy turned to greet us, her face beaming like some previously dying plant resurrected, blossoming again with those bright and beautiful eyes full of light. Even her cheeks glowed, the richness rushing back into her complexion.

"Hi, Pearl," Pierre said. His voice sounded strained, like the voice of someone who had a bad sore throat, but it was his voice and he was looking at me.

"Hi, Pierre." I hugged him. "How do you feel?"

"I'm tired, but I'm hungry," he said. He threw an angry gaze toward his nurse. "They won't give me anything good to eat until the doctor comes, they said. When is she coming already?"

"Not for a while, Pierre. It's four in the morning," I told him and laughed.

"Four in the morning? I've never been up that late, have I?" he asked, looking from Mommy to me.

"No."

He looked past me and saw Daddy on his crutches in the doorway. Pierre's eyes grew bigger than silver dollars. "Dad, what happened to you?"

"Oh, I slipped and fell down the stairs," Daddy said nonchalantly. He hobbled up to the bed.

"Does it hurt?"

"Not much anymore. Later I'll let you sign your name on my cast."

Pierre smiled. Then, just as quickly as that smile came, it faded. "Jean can't sign it," he said.

"Then you'll sign it for him," I replied quickly, before the tears could come to anyone's eyes.

"Yes," Pierre said, thinking. "I will. I'll sign everything 'Pierre and Jean' from now on," he said excitedly.

"Well, people might not understand that, Pierre. When you sign your name, it's enough that you know you're signing for Jean, too, okay?"

He thought a moment and then reluctantly nodded.

But I sensed that from that moment on, everything Pierre did in his life, he would do for his dead brother, too. He would drive himself to do twice as much twice as well. He would try to live two lives. It would take a long time for him to bury Jean. When he did that, Jean would die again for him, and he would suffer the tragedy a second, maybe even harder time.

Pierre couldn't believe how long he had been sleeping. We told him as much about his condition as we could. He was smart enough to understand most of it. I promised him that when he was up to it, I would explain it in more detail. He loved to learn, and it occurred to me that he, perhaps as much as I, had the potential to be a good doctor.

We remained with him until he got tired and closed his eyes again. Mommy was terrified he would slip back into unconsciousness, but the nurse and Dr. LeFevre, who arrived hours earlier than usual, having been told of Pierre's recovery, assured us the worst was over.

"But there is much to do," she added quickly. "He's going to need loads and loads of tender loving care and therapy. It will take time. Don't expect him to put on his running shoes and go off to join other children his age right away," she warned.

"We'll do whatever it takes to help him get well again," Mommy pledged.

Although it was still quite early and none of us had had enough sleep, we were too excited to just go home to sleep. Daddy took us out for breakfast, and we discovered that we were quite hungry. We hadn't done much more than nibble at our food the past day or so.

It was good to see my parents reanimated, talking excitedly about the things they were going to do to prepare for Pierre's homecoming. Mommy thought it might be wise to hire a tutor for him as soon as possible, and Daddy suggested some short sight-seeing trips. I warned them about moving too quickly and advised them to wait to see what the doctor thought before we made any decisions or took any actions.

"Look who's become the wise old lady," Daddy kidded and then reached for Mommy's hand across the table. "And look who's become as giddy as a child."

She smiled at him and they exchanged that magical look I had seen so many, many times before, a look I envied and dreamed of having between me and someone wonderful . . . someone like Jack.

Jack! I thought.

"Daddy, we've got to get home soon. Jack will be arriving."

"Jack?" Mommy said. "Oh, I had forgotten."

"How could you forget Jack?" Daddy teased.

"You stop it right now, Daddy," I warned. The two of them laughed. It was the sweetest music I had heard in a long time.

Just as I feared, when we returned to the house, Jack was already there.

"You have a guest in the sitting room, mademoiselle," Aubrey told me. I thanked him and hurried down the corridor.

Jack looked lost and unsure of himself seated on the velvet settee in our grand sitting room. He wore jeans, boots, and a cotton plaid shirt, but his dark hair was brushed neatly, not a strand out of place.

"Jack!" I cried, rushing to him. He almost didn't get to his feet before I embraced him. I kissed him and held him for a moment.

"Whoa," he said.

"I'm sorry I wasn't here when you arrived," I said, laughing. "But we had the most wonderful news this morning. Pierre came out of his coma. We've been at the hospital since very early this morning."

"That's fantastic." He looked up as Daddy came to the doorway on his crutches. *"Bonjour,* monsieur," he said.

"Bonjour." Daddy came in as quickly as he could and extended his hand. "I want to formally thank you for all you have done for my daughter and for my wife," he said. "I am in your debt."

"Oh, no, monsieur," Jack said gazing at me. "I am in yours for having such a wonderful daughter."

Daddy raised his eyebrows and turned a small smile at me. Blushing, I turned and saw Mommy in the doorway.

"Bonjour, Madame Andreas. I am glad to hear the good news," Jack said.

"Thank you." She came in to greet him. "If we don't behave like proper hosts, please forgive us. We're so full of mixed emotions. It's exhausting."

"Oh, please, madame. Don't think twice about my being here, and if I am in the way, even slightly, I will be gone before you can blink your eye, hear?" he said with his Cajun intonation.

Mommy seemed to drink in his accent, and I suspected that memories of her Cajun life were rushing over her. "I doubt my daughter will permit you to get away that soon," she said with a twinkle in her eyes.

Now I did blush, and so did Jack.

"Are you hungry, Jack? I'll have something fixed for you," Daddy said.

"No, thank you. I ate just before I arrived, monsieur."

"Well," Daddy said. "I guess I had better see to my business concerns so someone can pay the mortgage around here," he jested.

"I'm going to show Jack around New Orleans," I said.

"Good idea," Daddy said. "Why don't we take him

to one of our finer restaurants for dinner tonight. I'll make a reservation."

"Please, monsieur, don't plan anything special for me," Jack said.

"What are you talking about?" Daddy asked. "This is New Orleans. Everything we do for everyone is always special," he said. He turned to me. "Run him by your mother's current exhibit in the French Quarter," he suggested.

"Oh, Beau, there are many more interesting things for her to show him," Mommy said.

"I'd really like to see the exhibit," Jack said.

"Very diplomatic, monsieur," Daddy said. He gazed at me again. "You'll see that Jack is settled in the guest room?"

"Yes, Daddy."

"*Bien.* Have a good time," he said, and then he and Mommy left us.

After we put Jack's things in the guest room, I took him to my room. He stood by the window and gazed out at the gardens, the pool, and the tennis court, watching the grounds people clear away fallen palm fronds and manicure our hedges and flowers.

"You're right," he said. "This isn't what I think of as city life. You have a beautiful home, Pearl. And your room and your closets . . . practically as big as my whole trailer. You've grown up in a magical place, a castle," he said with a sad note in his voice.

I knew what he was thinking and what was happening. He was becoming overwhelmed with our wealth and feeling inadequate. He was sorry he had come.

I went up to his side and threaded my arm through his as he gazed down at the grounds.

"None of this means anything if you can't share it with the right person, Jack. I know a great many sad rich people who would trade most of what they have just to have a sincere, loving relationship."

"You say that now, little princess, but I wonder what you would say after you'd lived without servants and fine foods and cars and clothes."

I felt the heat rise to my cheeks, and I spun him around to face me.

"I'll tell you what I would say, Jack Clovis. I would say I love you, and all the servants in the world and all the fine clothes and cars couldn't compensate if I lost that love. I'd say that there's nothing more beautiful than a sunset when I'm in the arms of someone I love and nothing more precious than waking up in those arms, whether I'm sleeping in a trailer in the bayou or in a mansion in New Orleans.

"Being rich doesn't make falling in love impossible. I'm not sorry my parents have done well, but falling in love with someone who really is in love with you— that's *really* being rich, Jack. Maybe that sounds like a schoolgirl's fantasy, and maybe you're right that most people would regret losing their pleasures and comforts, but I'm not most people.

"Don't you forget I'm part Cajun, too, and my blood can be traced back to those swamps you cherish."

Jack's face broke into a wide smile. "You're not kidding about your Cajun heritage," he said. "I remember I said I didn't want to risk your wrath. That was a smart piece of advice I gave myself. I should have listened."

I softened. "Just see me for who I am and not for what my family owns," I pleaded.

"Okay. I'm sorry," he said. "That's the last time I'll make a big deal of this overgrown shack."

I laughed and hugged him. "Let's go. There's nothing like showing someone else your hometown," I told him and hurried him out and down the stairs.

I took him on a whirlwind tour. First I drove him past Loyola and Tulane. We stopped at the Audubon

360

park and zoo, and then he said he wanted to ride a streetcar. I drove back to the house, and we walked up to the stop and took the streetcar to Canal Street. We crossed into the French Quarter and had po'boy sandwiches at a sidewalk café near the river where there was something of a breeze. For a while we just watched the steamboats and barges going up and down the Mississippi and listened to the street music performed by guitarists and harmonica players, and trumpeters.

"It's nicer here than I expected," Jack offered, but there was still some hesitation in his voice.

"What is it you miss the most, Jack?" I asked. We were holding hands, but he suddenly seemed hundreds of miles away.

"The stillness, I guess. Nature, the animals, even the dangerous ones. And your well," he added. "They're drilling for a different kind of oil in these streets, hawking from the storefronts, pushing their wares." He shrugged. "I guess you gotta be what you are . . . but it really is pretty here," he added.

I thought about what he'd said and wondered if the gap between us was too wide. We lived only hours away from each other, but the way we were brought up had become part of us and had given us a different view of the sunrise and the sunset. How strong was love? Could it bridge the gap and show us how to really know each other?

We did have a wonderful day together, though. Late in the afternoon, after we visited Mommy's new exhibit, we had coffee and beignets at the Café du Monde. Jack smiled and said Bart was right: their baker, back in the bayou, was right up to par. His loyalty made me laugh, but it made me a little sad, too.

Before dinner we all visited Pierre again. He was more animated, and he liked Jack, especially when

361

Jack promised to show him how an oil well brought the oil up from the depths of the earth.

"Can we go up there as soon as I get out of the hospital, Pearl?" he asked me excitedly.

"Not as soon as you get out, Pierre. You have to get strong and healthy first. Then we'll go," I said flashing a look at Mommy.

"We'll all go there. I promise," she said, smiling at me, and I had the feeling she had killed all the demons that had kept her from visiting her past. We would go back often.

Jack was concerned that he didn't have the proper clothing for the restaurant Daddy had chosen. He mumbled about it, but Daddy overheard and told him not to worry. He considered him, nodded, and suggested Jack try one of his older sport jackets.

"I bought this a while ago, when I had a trimmer figure," he explained. The jacket fit Jack well. Daddy loaned him a tie, too. Jack was reluctant to take the clothing, but did so at Daddy's insistence.

Our dinner was spectacular. Daddy went overboard to impress Jack and to celebrate. After our rich desserts, Jack leaned over and whispered, "I bet the bill for this dinner is as much as I make a week." He laughed, but once again I felt the gap between us.

Mommy and Daddy drank a little too much wine. They were both giddy and pleasantly tired by the time we arrived home. Jack and I went out to the patio and pool, and they went upstairs to fall asleep in each other's arms.

It was a particularly starry night, no moon but a myriad of twinkling lights.

"Most of those stars are bigger than our own sun. But when you're far away, bigger things look small. Then, when you get closer, you see how small you are," he said. I knew what he was saying.

362

"No matter how far away I am from you, Jack, you will never seem small to me."

He laughed. "I only went to high school. My daddy taught me all I had to know about being an oil rigger. The fanciest party I've been to is a wedding, and I bet the whole affair didn't cost as much as tonight's dinner in that restaurant. And you're going to be a doctor."

"Don't make me regret it," I replied quickly.

"Why would I do that? I think it's terrific. You know what you are," he said, suddenly turning to me. He gazed up at the stars and then at me. "You were named Pearl, but you're really a diamond—a diamond in the rough. They're going to polish you and make you dazzle just like those stars."

Before I could speak, he raised my hand to his lips and then he leaned over to kiss me.

"Thanks for a great day," he said. "I guess I better go to bed. I've got to get up early and drive back."

"You're staying only one day!" I cried. He nodded. "But . . . can't you stay one more?"

"You've got a lot to do here, Pearl. Your family needs you. You can't be spending your time entertaining me, and I do have to get back."

"But your visit's too short. I don't know when I'll be able to get up to Cypress Woods. Pierre won't be home for a few more days and—"

"I'm sure you'll come when you can. I'll call you, and you can call me." He stood up. Reluctantly I did so, too. We held hands and walked back into the house. The lights had been turned low. Without speaking, we ascended the stairway and stopped at Jack's room.

"Is there anything you need?" I asked.

"No. I'll be fine. Thanks again for a great day," he said and kissed me. Then he went into his room and closed the door. I looked down the hallway toward Mommy and Daddy's closed door. They were probably asleep in each other's arms by now. I sighed and went to my own bedroom. After I changed into my nightgown, I slipped under the cool sheet and stared at the ceiling.

Had Mommy been right? Had my great love affair been stimulated only by my vulnerability and emotional strain when I was in the bayou? I felt the cold tears filling my eyes and turned over to bury my face in the pillow.

Then I thought about the night Jack and I had spent together in the old Cajun mansion, how passionate and loving we were with each other. I remembered how wonderful and happy I felt when he found me in the swamp and how loving and tender he was afterward.

I couldn't bear the ache in my heart. Telling myself I wouldn't stand for it, I decided to get up and go to Jack. Quietly I walked across the corridor to his room and opened the door. He was lying on his back, staring up at the ceiling. I could see his eyes were open.

"Jack," I whispered.

"Hey, what's up?"

I rushed to him and threw my arms around him. We held each other quietly for a long moment.

"I don't want us to lose each other," I said through my tears.

He smiled. "Maybe we won't," he said. We kissed.

"We won't," I said determinedly.

"I want to believe that, too, but I'm not smart enough to see past tomorrow, Pearl. Let's wait on the promises so we don't hurt each other, hear?"

"I won't ever hurt you, Jack."

"That's a promise," he warned.

"I'm not afraid."

"Well, I am. I can't help it. Even when we drill in a

known oil field, we got no guarantee until that bit hits that vein. We aren't deep enough into each other's lives yet, Pearl," he said wisely.

"Just hold me, Jack. Hold me and dream of only good things. Soon enough my life's going to be filled enough with facts and statistics, piles of details and piles of data and objective proof. I want some dreams, some fantasies, too."

"Sure," he said.

He held me and kissed me, and I fell asleep for a while. Before morning I returned to my own room, calmer, more contented.

Daddy and Mommy were surprised to hear Jack was leaving. At breakfast, he explained that he had planned only to be away from his job for only one day. Daddy made him promise he would come back soon.

Jack returned the sport jacket and tie to Daddy, thanking him, but Daddy asked him to keep the coat.

"I doubt that I'll get back to that size and you just might be going to more formal affairs in the future."

"But, monsieur—"

"Please," Daddy insisted. "It's nothing compared to what you've done for me." Reluctantly, Jack took the jacket.

Before Mommy and I returned to the hospital to visit with Pierre, I said good-bye to Jack in front of the house.

"I forgot to give you back your clothes," I reminded him.

"Can't trust you city folk."

I laughed.

It was a very sunny morning without the usual haze. Everything looked brighter, cleaner, and the air was filled with the scent of flowers and bamboo. We could hear the city coming to life, the streetcar rattling, cars honking horns, someone shouting down the street, and lawn mowers and blowers being started.

"I'll see you before I start college, won't I?"

"Absolutely," he said. "Besides, you should visit your well more often, get to know her. And bring Pierre."

"I will."

We kissed.

"Safe trip," I said putting my finger on his beautiful lips and drinking in the softness in his eyes. "I'll miss you."

"Me too." He got into his truck. "I hope I don't get lost in these city streets," he complained.

"A man who can find his way around those swamp canals shouldn't have any trouble navigating the streets of New Orleans," I said.

Jack laughed. Then he put on a serious expression and gazed at me.

"I don't know if I have a right to love you, but I sure think I do," he said.

"You have more than a right, Jack Clovis. You have an obligation. You *better* love me."

He flashed that wonderful smile, the smile that would have to last me for some time, and then drove away.

I started to cry, but then drew back my tears and took a deep breath. I had to be strong for Mommy and Daddy. We had a long road ahead with many steep hills to climb and many sharp turns.

Two days later we brought Pierre home from the hospital. He was shaky, but he wanted to walk. I held his hand and guided him. He wanted to go out to the gardens. I knew why. He wanted to look at the tree house he and Jean and Daddy had built long ago. The doctors thought he should get as much air as he could. They said it would make him tired, at least for the first week or so. It did. He fell asleep in his chair after lunch, and I carried him up to his room.

But he was outside every morning. I spent a great

deal of time with him, reading to him, playing board games, answering his questions about his illness. He went to therapy once a week and had a good checkup from Dr. Lasky, who was impressed with Pierre's physical recuperation. "The mind is far more powerful than we can imagine," he told Mommy. She was the one person in the world he didn't have to tell.

Epilogue

Two weeks after Pierre came home, Mommy decided to visit Jean's grave again. I went with her. She set out some flowers and stood gazing at the tomb, a small smile on her face as she recalled his antics and the way he threw his arms around her when he was frightened or sick or just wanted her love. But I knew why she wanted to go there. It wasn't just to remember. It was to say thanks, for she believed in her heart that it was Jean's spirit that had turned Pierre around and sent him back to us.

When Pierre was strong enough to make the trip, we went to visit Jack at Cypress Woods. Jack spent a great deal of time with him, showing him the machinery, explaining how everything worked. Daddy and Mommy walked around the neglected grounds and the house, and then we all went for lunch in Houma and ate crawfish étouffée.

A few weeks later I began my college orientation. Pierre was strong enough to return to school in September, although he was still seeing a therapist once a week. He was having a hard time adjusting to life without Jean at his side. Often I would find him off by himself, and I knew he was talking to Jean. Finally, Dr. Lefevre decided it would be good for Pierre to visit Jean's grave.

At first he resisted. I talked to him for a long time about it until he finally relented, and we all went to the cemetery with him. He just stared at the tomb and read Jean's name over and over. He was very quiet for the rest of that day, but I did see a change in him in the weeks that followed. He became more outgoing, was willing to have friends over and to visit with them. He grew taller and leaner and continued to be a very good student.

The summer never seemed to end that year. It was hot and humid right into the first week of December. Jack came to see me at college, but he was uncomfortable on the campus and was happier at the house or visiting the sights. Pierre loved him and was never so happy as when Jack visited us or we went to visit him in the bayou.

Late that spring, just after April Fool's Day, Aunt Jeanne called to tell Mommy that Gladys Tate had died. She said the family was thinking of restoring Cypress Woods.

"Paul would like that," Mommy told her. "He was very proud of that house."

"I know Pearl visits from time to time," Aunt Jeanne said. "Maybe you could come along sometime, and we could spend some time there. I'd like to hear your suggestions for fixing the place up."

Mommy told her she would think about it. She related the conversation to us at dinner.

Daddy listened and then said it wasn't a bad idea. "They don't know anything about real estate," he told her.

He knew how much Mommy wanted to be part of the restoration and made it easier for her. I was happy because that meant I would have that many more opportunities to spend time with Jack.

Something subtle began to happen to me as I made more and more visits to the bayou. In the beginning I believed my horrible experience with Buster Trahaw and my frightening time in the swamps had left me with such a bad taste for the bayou that I would never see anything pretty or pleasant about it again. But when I was with Jack and he and I walked over the grounds or drove on the back roads, it was different.

Just as I was eager to show him my city world, he was eager to show me nature, to point out the different flowers and animals. He had a Cajun guide's eye and could spot sleeping baby alligators, brown pelicans, marsh hawks, and butcher birds. I would have to stare and stare and sometimes be taken by the hand and nearly brought right up to them before I saw what he saw. Then I would nearly burst with astonishment.

I saw the bayou during every season, met many of the local people, and got to know and like them. I felt they liked me too, especially because Jack was bringing me around. I enjoyed their stories and their expressions and earthy humor. It was always a refreshing change from the hubbub of city life and the complexities of college.

In the late fall of the following year, Jack surprised me and Mommy by showing us what he had been doing during his spare time: he had been restoring the old shack. Now it truly looked like the toothpick-legged Cajun home in my fantasy. The new tin roof gleamed in the sunlight. He had replaced and stained the railings on the gallery and the steps, removed the broken floorboards, replaced the windows, and cleaned up and trimmed the grounds. He had even restored the racks where Mommy and Great-Grandmere Catherine used to sell their handicrafts and gumbo to the tourists.

Mommy beamed. She clapped her hands with joy and amazement and went through the shack declaring her astonishment and pleasure. Jack had repaired the old rocker, too. Mommy said she could stand back and easily imagine her grandmere sitting in it again. While she relaxed on the gallery and reminisced, Jack and I walked to the water. He held my hand.

"See that current there?" He pointed. "Watch. In a minute you're going to see a big snapper. There she is. See her?"

"I do, Jack. Yes."

I took a deep breath and looked down the canal to where it turned into the deeper swamps. Jack saw the direction my eyes had taken.

"You can get to Cypress Woods from here in a pirogue," he said. "I'll take you for a ride next time."

"My uncle Paul used to take my mother that way," I said. "She told me so. You think there's some power that makes us want to retrace the steps our parents took?"

"Power? I don't know. Maybe. I don't worry about it. I do what feels right, feels good," he said. "Is that too simple for you?"

"No." I laughed. "You still think I'm too brainy, don't you?"

"Well . . . you're getting better," he teased. "And growing more beautiful with every passing day."

I looked at him for a moment and then we kissed. On the front gallery, Mommy was sitting in Great-Grandmere Catherine's restored rocker, drifting back through time and reliving her youth. I was sure she heard and saw again the people she had loved.

And I realized how important it was not to lose the precious moment when it came.

"For a while, Jack Clovis, you had me wondering where I belonged."

"Oh. Where do you belong?" he asked, his dark eyes searching mine.

"In your arms."

"Even here?"

"Especially here," I said. He put his arm around me. A flock of rice birds rose from the marsh and flew past us, so close we could feel the breeze from their flapping wings. It was just the way it had always been in my old nightmare.

Only now the demons were gone.

And I was truly safe.

POCKET BOOKS

The Rain Series
VIRGINIA ANDREWS®

RAIN

Book 1

Life isn't getting any easier for Rain Arnold. The ghettos
of Washington D.C. are a daily reminder that she must
struggle to hold on to her dreams. Unlike her tearaway
sister, she has battled against the odds to do well at
school and to be a good daughter. But Rain can't
suppress the feeling that she has never really belonged,
that she is a stranger in her own world.

Her instincts are confirmed when she overhears a
revelation from the past. A long-buried secret is about to
change her life beyond recognition. Suddenly everything
Rain has ever known is left behind, and Rain is sent to
live with the wealthy Hudson family. Just as she never
felt a part of the troubled world she was raised in, Rain is
also out of place in the luxury and privilege that now
surround her. Will Rain ever be able to fulfil her hopes
and ambitions – and find a place to call home?

0 6710 2964 9

£5.99

**POCKET
BOOKS**

The Rain Series
VIRGINIA ANDREWS®

LIGHTNING STRIKES

Book 2

Torn from the embrace of her poor but loving family,
Rain Arnold now lives surrounded by opulent riches but
feels more like an outsider than ever before. Enrolled in
one of England's most prestigious drama schools, she is
sent to London to live with her great-aunt Lenora.
Treated little better than a servant, nevertheless Rain is
happy; she has new friends, and a new determination to
succeed in her chosen career.

But soon Rain realises that something is dreadfully
wrong. She hears footsteps at night, and the high-pitched
laughter of a little girl. She sees strange lights in rooms
that are supposed to be closed off. Behind the icy sheen
of wealth and privilege lies something unspeakable.
Something that could turn Rain's most precious dreams
into an inescapable nightmare . . .

0 7434 0914 0

£6.99

**POCKET
BOOKS**

The Rain Series
VIRGINIA ANDREWS®

EYE OF THE STORM
Book 3

After a successful first year in one of London's finest
drama schools, Rain returns to America to cope with the
death of Grandmother Hudson, the only family member
who truly loved Rain for who she was. Now Rain finds
herself the controlling heir in her grandmother's will,
inheriting the vast millions of the Hudson wealth. Rain
can hardly believe it. Is this a gift or a test?

All she knows is that she is alone to face the rest of the
Hudson family. They will not allow Rain to inherit the
fortune that is their birthright. They will do whatever it
takes to remove this parasitic young woman from their
lives. Rain knows how to fight. And she is not afraid to
try. But the battle for her grandmother's estate is only the
beginning. Rain will soon face a tragedy of her own – a
devastating blow to her dreams that will leave her
shattered. And finally, Rain will have to come to terms
with her own fears to discover the person she truly
wants to be.

0 7434 0915 9

£6.99

**POCKET
BOOKS**

The Rain Series
VIRGINIA ANDREWS®

THE END OF THE RAINBOW

Book 4

Rain's precious daughter, Summer, is about to turn
sixteen. Like all girls her age, Summer dreams of
growing up and making her own life, of falling in love
and finding her soulmate.

But a devastating tragedy will force Summer to stare into
the cold eyes of adulthood long before she is ready. A
tragedy that will force her to flee the only place she has
ever called home.

All her life, Summer has lived on the Virginia estate
where the Hudson family's secrets have lurked among
the shadows for generations. Now it is time for Summer
to discover secrets of her own. Some she will keep. Some
she will share. And some will haunt her for the rest of
her life . . .

0 7434 0916 7

£6.99

**POCKET
BOOKS**

This book and other **Virginia Andrews** titles are available from your book shop or can be ordered direct from the publisher.

Please send cheque or postal order for the value of the book, free postage and packing within the UK; OVERSEAS including Republic of Ireland £1 per book.

OR: Please debit this amount from my:

VISA/ACCESS/MASTERCARD ....

CARD NO ....

EXPIRY DATE ....

AMOUNT £ ....

NAME ....

ADDRESS ....

....

SIGNATURE ....

www.simonsays.co.uk

Send orders to: SIMON & SCHUSTER CASH SALES
PO Box 29, Douglas, Isle of Man, IM99 1BQ
Tel: 01624 83600, Fax 01624 670923
www.bookpost.co.uk
Please allow 14 days for delivery.
Prices and availability subject to change without notice.